THE QUIET ARMY

ELUDING DESTINY

BOOK SIX

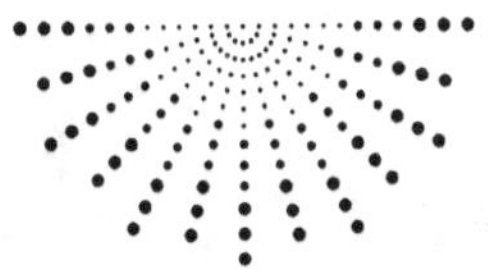

CHARLIE NOTTINGHAM

LIQUID MIND PUBLISHING

THE ELUDING DESTINEY SERIES

Eluding Destiny

The Horrors That Created Us

Aftershocks

The Precipice

Land of Light

The Quiet Army

Sacred Sins

Flash Back

The Shift

Lost to Time

Gods Among Us

The Cover Up

Blank Slate

Sign up for Charlie's newsletter and receive a free copy of the Eluding Destiny prequel, Blood Bar:

https://liquidmind.media/eluding-destiny-prequel/

CONTENT WARNING

This book contains detailed sex, mentions of drug abuse, addiction, captivity, rape, suicide, gore, violence, torture, homicide, and other adult language and situations,
It is intended only for mature audiences.
Reader discretion is advised.

PROLOGUE

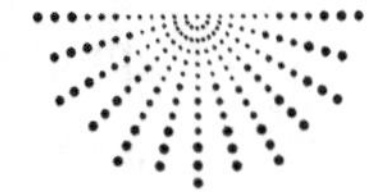

MARCH 2022

He was waiting.

Mommy said it'd be a few more days, and Micah was waiting.

Laying against the cool cement, his lips lifted in a smile. He thought about that great blue sky she'd shown him. He thought about that music Daddy had let him hear. He wondered what that big white dog's fur would feel like between his fingertips.

He liked animals; they were sweet. And they never hurt him, not on purpose. Well, the little mouse he'd found at the last place—Stew, Uncle Chris had named him—had bit him once. But it was okay. It didn't hurt that much.

He missed Stew. But it was okay, because soon, he'd meet that big white dog. Just like Mommy promised.

Sleeping was hard that night. He didn't know why; he just couldn't sleep. Uncle Chris was snoring though. He did that a lot. Maybe that's why he couldn't sleep.

It was dark too. He didn't like the dark because he couldn't see much in the dark. And this place was always dark. The last place had more windows. This one only had one, and there wasn't a lot of light at night. He could see the moon though. It was a pretty, almost yellow color. He liked yellow too. It looked happy.

Micah liked happy stuff. He tried to be happy all the time. That wasn't always easy, but it had been the last few days, because Mommy said she was coming. That he'd finally get to go home.

That he'd get to listen to his daddy play music, and that he'd get to meet his sister, and his baby cousin, and all of his aunts and uncles. And Aunt Leah, he really wanted to meet her. Her hair was pretty; it was the first place he'd seen the color purple. He liked purple, too. But he liked yellow better.

He rolled to his side, still looking out the window. He saw something. It was fast; he didn't see it good, but it wasn't a guard—they had short hair.

A quiet gasp left his lips. He scurried to his feet. They were cold, and they scraped against the cement, but he didn't care. It could be Mommy and Daddy.

He craned onto the tips of his toes, squinting out the small, dusty glass.

But there was nothing there.

He frowned. Maybe it *was* a guard.

It was okay though; they'd be coming soon.

He heard something. Words, he thought, whispers. He didn't know what they meant, but he heard something.

Maybe it wasn't a guard. Maybe it was the doctor. Micah didn't like the doctor. He did love him, but he hurt him, so he didn't like him anymore.

That was why he couldn't wait to be with Mommy. Mommy would never hurt him, she promised she wouldn't.

Then the big doors clattered open. Bright white lit the room, coming from someone's hands. He squinted.

Another gasp. He smiled wide.

Her long dark hair fell over her shoulders. Two big green eyes glowed above her white hands. Those pretty flowers on her arms reminded him of the ones he'd seen out the window of the last place.

He ran from the window to the middle of the room, starting to the door.

"Mommy?" he asked.

A long breath fell from her lips. The white light in her hands went out. She smiled wide, and he smiled back.

It was her; it was really her. She did it, she made it. Just like she promised. She was here. She was going to take him home and he was going to meet that big white dog and his little sister and all of his aunts and uncles.

"Micah." Mommy took a step forward. But she stopped. Her brows fell, hands touching the opening of the door, but it was like that window. Just like Micah couldn't get through that, she couldn't get through this.

But she was here. She'd figure it out. She promised she would. It was okay; Mommy could do anything.

Then someone behind Mommy turned. And Micah's mouth fell wide open.

He looked just the same too. Like Uncle Chris, but different. His eyes were so big and blue, and his hair was long and black, and he was so tall.

He darted across the floor, yelling, "Daddy!"

Daddy smiled too. But his smile looked a little sad. Like Uncle Chris when he told Micah to close his eyes and not to look. That always meant something bad was going to happen, and he didn't want Micah to get hurt.

"Micah," Daddy said. He reached toward the door too, but it did just the same as it'd done for Mommy. It was like glass. They could see each other, but they couldn't touch.

It was okay though. It'd be okay, they were here now.

White light shined in Mommy's hands. She started talking again, speaking a bunch of words Micah didn't understand.

Just like he thought. Mommy was gonna fix it. That's what she was doing, she was fixing it. She was gonna get through that glass and get him home. He just had to—

A big, strong hand grabbed Micah from behind, yanking him backward. He screamed, heart beating so fast that it hurt. Could a heart hurt? Because his did. It felt like it was falling and hurting at the same time.

Cold metal touched his throat.

Daddy's mouth fell open, both hands reaching out to the glass. Mommy's eyes filled with tears, no longer speaking those strange words. The light in her hands went out.

"You didn't think it'd be that easy, did you?" the doctor's voice said outside.

"Don't hurt him," Mommy said, looking at the person holding Micah. "Please, Amy. Please. Don't hurt my baby."

"We won't," the doctor said.

Daddy turned and stood against Mommy's back. Good, that was good. The doctor hurt Mommy; Micah didn't want him to hurt her again. He didn't want Daddy to get hurt either, but maybe Daddy would keep Mommy safe. Like Uncle Chris kept Micah safe.

"Not yet, anyway," the doctor said. "Nice to finally meet your acquaintance, Jeremy."

"Fuck you." Daddy's voice sounded different than it did when he talked to Micah, he sounded mean. But Micah wasn't mad. He didn't like when people were mean, but the doctor was mean, so Daddy had to be mean back.

"Is that how you're going to talk to the man who holds the fate of your son's life in his hands?"

It got quiet for a moment.

Micah kept looking at Mommy. He'd never seen her look like that. Her eyes were so big, water gushed down her cheeks, and her lips shook.

She was so scared. Micah was scared too, but he didn't want Mommy to be scared.

"Thought so." The doctor blew out one of those long, slow sighs. He did that a lot. "You sure love killing my men, Laila."

Mommy's hands shook, touching that glass wall. She mouthed, *It's okay, baby, it's okay.*

Micah believed her. He always believed Mommy because Mommy didn't lie to him. Mommy loved him; he knew she did.

He was scared, but if Mommy said it was going to be okay, It'd be okay.

The doctor said something else, but Micah didn't really hear it. He just kept looking at Mommy. He wanted her to hold him. He wanted to feel her for real. He never got to touch her for real, and he wanted to so bad.

Blue light shined from Daddy's hand. See, just like Micah thought. Daddy would keep them safe.

"Come on, Jeremy, don't make me do it like this," the doctor said. "Now isn't the time, you have things to learn first."

"I'm not leaving her," Daddy said.

Good, don't leave Mommy.

"You're not," the doctor said. "You have things to learn together. But you're going to be unconscious until I get you into a secure location."

"Just let me hold him." Mommy glanced behind her. "Please. Please let me hold my son."

Micah wanted that too. Maybe she read his mind. The doctor was nice sometimes, maybe he'd let Mommy.

"You will, Laila," the doctor said. "You'll see him soon."

"You won't hurt him if we go with you?" Mommy whispered.

Micah's heart hurt again. He wanted to yell and tell Mommy to stay, but he couldn't. The doctor didn't like when Micah yelled.

The doctor said, "Not yet."

Mommy's eyes started to water again. Her whole body began to shake. Micah's did too. Now he was really getting scared. She wasn't saying it was okay anymore.

"But this gives you more time to try and think of a way to stop me," the doctor said. "Maybe you'll figure it all out and beat me to the punch. You have before. I expected you to be in my custody far longer last time around. This time, I'm not expecting an extended stay."

Did the doctor know then? Was he finally going to let Micah see Mommy? He always said, 'one day.' Maybe that day was today.

"Then why are you doing this?" Daddy said. "Why don't you just stop? You know that we get him back, you've told us this. Why are you still fighting?"

"Because if I don't do this, you don't get them back. I may hate you, Jeremy. But…" the doctor said something else, but Micah didn't hear it. His heart was hurting his ears.

He didn't get that. The doctor always said that, that he hated Daddy. Daddy was nice. Why didn't he like Daddy?

"You're not going to hurt her again," Daddy said.

Good, don't let him hurt her.

"If you want to hurt someone, you hurt me. You don't touch her."

No, don't let him hurt you either.

The doctor said something else, but his voice started to blur into the silent noise of the night. The only things Micah could hear were Mommy's, Daddy's, and that thumping in his ears.

Mommy looked even more scared now. Her legs were shaking so bad, like Micah's did when he was scared. Daddy had his arm around her from behind, and it looked like that was the only thing keeping Mommy on her feet. That worried Micah. Why did Mommy look so scared if she was going to get him out of here?

"What's in it?" Daddy said.

"Oh, you'll know soon," the doctor said. "Don't dump the whole thing in there. Don't want you dying on me."

Daddy was quiet for a second. He said, "What are you giving her?"

The doctor said something else that Micah didn't hear good, but he said, "You're getting the fun stuff."

Micah knew that wasn't true. There was nothing fun here. The only time he had fun was when Uncle Chris and he were alone, and they played games.

"No." Mommy took Daddy's hand. "No."

"I'll be okay." Daddy touched Mommy's back, still holding her up. He smiled, but it looked sad still, not like it did the other times. "It's okay."

Mommy didn't say it that time, but Daddy did. It was going to be okay. Micah felt a little better now; Daddy said it was going to be okay.

The doctor said something else Micah didn't understand, and Mommy shook her head fast. She grabbed Daddy's hand tighter, looking at him now. She was crying still.

But Daddy smiled. "It's going to be okay."

He said it again, that it was going to be okay. That made Micah feel a little better again.

Mommy grabbed Daddy's shirt. He squeezed her back tighter, holding her close.

Micah wanted to be held that close too. He wanted them to hug him. He wanted this to be over. He wanted it to be okay.

Then the doctor came into view. He pushed something into Mommy's arm.

Daddy shoved him away. That made Micah happy; he didn't want him to hurt Mommy again. Daddy would keep her safe though. He'd keep Micah safe too; he said it was going to be okay.

Then Mommy started to fall.

Oh, no.

Daddy caught her though. See, he'd keep her safe. He was nice. He was good. He'd keep Mommy safe. He wouldn't let the doctor hurt her again.

The doctor said something Micah didn't hear again.

Then Daddy said, "Do you have a gurney I can put her on?"

"Your brother will grab the two of you after you're unconscious." He glanced at Micah inside.

What did that mean? What was a gurney?

Daddy glanced at Micah. He looked back to the doctor. "I don't want Micah to see this. Close the doors."

The doctor nodded.

No. No, no, no. They couldn't leave. He liked seeing them, it made him feel safe. They couldn't leave.

"Daddy," Micah whispered. His lip quivered, warm liquid spilling from his eyes. "Daddy, I'm scwade."

"It's going to be okay, buddy." Daddy smiled but tears rolled down his cheeks. "We're coming back for you."

He said it again. He said it'd be okay. That made Micah's heart hurt a little less.

Micah's little teeth began to chatter. "Pwomise?"

"I promise." Daddy smiled a little bigger, nodding fast. "You hang in there. We're coming back—"

"Alright, that's enough." The doors flung shut.

CHAPTER ONE

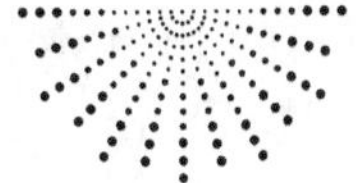

OCTOBER 23, 2021 - LAILA

"This is bullshit!" Lydia's voice echoed from the living room of the main house. She stormed into the kitchen. My eyes widened, turning to Jeremy. He pressed his smiling lips together. Ray's voice followed.

"Don't talk to me like that, little girl," he yelled as she stomped past Jeremy to the fridge.

"Well, quit making bullshit rules and I'll quit calling them bullshit." She pulled a tub of ice cream from the freezer.

"It's for your own good—"

"I left with Laila that day because I didn't want to be a prisoner anymore." Lydia slammed the silverware drawer.

Damn, bitch, don't bring me into this.

Not that I blamed her though. I understood being overprotective with children better than anyone, but mine was six months. His was fourteen. She needed a little freedom.

I considered chiming in on her defense but figured it best to do that later. Not in the middle of their throwdown. For now, I'd just sip my warm coffee and continue spoon feeding my wide-eyed baby bites of fragrant bananas.

Lydia's glowing gaze turned to Ray in the doorway. "I've left this house eight times in the past month and a half. You pulled me out of school. I can only see my friends if I have a chaperone. And now you won't even let me go to a party I RSVPed for months ago. Don't tell me that this isn't fucking bullshit, Dad."

"Lydia Marie!" Ray yelled.

"What?!" she hollered. "What, Dad? I'm not old enough to say fuck and shit? Is that what you're going to say? Because I've seen more shit than you have. Quit acting like I don't understand things. I know a lot more than you think I do. I'm not the three-year-old that went missing a decade ago. I'm a few years from being an adult now—"

"If you make it that far!" he yelled. "I'm trying to keep you safe, Lydia. Some madman was standing over your bed in the middle of the night; I can't risk something happening to you again—"

"So, what—You're just going to lock the princess in a tower until a knight in shining armor comes to save her? Newsflash, Dad, nobody's coming. No one's coming to slay the dragon and free me. So why the fuck am I still locked up?"

"Kids still say newsflash?" Jeremy lowered himself to the breakfast nook beside me.

"Apparently," I murmured.

"We just need a little bit more time, Lydia—"

"No, I need to learn how to defend myself," she snapped. "Laila's powerful enough to crack the ground open and drop someone inside of it. She can get in someone's head and make them shoot themselves. I can do that too, but you don't even want me to learn. You want me to be a little bitch who sits around waiting to be rescued."

Eh, she wasn't wrong. She could do all of that, and it was about time that she learned how. But since it was the second time she brought me up, maybe I could help lower the tensions a tad.

Ray's nostrils flared as he took in and expelled a few calming breaths.

"Do you want to go to the mall with me and Milly?" I asked. "I'm looking for something to wear to the survivor's banquet next week. Maybe we can find something for you too. We'll get lunch and try that new rolled ice cream place."

She turned to Ray and crossed her arms against her chest. "Is that okay, Daddy Dearest?"

He narrowed his gaze. "Yes, Lydia. That's fine."

"When are you leaving?" she asked me.

"Probably an hour unless you need longer."

She pushed the lid back onto the ice cream and dropped the spoon to the sink. "I'll go get dressed then." She stomped up the steps.

My gaze shifted back to Ray rubbing his tired eyes. I chuckled. "Teenagers, right?"

"Ya know, when that little girl is putting you through hell, I'm going to laugh at you too." He sat across from us.

I turned to Milly in her highchair and smiled. She giggled, slamming her plastic spoon into the banana mush on her tray. "You're not going to give us any trouble, huh, Mills?"

That was incredibly far from being true. She was going to be hell through her teenage years. But that's a story for another time.

"I get pulling her out of school, but do you have a plan to get her back in?" Jeremy asked. "I get being worried, but seclusion isn't good for someone who's been in captivity. There's no one around here that's close to her age either; that's got to be really hard."

"What am I supposed to do, man?" Ray asked. "Her mother shot her in the chest. The lunatic she's working for held almost a thousand people captive for more than a decade. I woke up to someone standing over her bed. I can't lose her again. Of all people, you should understand that."

"Sure," I said. "But she's right. No one can be her personal bodyguard. She needs to know how to defend herself, Ray."

He scoffed, tightened his jaw, and leaned back in his seat.

"Why are you so against her being who she is?" Jeremy asked. "It's the biggest part of her."

"Because I want her to be safe. I want her to have a normal life," Ray said.

Too little too late. Lydia was never going to be what Ray described as 'normal.'

"Then you should have married a human," I said. "Threats are going to follow her wherever she goes because of what she is. You can't change that. But you can make sure she knows how to defend herself if she has to. Let me work with her. I'll teach her how to keep herself safe. If someone would have taught me to use my powers, my life would look a hell of a lot different than it does right now."

He pursed his lips. "She isn't you, Laila. I don't want her to get overconfident and think that she's invincible."

"If you know what you're doing with powers like that, you almost are," Jeremy said. "But yeah. It's important to know that you aren't."

"And I can teach her that," I said. "I know the importance of that lesson better than anyone. She has to learn, Ray."

"You don't want to look back one day and wish that she knew how to protect herself," Jeremy said. "It can mean life or death. Trust me. You'd be stupid if you didn't let her learn."

Ray ran his hand against the dark five o'clock shadow on his warm, umber skin. He dragged his fingers through his jet-black hair. "I'll think about it. But that party for the survivors, kids her age will be there, right? Kids like her?"

"Sure," I said. "Another friend of mine, his brother and sister are around Lydia's age. Maybe I can introduce them. Emma's kind of a shit head, but they're good kids."

"Alright," he said. "Alright, good. Maybe they could come here and hang out some time if they all get along."

"Maybe." I gave a gentle smile.

"Hey, guys," Jenna called, followed by the front door creaking shut. "Is Adam here? He wasn't at the diner."

"Yeah, he's upstairs with Leah," Jeremy yelled.

"Bring that baby in here first, though," I called.

She came through the doorway pushing the stroller a moment later. Her blond hair was pulled into a messy, knotted bun at the top of her head. She had deep purple bags under her blue eyes behind her messy, rain droplet covered glasses. "He's finally asleep. If you wake him up, he's your responsibility for at least the hour length of his nap."

"That's okay. Huh, Luka?" I grinned, stood, and looked at him sleeping in his car seat. His pudgy little cheeks, his soft blond baby hairs, the sweet blanket framing his face.

"I'm not kidding, dude." Jenna's eyes darted over me. "This baby has colic. He never stops crying."

"Message received." I raised my hands in surrender. "I'll just admire how cute he is when he sleeps. Is that acceptable?"

"Thank you." She sighed, rubbed her temples, and started up the maid stairs.

Milly turned to her cousin and babbled with a gesture to the stroller. "Luka's sleeping. We've got to be quiet." I held my finger over my lips.

Jeremy wiped bananas from her face. "I think she needs a bath."

"Probably a good idea." I lifted her from the highchair. "You're still going to the diner to fix that door in the men's room, right?"

"Yeah." He reached into the diaper bag, pulled out a set of clothes, and a diaper while I made my way to the sink. "Shouldn't take me long though. Maybe we could meet up at the mall for lunch."

"That sounds good. Can you go grab me a towel?"

<hr>

Our day-to-day life had been pretty simple since Milly's birth. Most were like this. Simple, peaceful, and happy.

I hadn't returned to work, but Jeremy had. Max's mom was diagnosed with cancer late in the summer—unfortunately one of the few diseases I couldn't heal—so he had to back down on hours. That left a lot of management issues up in the air. Jeremy seemed happy to take on the work though.

I think in some non-misogynistic way, doing the work that paid for the roof over our heads gave him a sense of pride. Jeremy always struggled with some self-esteem issues, but I think feeling like "the man of the house" was helping him move past them. I didn't mind either. I enjoyed the time I got to spend day in and day out with my daughter.

Aside from the day that we accessed our past lives, I hadn't been more than a room away from her for any length of time. The only exception up until that point was mine and Jeremy's date on our second anniversary. We were only gone for two hours, half of which was spent waiting in the line at Applebee's to get a table. We should have just ordered it because we kept calling Leah and Hannah to check on Milly and spent the whole two hours being nervous wrecks.

Our lives were seemingly normal during those months. But dark clouds still loomed over us from time to time. Many nights were still spent crying on the floor in my shower. However, Milly had a way of shining a light when the clouds rolled through.

We'd been in contact with a higher-level Demon back in August. She made arrangements for us to meet with Lucifer that coming April. Her exact words were, "I'll let you know if there are any cancellations before the scheduled date, although it's highly unlikely."

We reluctantly accepted because we didn't have much other choice. It was the only lead we had. If it would've been someone less important, I would have demanded a sooner appointment. But it was Lucifer. *The* Lucifer. I was in no place to demand shit.

There hadn't been any news on the apocalypse nor information on my missing child and brother-in-law. I wish I could say that I was still searching high and low for a way to find them. But in all honesty, I'd looked everywhere that I could think to. The only chance I had left was literally the devil. I hadn't given up, but I was out of places to look until our meeting.

CHAPTER TWO

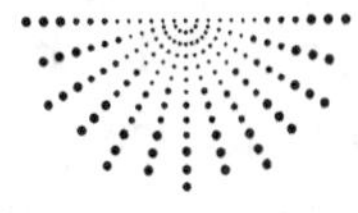

LAILA

The smell of Chinese food mixing with pizza and French fries filled my nose, creating a pleasant mixture that brought me back to my high school days. Blue raspberry ice slid down my throat, sending a shiver down my spine. Such an odd thing, really. Blue raspberries didn't exist. They were an entirely artificial flavor. And yet, they had to have been my favorite. I looked out over the busy food court and tried to listen to Lydia over the loud bustle of the crowd.

"It just isn't fair." Lydia chomped into a pretzel. "I get that he's scared and everything, but if he wants me to be normal, he has to treat me like I'm normal. Normal kids go to football games and movies. They get to see their friends and go out on dates. And it isn't fair. I didn't choose any of this."

"So that's what this is about." I grinned and set my slushie into the cupholder of Milly's stroller. "You've got a boyfriend."

She rolled her eyes. "I don't have a boyfriend."

"Girlfriend?" I asked.

"What? No."

I gestured toward her buzzing pocket. "Then who's blowing up your phone?"

She took another bite of her pretzel. "He's not my boyfriend."

"Uh-huh." I smiled. "What's not-your-boyfriend's name?"

"Ethan," she muttered. "But don't tell my dad, alright? He's crazy. He'll probably show up at his house with a gun and bust him for weed."

I laughed, walking past the escalator. "So was Ethan going to be in attendance at this party you're so mad about not getting to go to?"

"That's not why I wanted to go. Alexis was my best friend in Buffalo. I just up and moved back here out of nowhere," she said. "My life is just crap. And I don't get it. What did I ever do to anyone? Why does this have to happen to *me*? I was finally starting to find a place that I fit in back home. I made friends, I had good grades, I was even on the cross-country team. And now, my only friend is some old lady and her baby."

My gaze narrowed. This kid was always calling me old. And I was not old. "I'm only twenty-three, you know. I'm actually pretty young."

"Well, yeah. But you're still old compared to me," she muttered.

"Fair enough," I said. "Well, listen, kid. I'm working on getting your dad to let me help you learn a thing or two. The way I see it, you've got the power to protect yourself, you should learn to use it so you can go to a birthday party without a chaperone once in a while."

"And he keeps saying no, huh?"

"I'm working on it," I insisted. "But, if he doesn't budge soon, we're going to start training you with or without his permission. You're a powerful kid, Lydia. I'm not going to let you make the mistakes I made. You need to know how to fight because one day, you might have to. If you never have to use what I show you, then great. But it's better to know how and be safe than to wish you had and be sorry."

And I meant that from the bottom of my heart. We didn't know what the future had in store for us, but there was a lot of talk about an apocalypse coming. I'd never ask a teenager to fight alongside me in that. But that didn't mean I didn't want her to at least know how to protect herself.

"That's what I've been saying," Lydia said. "See? I knew there were some smart boomers out there."

I stopped the stroller and turned to meet her gaze. "Were you saying that as a joke or do you really think that I'm that old? Because I'm not even old enough to be classified as a millennial. I'm gen Z, bitch."

She laughed. "I'm just kidding."

Didn't sound like she was kidding. "Ha-ha, you're so funny."

"Lydia?" a young voice called behind us. "Lydia Ramirez?"

We turned. A few feet from the escalator stood a young, awkward looking preteen with two long brown braids on either side of her head. She wore thick framed glasses over pearly white skin coated in big, angry pimples. When she smiled at Lydia, two big dimples appeared in her full cheeks. Lydia gasped, she smiled wide. She bolted that way and threw her arms around the girl in a tight embrace.

"Isabella!" Lydia said. The two young girls rocked back and forth in a tight hug. "It's been forever."

Isabella pulled back. "I know. You never come to visit anymore."

"Yeah, it's a really long story." Lydia huffed. She turned to me. "I'm sorry. Laila, this is Isabella. Isabella, this is Laila. She's a friend of my dad's."

"Nice to meet you." I smiled.

"Yeah, I've heard a lot about you. It's nice to meet you too." Isabella reached out to shake my hand.

"Yeah, I think Lydia's mentioned you a couple of times too."

If memory served, Isabella was the odd little friend Lydia made here shortly after she got out of captivity. Ray mentioned her, actually. She was the one who liked to go on hikes, find animal remains, and reassemble them as free-standing skeletons.

Weird, sure, but I was here for it. That was better than what I was doing in my freshman year of high school.

"Are you guys in a rush?" Isabella asked. "'Cause my parents just gave me twenty bucks to go to the arcade. Do you want to come?"

Lydia gave me a grin. "C'mon, Lai. It's fate. I was literally just saying that I wanted to see some friends."

I shrugged. What was the harm? If Ray were pissed about it, he could take it up with me. But the poor kid needed to see someone her age. She needed some normalcy. "Sure, you guys can hang out at the arcade. There's a pizza place in there, right?"

Lydia nodded.

I reached into my back pocket and handed her a twenty-dollar bill. "Just stay close, alright?"

She grinned. "Thanks, Laila."

"Get out of here." I smiled.

But stay where I can see you. And if anyone so much as looks at you funny, you tell me.

You're the best. She smiled over her shoulder.

Maybe we'll go see a movie or something when we leave. Me and Jeremy'll sit in the way back.

Lydia's smile widened. Her brown curls bobbed in a quick, inconspicuous nod. I smiled back. She and her friend darted through the big glass doors into the noisy arcade. Milly looked around, taking in the room lit with bright multi-colored lights and a thousand exciting sounds.

I liked Mom life. I didn't think it would, but it suited me pretty darn good.

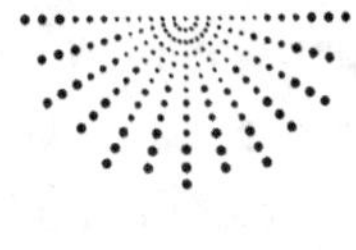

CHAPTER THREE

JEREMY

Loud pop music—that I couldn't recognize if my life depended on it—played from the speakers that hung at the neon light lined ceiling. The smell of popcorn mixing with teenage boy BO wafted from the trampoline park a few feet to my right. My damp Chucks squeaked against the linoleum before I stepped onto the colorful carpet and rubbed them dry.

Squinting through the dark room barely lit by more than game machines, I looked around for Laila. I was about to pull out my phone when I heard Milly's sweet, bubbly giggle. I'd recognize that anywhere.

I headed that way. Milly saw me first, big smile stretching into the apples of her cheeks. Short brown curls hung in her vibrant green eyes, spit-up spilling from her little lips. Smiling back, I flexed my fingers in a wave. She giggled and plopped her head to Laila's chest.

"Hey, you." I ran my hand along Laila's bicep and leaned down to kiss Milly's forehead. "Where's Lydia?"

"Over there." She gestured to the ski-ball area in the corner by the pizza counter. "We ran into one of her old friends, so I gave her twenty bucks to come in here and play some games."

"Sounds fair." I grabbed a piece of pizza from the table and set it on the white paper plate beside it. My gaze caught Laila's steady stare on Lydia as she nibbled a piece of pepperoni. "You alright over there?"

"Why wouldn't he want her to know how to protect herself?" she said quietly. "Same with Jenna and Luka. I just don't get it. What we can do is a gift. Yeah, a burden too, but if you don't master it, it's nothing but a burden."

I understood Ray's perspective. Being a parent is never easy, but it is especially hard if your kid has abilities that you don't. Milly burning me when I changed her diaper was plenty of proof in my understanding. But I agreed with Laila more. Laila wouldn't have been taken that day had I encouraged her to perfect her abilities.

"Why are you afraid to buy your kids their first car?" I asked. "It means that they're growing up. It means that they don't need you for everything anymore. He'll come around. Jenna, I'm not so sure about."

"Well, lucky for Luka, the only Witch Jenna knows won't cast on kids," she muttered. "It wouldn't be fucked up to teach her to use her powers better without his permission, would it? It's not like it isn't what's in her best interest. She's important in all of this too. It's not like a time is ever going to come where she isn't Fae. She's always going to be in at least a little bit of danger. Even if they weren't doing anything to her, there's got to be some reason she was having all those weird night terrors that mysteriously vanished when she came to live here."

"Amy was probably fucking with her head while she was sleeping," I said. "Dropping thoughts, searching for information. Who knows? I still don't feel great about them going home until Ray can afford to get a spell up like we have. But yeah, she definitely needs to learn to defend herself. I say give him another month. If he doesn't give you the okay, just tell him you're doing it anyway. I feel shitty to even say it, but it really isn't Ray's call. Learning to use her abilities is something she's going to need to know for the rest of her life. Ray doesn't get that because he's got her wrapped up in this imaginary bubble of humanity. I get that he doesn't want her to grow up but being what we are is pointless if all that you can do is grow some pretty flowers and read some meandering thoughts."

She chewed her lip, squinting slightly.

Judging by that face, this wasn't just about Lydia. She had something else going on in that pretty head of hers. But life had been good lately, so I wasn't sure what.

I frowned, reaching out to take her hand. "What's the matter, baby?"

"Nothing." She pulled a smile to her lips. "I'm fine. Just a lot on my mind."

"Like?"

"Like what I'm going to say at the dinner next week. Really weird concept, you know? Standing in front of all of those people and telling them I think that the man responsible for all of this did it to give them a reason to be loyal to me?"

The survivor's banquet. I was looking forward to it, actually. Most gatherings of supernatural races were at Chamber's meetings in uppity mansions. But meeting others like us, bottom level guys who did the grunt work like us, was a nice thought. They were the ones who really mattered, not the high up people in their fancy homes.

Plus, if these people were anything like the other survivors we met, they weren't going to look at Laila and cast blame. Regardless of why Peterson had done what he had, Laila was the one that saved them. She was one of them. She got the same scars in there that they did. She lost her baby in there. Even if this had all been a setup to make Laila their idol, the fact remained. She was innocent to his intentions. Each step she took was to help them; never to hurt them.

"You don't know that for sure," I said.

"That's what he said." Her lips vibrated together in a trill. "They deserve to know that."

"Sure. And then what they do with that information is up to them. You're not forcing anyone to follow you into battle," I said. "You're not telling them they have to be your army."

"Do you think that I should tell them what we know about the apocalypse?" she asked. "I think everyone's talking about it anyway."

"Since we know jack shit, yeah, I don't see why you shouldn't." I took a bite from my pizza. "I mean, we know that Micah's connected to it somehow. But we don't know why, and we don't know how. Who knows? Maybe we'll tell everyone, and it'll jog some memories. Maybe someone heard something or saw something that could help us."

"Maybe," she said. "I'd like to think that we're on the same side. But I'm worried that after I publicize this, they're going to always have that wonder in the back of their heads. Did she play a part in all of this? Is that how she was able to save us? Does she work for him?"

"I really don't think they'll see it like that. Our family is the only one left with people still inside. They're out. They don't have shit to be mad at you for. If they hate you for telling them the truth, then fuck them. But I really don't think they will."

She brushed hair from her face, gaze still a little distant. "I guess we'll see. Oh, I told Lydia we might go to the movies when we're done here."

Her expression lightened then, and I smiled in return. "How about roller blading? There's a rink right down the road. Seems less disruptive with the baby."

"Yeah, that sounds good. But you've got to hold Milly because I don't trust myself on skates." She grinned.

"You've got yourself a deal." I smiled back, leaned forward, and pushed my lips to hers.

The past four months were filled with the most consistent happiness I'd seen in years. We had bad days from time to time. But mostly, they'd been good. Life felt normal unless I got caught up in a rough bout over my son.

In most regards though, life was good. Laila and I were in a better place than we'd ever been before. The romance between us felt entirely different than it once had. We were still passionately in love, but it wasn't as much about us as it'd once been after having a baby.

We were partners in everything. She helped me with things for the diner that I didn't understand, and I helped her cook dinner and wash the dishes. We'd grown out of the intense screaming matches and makeup sex on the kitchen counter onto seriously considering going to bed at seven p.m. on a Saturday night. We'd been having sex at least twice a month because it seemed like the thing we should do even though both of us were way too tired to really get into it.

I guess you could say we aged quickly when Milly entered our lives. We were just beginning to see what grown, mature love looked like. Truth be told, that version would always be my favorite of us. Being young and falling in love was a fun and adventurous time, but this was where I always wanted to end up. Being married with a simple, boring little life. Only one detail could have made it better. Having my son here too.

Still, in most areas, life was great. Getting to watch my daughter grow from a baby who couldn't even hold her head up into a wiggle worm that crawled around the floors of our new home was the coolest thing I'd ever experienced. She was babbling all the time, she was eating solid foods now, she had just started to crawl. She couldn't make it very far yet, but she could do it, and I was prouder than I'd ever been of anything.

I was just happy.

CHAPTER FOUR

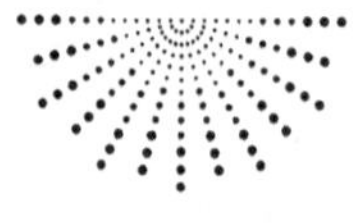

JEREMY

Bouncing Milly against my chest, I looked around the crowded skate park. It was just like it'd been when I was a kid. The chipped wooden floors, the disco ball in the center of the domed roof, the shitty little food court.

Stuff like this made me feel so light and airy. Family fun types of things, I mean. Milly was still too young to enjoy it, but Laila was practically a grown child. She made it fun.

Still, I wished Micah were out there with her. I wondered if Laila and I would have to switch places though, because she damn sure couldn't teach a kid to skate. She could hardly do it herself.

"I'm doing it!" Laila exclaimed from the edge of the skate area. She gripped one of those PVC pipe training braces for little kids, struggling to move her feet from side to side.

I laughed and took a sip of my pop.

Lydia skated circles around her. "I mean, not really."

"Shut up." Laila grinned. "I'm great at this."

"That's the spirit." Lydia raced past her.

"Do you want nachos?" I called to her over the barrier. "I'm in the mood for nachos."

"Sounds good, baby," she said. "Ray's meeting us here soon, right?"

"Yeah, he just called. He said he was almost here. Should I grab a table?"

Milly placed her little hands on the bar that separated the skating area from the walking section from her perch in the baby carrier on my chest. Laila grinned over her walker, gripped the bar, and leaned forward to press her lips to Milly's cheek. Milly giggled. Then Laila pulled back to meet my gaze.

"Yeah, that sounds good. Can you get a pitcher of water too?" she asked. "I'm dying out here."

"Will do." I smiled and touched my lips to hers.

She grinned. She swiveled back and returned to her walker. Her feet wiggled from side to side as she tried to get started again. I laughed.

Just as I started to turn away, she stumbled and fell face first, pushing the walker a good ten feet forward. I felt the ache in her knees as she exclaimed, "I'm good!"

I chuckled again. Lydia returned in a fit of laughter to help Laila to her feet. As I started to the concession's stand by the entrance, I saw Ray make his way inside. He pulled his jacket over his arms, and I lifted my hand over my head in a gesture our way. He waved back, gave a friendly smile, and started through the busy crowd.

Just as I found my way to the end of the line, Ray came to stand beside me. "You want me to grab you anything? We already are, but I'm getting nachos."

"Yeah, get some fries." He reached into his pocket and handed me a ten-dollar bill. "Even if the kid already ate, she's going to want more. Trust me."

I chuckled. He rubbed his forehead.

"Rough day?" I asked.

"They're all rough days. Do you guys have a table yet?"

"Nah, you can go grab one though. I'll be over in a minute. Are you skating?"

"No, I had to tackle some little shit in the field today. My back's killing me," he muttered.

"Laila could probably take care of that for you when we leave."

"Usually, I'd pass, but I think I really fucked something up this time," Ray said. "Enjoy being young while you can."

"Is that Isabella out there?" Ray gestured to the roller rink, chewing on a fry.

"Maybe, I didn't catch her name. Weird kid with the glasses and the rich parents?" He nodded, and I said, "Yeah, I think. I guess they ran into each other at the mall, so Laila told her to come skating with us."

Ray huffed out a laugh. His head shook a bit. Beer spilled from the edge of his plastic cup as he raised it to his lips. "Funny how when I first met Laila, she was a murder suspect. Now she's just about the only person I trust to take care of my kid."

Ah, my opportunity. I'd been on Lydia's side about this for a while. She wanted to utilize what she was, and no one should take that away from her.

And I knew how guys like Ray were. The macho, manly, 'I know what's best,' type. He listened to Laila on most things, but he hadn't given in on this one. Maybe hearing it from a man would lighten his perspective.

"You know she'd be fine to go out once in a while," I said. "Maybe not something like school that's routine. But at least a movie with a friend every couple weeks."

He rubbed his fingers into his scalp. He gazed at his daughter skating with her friend. "I'm a shitty parent, huh?"

"You're a good dad. But you are overprotective."

"But what am I supposed to do?" He leaned over the table and lowered his voice. "I didn't want to come back here either. But we didn't have a choice. She wasn't safe back there, and I can't afford putting a spell like yours up at our house. I had to take a massive pay cut when I moved back; I can barely afford the mortgage for the house I'm not even living in."

If money were the issue, Laila and I could help. We had more than five hundred grand in the bank.

"Helena might be willing to work out some type of payment arrangement or something. A lot of the ingredients are what makes it so expensive, but maybe Laila and I could—"

"No," Ray said. "No, I'll figure it out. Thank you, but no."

Like I thought. The macho man type. "Why are you so against her learning to defend herself? It can't be about wanting her to be normal because we all know that the way she's been living for the past few months is definitely not normal."

"It's not like this is what I want either, Jeremy," he said. "But the fact is that she is a fourteen-year-old girl living in a world that's nothing like the worlds of most fourteen-year-olds. I get it, alright? She wants to go out and have fun with her friends. She wants to go to parties without me and she wants to go to school. But she isn't like other fourteen-year-olds. I want her to be, but she isn't. It isn't safe for her without someone like you guys there."

That was the thing though. We couldn't *always* be there. We had been, because life had been easy lately, but I knew that wouldn't last forever.

"She's always going to be at risk, Ray. You know this. Laila was twenty-one when they kidnapped her, and she was still more than twice as powerful as Lydia will ever be."

"That's my point. Lydia's never going to be as strong as Laila—"

"So do you plan to have a security detail on her for the rest of her life?"

"Of course not, but—"

"Do you know why they got her that day? Laila? The day that she was kidnapped?" He fell silent. I leaned over the table and lowered my voice. "It wasn't because she was weaker. It was because they were smarter. She didn't know what she was doing, and they knew that. They waited for the moment that she didn't have someone like me to be there because they knew that moment would come eventually. And when it did, they took their shot. But if she would have had just the slightest clue of what the fuck she was doing, none of that would have happened. She could've killed them. She could've called me before she got out of that car, and *I* would have killed them. Instead of investigating her disappearance, you would've been investigating the mysterious murders on some back road."

Ray leaned back in his chair and took a swig of his beer.

"We can't always be there to protect them," I said. "But if I were in your shoes, my utmost priority would be getting Lydia to be as strong as she can be."

He gestured to Milly in the stroller beside me. "Is that what you're going to do with her?"

"That's the plan. Same way my parents did with me. Do you know how many times I used my powers to jump a car before I was five?"

A quiet laugh left his lips. "Really?"

"Really," I said. "Look, I get that it's scary to think about her doing things that could potentially hurt someone. But if she's taught how to use them properly, she may never have to. Leah's done so much to keep us safe, and she's never hurt anyone because she's never needed to. When you can control thoughts, you can protect yourself and keep other people safe at the same time."

Ray ran his tongue along his teeth. "She could use that shit on me, couldn't she?"

"Probably already has a time or two," I said. "She ever touch your hand and look really deep into your eyes?"

"Oh yeah, I know about that one. But I've realized she did it every time so far. That's what I'm scared of though. She can make the decision to control me whenever she sees fit."

"Give anyone a gun and they can too. That doesn't mean that they will unless they aren't taught to do otherwise," I said. "The thing is, her gun can't be taken away. She *has* to learn to use it, or chances are, she's going to hurt the wrong person. Maybe you, maybe a friend. Maybe even one of us. But one way or another, you don't have much choice. When a kid learns to walk, we don't cut off their feet because they can run from us. We teach them to stay close."

He rubbed the back of his neck as he turned his gaze back to mine. "I know she isn't Amy. But she's got half of her in there. And I'd be lying if I said that the thought of her becoming that powerful didn't terrify me."

Ray equated Lydia to Amy? The woman who shot her twelve-year-old in the chest? The woman who put up a wall in Laila's mind that kept us from helping her in there? No wonder Lydia was being such a little shit to him, I'd be offended if he compared me to that cunt too.

I raised a brow. "That's what all of this is about? You're worried Lydia's going to be like her mother?"

"It's not that I think that she will. I'm just worried that she could," Ray said.

"Then let her learn from the best. Let her learn from someone who knows firsthand when you need to fight and when you need to walk away," I said. He frowned. "But she chose to leave with Laila to be with you. She wasn't even five when she was taken, Ray. And she still chose you over her. Comparing Lydia to Amy isn't fair. Those types of thoughts are probably why you're having such a hard time with her in the first place. Since she hasn't been taught *how* to stay out of other people's heads, she's probably already heard you think that."

His eyes widened. "Shit, really?"

"Probably," I said. "If you think biting your tongue is hard, just wait. Holding back thoughts is a hell of a lot harder."

He bit his lip and shook his head.

I bit into a nacho. I was just getting ready to tell him that we were gonna train her with or without his permission soon, but then a loud thud sounded in the skate area.

Gasps and quiet yells erupted from the far-left corner of the rink. The fluorescent glow flicked on over the black lights. The music stopped. Someone blew a whistle and instructed the busy crowd to stop skating.

"Do you see Laila and Lydia?" Ray asked.

I shook my head, scanning the hectic, shuffling people as they scurried off the rink. Ray stood and started toward the crowd. I squinted in search of Laila. I was looking for her dark brown hair when my gaze caught in the center of the cluster of people.

My heart hammered. I blinked hard to make sure I wasn't hallucinating. The low lighting made it difficult to make out much, but I saw him.

At first, it was just a head wavy black hair. He stood just around three foot tall, moving his head from one side to the other as if he were searching for something. It was when he turned his head to the side that I recognized him because I got a quick glimpse at one of those big blue eyes.

More than just his appearance, I felt him. I thought I did, anyway. Because there was a sudden burst of bright energy through the room. Not the kind anyone could see, but the kind that anyone supernaturally inclined could feel.

Micah.

I grabbed Milly from the stroller and started through the maze of tables and people on roller skates. My eyes glued on him as I struggled to move through the swaying, rustling crowd of preteens and middle-aged couples out on date night. At first, I was sure that I was hallucinating.

I was either crazy, there was a kid out there who looked a hell of a lot like my son, or Micah was—for whatever reason—at this roller rink.

But then, I saw a tall man in a black hoodie and sunglasses rip him from the ground.

I pushed through the crowd of shifting people until I was almost at the barrier. My fingers wrapped around it and I shoved like hell with one hand, clutching Milly against my chest with the other. But they were moving too. I thought about calling out his name, but I knew that wasn't Chris. If he realized that I saw him, he'd run faster.

He fought and yelled against Chris just as hard as I fought to get through that slow moving crowd. I spat 'move' and 'get out of my way' more times than I could count but a please probably would have gotten me a lot farther. Because they made it through the double glass doors just as I was breaking through the most congested part of the crowd.

I took off in a sprint and called out, "Micah!" just as a large man slammed into my shoulder and knocked me to the side. It couldn't have been for more than two seconds, but for that instant, his gaze met mine and he stopped screaming.

I saw my son, and my son saw me.

It was them. I knew it was.

Around Chris's big black hoodie, I couldn't make out much. But I knew those eyes. They were mine. They were my brother's and sister's and father's. That was my kid, and he was right there.

But I was in a crowd of people with a screaming infant. I couldn't teleport to him, not without exposing us.

The man doted an apology. I hurriedly recollected myself and kept moving toward those doors.

They were out of sight, but I kept running despite the screaming baby in my arms it probably looked like I was kidnapping. Just as I made it outside, I saw him again. Only for a fraction of a second over Chris's hooded shoulder as they rounded the edge of the building, but I saw them. I don't even remember running the length of that building. All that I remember was making it into that alley and spinning in a circle in search of them, or their energy signature, or anything. Just something.

But there was nothing.

I stood in the middle of that alley between the roller rink and the bowling center gasping in heavy breaths as Milly screamed bloody murder in my arms. One hand clutched her tight, and the other, my racing heart. I spun in another circle.

Gone. Just like that, they were gone.

I heard Laila's voice at the edge of the building.

"Baby, what's going on?" Her eyes glimmered with concern as she drew closer.

I heaved in and let out slow, deep pants. "I think Micah was just here."

CHAPTER FIVE

LAILA

We sat on the concrete barrier just outside the roller rink with heavy hearts listening to the cars whoosh by a few hundred yards away. I tightened my poncho over my shoulders and squeezed Milly closer against my chest as the cool autumn breeze brushed my nose. The few meandering snowflakes that fell from the clouds glistened before descending to the warm cars around the parking lot and turned to water droplets.

"I don't understand how it's possible," I muttered.

Jeremy took a hit off a cigarette with shaking hands. He didn't smoke often, but it was either that or a joint to calm down, and that wasn't the best idea outside of a roller rink. "Maybe I'm wrong. Maybe it wasn't them. But it looked a hell of a lot like my brother and an older version of the little boy in that picture we have hanging on the mantel. And I... I think I felt him."

I hadn't. But there was a reason Jeremy could have and I hadn't. Nastya was one powerful Witch, she was more than capable of concealing his powers. Normally, that'd mean he felt as powerless as a human. But at a close proximity, which Jeremy had been, someone as powerful as Jeremy could still pick up on it.

The thing I couldn't understand was how he made it here. I hadn't been able to escape those barrier spells, how could he? And *why* would he? More importantly, why hadn't he sooner?

My head shook. "I saw the memory. Either you're losing your shit or that was them."

"Hopefully the latter," he muttered. Milly fussed beneath the blanket over my shoulder. Jeremy lifted his jacket over my arms. "I didn't hurt her when I was running, did I?"

"No, I think you just scared her a little." I lifted the blanket to meet her gaze beneath it. Her eyes were heavy. Her fingertips balled to fists and rubbed against them. "She's okay."

"What was happening in there anyway?" he asked.

"Lydia fell trying to do some trick. She got her ankle pretty good. I think she broke it. It was turning black and blue before I made it out here. Ray's filling out an incident claim with the manager. When they're done, I'm driving her home and healing it. She's got to suffer for a few more minutes though."

"Huh." His lips pursed in thought.

I turned my head to the side a bit. "What're you thinking?"

His gaze was at the cars ahead as he took another hit off the cigarette. "Lydia and Micah are bound, right?"

My brows puckered. Then they raised.

Of course.

"He felt her get hurt," I whispered. "He came to heal her."

"Maybe," he said.

A quiet laugh left my lips, eyes filling with tears. "That—That means he teleported here." I smiled. "That could mean that he could get out if he knew where to go."

"It could." Jeremy took another hit off the cigarette.

"But?"

Fast, shaking breaths left his nostrils as he stared at the ground. His palm clenched, and his jaw tightened to a straight line.

"What is it?" I asked. "This could be a good thing."

"It could. It could but..." His palm ran along his thick scruff. He cleared his throat. "But I'm just worried about what they're going to do to him for what he just pulled."

Another thought dawned on me then. I couldn't see Micah well in Jeremy's memory, but I did see his clean scrubs over his shoulders. And I saw his neck.

He didn't have the implants.

"You don't have to do it this way," I told Lydia, pushing sweaty curls from her blue eyes. "We can take you to the hospital and you can just get a cast."

"No." She blew out slow breaths. "No, I'm okay. I know I'm screaming, but I'm okay."

Ray looked at me and swallowed hard. He had to work at the police station for six months before he could get health insurance. One of our hospitals was still a possibility, but Lydia didn't want to wait for it to heal.

"Can you try biting down on this then?" I rolled a blanket from the edge of the couch into a ball and handed it to her. "I know it hurts, but it's really hard to focus when someone's trying to kick you in the face."

"Well, it's not like I'm doing it on purpose," she grumbled.

I looked between her eyes. "You ready?"

She nodded and bit down on the blanket. Ray gripped her shoulders. Jeremy grasped the ankle that wasn't swollen to twice its size. I put my palm around her inflamed skin.

As I let the warmth flowed from my fingertips and her body began to flail, I squeezed her swollen ankle tighter. Her screams grew louder and more intense. It was admittedly a bit more brutal but the way I saw it, she was in excruciating pain regardless. May as well get it over with sooner rather than later.

She yelled profanities through the makeshift gag for about ten minutes until the pulsing ligament returned to its former glory. When I finished, she shot up and danced around the living room in awe.

Lydia reminded me so much of myself when I first started coming into my abilities. She was raw, yet so full of wonder at the magic within us. I still feel that way now from time to time when I swirl a ball of fire in my hand or when I float into the clouds and drift around for a while. But at that time, although still grateful for my gifts, I couldn't say that I wasn't jaded by them. After all, if it weren't for them, Jeremy and I would be living normal, happy lives with both of our children.

"Lydia, are you feeling okay?" Jeremy asked.

She smiled and gave a quick nod. "Yeah, I'm great. Good as new."

"Yeah, but are you feeling anything else?" Jeremy asked.

Lydia tilted her head and placed her hands on her hips. "What do you mean?"

"Are you feeling any pain that isn't yours?" I asked.

"What?"

"I'm pretty sure I saw Micah back at the roller rink," Jeremy said. "I think he was there because he sensed you get hurt. He wanted to help you but then Chris grabbed him, ran outside, and they were gone."

Her breaths slowed, wide eyes somewhere between shocked and terrified. "Are you sure?"

"Pretty sure," I said.

"No," she said softly. "No, I haven't felt anything. But I'll let you know if I do."

"Thanks," Jeremy muttered.

She was silent for a moment, eyes shining with sympathy. "You don't think they'd hurt him, do you?"

Yeah. I did. I knew they would. I'd seen them kill an eight-year-old. Micah may have been their savior, but to Peterson, I wasn't much different. He had no problem hurting me when I didn't submit to him. I had no doubt they'd hurt Micah.

Although, I was relieved they hadn't yet.

"I hope not."

CHAPTER SIX

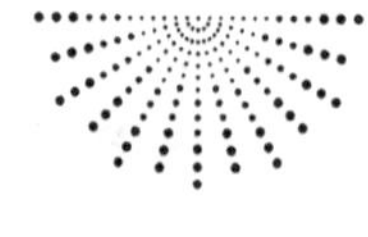

LAILA

"But how do you know that it was even him?" Hannah asked.

"I guess I can't know for sure." Jeremy ran his hand over his mouth. "But it looked like Chris. And he... I mean, it looked just like him. The exact kid in that picture. Just a little bigger, longer hair. But it was him. I'm telling you, it was them."

"If Micah can teleport, that changes things, doesn't it?" Hannah said.

"Not really. I assumed that he could," I muttered. "What stands out to me is the fact that he could trace Lydia's energy to end up there. Do you think Lydia could do the same if the roles were reversed?"

"Probably not." Leah swallowed a gulp from her scotch. "Lydia's got a drop of the power that Micah has."

I took a sip from my coffee. My fingertips combed my scalp to the tips of my hair. Jeremy's gaze caught mine. His lips lowered. He made his way around the island and rested his chin on my shoulder. I rested my head against his as his hands made their way around my waist.

This could be a great thing. Or it could be a really bad thing. If Micah were getting the hang of his abilities, maybe he'd be able to help us find him. But if Peterson knew what he was trying to do...

"I've got an idea." Kai rubbed his hand over his mouth. His gaze shifted to Ray. "But ye aren't going to like it."

I cocked my head to the side a bit. "What is it?"

"This shield." He made a gesture around the room. "The one we've got 'round the land here. The future generations can come through it, right? That's why Milly and Luka can come in and out as they please like the lot of us."

"Yeah," I said. "But Micah doesn't even know where here is. He wouldn't know how to get here if he wanted to."

"No," Kai said. "But he can feel where Lydia is."

A quiet gasp dropped into Jeremy's lips. His head sprung up. "If Lydia gets hurt, he'll feel it and he'll come for her."

Kai nodded.

"And if we do it here inside the barrier, Micah could get inside but the others couldn't," Hannah said.

"We'd still have to get Chris." Leah chimed in. "But they'd be trying to get Micah back anyway. They'll be at the perimeter trying to figure out how to get in. Then we can pick them off. Kill Amy and Nastya, then there's nothing bound to Chris. Even if Peterson doesn't show. We'd have Micah and Chris."

"We can take him out later," Jeremy said. "But if we can get Micah inside the barrier, we can go back for Chris. Hell, Micah might be able to show us where he is."

My eyes widened. A plan? Is that what we had? After all this time, did we finally have a plan? One that might actually work?

Ray crossed his arms against his chest. "I don't know how I feel about this."

I scoffed. "What?"

"I don't like the idea of using my daughter as bait," he said.

My eyes lit to bulbs in their sockets, hand clenching at my sides. I'd given everything to find his daughter. And I would never truly put her at risk. She would be fine. We had a million healers; nothing permanent would happen to her.

Jeremy turned to meet his gaze. "Bait to a two-year-old. It isn't like she'll be in danger. She'd be hurt for the few seconds it'd take for Micah to come to her. Then someone will heal her and we'll both have our kids back."

"I'm just not comfortable with putting her at risk—"

"You can't be serious right now." I stepped down from my perch at the island. "She wouldn't be at risk. She'd be safe. She'd be inside the perimeter. No one would be able to hurt her."

"You don't know that," Ray said. "Who's to say they wouldn't do some other crazy spell? How do we know it'd be foolproof?"

"Nothing's ever foolproof," Jeremy said.

"Then why should I risk my kid's life?"

Leah eyes glowed too. "Micah risked his for hers."

"And that's admirable of him but—"

"But what?" I nearly yelled, starting toward him. "Do you know why all of this started, Ray? Do you know what this traces back to? You. My life went to shit because of *you*. You begging me to help you find *your* kid and *your* wife. I don't pull this card often, but who the fuck do you think you are to tell me no? I gave up everything to save your family. I'm still doing everything in my power to keep your kid safe, and you're really going to fight me on this?"

"It isn't that black and white—" Ray began.

"Bullshit." I took a step closer to look between his eyes. I could feel his fear radiating toward me, but I didn't feel an ounce of guilt for it. He needed to be scared because I wasn't backing down. "I think you've misunderstood, Ray. I wasn't asking for your permission. I'm informing you as a courtesy."

He clenched his jaw. "You're going to—What, exactly? Torture my fourteen-year-old?"

"With her permission," I said. "Or without. But yeah, Ray. I'm going to do what I have to do. Unlike you, I don't have someone to do the dirty work for me. To get my kid back, I actually have to work for it."

His brows crunched down, nose crinkling.

"Yeah, look at me like I'm the villain." I narrowed my gaze. "I really don't give a shit. In my shoes, you'd do the same, and don't pretend for a second like you wouldn't."

He gritted his teeth. "You're not the person I thought you were."

"Neither are you," Jeremy snapped. "You're a cop, you're supposed to protect and serve. But all you care about is giving your kid a soft and cushy life."

"I care about keeping my daughter safe—"

"No, you *only* care about keeping your daughter safe," Jeremy snapped. "What about our kid, huh? He doesn't matter to you?"

"I gave up over two years of my son's life to bring your kid home." I clenched my jaw. "How *dare* you? My kid would still be here if it weren't for you. I'd have enjoyed the past two and a half years but because of you, my life has been shit. And I need one thing from you. One fucking thing that still lets you keep everything you love, and you have the fucking balls to tell me you won't put her at risk for a few seconds? Fuck you."

He clenched his jaw. "I'll talk to Lydia in the morning. Can you give me that? Or do you want to start attacking her in her sleep?"

I rolled my eyes and started to Milly in her stroller. "Be ready by nine."

CHAPTER SEVEN

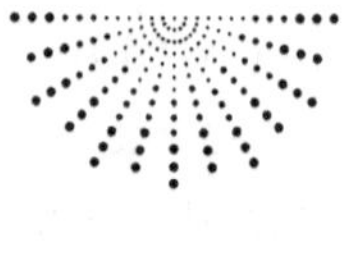

JEREMY

"Who the fuck does he think he is?" Laila bitched while pulling on her pajamas. "He's such an ungrateful little dick—and I do mean that in the literal sense. After all the shit I've done for him, he's seriously going to pull some shit like that?"

"I know, babe," I said.

"What—Does he think I'm really going to hurt Lydia? Does he really believe I'd let something happen to her?" She yanked one of my T-shirts over her head. "Have I ever let anything happen to that little girl?"

"No, you haven't," I muttered.

"And that's another thing. It's not like she's a baby. She's a few years from adulthood, she can make the decision to help us on her own. I know she's going to be fine with it. But it's the point. He doesn't have the fucking right."

"I know, baby," I said again.

Obviously, I agreed with everything she was saying. But I also knew my wife. When she was bitching, it was best to just nod and tell her she was right.

Plus, I was in the midst of changing Milly into her pink, fuzzy sleeper. And the damn thing wasn't cooperating, so I was a little side-tracked. I squinted, trying to figure out why there was a button remaining at the top.

Ah-ha, there it is. I missed the second from the bottom.

Aside from that though, I didn't want her to get her hopes up. There was a good chance this wasn't going to work. After what he'd done earlier, I was sure they'd have him under close watch until they were sure he wouldn't do it again. Otherwise, he would've shown when Laila was healing Lydia. That didn't mean it wasn't worth a shot. Lydia would only have to endure a moment of pain. And if it worked, that'd be the best thing imaginable. But we didn't get happy endings like that. Any happiness we got, we had to bust our asses for.

She exhaled deeply as she came out of the bathroom running a brush through her hair.

"I'm sorry. I know I'm being annoying. It just really pissed me off." She sat on the bed. "I can see his perspective. Nobody wants their kid to be in pain. But this isn't just about Micah. We get him back, and they'll be looking for him. We can lead them straight into a trap and finally shut the door on all of this. This could all be over. They could go home and Lydia could lead a normal life. This could be the answer to everything."

"Lai." I took her hand. She looked up to meet my gaze. I frowned. "I hope that this works too. But we should be prepared in case it doesn't. They're probably taking extra precautions as we speak to keep it from happening again."

Her gaze turned down. "Yeah. Yeah, I know. But it's worth the shot, isn't it?"

"As long as we don't have to hold a fourteen-year-old down to try it." I pushed hair behind her ear. "I can't see why it wouldn't be."

She bit her lip and gave another nod. "I wish I would have gotten to see him."

"I wish I would've moved faster," I muttered.

Laila laid her head against my chest. "Why does life feel easier when we don't have any leads?"

"Because there's no empty hope."

"You're sure you're okay with this," Ray said to Lydia.

"Yes, Dad. I'm fine." She rolled her eyes and turned to Laila. "So who's doing it? It's got to be one of you because I don't think I have the balls to hurt myself."

Wasn't gonna be me. Sure, I'd thrown plenty of punches in my day. But rarely at girls, and never at kids.

Laila looked at me.

"Uh-uh. This one's on you, baby."

"Neither of you should do it." Leah stood from the stool at the island. "Micah's going to see it. If he sees you hurting her, it's going to give him the wrong impression about the type of people you are."

"Ray ought to do it then. Seeing as how he's the one who doesn't want to do shit to help end this," Laila mumbled.

He rolled his eyes.

"I'll do it." Leah lowered herself to the chair at the end of the breakfast nook with a knife in her hand. "This is a first for me so try and cut me some slack."

Lydia chuckled and extended her hand out to Leah. "Hit me with your best shot."

"Is a calculated injury our best bet?" I asked. "Because it was probably the shock of the pain that alerted Micah. He might think a slow careful cut doesn't need healed."

Ray licked his teeth. "Then what do you recommend, Jeremy?"

Lydia's gaze met mine as Leah grabbed the heavy ceramic fruit bowl from the table and slammed it into the back of the girl's palm. Her eyes widened, and she grunted out in pain.

"You said hit you with my best shot, kid," Leah muttered.

Lydia grumbled to herself as she examined her swelling hand. Laila and I looked around with hopeful gazes for a moment. But that deafening stillness continued to radiate around us.

No one appeared. No one left. Everything remained as it had been a moment prior.

"Do it again," Lydia said. "Maybe it didn't hurt enough."

"Are you sure?" Leah asked.

Lydia placed her inflamed palm onto the table. "Go ahead. I'm alright. You're going to heal it when we're done anyway."

"Alright, if you say so." Leah picked up the bowl and thrust it into her palm once more. I winced at the crunching sound as the corner clacked off of the wood.

Yet again, nothing changed. Micah didn't show.

"I'm good," Lydia insisted with tears rolling down her cheeks. "I'm good, do it again."

Leah looked to Laila. She gave a nod. She took in a slow breath, closed her eyes, and slammed the bowl into Lydia's skin once more. That time, she couldn't help the agonized moan that left her lips. Every part of her hand that wasn't dripping blood already turned black and blue.

And once again, Micah didn't show.

I figured that would be the case. Last night was a fluke they wouldn't let happen again. I hoped I'd be wrong. But we all knew it.

"It's okay, keep going." Lydia wiped unwilling tears from her cheek with her good hand.

There was no point. And watching Lydia's hand get turned to mush wasn't exactly encouraging either. Especially not when I considered the fact that my two-year-old was feeling that pain.

If he could've come, he would have. Instead, he was sitting somewhere in misery. Probably terrified for the girl whose pain he was feeling but couldn't help.

We had to stop. It was worth the shot, but we had to stop.

Leah turned to Laila with a questioning gaze. Laila nodded.

But I said, "It's not working. He would have shown by now if he were going to."

"We don't know that," Laila said.

"Then let her sit like that for a few minutes. But she's already hurting, there's no point in hitting her again," I said.

Laila was quiet for a moment. "I guess that's true."

We sat there for thirty minutes waiting for Micah to appear before Lydia found herself in too much misery to go on without being healed. Then we told Lydia how grateful we were that she was willing to help us. She smiled with bloodshot eyes and nodded. Then we went back to the house and collapsed onto the couch with Milly.

Sitting around our beautiful and comfortable home that day felt like sitting in the rubble after a bombing. Laila battled a pretty fierce panic attack while cooking dinner, and I struggled to retain my composure. I held Milly a little tighter as the heavy weight of another failure pushed down on my shoulders.

Our hopes hadn't been lifted very high. We knew it was a long shot. But yet again, those hopes fell harder than they rose. We were back to square one. Yet again, it was time to go back to pretending that everything was okay.

CHAPTER EIGHT

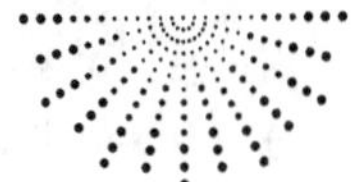

OCTOBER 30, 2021 - JEREMY

My eyes shifted over Laila in the mirror as she pulled on her knee length blue dress. It had short sleeves and dipped in tightly at her waist. Small white buttons started in the middle at the bottom and worked their way to the top where they still hung open. She stood in front of the floor length mirror running her straightener through the long hair that hung loosely against her bare chest.

Her tits looked great all the time, but they were fucking amazing when she was breastfeeding. Got a little weird when I licked her nipple and milk shot into my mouth, but they were fun to play with.

Her gaze found mine, and she grinned. "What?"

"Just looking at your boobs." I smirked.

She laughed. "Well, enjoy them now because they're going to be gone soon."

"I thought you wanted to wait until she was a year," I said.

"That was before she had teeth. She's bit me twice this week." She laughed while fastening the remaining buttons up her chest. "She's getting cut off."

Damn. I'd miss those.

"That's fair." I took a few steps forward and put my arms around her waist. Our gazes met in the mirror, and I smiled. "You look beautiful."

"You don't look so bad yourself. I've said it before, and I'll say it again. You should wear button-ups more often." She grinned. My smile widened, and I tightened my hands at her hips. I slid my palm to the front of her dress. I pressed my lips to the side of her neck while my fingertips crept up the front of her skirt. Laila laughed, shaking her head. "We have to be out of here in thirty minutes."

"I only need five." I grinned and slid my hand into the front of her panties. I traced the tips of my fingers against her lips down to her opening, wetting them. I slipped them back up to her clit.

A heavy breath fell from her lips. Her eyes closed, and her head rolled against my chest. Fuck, that was hot. "You always say that and then we show up late."

"I promise I'll make it quick," I whispered, touching my lips to her neck. My fingertips spun faster, feeling her clit grow firm beneath them. I watched her mouth fall open in the mirror, and my dick hardened against her ass. "Ten minutes tops."

"See, that's twice as much as your original offer." She rolled her head back, eyes meeting mine, a grin across her lips. I slipped two fingers inside of her. A gasp left her lips as a smile came to mine.

"Twice the fun." I grinned.

She bit her lower lip and leaned into me. "If you aren't done in ten minutes, I'm leaving with or without you."

"Deal." I teleported in front of her, grabbed her hips, and lifted them against mine. She laughed as I set her down on the vanity a few feet away.

***

"I know everybody is super excited to be here," Haley yelled into the microphone from the small stage of the banquet hall. "And I feel you guys; I'm hype to be here too. You all have a lot of questions, and I'm sure that Laila and her family will be happy to answer them for you. But before we get to that, try to enjoy your meal, and get to know the person beside you. This is a little overwhelming for her though so let's try and be considerate before we jump down her throat with questions, alright?"

"Well, she didn't have to say it like that," Laila muttered beside me.

"What was wrong with that?" I laughed, lifting the spoon of bananas into Milly's mouth.

"That made it sound like I don't want to talk to them."

"No, that made it sound like thousands of people wanting to meet you is overwhelming because it *is* overwhelming," I said. "We've got this hall for six hours. Even if you only spend a minute with each survivor, you still don't have enough time to meet them all."

She let her lips vibrate in a trill. "I guess. I just don't want anyone to think I'm picking favorites."

"Leah and Haley are handling the meetings; all you've got to do is relax," I said.

"I guess so."

Laila wanted this deep, personal connection with every person in that room. And I applauded her for it, it was sweet. But that was not physically possible. She couldn't be all of their best friends. It just wasn't possible.

"Did you go over what you're going to say?" I gestured toward the stage.

"Yeah, I've got my notecards in my purse."

"Are you still starting with the story of why we started looking?"

"I'm starting at the part where Ray showed up and told me about Lydia and working my way up all the way to last night," she murmured.

"You're telling them everything?"

She bit her lip and dipped her head in a slow nod. "If I don't tell them the whole truth now, there's a good chance I'm going to have an angry mob on my hands later. So yeah. I'm telling them everything."

In fairness, it's not like she was wrong. But that was a tad concerning. Yeah, in my eyes, we'd done everything right. But things we'd done, and still were doing, could definitely be misconstrued.

I gave a careful nod. I looked out over the room full of rustling and laughing joyous people. "So you're going to tell them that Anastasia La Fay is who concealed their locations."

"Yep."

"And you're going to tell them we're working with Moriah La Fay."

Her breath caught as her eyes pulled open a bit. "Shit, I didn't even think about that."

My lips pressed together. "If you explain it in chronological order, I'm sure they'll understand."

"Couldn't that put a target on her back though?" She turned her gaze to mine. "Telling all of these people about Nastya?"

"It could," I said. "I'm not necessarily concerned about these people going after Moriah. They're no ones and the La Fays are on the Chamber. I'm more concerned about what Nastya will do to her when she realizes she came to us with her information."

"No, I'm not worried about that. That letter she wrote Moriah; I think it was always intended for us. Peterson knows what's going to happen before anyone. That said, it stands to reason that so do Nastya and Amy. They gave us that letter. That's why Nastya sent it to Moriah in the first place. She knew she'd bring it to us."

"Either way. Think we should let Moriah know before you make that kind of announcement?" I asked.

"Yeah, I think I'll go call her real quick." She started to her feet. "You've got Mills?"

Just as I was about to tell her to go ahead, yelling erupted a few dozen yards away. I couldn't make out much of the woman's words, but I heard my wife's name and hysterical crying.

I squinted at the end of the buffet table where Adam was trying, and failing, to calm a screaming Latina woman. I lifted Milly from the highchair and stood as Laila started toward her. Her yells and gaze softened when she saw Laila. I fixed Milly on my hip and cleared the distance between us.

"I was coming to grab you guys." Adam's blue eyes widened.

The woman took Laila's hands and began speaking in Spanish too quick for even me to translate. Tears cascaded down her cheeks.

It was when her gaze turned to me that I put two and two together.

I knew those chocolate eyes. I knew that prominent hooked nose. I knew those high cheekbones and chubby cheeks.

But I didn't know them on her.

That realization sent my stomach falling from my body.

"Mi hijo. Tu sabes mi hijo." *My son. You know my son.*

That part, Laila made out. The moment she did, she stopped breathing for a second. She couldn't find the words. Neither could I.

With tears in her eyes, Laila whispered, "¿Daniel era tu hijo?"

My stomach sunk. Fuck, was I going to have to tell this woman that her son was dead? Did she not know yet?

Daniel's death had torn me up too. But it didn't hurt me anything like I saw it hurting this woman. Her eyes were full of tears, her lips were quivering, and her hands were trembling.

"Si." The woman nodded quickly. "Si. ¿Sabes lo que le pasó?

Laila turned to me for translation. I said, "She asked what happened to him."

She turned back to the woman and pressed her quivering lips together.

"¿Sabes que murió?" *Do you know that he died?*

"Si. ¿Pero qué paso? ¿Usted estaba allí? ¿Estabas allí cuando murió mi bebé?" *Yes. But what happened? Were you there? Were you there when my baby died?*

Laila's eyes watered. "Si. Si, señora." She turned her gaze to mine and wiped a tear from the corner of her eye. "Her accent's thick, can you translate?"

I nodded softly.

"We found your son on a back road late at night in late January of 2019. He ran out in front of our car, and we hit him." I watched the woman's expression carefully as I translated. "He had an injury on his leg, so we took him back to our house to heal him. Once he was healed, I got him something to eat and a bath. We got him in some new clothes, and he fell asleep on our couch watching Spongebob."

Nodding, tears pearled down the woman's face.

Laila continued, "We were able to file for emergency custody to keep him while we looked for his parents, or rather, while we looked for you." She paused for me to translate. The woman smiled and gave slow nods. "We had him for just over a month before…" Water had started to bubble against her cheeks.

"But while he was with us, he was very happy," Laila murmured. "Would—Do you think it would help you to see those good memories of him?"

The woman nodded again, giving a joyous smile. Laila forced a smile back. She opened her eyes and extended them to the woman, closing her eyes. Her palms clasped around Laila's. In a matter of moments, the woman was in an all-out bawl with tears gushing down her cheeks.

My chest grew heavy, stomach aching. I held Milly a little closer. The pain this was causing her, I couldn't completely understand. But I dreaded the day that I lived something comparable to what she was in that moment. There was a very real chance my son was going to die, and the only opportunity I had to know a fragment of who my son was would be from someone else's memories of him.

When their eyes gradually opened, Laila pressed her trembling lips together and blinked through the tears that clouded her vision.

"I was trying to keep him safe that day," Laila whispered. "I got in that van to keep him and my sister safe. But I failed. I failed Daniel, I failed you, and I failed my son too. And no apology will ever be enough to show you how truly sorry I am, but I'm going to say it anyway because I am so sorry. I'm so sorry he's gone. I am so *so* sorry that I didn't keep him safe."

I translated for a moment. Then the woman shook her head and pulled a forced, tear-filled smile. "Esa no era tu trabajo. Era mío. Soy el que falló, no tú."

"What'd she say?" Laila asked.

"That wasn't your job. It was hers. She's who failed him, not you," I said.

Laila's eyes softened. "Tell her I wish neither of us had to blame ourselves for the loss of our sons."

As I spoke, her brows creased a bit. She turned her head to the side and said, "¿Tú también perdiste a tu hijo?"

"She asked if you lost a son too," I muttered.

Laila cleared her throat and gave another nod. "I—Um... That day, the day that Daniel died, that was the day that I was taken. I was about five months pregnant. We—We were... Well, I'll tell the full story when I give my speech. But they told me that if I didn't get in their car, they were going to kill Daniel and my sister." She paused, searching for a way to say it. "So I got in the car."

"Estabas embarazada?" the woman asked. *You were pregnant?*

"Si," I murmured.

"¿Y arriesgó la vida de su hijo por la mía?" *And you risked your son's life for mine?* The woman's pained gaze grew to something I couldn't quite place. Almost pride, but not quite. Maybe gratitude? Admiration? The closest way I could describe that expression was looking to Laila as if a god.

I forced a smile. "Si, senora."

A soft gasp dropped into the woman's lips. She gently clasped Laila's around her shoulders. She pulled her close into her chest and repeated, "Gracias," at least thirty times.

"What'd she say?" Laila mouthed over her shoulder.

"She asked if you risked your life for her son's." I gave a gentle smile.

Her face fell to a frown as she held the woman's shoulders.

Yeah, what she did was an act of heroism. But that didn't mean she was proud of it. And she didn't realize that's what she was doing when she did it.

CHAPTER NINE

LAILA

Speeches.

They weren't my thing.

I wasn't bad at them, but this one felt like I was splitting myself open and pouring it over the crowd. Looking down on all of those people felt so weird. Their eyes were wide in amazement, their lips turned up in a smile—as though I was some celebrity about to perform a show for them.

What if they hated me after I told them the truth? Not that I wanted them to admire me—that part felt really strange anyway. But what if they believed I was aligned with Peterson after they heard the truth? What if they thought that I played some part in what happened to them? What if they believed I was a villain too?

Bracing myself for that possibility, I breathed out a slow, even breath. They had the right to know regardless of how it made me feel once they did. I lifted the cold microphone to my lips.

"Hi, everybody," I said. "For those of you who don't know me, my name is Laila Callidy. And I'm really happy to be here, but I hate speaking in front of people so try and bear with me a little bit, alright?"

There were a few murmurs from the crowd, but they all smiled. Standing there and looking at all of their admiring expressions, I had to fight my urge to run off the stage. They looked at me like I was Christ himself. But I was so far from being a savior. I wasn't even close to being the person they built me up to be in their minds. Explaining that to them felt like telling a child that Santa isn't real.

"Okay, so I'm going to tell you my story. I won't get into the gory details; we all know that we were tortured, and we all have the scars to prove it." I rubbed a sweaty hand against my thigh. "So let me start with when we realized that you guys might still be out there somewhere. It came to us—me and my family—I mean, after a cop who was investigating my friend's murder caught me using my powers on film. Rookie mistake, I know. As the story goes on, you'll see that I made a lot of those.

"But he told me that his wife and daughter had been missing for a number of years. Apparently, before she went missing, she had a premonition. She told him that a girl who 'could hold fire in her hands' would reunite the three of them one day. He agreed to sweep my slip-up under the rug under the condition that I look into their disappearances. So that's what we did. We ran a few spells that kept coming out to the same conclusion. His family was out there, but their location was being concealed. So, we used the same spell a few more times on a few other people. And my brother in-law, who we thought was dead, showed the same outcome.

"I guess that's when it became so important. I never even met Chris. But he was my now-husband's brother, and I wanted to do what I could. I had no idea it would lead us where it did though."

I pulled the microphone from my mouth and ran my hand along my tense jaw. They were all looking *up* at me. And I didn't like it. I was no better than them. We were equals.

So I lowered myself to the end of the stage and draped my legs over the edge. Still, my eyes were slightly higher than theirs. But we were closer to an equal level. That made me a bit more comfortable.

"We started digging. We looked into similar cases, people who disappeared and left nothing but a shit ton of blood behind. We found a lead here, a fragment there, but almost nothing concrete. Then we were driving home one night, and we hit a little boy with our car.

Daniel. His name was Daniel. We took him home, my brother healed him because I wasn't very skilled at the time, and then we got him some food. But when I went to give him a bath, I found the scars. That's when I realized that it was them.

"So we tell our cop friend about it. He gets us temporary custody, and Daniel starts living with us while the cops are looking for his parents. A little over a month goes by before my abduction."

My lip involuntarily quivered. I cleared my throat.

"I was about five months pregnant then. The night that it happened, my husband was going to get our engagement rings from the jeweler a few towns over. I went out with my sister in-law Hannah to get my nails done and dinner with Daniel. But on our way home, they... They were driving a van behind us. Then they sped past me and slammed on their breaks. I couldn't break in time, and I rear-ended them. But when I got out of the car to exchange insurance informa-tion, I..." I struggled to refrain from letting myself break down, blowing out a careful breath to maintain my composure. "The driver had a gun in his hand. And then the passengers got out of his car and ripped Hannah and Daniel from mine. They told me that they'd let them live if I got into their car. I shouldn't have believed them, but I did. I got in the car because I was naïve enough to think that I could handle it.

"So I wake up in my cell and it begins. I won't go into the details with that either because we all know what it was like. But... A lot of things happened to me in there. A few weeks before we escaped, I tried to get out during the stress tests, and I was shot. Right here in the leg." I pulled up my skirt a little to show the scar to the crowd.

"I want to say it was about three weeks later when I prematurely gave birth to my son. That was the most important part. But even more important than that is that when he was born, he didn't cry. But his whole body was glowing like my hands do when I heal.

"I'm not really sure what was going on inside of me, but as soon as I lifted him up and held him to my chest, I looked down and I... I was bleeding. A lot of bleeding. I only saw it for a second or two, so I didn't even realize what was happening until I was passing out. When I woke up, Peterson told me that my son died. My cellmates thought that he did too, or I wouldn't have believed it. I *shouldn't* have believed it because I found out more than a year later that he was still out there." Another pause. "So then we get into it, and he knocks me out with some sedative, and I wake up in my cell."

"But see, I'd been planning an escape for weeks. What was holding me back was this bullet wound in my leg that kept me from walking. I knew that to get everyone out, I had to be able to move or it would be useless. When I woke up though, I realized that my leg was healed. So were the cuts left on my back and... Well, everything. I was back to normal. So I knew that was our shot. Before the next stress test day came around, I was getting us out. I had the opportunity, so I took it.

"Then we get home. Yay, homecoming. Blah, blah, blah. Then was the bombing that took place at our last gathering." Another slow breath left my nostrils, and I licked my teeth. "What Peterson did that day was to prove a point to me. He wanted to show me that he could take anything from me whether I was tied to his table or not. You guys... Don't take this the wrong way, but you were my consolation prize. My son gave his life so that we all could live, or at least that's what I thought at that time, and he wanted to take that from me too. He wanted me to have nothing.

"After that, I fell into a deep and dark pit of depression. Ultimately, I climbed out of it. But I was in that place for a while, and it wasn't easy. While I locked myself in my apartment, my husband locked the bomber up in our basement.

"I only spoke to that man once when we were on the outside. But at that point, he wasn't much of a person anymore. His body was dead, but Peterson was in his head. And he was kneeling on the floor reciting scripture from the Bible. More specifically, he was reciting the biblical book of Revelation.

"We took it with a grain of salt. But after that, everything grew very quiet. For almost a year, things were silent. I learned from another survivor that my son was still alive. But still, I had no leads to follow. I fell into another abyss of depression for a while then too. But I kept looking. Until one day, a woman named Moriah La Fay showed up at my door with a letter, a baby's sock, and a lock of my son's hair.

"I mention her name not because of her family's notoriety but because of what I found in that letter. It had been signed by Anastasia La Fay. I brought a copy of it with me in case anyone wants to go over it and let me know if they see something we haven't. But essentially, that letter was a death note. Not a suicide letter, but a future confession of what they planned to do to my baby. It was all about my son. The son I just learned was still alive somewhere. But not only was it about his death, but the purpose of it. I still don't know what they mean exactly, but they refer to him as the lamb. Using his blood to wash away the sins of the people. Whatever the fuck that means."

I had to pause to recollect myself. A slow breath settled into my lungs as I wiped the tears that escaped my eyes. I cleared my throat once more. I raised the microphone back to my lips, holding my gaze against the pink polish on the tips of my toes.

"When I found that, I... Well, I don't know. I was a mess. For months. Still kind of am, if I'm being completely honest," I muttered into the microphone. "A couple more months go by and I keep having these nightmares where an older version of my son is telling me repeatedly that I have to go back. And I'm not proud of this, and I'm not in any way condoning this behavior. But I ended up doing some hallucinogens with a friend. I see my brother in-law, who I only met inside there, and he tells me that if I want to find them, I have to look. I have to go back. So I do.

"I go back to the building where we were being held. Everything started out fine, but then we split up. Another rookie mistake, I know. But for whatever reason, a guard was there. He ended up stabbing me. My husband takes me home, gets me healed up, and we go back the next day once I'm sober. And we find something. Not what we were looking for. But something."

I fumbled in my purse until I found the book.

"Now, I'm sure none of you know this. But I'm a writer. Never been a great one, but that's what I am. I love words. And I used to fantasize about writing a book, but I found out what I was, and my life took a different route, so I kind of left writing behind. But that day, we found this book.

"Not so weird from where you guys are standing. But if you look a little closer, you can see the by line. And that's me and my husband's name." I pointed to the cover as my gaze shifted around the crowd. "Spoiler alert, we haven't written a book, guys. But somehow, we wrote this. It's the story of how we fell in love, and in it are things no one but me and Jeremy know. Yet, here it is. A book I never wrote written by me. But the even weirder part? The publication date is 2062. Forty years from now."

The puzzled gazes in the crowd grew more confused as I laid the book beside me.

"We thought this was it. This was what my nightmares were leading us to. It didn't help us find our family, but it taught us that the man behind all of this isn't from our time. But then the friend who went with me the first night found some pictures on his phone. There was an orb in every photo of me. So we went back to the building again. But this time, we brought a Witch who could follow the path my brother in-law walked. And when she did, she showed us to a small engraving near the landing strip in the back. It was a code my in-laws created as children. It took my sister in-law a night to decipher it, but when she did, she realized they were coordinates. Chris carved them into the wall the day that we escaped.

"We had a little battle with Peterson and his sidekicks before we pinpointed the exact location of the remaining survivors. Then we took it."

"*You* took it," a voice called from the audience.

Claps and applauses ensued.

But I shook my head. "I didn't do any of this on my own. I don't want you to think that I did. My family worked just as hard as I did to set you all free. I know that I'm the face you guys put to it, but there was a lot of research and other work going on that you guys didn't get to see. My husband, my brother and sister, all of my in-laws. This was a group effort. I know that I'm the one who blew off the roof, but I couldn't have done it all. I couldn't have gotten you all out without each and every one of them. But I especially couldn't have done it without my son and brother in-law, Chris. He's lost everything to that man. He was taken at eighteen almost a decade ago now, and he's the only one of us still in there aside from my son."

A voice called from the crowd, but I didn't hear what they said. I squinted a bit and turned my ear toward the crowd. "Sorry, what was that?"

"Your son," they called back. "What's his name?"

"Micah. My son's name is Micah," I said into the microphone. My lips curved into a smile. "Believe it or not, there's a lot more to the story. I don't know how much more detail I should go into, but there is one thing that I know you all deserve to know."

My hand ran against my mouth. "When they took me, I was treated vastly different from the rest of you. Peterson, I don't know how many of you guys have met him, but he... He was, like, infatuated with me the moment that I got there. I met him three times inside. When he put in my implants, again when I was shot, once at my cell door, and again a day or two before we escaped. And he always phrased things very strangely. He'd say these things that sounded a lot like riddles then but now, looking back on it, I don't think that they were. I think he meant everything he said in a literal sense.

"The day we took the second compound, my husband and I were driving down the road. We were both pretty heartbroken because we were sure we'd have our son and Chris back that day. It's not that I wasn't happy about finding you all, I was. But... Well, I lost my son once again which is a pretty bitter pill to swallow when you blame yourself for losing him.

"Anyway, my husband and I were driving, and I said something about how I never wanted to be like this. I never wanted to be a murderer or a vigilante or whatever you want to call me. I didn't want this. But he said something about how it's not like I chose to do these things. I did them because I had to. That I was put in a situation where I had to fight. I had to become a mass murderer to save all of you.

"When he said that, I had this flashback to something Peterson said the day that I met him. He kept raving about who I was and who I would become. He said that everyone he was holding was important but especially me. He told me that he was trying to teach me. He wanted me to master my capabilities, that's what the stress tests were for. To teach us all how to use and control our abilities. He said something else that didn't make much sense to me then. I can't remember his exact words, but it was something along the lines of how one day, you would all be mine. I thought he was just crazy at first.

"But we found that book and realized that all of this is far more intricate than I first thought." I paused to consider how to go on. "Now I could be wrong about this. This is just a working theory. But... I think when he said that all of you would be mine, he meant that literally. I think he did this... All of this, I mean, as a way to bind us all together. I think that he wanted you guys to trust me. He wanted me to save you all so that you would be loyal to me.

"And I know how that sounds. I know it paints a pretty ugly picture of me. And again, I could be wrong. He may have had an entirely different reason for everything he's done. But if I am right, if he did what he did to all of you to make you want to follow me, I want you to know that you owe me nothing. I didn't help you guys for your loyalty, I helped you because you needed help. That's it. Plain and simple. No one has to be loyal to me, or love me, or even respect me. No one has to look at me like you owe me something because you don't."

I gazed around between the faces for a few heartbeats. I wasn't sure what I expected. Uproar, perhaps, but that didn't come. Instead, they listened with watchful gazes. They were thinking. Maybe the uproar would come a moment later. Or maybe it wouldn't come at all.

I cleared my throat and continued, "But there you have it. There's my story. That's the basic synopsis on how all of this began and where I've ended up. I probably missed some details but there it is. Is there anything I left out that you all want to know?"

Hands raised and tons of people stood to their feet. A young girl near the front waved her hand in the air like a flag was clenched between her fingers. I pointed to her. "What's your question, sweetie?"

"How did everyone know we were breaking out?" she called. "All the people who helped us get to the hospital, I mean."

"That's a good question," I said. "So for those of you who don't know for sure, the rumors are true. My husband is my par animo. At first, the Fae who was working for Peterson managed to put a block in my mind that kept Jeremy from finding my location. But he found a way to get me a message by carving words into his skin. I'd trace out the letters and put it together. Once I felt that barrier in my mind, I started planning our escape. When I woke up healed in that cell after losing my son, I told Jeremy to get everyone ready. I broke out of my cell and killed the guard on watch before knocking down the wall in my mind. That told him where we were, and they started moving people in."

She nodded and sat back down. Then an array of others stood.

They asked so many questions, most of which I hadn't expected. A few pertained to our captures, but most of them were mundane. They wanted to know my daughter's name and my favorite color. They wanted me to introduce them to my family. They asked what I did for fun. They asked what my favorite band was and what shows I liked to watch on TV.

Then they asked about my son. When I stammered over the few vague memories I did have of him, their final question left my heart fluttering. "What can we do to help?"

Although I told them I didn't want to be their savior, they chose me as such anyway. I didn't ask for an army. I never asked for anyone's loyalty who wasn't my family. But they handed it to me on a silver platter because even though I didn't want to be, I was their hero. I was the one who led them from captivity back into a life of freedom.

My hatred for Doctor Robert Peterson fueled the fire within me over the course of the prior two and a half years. I would never stop hating that man for what he did to me, my son, my family, and the other survivors. But he was right about one thing. I was thankful they were on my side.

Because one day, I was going to need that army.

CHAPTER TEN

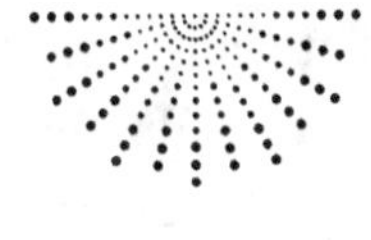

LAILA

I looked out over the quiet banquet hall, breathing in and out slow. Everyone had been pretty considerate; the mess to clean up wasn't that large. But the ambiance had been so beautiful. All those smiling faces, so grateful for the lives they had now.

It almost felt like we were all a family. We all knew about the horrors we'd faced together. We were all bound together by our tragedies. And it was awful when I remembered that Peterson had done so intentionally, but they weren't just numbers. They were people. Individuals with their own stories and lives, and now, we all understood one another in a much more profound way.

The irony in it was that the Chambers existed to unite the supernatural races. But this hadn't been a gathering of the top fifty most relevant creatures in our world. This had been an assemblage of the little guys that truly mattered, and everyone left feeling more unified than ever before.

"That was kind of amazing," I murmured.

Leah shoved paper cups into a black contractor bag. "It went a lot better than I expected."

"Hell of a lot better than last time," Celena muttered.

"I didn't expect them to be so understanding." Brody lowered himself to the edge of a table across from me. "They didn't seem to give a fuck about the fact that you're probably the reason this happened to them in the first place."

"We don't know that's true," Kai murmured.

"We don't know that it isn't either," Brody said.

"Because we know that you didn't have any more choice in this than we did." Gwen leaned against the table beside Brody. "No one could blame the person who saved them from years of misery."

"I'm glad you all see it that way," I muttered. "I was worried when that came out, they'd think that I willingly helped him."

Gwen shook her head. "No, everyone is abundantly grateful for what you did. No one blames you for anything. You're the only one who's still suffering, after all. If you did anything to cause this, you'd have gone to great lengths to cover it up."

I supposed that was so.

I adjusted Milly against my chest. When I lifted her, she chomped down on my nipple. "Motherfucker, Mills." I pulled her off my chest. Her green eyes met mine beneath furrowed brows. And she erupted in cries. But she could fuss all she wanted—she wasn't gonna bite my nipple and still get to keep going. I pulled my dress back over my boob.

My gaze went to Jeremy packing up a box of cookies a few tables down. "Baby, did we bring any milk?"

"Yeah, I left it in the fridge in the back. She bit you again, huh?" he called.

"Yeah, the little shit," I muttered. "She got me good this time."

He made his way around the table and lifted her from my arms. "I'll go feed her."

"Alright, cool. I'll keep cleaning up in here."

As Jeremy walked away, my gaze caught on Gwen. She tried hard not to look my way, clearly holding her breath. "You alright over there?"

She cleared her throat, and her gaze turned up to mine. Her pupils dilated to the size of saucers. "You're bleeding."

I looked down. I felt the wetness on my bra I'd cracked up to milk spillage. I pulled my shirt out to examine it. A slight pinkish color had mixed into the light cream-colored milk. "Oh, shit. That little turd made me bleed."

Gwen's gaze stayed steady on my chest as slow breaths made their way from hers.

"Are you good, girl?" I asked.

"Fae blood's like candy to us," Celena said.

"Yeah, Celena's is all I drink anymore." Wyatt chimed in from a few tables away. "But yours is probably better since you're not part wolf."

"Yeah, if you ever have a little to spare, you could help a sister out once in a while." Celena grinned.

"Wolves don't feed as often as we do." Gwen cleared her throat. "It's a little easier for them to control the hunger."

"Look at that." Adam teased from a few tables away. "You and your girl have now both fantasized about licking Laila's tits, bro."

Brody rolled his eyes and turned to Gwen. "Do you want to go eat, babe?"

She nodded quickly, bringing herself to her feet.

"We're going to head out. I'll see you guys at home." Brody and Gwen joined hands.

"Sure." I smiled. "Nice to see you, Gwen."

She nodded again, unable to meet my gaze. Then they disappeared.

"Here." Leah handed me a glass of wine. "It's been a long couple of years. But all of this, all of those people... It doesn't bring Chris and Micah home. But it makes it all feel a little more worth the fight, doesn't it?"

A small smile pulled at my lips. "Cheers."

***

Warm cotton caressed my bare legs. Soft light from the alarm clock and the bedside lamp shined through our bedroom. I slid my fingers along Milly's soft fingers as her eyes fluttered beneath their lids. Leaning down, I kissed her forehead and breathed in a long whiff of her lavender body wash.

"When do you think we should start putting Milly in her bedroom?" Jeremy asked, plopping onto the bed beside me.

"When she's married," I said.

"Might have to upgrade to a daybed then." He smiled.

I laughed and leaned back against the pillows. "When do *you* think we should move her to her room?"

"Google said between three and six months." He lifted Milly from my arms into the basinet. "And she's looking a little snug in here."

I knew she was probably ready to sleep in her own room. But I still held onto this irrational fear when she wasn't with me. When she was with Jeremy, I didn't worry. But the thought of her being all alone in that big room made my stomach spin. Still, I could teleport to her at any time. I was a mom though—one who already lost a child. The thought of something happening to her terrified me.

But we had the spell around the perimeter, and no one had penetrated it.

I said, "Maybe we could bring the crib in here first. That way she's not a whole floor away just yet."

"Yeah, that's what it said to do online. It also said that we should sleep with the crib sheets before we put them on so that they smell like us. I don't think it'll be too hard for her though 'cause she's already sleeping six hours straight a night." He lowered himself to the bed beside me and pulled the blanket up to his chest. He met my gaze and grinned. "Did I tell you I think she tried to say 'da-da' yesterday?"

My mouth dropped open. "Nuh-uh."

He grinned. "It was more like 'duh' but she's trying."

"No, Mama has to come first," I pouted. "That's not fair."

"Bet she'll say Dada first just to piss you off."

"Fuck off." I playfully smacked his chest. He laughed and swung his arm around my shoulders. My lips heightened in a smile as I nuzzled my head against his chest and gazed at Milly dreaming peacefully in her basinet. "She's getting so big."

"She is," he murmured.

As I looked over her, my mind went to Micah. We should have already had the experience to know when to move Milly to her own room. We should have gotten to watch Micah crawl around on the floor. I should have been able to bitch about him biting my nipple and making the hard leap to get off of breastfeeding.

"Can you show me that memory of Micah again?"

He twined his fingers between mine. "Sure, baby."

I closed my eyes and engulfed myself in the glimpse of my son. Those beautiful blue eyes gazing at his father in question. The long black waves that framed his little cheeks. His sweet little lips and those long black eyelashes. It was only a flash; it wasn't the clearest visual. But it was a recent idea of how he looked, which I found both comforting and agonizing.

My mind stayed frozen on that frame for what felt like hours. I wished I could stay in that second for a century. I just wanted to see that little face and bring a smile to that confused expression. If I could just see him smile, I would do anything. But I couldn't.

All that I could do was admire his perfection in a vague memory.

CHAPTER ELEVEN

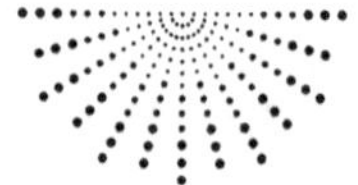

NOVEMBER 6, 2021 - JEREMY

I hummed along to Elton John playing on the diner speakers. My ass ached against the cool tile floor, shimmying a cabinet door beneath the sink into place.

"Hey, did you sign off on those papers from the bank?" Max asked from the doorway to the office.

I propped the cabinet door against my shoulder to lift the screw from my lips. "Yeah, they're in an envelope on the desk. I'll take them with me when I leave and drop them off on my way in in the morning. You still need off tomorrow, right?"

Max had been taking a lot of personal days lately. His mom was in a really bad way—she'd been diagnosed with cancer over the summer. It didn't look like she had much time left. Laila and I both wanted him to get as much time with her as possible before that day inevitably came. I didn't mind picking up the work. God knew he'd done so much for us over the years, it was time we started picking up some slack.

"Yeah. Yeah, sorry for giving you guys such short notice. The spot opened up for that trial at the last second because one of the patients died. I would have given you two weeks' notice if I knew sooner."

"Don't worry about it, man." I jammed the screw into the pre-drilled hole on the cabinet, screwed it into place, and raised my voice above the hum. "I don't mind picking up the hours. How's she doing by the way?"

"Not good," he muttered. "Just got moved into stage three."

"Damn, I'm so sorry. It's progressing quickly, huh?"

"Yeah, pancreatic does, I guess. That's what the doctors keep saying anyway. They're talking about palliative care, whatever the fuck that is."

"That's a good thing actually. Palliative care is statistically proven to help cancer patients live longer." I set the drill on the floor and stood. "No one's talked about hospice, right?"

"No, thank God," he said. "Look, I wanted to ask you something. And if not, I completely understand."

I wiped sweat from my forehead and leaned against the counter. "Sure, what's up?"

"Our sewage pump broke down on us last week. Normally I'd have the money to get it taken care of, but it was two grand just to get into the trial, plus the plane tickets and the hotel room so I'm, like, flat ass broke. You know I hate to ask for favors, but I'm just really struggling right now. Is there any way I could get an advance on next month's pay? You know I'm good for it, I just don't know what else to do. We've been shitting in a potty chair and showering at the gym and Mom's too sick to do all that."

Damn, what were they doing with the shit in the potty chair? Burying it in the backyard? He should've asked the second it broke. Helping out friends and family wasn't something we minded doing. Max was Laila's best friend; I didn't even need to ask if she'd be okay with it. She'd probably get pissed at me for not immediately telling him yes in the first place.

"Yeah, of course, man. But how are you going to pay for your bills next month then?" I asked.

"I don't know. I'll figure it out."

"How about you just take the money as a bonus?" I wiped my hands against my jeans and stifled a yawn. "You've done a lot here over the years, you deserve it."

"Are you sure?" His round cheeks grew red. "I know you guys just built the house, and you're trying to replenish your savings and everything."

"We're doing alright. I'm sure Laila'll agree that you need it more than we do. How much do you need?"

"It's gonna be around twenty-five hundred. I have a couple hundred though. Really anything would help."

"Stop by the house when we close up, and I'll get it out of the safe for you," I said.

"You don't want to check with Laila first?"

"I'll text her, but I doubt she'll care."

"Alright, well thank you. I'm going to find a way to pay you back one way or another though."

I adjusted my ponytail. "I really wish that you wouldn't. You've done so much to help us over the years, Max. This is the least we could do."

He sighed as the bell rang above the door at the front of the diner. "Well, thank you. I really appreciate it. Do you need any help with those doors?"

"Nah, they were just loose. It's all good," I said. "Let me go seat that table real quick."

"Sure," Max said.

I started through the swinging stainless steel door. Just as I was about to spout off my usual 'Have a seat wherever you'd like,' spiel, I saw Ray rubbing his eyes at the bar.

"Oh, hey. Do you want a cup of coffee?" I asked.

"Got anything stronger?"

I laughed. "If you want to go pour it. Pretty sure that door to the basement's open but if not, you can go through the kitchen."

"Oh, shit. I'm sorry. I completely forgot for a second there."

I smiled, giving a shrug. I'd just hit a year of sobriety—something I was elated about. But I couldn't be that close to liquor still. Seeing other people drink didn't bother me. Actually touching the bottle was another story.

"No, you're good. I was alright pouring drinks before my last relapse. It's still pretty fresh though."

"How long's it been now?"

"Just shy of fifteen months," I said. "No six years. But hey, I'm pretty proud either way."

"Yeah, absolutely. That's great."

"You can go ahead and grab a drink though. Seeing other people drinking doesn't bother me," I said.

"I'll just get one when I get home. I'm in the cruiser anyway. But could you grab me a Coke?"

"Yeah, no problem."

As I started toward the soda fountain, I saw Ray lift his arms through his jacket out of the corner of my eye. When he did, I caught a glimpse of a big splotch of blood on the side of his neck. "Jesus, are you alright?"

"What?" I gestured to his neck. He touched it, then closed his eyes and sighed. "I thought I got it all off, damn it."

"Not yours I take it?"

"No. I got called in on a domestic dispute. Some guy was drunk and beating on his wife. It was pretty bad when I got there. He tried to tell me I couldn't come in without a warrant; I told him I could because a call was made from inside the home. I heard a kid yelling in the back, so I told him to let me in again and the fucker socked me. He could barely stand, it's not like his punch did much. But I had to take him down. I kept telling him to stop resisting, but I couldn't reach my taser so." He lifted a shoulder.

I raised a brow. "So you used excessive force?"

Laila and I had both attended a number of protests and rallies over police brutality over the years. Our opinions on it were pretty firm. Cops should know how to deescalate without immediately reaching for their gun.

Still, I supposed if I heard a kid screaming, I probably wouldn't have done much different.

"Don't give me that look. You and Laila kill people all the time."

"Hey, dude was beating his wife and kids. I don't care what level of force you had to use," I said. "Just, ya know. Be careful. Video of you doing something like that pops up on the internet and you're never getting a job in law enforcement again."

"Yeah, I know. The kid and the wife locked themselves in the back room, no one saw anything. Not my proudest moment though," he muttered. "But dude wouldn't stop hitting me either, man. I know in some situations, cops use force they don't need to. But I didn't have back-up. It felt pretty necessary at the time."

I supposed the was fair. "Probably should find a way to channel your anger though. If you're looking for a place to let your anger out, I could use someone to spar with. I won't fight Lai, and Brody punches too hard. Adam's got a newborn with colic so he's out too."

"I don't know, man. You hit hard."

He wasn't wrong. I may not have been a big guy, but I had three brothers. If that hadn't taught me to fight, killing Demons and Were-wolves since I entered adulthood definitely did the trick.

"Pussy," I muttered.

"And you have an unfair advantage."

"You should learn to fight a teleporter. You might need to one day."

"I was more so referring to the ten-year age gap," Ray said. "Get to be my age and fighting isn't something you do for fun anymore."

It's not like I was a teenager; I was almost twenty-seven. Ray was my peer, not my elder.

"*Your age.* What are you? Thirty-five?" I laughed. "And I don't do it for fun. I do it because in our lives, it's important to know how to fight."

Ray bit his lip. "You aren't going to hit me as hard as you hit me after you found out me and Laila slept together, are you?"

It wasn't that I liked the fact that that had happened. I just liked to pretend that it hadn't. We all knew it didn't really matter in the grand scheme. But if he didn't want to get punched in the face again, he could shut the fuck up about it.

My gaze narrowed. "Mention it again and we won't make it to sparring."

"Duly noted," he muttered. I handed him his drink and turned to the coffee pot to pour myself a cup. "So how was Lydia for you guys today?"

"Huh?"

"Lydia was with Laila today. They were going to see a movie," Ray said.

I did a mental memory search, but Laila didn't mention anything about a movie. Milly and theaters weren't a good combination. "I don't think so. Laila's at her mom's with Jenna and the kids. I'm pretty sure Lydia was at the main house when I stopped by this morning."

His breaths stopped. "What?"

"I mean, I could be wrong. Let me call her and ask." I reached for my phone in my pocket as he reached for his.

He hurriedly slid his out too, tapping for a minute. "It says she's at the house. I better call her."

CHAPTER TWELVE

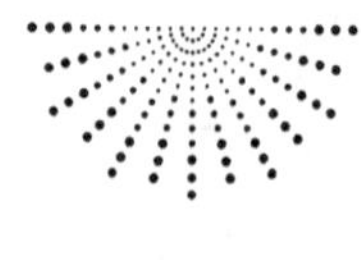

LAILA

The soft yet spicy scent of Mom's chili filled my nose. Pretty hues of orange and yellow from the sunset shined in from the patio doors to the terracotta flooring. Milly cooed in her highchair, plopping her spoon into the red mush on her tray.

"Why?" Jenna huffed, looking down at Luka in my arms. "Why do you only shut up when we're around people?"

"He can probably pick up on how tense you are," Mom muttered.

"Well, you'd be tense too if you hadn't gotten more than three hours of sleep in the past two months," Jenna snipped.

She was always a bitch. But she was so much crankier since Luka was born. I'd asked if she was okay a hundred times—worrying she was going through post-partum. But she said she was fine, just annoyed. Not that I blamed her. Luka was a grouchy infant. Colic isn't fun. I'd gone into his head a time or two to feel what it was like, and I couldn't blame the kid. It hurt.

"Why don't you let me and Jeremy take him for a night?" I asked. "You and Adam could go out and have a night on the town. Maybe rent a hotel in the city. Or somewhere else. Your boyfriend can teleport, you know. You guys could go to Paris."

She rolled her eyes. "I haven't showered in four days and you want me to go to Paris."

"Alright, does somebody need a little nap-nap?" I grinned.

Her eyes narrowed. "I'm going to hit you."

"No, I'm holding a baby. I have immunity," I said. She leaned forward and flicked me in the forehead. I let my finger get hot before quickly poking her in the arm.

"Fuck you. That hurt, bitch."

"See? And you wondered why your father bound your powers," Mom said.

"She started it," I said.

"Well, I'm *so* sorry that I'm cranky, but not all of us have little angel babies. Some of us have devil spawns," Jenna said.

"Don't talk about my grandson like that." Mom leaned down and lifted Luka into her arms. "It isn't his fault."

Milly was not a perfect baby. I suppose she was perfect to me, but my situation was vastly different from Jenna's. Her cry was the best sound I ever heard. For two years, I dreamed of hearing my child cry. That cry sounded like love and joy.

Adam wasn't the doting father that Jeremy was either. He loved Luka and all, but he acted like a more typical dad. He smiled at him, held him for a while, changed his diapers, and fed him his bottle. But Jeremy spent any free moment he had doing something with Milly. He enjoyed parenthood as much as I did. The two of us were built to be parents.

Jenna would get there soon enough. But parenthood comes easier to some than others. It'd take her some time to adjust.

"I'm serious, Jen. Me and Jeremy can take him for a night. Or at least a couple hours so you guys can have a little peace and quiet." I looked over Luka sleeping in Mom's arms and smiled. "You could use a little stress relief, and we could use some time with our nephew."

"Maybe," she said. "I don't know what Adam's schedule looks like."

"Well, I'll talk to him when I stop by the diner. I'm sure he'd be down. You're parents, but you're still young. You guys could use some quality time together." My phone rang in my pocket as I went on. "Plus, you guys can finally bang again. You ought to get on that."

"I ought to get back on the pill first," Jenna mumbled.

I chuckled and pulled my phone out. Jeremy's picture lit up the screen. I answered the call and held my phone to my ear. "Hey, you."

"Hey, what are you doing?" Jeremy asked.

"Sitting here with Mom and Jen. What's up?"

"I was just finishing up those cabinets in the kitchen when Ray came in. I guess Lydia told him she was with you. She isn't, is she?"

"No." I furrowed my brows. "Is she at the house?"

"Her phone says she is, but Leah says she isn't," Jeremy said. "Do you have any idea where she could have gone? Ray's freaking out."

My heart began to race. "No, I have no clue. But she's fourteen. She probably just wanted to go hang out with her friends. Did he call Isabella? I know they've been talking a lot."

"Yeah, he's calling her parents now," Jeremy said. He paused as Ray talked in the background. "Chill, dude, I'm getting there. Babe, Ray wants to know if we can split up and drive around looking for her. Maybe you could look in people's heads to try and pinpoint where she is."

"Yeah, of course." I stood. "Let me get Milly packed up and I'll meet you guys at the diner."

"Okay, I'm going to call Wyatt and Celena to see if they can try to find her scent. She's Fae; it shouldn't be too hard to track her down."

"That's a good idea," I said. "Alright, I'll see you soon. Love you."

"Love you too," he said.

I ended the call, grabbed the wipes from the table, and started scrubbing chili from Milly's hands and cheeks.

"What's going on?" Jenna asked.

"Lydia told Ray she was with me and her phone is at the house, but she isn't." I hurriedly pulled Milly's shirt back over her shoulders and lifted her into her car seat. "She's probably just with a friend, but I'm going to go help look for her."

"I bet she's with a boy," Mom said.

"Yeah, probably," Jenna said. "That's what I lied to you and Dad about when I was fourteen."

"The kid she's been talking to lives in New York, so I doubt it. But I'm going to talk to Jeremy about Adam's schedule so we can make plans for my night with my nephew. We're going to make something work."

Jenna sighed. "We'll see."

"You go on and on about how much of a pain in the ass this baby is, and you don't even want to go to dinner without him?" Mom laughed.

"I love him." Jenna's face said Mom's kindhearted comment was deeply offensive. "I just miss sleeping."

CHAPTER THIRTEEN

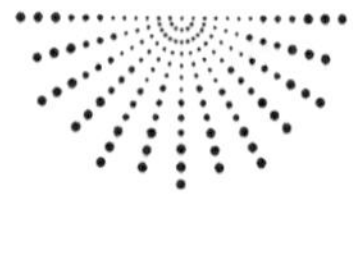

LAILA

"When did you see her leave?" Ray said quickly as he and Wyatt loaded into my car. "Four thirty you said, right?"

"Yeah, about," Wyatt said. "I was on a run, so I didn't talk to her. But yeah, it was some time around there. She was walking down the driveway."

"Why didn't you stop her?" Ray said as he dialed quickly on his phone.

"Stop her from what?" Wyatt cracked his window for a breeze. "The kid's not allowed to go for a walk?"

Ray gritted his teeth and clicked the seatbelt into place.

That settled it then. She left on her own accord. I was sure she was fine. She had left her phone because she knew her dad could track her with it. The poor kid just wanted an ounce of freedom. The normalcy Ray rambled about but wouldn't allow her to have.

"You need to chill, dude," I said. "She's a kid. For all we know, she's hanging out with her friends at the library."

"Or she's lying in a ditch somewhere. Or they took her again. Anything could have happened to her, Laila. I don't need to chill; I need my daughter to be safe in her bed."

"More like you need her to behave on her leash," Wyatt muttered.

Ray turned with a tight jaw. "What?"

Wyatt shook his head. Ray's nostrils flared as he turned back out the window.

I did see Ray's perspective. We'd both lost a child, and the thought of losing them again was nearly unfathomable. That's why I was so protective of Milly too. The thought of her growing up and no longer being under my supervision terrified me. But even so, he was going overboard. He gave her no room to breathe, let alone live. And although I saw his perspective, I could also see Lydia's. In her shoes, most would have done the same thing.

"I'm sure she's fine, Ray. We're going to find her," I said.

We spent the following two hours driving around our tiny town with the windows down. Wyatt stuck his head out of the window on multiple occasions to 'get a better whiff' but it did no good. We even stopped at a few parks for Wyatt to take a closer look but still came back with nothing to go on.

Celena called to tell us that she followed her scent to the end of the driveway, but it disappeared just outside of the perimeter. That conclusion terrified me at first until Celena said she picked up the scent of motor oil near where Lydia's scent ended. Since our back road didn't get much traffic, I knew what that meant.

She wasn't kidnapped. Someone picked her up. Ray proceeded to go through her phone where all of her conversations had been deleted. That gave me all the information I needed to know. Mom was probably right; she most likely met up with a boy and left her phone at home so Ray couldn't track her location, as she knew he would.

Wyatt said something about how we should call it a night because she'd probably be back soon, as most teenagers are when they sneak out. I was about to agree when Ray flipped his lid. He screamed that we couldn't just go home when his daughter was still out there somewhere. It felt ironic to agree, but I did because in his shoes, I would have done the same.

At a quarter after eleven, I got a call from a New York number I didn't recognize. As it flashed against the touch screen on my dashboard, Ray stopped breathing for a moment. I prepared for the worst and clicked accept.

"Hello?" I answered.

Heavy breathing ensued before Lydia's shaken, somber voice spoke through the speakers. "Laila, it's—It's me. It's Lydia. I—I, I need your help. Something happened."

"What's going on, sweetie?" I pulled off to the shoulder of the road. "Where are you?"

"I—I'm not sure. We're—We're at a park somewhere." She stammered and stuttered, voice shaking with tears.

"We who?" Ray nearly yelled. "Who are you with, Lydia?"

"Is that my dad?" Lydia asked.

"Yes it is, and you're in big trouble—"

"Shut up, Ray," I said. "You can text me your location, can't you?"

"Yeah, just hurry up. My friend's hurt and I'm scared," she said.

I shifted the car into park. "Alright, sweetie. I'll be there as soon as I get your location. Is it clear for me to teleport in?"

"Yeah." She struggled to take deep breaths into her lungs. "We— We're in the woods. No one's around."

"Well, if you thought you had no freedom before, you just wait until—"

"Please just shut the fuck up, Ramirez," I snapped with a shake of my head. Lydia's cries got louder, and she ended the call.

"I don't tell you how to parent your kid," Ray said. "Don't tell me how to parent mine."

My forehead scrunched up as I turned to meet his gaze. "That wasn't about parenting; that was about compassion. Yes, she broke your rules. And yes, you have every right to punish her. But maybe wait until she's—Oh, I don't know. Not stranded with her injured friend with no one there to help her."

"You worry about your kid, and I'll worry about mine."

My gaze narrowed as I thought about the irony of that statement.

His daughter was half of the reason I didn't have my son. I gritted my teeth together as my phone dinged with Lydia's message.

"Wyatt, could you take Milly to Jeremy and then the car back to the house? He said he was right down the road." I glanced at him in the back seat. "She's already asleep, I don't want to wake her if I don't have to."

"Yeah, that's fine. I'll call Celena now and tell them to call off the search," Wyatt said.

"Alright, thanks." I looked down at the coordinates, typing the address into Google Earth. Once I got a clear image of the wooded park, I put my phone back into my pocket. Ray extended his hand. "Fuck off. You wanted my help so I'm handling it."

"You can't just—"

I was gone before he could finish his sentence.

CHAPTER FOURTEEN

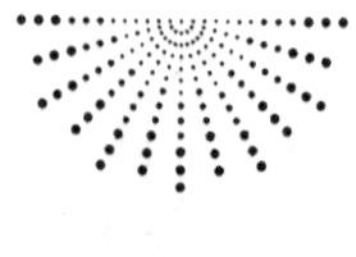

LAILA

The cool late autumn air sent a chill to my skin as I landed in the muddy mountain dirt. I took a look around, but the sun had set hours before, making it impossible to see my hand a foot from my face. A flame came to my skin for a source of light. Raindrops turned to steam when they touched the fire.

"Lydia," I yelled. "Lydia, it's me. It's Laila."

"Over here," she called from a few dozen yards away. I sensed her energy and focused on it. Once I pin-pointed where it came from, I teleported to her. The fire remained aglow in my palm as I landed beside her at the edge of a rocky cliff side.

Her thick black curls caked mud to her cheeks. A stream of blood pearled from her forehead down her blotchy, tear covered face. But there was no wound where it started.

She kneeled next to a young boy who couldn't have been more than sixteen. Blond hair hung around his blood splattered cheek that rested against a large rock. Blood drizzled from his elbow to the pile of stone beneath him.

"What the hell happened?" I lowered myself to the ground beside her. The fire in my hand turned to a bright glowing white, preparing to heal him.

"Wait." Lydia grasped my wrist with wide eyes. "You have to wipe some of his memories first."

I cocked my head slightly. "What happened, Lydia?"

She pressed her trembling lips together as more tears flowed down her cheeks. "He—He was here."

My breath caught as I looked between her pale blue eyes. "Micah?"

"Ethan fell, and I was trying to help him back up, but I fell too and I—I hurt my leg really bad. The—the bone was sticking out and I w-w-was sure I was done for but—but..."

"Micah came and healed you," I whispered.

Lydia was silent for a moment, eyes watering. "Chris showed up, but it wasn't Chris. And Micah threw some type of energy at him but he—He just grabbed him up and they were gone. And Ethan fainted when he saw it but he—he did. He saw it."

He did it again. It'd been a few weeks; we should have tried again. Maybe it'd have worked. Damn it, we missed our shot. God fucking damn it.

But in the same breath, I was proud of him. He saved someone's life again. My baby was a little hero. I wished he didn't have to be. I wished he could just be a baby like he was supposed to be. But I was still proud that his heart was that big, especially in a place where kindness had been beaten out of me.

My eyes filled with tears. I gave a quick nod. I couldn't bring myself to say a word as I enveloped myself into the boy's mind and altered the final moments before he fainted. He'd wake up thinking he fell, hit his head, and passed out. He'd have no recollection of the toddler who appeared and shot energy from his palms. I placed his thoughts into a heavy trance of sleep and quickly healed his broken arm but left the cut on his cheek so that there'd be an explanation for the blood. When I finished, I ended the trance inside of his head.

"What happened?" he asked, eyes dazed.

"You fell and hit your head," Lydia said. "I called Laila to come and try to help me wake you up so we didn't have to call our parents."

He blinked hard, gently pulling himself up.

"Easy there," I said. "Don't want you fainting again."

He ran his hand against his elbow. "I just hit my head?"

"Yeah," Lydia assured him.

"Weird," he muttered. "I remember my elbow hurting."

"Maybe you pulled a muscle on the way down," I said. "But you're feeling alright?"

"Yeah. Yeah, I'm good. Just a little dizzy," he said. "But yeah. Yeah, I'm okay."

"Are you going to be okay to drive home or should I call your parents?" I asked.

"No," he said quickly. "No, I'm okay."

I started to my feet. "Drove all the way from New York without their permission?" He didn't respond. I extended my hand to him. "Not a smart move, kid. But I was young and dumb once too. Just learn from your mistakes, okay? Someone could have really gotten hurt, and you would've been a whole state away. Plus, Lydia's dad's a little crazy. You take his daughter somewhere without his permission again and he just might kill you."

He stood and locked his gaze with the ground.

"Go ahead and walk your friend to his car, Lydia. I'm right behind you." I gestured toward the trail a few dozen yards away.

She pulled a smile to her lips. "Thanks, Laila."

I forced a smile as they headed to the trail.

As I walked behind the couple of kids playing with puppy love, I found myself fantasizing about her little hero. Micah was getting smarter. Smarter, and stronger. I pondered how he managed to escape the barrier spells that even I couldn't. Wherever they were, Nastya was still using them. I tried that simple locator spell at least once every week and it always came back with the same results. Helena's all did the same. So how did he get out?

His thoughts were becoming far more complex. Maybe I could make a connection to him through Lydia. Maybe if I focused hard enough, I could contact his mind. That's all I needed. Just one minute in that little head.

But I had to stop myself. I had to handle any situation with Micah like diffusing a bomb. If I let my emotions rule my decision making, I would lose again. I'd learned my lesson before, and I wouldn't make the same mistakes. I wouldn't get my hopes up either because every time that I had before, they came crashing down around me like a meteor shower.

I stayed at the edge of the trail while Lydia approached the Oldsmobile and kissed her friend goodbye. It brought a smile to my lips when I saw those two share a closed-mouth, innocent kiss. That was all Lydia wanted. Normalcy. To love and to be loved for the first time as any young girl does.

The same normalcy I wanted for my babies.

Then the boy loaded into his car and backed out of his parking space. He honked goodbye as a cloud of dust billowed behind him on the gravel road. We watched his headlights bounce in the dark for a moment. I turned to Lydia. "Your dad's being a real dick about this."

Her gaze turned to the ground. "I guess he has a good reason."

"He does," I said. "Wasn't a smart move."

"I just... I never get to do anything," she muttered. "I should be in high school right now. I'm missing my freshman year. I shouldn't have to worry about my mother or one of her insane friends trying to kill me."

"And I should be going home to my son and daughter," I said. "But we aren't the icons of what a life *should* look like, Lydia. Our lives are bullshit. But unfortunately, they're our lives. We don't get to start over and have a new one no matter how badly we wish we could. You've got to accept the hand you're dealt, baby girl."

"I can't call a re-deal?" she said with a half grin.

"If it worked like that, I'd have done it years ago."

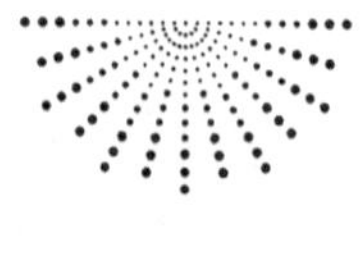

LAILA

"What the fuck were you thinking?" Ray yelled with a darting gaze at Lydia. "Why would you lie to me like that, Lydia?"

"Because I knew you wouldn't let me go," she mumbled.

"You're damn right I wouldn't. Look at you, you're covered in blood and you have leaves in your hair and mud everywhere. What were you doing with that boy anyway?" He narrowed his gaze. "Who is this kid?"

"He's my friend," she said.

"Your friend, huh?" He looked down at her phone in his hand. "Well, is he gay? Because I don't know any straight boys who use this many hearts in a message about their breakfast."

He must've gotten into her social media accounts for those messages because she'd deleted all of her texts. And sure, I knew I may end up going through my kid's phone at some point, but it still felt pretty fucked up. He'd deprived Lydia of every bit of privacy she had.

"I don't know any gay boys who do that either," I muttered.

"Laila." Ray clenched his jaw.

"Sorry."

"Is this kid your boyfriend?" he asked.

"No."

"Well, it looks like it from where I'm sitting," Ray said.

"So what if he is?" Lydia blurted. "Why does it matter?"

"Because you didn't talk to me about it—"

"Talk to you? How am I supposed to talk to you about shit, Dad? You don't care about what I think, or how I feel—"

"That isn't true—"

"Sure it is. But that had nothing to do with it. It isn't because I didn't tell you; it's because you want to control me. You don't treat me like your daughter. You treat me like one of those convicts you put behind bars. You want power over me because it terrifies you that I'm strong enough to do whatever I want. I usually don't break the rules out of respect for you, but the one time I do, you act like it's the end of the—" She gasped and grabbed ahold of her wrist.

I stood from the breakfast nook beside Jeremy. Her gasp turned into a quiet moan as she looked down at her hand with wide eyes. "Are you okay, hon?"

Just then, an ear-piercing scream left her lips. She stumbled from the bar stool and plummeted to the ground. Ray and I rushed to her as her scream grew louder and even more agonized. But I looked at her wrist and saw nothing.

Then the thought rang between my ears.

Micah felt her pain, and she felt his.

My heart hammered against my ribs. Her eyes closed, grasping her hair in fistfuls on either side of her head. She writhed and screamed against the pain that wasn't hers. "No!" Her head shook. "No, stop! Stop!"

I grabbed her shoulders and looked over the terror in her expression. Her brows pulled together, the water drenching her cheeks, her lips trembling. My breathing grew uneven as I put my arms around her and tugged her into my chest. The tears in my eyes escaped as I closed them.

My baby was in pain. He was hurting, and I couldn't help him. I couldn't hold him. Holding her was the closest I could get.

Slow pants heaved from my chest. I made the horrible decision to dip into her mind. Those memories still haunt me today.

I could see through his eyes. For a moment, I saw what my two-and-a-half-year-old son could see.

Above him to his right stood the man I hated more than I hated Hitler. He wore his own face this time. His expression wasn't angry nor merciless. His gaze against Micah's forearm looked as mine did when packing up leftovers or sweeping the porch. Careless and unbothered.

Amy stood on the left clenching his tiny shoulders against the metal table with braces too large to keep him steady. She held a gentle smile and murmured soft words I couldn't hear over the sound of his deafening screams. It was the same way I must have looked to Milly when I held her down for the doctors to give her vaccines.

Nastya held either of his legs at the foot of the table. She too wore a simple, unbothered gaze. It was as if she had no care in the world that they were cutting into the flesh of a toddler.

"It huwts!" Micah cried. "I no do it again."

"You said that last time, Micah." Peterson met Micah's gaze. "If you don't do as I say, I have to take something from you. That's just the way the world works."

"But it huwts," he continued between gasping cries. "It huwts."

His voice. My baby's voice. Soft and sweet, so gentle and kind. My eyes filled with tears, chest so tight that I wasn't sure I was breathing.

Peterson hushed before he stroked a bloody glove covered finger against Micah's cheek. "It'll be over soon."

He pulled back and lifted the small black dot to his finger. Micah shook his head and continued to beg before he gripped the skin between his middle and forefinger and yanked the skin apart. He screamed the loudest, most pain filled, horrible sound I'd ever hear.

I don't know why I stayed there as long as I did. I should have flung myself from those thoughts the moment that I realized what was happening. But I couldn't bring myself to. I had to stay there because that was the closest I'd been to my son since the moment he was born.

Those would always be the most painful twenty minutes of my life.

If I could do it over, I would have saved myself the pain and found peace with the summary. But as they say, curiosity killed the cat.

When he finally fainted from agony, I found myself in a panic attack on the floor beside Lydia. Her hands cupped over her mouth as floods descended from her eyes. Jeremy kneeled in front of me with wet, salty water covered cheeks. His hands quivered on my biceps as he said words I couldn't hear over my hyperventilating gasps. His hurt, heartbroken eyes were the only things I saw.

I leaned forward and wrapped my arms around his shoulders, struggling to bring air into my lungs. His hand slid along the back of my hair. He squeezed me tight against him with the other. I felt a soft glow from his palm that normally would have left me feeling euphoric but only gave me enough peace to breathe normally.

Once my tears were only glistening, Jeremy placed his hand on Lydia's shoulder and did the same. With her restored composure, Tink approached me with her tail between her legs and sad eyes. She leaned forward, licked the tears from my cheek, and the snot from my nose. More tears formed in my eyes. I reached out to pet her scruff, resting my head against hers.

"What just happened?" Ray whispered from the counter.

"They put the implants in Micah," Leah whispered with teary eyes a few feet in front of me.

Celena stood beside her gently rocking Milly in her arms. Hannah and Kai sat at the breakfast nook with looks of sympathy and guilt. Wyatt was unable to meet my gaze from where he stood at the wet bar. Mary was chewing her thumb nail by the rear doors.

Ray's eyes peeled further open. "For healing Lydia."

I nodded, swallowing hard at the lump in my throat.

"This is why you should have listened to me," Ray began to the traumatized girl on the ground. The moment he said it, Lydia's glistening tears flipped back to quaking sobs. "None of this would have—"

"Shut the fuck up." I hurriedly brought myself to my feet. "Stop with all of your bullshit about wanting to keep her safe. None of us are ever going to be fucking safe. We're all always at risk. This isn't Lydia's fault."

"That isn't what I meant—"

"That's what you said. And you don't get to toss around the blame card." I felt my eyes radiate in their sockets while I made my way to him at the end of the island. "If this is because of anyone, it's you. If you treated your daughter like a person instead of your captive, this wouldn't have happened. If you let me teach her what the fuck she was doing, she would have used the Earth to protect her and she would have never fallen and gotten hurt in the first place. This is *your* fault." I pushed his chest, tears rushing down my angry, wrinkled cheeks. "This is all your fucking fault. You're the reason I lost my son in the first place, and now you think you have the right to blame one of the only things that made my loss worth it?"

"I didn't mean—"

"Shut up. Just keep your fucking mouth shut."

Another voice cut through the room, one that'd been silent since this started.

"Laila." Mary stepped around from the other side of the counter. "Laila, let's take a walk."

Ray looked between my eyes with a gaze that fell somewhere between guilt and fear. I angrily wiped my cheeks as Mary took my arm. "Can you watch the baby for a little while, Jeremy?"

He licked his lips. "Yeah. I'll take her back to the house and get her to bed."

"Thank you," she said. "Come on. You need some air."

CHAPTER SIXTEEN

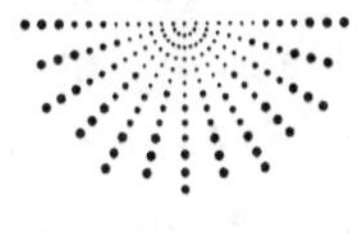

LAILA

The stars twinkled in the dark blue sky above me like fireflies over a grassy field in the summertime. A bluish white glow shined on the naked trees Mary and I meandered through in silence. The dead leaves crunched together beneath the soles of my feet before imprinting into the mud.

Mary extended a small metal flask my way. I arched a brow, took it, and met her gaze. "You drink?"

"An acquired taste," she muttered. "I'm a Demon now. This is what we're supposed to do, isn't it?"

I unscrewed the lid and lifted the drink to my mouth. A grimace stretched across my lips when the cinnamon flavor touched my tongue. I swallowed quickly before it turned to a cough. "Ew, is that Fireball?"

"Goldschlager." She laughed. "You don't like it?"

"I used to." I coughed again. "But I can't do cinnamon in my liquor anymore."

"That's a shame." She pulled another flask from her jacket pocket.

"Damn." I chuckled. "You keep that muh-fucking thing on you."

"What?" Mary extended it to me, face screwed up in confusion.

I laughed and opened the flask. "You should really get on social media. You probably have no idea what we're talking about ninety-nine percent of the time."

"I think a dictionary of your lingo would suffice," Mary muttered.

"They have one of those, ya know. Hell, just get a cell phone."

"I have a cell phone."

"You have a flip phone. It's not the same thing." She waved me off. I lifted the bottle and sniffed. "What's this?"

"Whiskey," she said. "You like whiskey, don't you?"

"I do like whiskey." I took a long gulp. So long, only half remained when I screwed the lid back on. As the burn settled in my stomach, I looked up at the sky. "Me and Adrian were drinking Fireball the night that she killed me."

"Oh," she muttered. "I'm sorry, I didn't realize."

"We were only a couple hundred yards that way." I pointed ahead. "I marked the tree it happened under with a knife, but I didn't need the marker. I'll never forget that tree. Adrian died under it too."

"She did," Mary murmured.

For years, I'd wondered. I never had the courage to ask, and honestly never cared to with all things considered. Life had been too hectic to think about my high school best friend's murder. But the opportunity was there so I took it.

"Did you have anything to do with that?" I turned to meet her gaze.

She made a face. "You think I'd manipulate the mind of my daughter's friend into murdering her?"

I shrugged. "Stranger things have happened."

Mary frowned. "No, Laila. I had nothing to do with that."

Her expression did make me believe her. Truthfully, I never believed she was responsible for it either. I just had to ask. "Did you know what would happen to Micah yet?"

She lowered herself to a tree stump. "No, I knew nothing of the sort. I was still trying to wrap my head around the fact that the myth was true. About the par animarum, I mean. Let alone that I birthed one of the most powerful souls to ever exist. And that I helped raise another."

I used the wind to lift me to a low tree branch before situating my butt on it.

A quiet laugh escaped her lips. "Your father used to do that."

"What? Levitate with air?"

She nodded, and her smile slowly fell. "Yes."

"Wish I would have gotten to see it."

I didn't want to think about what I'd just witnessed. I wanted to think about anything *but* what I'd just witnessed. And there were many questions I'd pondered about Mary. The little interview would serve as a good distraction. "Did you love him? My dad?"

A soft, audible sigh left her lips. "I still do. I wish that things were different. But yes. I love him."

"But if you loved him, why didn't you just stay together?"

"I was told not to," she murmured. "I was obedient then. And he deserved the life he lived. He loved your mother, and she loved him the right way. A way that I never could. And he loved your sister. And he loved you. Kai as well. Giving him to Flora was the hardest thing he ever did."

"When did you find out what would happen to Micah?"

"I don't remember the day. But some point in 2016," she murmured.

I cocked my head to the side. "Then why did you wait so long to act?"

"I didn't. The siren was a last resort, Laila. I was desperate at that point. I'd been doing other things to drive a wedge between you. I had Jeremy work as many cases out of town as possible. I had Olivia make advances on Jeremy on several occasions when he visited the hospital —all of which he rejected. I even considered coercing him into a relapse. Now, I know that what I did caused only harm. But at that time, the siren scenario seemed more humane than that. It would have been if he never figured it out. I know you don't want to hear this, but she was a beautiful woman. He did *want* to do it."

"Well, sure. So did I," I said. "That doesn't mean it was acceptable."

"No, I know," she muttered. "And I hate that I did that. If I could rewrite the script, I would. I don't know that he'll ever truly forgive me. But I don't blame him either. I wouldn't forgive me in his shoes."

I took another gulp from the flask. "So your secret source. The one that told you about Micah. They're from the future, huh?"

She laughed. Sipping from her flask, her head shook. "Not quite. But something like that."

"And they haven't given you any more information?"

"Like I said before. They're very elusive."

"Why won't you tell me who they are?" I asked.

"Because that's not my secret to tell," she said. "They will reveal themselves to you in due time."

I squinted in focus. "So you were trying to break me and Jeremy up for three years before you realized the only thing that would work was forcing him into infidelity."

"Unfortunately," she murmured.

My teeth chomped onto my lower lip. I took another gulp from the flask. "Do you feel guilty for killing Moe?"

"To an extent." Her tone was nonchalant. "You don't know this, neither did he, but he didn't have much time left either way. A year, tops. And yes, he was enjoying his retirement. But he's enjoying his new life just as much."

I laughed. "Is that how you justify the blood on your hands? Knowing they'll be reincarnated?"

"It is," Mary said. "It should bring you solace as well. To know that the lives you took will start over without the knowledge of the horrible things they did in this one."

"I guess," I muttered. "It doesn't bother me that I killed them. It bothers me that I have nothing to show for it. I know that I saved the others. But this shit-show started because I wanted to find Lydia, Amy, and then Chris. Then Micah later. And Lydia's all I've got. I love that little girl, I do. But..."

"She's not your son," Mary murmured. "It doesn't make you a bad person to feel that way. It makes you a good mother."

"I'm doing alright with Milly. I don't think I can call myself a good mother though."

"You are," she said quietly. "You're a better mother than me. That's for sure."

True, but that didn't say much.

I took another swig from the flask. "When I died, how did you feel?"

"Micah isn't going to die, Laila."

"I hope not." I ignored the sting in my eyes. "But still. How did you feel?"

She huffed a bit. "Well, I was sad of course. I knew it wasn't your time. You were too young, and you had so much ahead of you. I didn't know what that would be yet, but from the moment you were born, I knew you'd be important. But more than anything, I had a lot of regret."

"Regret." I paused. "What do you mean?"

"I didn't know you well yet. I'd watched you grow up from a distance, but I... Well, I didn't start getting to know you until you and Jeremy got together. You certainly didn't know me. That's what was so hard, I think. You only knew me as the bitchy old lady that worked with your boyfriend's family. Although I was, and still am, that, I wished you had known me. The real me. That half of *you* that came from me." She paused. She cleared her throat. "I suppose that when Jeremy brought you home to meet all of us that day, I thought that it was fate's way of giving me a chance to finally be someone of importance to my child rather than simply assisting in their creation. I'd always been told to never interact with my children, but the sequence of events gave me no option. I thought it was my chance to have some form of a relationship with my child. I thought maybe you could love me as I loved my father. But the moment that I saw you die, I... Well, for a moment, I thought that it was fate's way of correcting its failure."

"I barely know you now," I muttered. "I do love you though. Even though I hate a lot of things you've done, I do love you. Because I know that you've got a lot of good in there. You've got some bad too. But so do I. And if I'm being honest, if I were where you were, if I knew what happened to me would happen to Milly... I can't say that I wouldn't have done the same thing you did. I probably would have just killed him though. But you loved Jeremy as much as you loved me. You were between a rock and psychopathic abductor. You tried to give us all the least painful option available. I get it."

She chuckled.

"What?"

"Just the irony," she murmured. Another laugh left her lips. "You'll understand one day."

CHAPTER SEVENTEEN

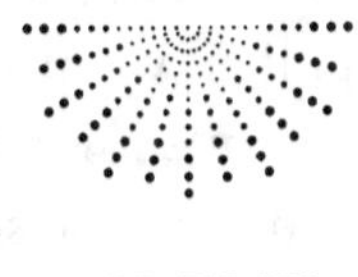

JEREMY

Milly fell asleep on the short drive back to the house and stayed asleep the whole way through me putting her in the crib. Usually, I hated when she fell asleep because I missed her so much while I worked. But after what happened to Micah, I wanted a breath of fresh air. I couldn't break down in front of my daughter, and I needed to.

Once I got the baby monitor turned on beside the crib, I grabbed the jar of weed I hadn't touched in months from the nightstand and made my way to the living room. I sat down, rolled a joint, and lit it at my lips. My hand instinctively reached for the guitar on the wall by the window. I found myself strumming in a trying attempt to avoid thinking about how my son must have been feeling in that moment. I tried really hard not to think about it. But that scream wouldn't stop ringing between my ears.

I didn't *like* the sound of a baby's cries, but they never really bothered me either. Even the obnoxious ones in the middle of the night. But I never heard a child scream the way that Micah did.

Milly'd been sick the month before with some bug that turned into an ear infection. She grabbed her ears with big teary green eyes, and I felt powerless. I just wanted to make the pain go away. I even told Laila to heal her. She laughed and said that she needed to work up an immune system. She was right; the pain of the healing would have been worse than the week of aches.

But I just wanted to make it stop, and I couldn't. Her cries during that week left my heart feeling heavier than a thousand-pound weight. But Micah's was far, *far* worse.

Rather than a heavy heart, hearing that moment of Micah's screams while they sliced into his skin left me with a hole through my chest. It was even more awful than when I felt them doing it to Laila. As a parent, the only thing I wanted was for my children to be safe. When we discovered his bedroom that he shared with Chris, I took on a false sense of security. My brother was there, he'd take care of him. And I know that he tried.

But he couldn't protect him from that evil excuse of a man and the two psychotic cunts that stood behind him. He couldn't even protect himself. All that he could do was give him care. Every single strength he had was taken away. His powers, his ability to see, even his ability to control his body. All that he could do was love him. Ironically, that's all that we could do too.

At one fifteen, the door creaked open as Laila murmured with Mary. I continued strumming as they spoke for a moment. Then Laila walked into the powder room.

Mary made her way to the couch. "Hey." She gave a forced, sad smile.

"Hey," I muttered as I set my guitar on the ground.

"How are you holding up?"

"I don't know. Not great, I guess." She was quiet for a moment, waiting for me to go on. "How am I supposed to feel?"

"There is no right or wrong answer."

"Well, I guess I feel pissed." I grabbed the half smoked joint from the ashtray and sparked it at my lips. "This life has been one bullshit event after the next, and I'm pissed. God or destiny or whatever the fuck it is that's been manipulating us for centuries is an asshole, and if I could punch them in the face, I would."

"I couldn't agree more," Mary muttered.

"I'm just sick of not being able to be happy. All those damn self-help books tell you to create your own happiness, but how the fuck am I supposed to do that when my son's being tortured and there isn't a god damned thing I can do about it?"

"It's okay to not be happy, you know. It's okay to be angry. It's okay to be hurt and sad. There's nothing wrong with that."

"It is when it's a broken record." I took another hit off the joint before setting it back down in the ashtray. "I can handle crisis. I can handle pain. I can handle most of the bullshit, but I'm tired of not being able to fucking do something about it."

Mary expelled a quiet breath. "I know what you mean."

"I just don't know what I'm supposed to do," I muttered. "I just... I don't know."

"Peace will come with time," Mary murmured.

I huffed. "That's shitty advice, ya know."

"I wish that I had good advice to give, but under these circumstances, I don't think that there is."

I gave a slow nod. "Yeah, I guess so, huh?"

Mary sighed. A thud sounded from the bathroom. Laila's voice followed, saying, "I'm okay!"

I gestured that way. "Is she drunk?"

Not that I'd blame her if she were. I just wanted to brace myself if I was going to be carrying her drunken ass to bed. It'd been a long while since that happened, and I'd hoped we were past those days, but I understood too.

"She's a little tipsy, but no. She isn't drunk."

After a moment, I said, "Well, thanks for helping her calm down."

"Sure. It was nice, actually. I think she likes me more now that I've fallen."

"Yeah, well, probably because you come off less hypocritical now. We all have issues with the holier-than-thou attitude the Angels have. At least if you're a Demon, the things you've done don't make you a hypocrite."

Her somber smile fell to a look of remorse. "I suppose that's true."

"But I guess it's a good thing for you two to have a relationship. You are her mom and everything," I muttered. "Plus, you've got a lot of common ground to walk on. The whole hurting the few to help the many mentality."

In hindsight, I realize that I should've phrased that differently. I meant it as dark humor. But it came out a little offensive. I'd mostly moved past what Mary had done, but she still hated herself for it.

She turned her gaze to the ground. "She's got my stubbornness too."

I chuckled. "Yeah, you're telling me."

"I didn't wake her up, did I?" Laila rubbed her damp hands against the thighs of her jeans as she came to sit beside me on the couch.

"No, she's out cold." I looked at Milly sleeping on the baby monitor. "There was a lot of excitement today."

"I'm going to head back to the house, guys," Mary said. "Sleep well."

"Thanks." I sent her a quick smile.

"Yeah, you too," Laila said. Mary smiled and headed toward the door. I turned to Laila. "I guess we knew that something like this would happen eventually."

"I didn't even think about the implants," I murmured.

"I did when I had those dreams last year. But I thought that they would have done it already." Tears formed in her eyes. "I knew that he'd have scars, but I didn't think he'd be old enough to remember it."

"He might not. He's not even three yet, you usually don't remember anything prior to five years old," I said.

"Trauma's different," she murmured. "He... He's just so little. How could they..." She shook her head. "Why didn't he just sedate him?"

"Why didn't he sedate you?" I asked. Her gaze turned to the ground. "Why did he record the stress tests? Because he uses them as a spank bank. He's a sick fuck. He likes seeing other people in pain."

Laila closed her teary eyes.

Damn it. Should've kept that thought in my head.

"I'm sorry. I'm not trying to pick at an old scab. It's just fucking frustrating." I rubbed my hand against my tense, scruff covered jaw.

"It's not a scab," she murmured. "It's still oozing. The bleeding slowed for a while, but it's never gotten the chance to heal."

My head dipped in a nod. I rubbed the back of my neck and reached for the weed on the table. While I started to roll another joint, Laila rested her head against my chest and twisted her arm around my waist.

"Is that how you felt when it happened to me?" she whispered.

"Yeah," I murmured, rolling the paper between my fingertips. "It was different though. It was still terrifying. But you're you. Micah's... He's a baby. You couldn't defend yourself either, but he... He knows her. He loves that bitch, and she helped hold him down. That betrayal... It—It hits different."

I raised the joint to my lips with one hand and tightened my arm around her shoulder with the other.

"We have to find him." Her voice was barely above a whisper.

I took a long drag. As I pulled it from my lips, she reached for it. I handed it to her. "You're done breast feeding?"

"Yeah." She took a hit before handing it back to me. "We have enough milk to ween her down. And I... I'm diving back in on the search for Chris and Micah. When we find out where he is, Milly's going to have to stay with someone in the family. It's probably best if we transition her to just bottles and baby food."

"I guess so."

We sat there in silence for a long moment or two. Laila held the video monitor in her hand, and we gazed down at our daughter sleeping peacefully a few rooms away. I think we both had the same thoughts running through our head while we passed that joint back and forth.

It was so close to the life that we deserved. So, *so* close. Only one piece of everything we ever wanted was missing, and we had to get him back. We had to complete the puzzle.

"We have to bring him home before he's gone forever," Laila whispered. "We have to kill them before they kill him."

I didn't say anything. Of course, she was right. But I didn't know where else to look.

CHAPTER EIGHTEEN

LAILA

Dreams typically are just that. Fictitious thought processes to work through daily struggles our conscious minds have a hard time grasping. I never held them to much merit, not even the dreams that woke me night after night the previous year. I listened to the psychiatrist. She said they weren't real, and I convinced myself that she was right.

Those rules may apply to humans, but our kind is far different. Dreams aren't just thoughts for us; they're almost their own world. Some are minuscule and miscellaneous, but there's a power behind the ones that aren't. I could feel the spiritual force that manifested them. But especially so when I was inside someone else's reality. The feel of vibrating energy acts as a fingerprint. If I'd felt that power once, I couldn't mistake it.

I'd been asleep for a while when I made my first astral trip to another person's dream. The odd part wasn't that I was there; I knew something along those lines was possible. The strange part was how I felt my spirit leaving my body and being pulled into his. My conscious mind was entirely aware of the fact that it exited my body. But I didn't feel panicked or scared because the moment that I felt it, I knew who was doing it.

When my vision became clear, I found myself standing barefoot in warm sand gazing out over waves crashing onto a golden shore. I squinted for a moment, knowing that I recognized the scenery from somewhere but unable to remember where. But there was no smell of ocean, only chemicals. Sanitizing agents, like hospital. A smell I knew all too well.

My confused gaze slid over the empty beach that seemed to stretch on forever, trying to make sense of it all. No one lay on towels or blankets beside the crashing waves, no music played, no activities ensued. The only things around seemed to be me and the ocean. I turned and our eyes met.

Micah.

He sat on the sand behind me in a white hospital gown with his arms wrapped around his knees. His big blue eyes shined back at me with an expression I couldn't quite place. It looked somewhere between fearful and hopeful, if that makes any sense.

"Micah?" My eyes widened. I rushed up the small incline of sand and dropped to my knees in front of him. "Is—Is that you?"

He looked at me over his knees and gave a slow nod. "Hi, Mommy."

My mouth lifted into a smile. I leaned forward and put my arms around his tiny frame. Part of me expected him to pull away, but he circled his arms around my back and tightened his hands on my shoulders. He squeezed tighter than I knew a two-year old was capable of.

And I *felt* it. I felt his arms around me, as real as I'd felt his sister's a few hours prior. I felt his heart pulsing against mine. I felt his breath at my neck.

His voice sounded a few pitches higher than it did in the dreams. But it was just as soft and sweet. His body was as warm as a hot July day. His hair against my cheek was as soft and luxurious as a rabbit's. He had that same familiar baby smell as his sister.

It was real. It may have been an astral reality, but it was real. This was my son. I was with my son. I didn't know how, and I didn't care why. All I cared about was the fact that I was holding my baby.

After a long, beautiful moment, he inched back and met my gaze. I smiled at him as tears filled my eyes. I cupped his cheek.

He lowered his knees, sitting criss-cross. That's when I saw the thick swollen flesh at the base of his neck tied together with thick black thread. I only looked at it for a second and didn't let my smile fall as I looked back up to his eyes.

"Where are we, buddy?" I asked softly, cupping his velvety cheek in my hand.

He moved his shoulders with his brows in something of a quick shrug. "We at the beach."

I laughed quietly. "Yeah. Yeah, I see that. But do you—Do you know where you are? Where you really are, I mean?"

He shook his head.

"That—That's okay. That's okay," I said, pausing as I looked him over. I didn't know what to say, but I had to say something. "Do you like the beach?"

He shrugged again. "I only seen it one time."

"Oh yeah?" I smiled. He nodded, and I continued, "Did you like it?"

He pointed upward to the blue sky. "I saw it up thewe."

"You were in an airplane?"

He nodded again.

When had that been? I considered asking, but I doubted he had any concept of time. I gave a smile instead. "I bet it looked really pretty from up there."

"I want to see it down hewe," he muttered.

I fought the urge to burst into tears. "Me and your dad can take you to see it one day."

He furrowed his brows and shook his head a bit. "I don't like Dad."

My face screwed up in confusion before I realized he was referring to Peterson. "No, sweetie. No, I mean your real dad. My husband. Uncle Chris's brother."

"Oh," he muttered.

"Has Uncle Chris told you about him? Have you seen him in his thoughts?" I asked.

He nodded, and I smiled. "I think you'll like him a lot when you get to meet him."

"Can we do that?" he asked. "Can I see you fow weal?"

I felt my eyes burn with tears. My smile widened, and my nostrils flared in a trying attempt to keep from crying. "There's nothing I want more than to see you for real."

"When?" His big blue eyes filled with tears, and I felt like I was looking at his dad the day I broke up with him. Those big eyes full of tears like that... The only word for it is heartbreaking. "I—I don't like it hewe no mowe."

Fighting back the water that desperately wanted to leave my eyes took more effort than anything in my life ever had. How could I tell him that he had to stay there? How could I explain to a toddler that he was stuck in a place where the people caring for him wanted to end his life? What was I supposed to say when I had no idea how to help him?

With tears in my eyes, I held his face in both of my hands. His little palms gently lifted to my wrists, looking at me with big, wet blue eyes. His begging gaze was convinced that I was the most powerful thing in the world. He thought that I was strong enough to do anything. It broke my heart because I *was* the most powerful thing in the world, and I was strong enough to do anything.

Anything but find him.

"I'm trying really hard to find you." I pressed my trembling lips together as I looked between his eyes. "I've been trying to find you for so long and I... I'm trying, baby, but I don't know where to look."

His little lips turned down in a frown as tears began to escape his eyes. "I need you," he whispered.

Those words were like being punched in the gut.

"I need you too." I wiped the tears from his cheeks with my thumbs. "How are you doing this, Micah?"

"Uncle Cwis show me." He rubbed his little fists against his eyes.

I squinted in thought for a moment. "You know how you brought me here?" He nodded, and I said, "Do you think you can bring Uncle Chris here too?"

"Not wight now," he murmured.

"But can you do this again? Can you bring him next time?" I asked.

"Maybe."

If he could, if we could get an adult, inside look at what they were doing, maybe we'd have a lead. Somewhere to search. Some stone to turn over.

"Okay," I murmured. "Okay, well can you give him a message for me?" He nodded, and I went on, "Tell him because of his message, everyone got out. We got everyone out except for you two."

He rubbed his blue eyes, and I said, "Can you ask him a question for me?" Micah nodded again. "Ask him if he knows anything that can help us find you. Anything at all. Even just a country."

"Okay," Micah murmured.

A slow, uneven breath left my lips as I looked between his somber gaze. I wanted that sad look to disappear forever. I *needed* to see him smile.

"Do you want to walk with me?" I nearly whispered, summoning a smile to my lips.

His gaze was still sad, but a slight smile pulled at his lips. "Can you cawwy me, Mommy? My legs huwt."

My heart ached, but I held my smile. "Yeah. Yeah, of course I'll carry you, baby."

His smile grew more legitimate, lips reaching his eyes. Like that was the best news he'd ever heard. He reached his arms out toward me. My smile grew. I brought myself to my feet, placed my hands in the creases of his armpits, and lifted him to my waist. He wrapped his arms around my neck, his legs around my waist, and his head on my chest. I placed one hand beneath his butt and the other at the back of his head. I closed my eyes and held my son for the second time in either of our lives.

He felt just as he had the day that he came into this world. Of course, he weighed a lot more than he did then. But his weight in my arms made the weight on my shoulders a thousand times lighter. His body was warm, even for me. He smelled soft and sweet, as if he'd just taken a bath. Chris probably had to clean him after the—

No, I couldn't think about that. I had to feel this moment. I had to stay inside of it.

"I'm going to bring you home, Micah," I whispered. "I'm going to find you, and no one will ever hurt you again. I don't know when, but I will. I promise you, I will."

"What's it like thewe?" he asked quietly.

I began walking down the warm sand. I lifted my hand from the back of his head to his arm. "Hold my hand, and I'll show you."

He put his palm into mine, and I closed my eyes. I gave him a visual trip through our house starting outside and working through the interior. I took him through the living room and into mine and Jeremy's room. Then back through the living room and up the steps. I showed him through each of the bedrooms but stopped in his. I made it through the room to the glass door that led to that balcony Jeremy loved so much.

He only gave us two doors to access that balcony. One from the hallway and another from Micah's room. I hadn't given the why of that much thought until I could feel Micah's amazement by it. That's when it clicked. He wanted our son to know that the outside world is only a few steps from wherever he was. He didn't want him to feel trapped.

"It's pwetty," Micah murmured in awe.

"It is, huh?" I whispered at his ear.

"Can you show me my dad?" he said so quiet that I almost didn't hear him.

I smiled. "Yeah, buddy. Yeah, of course."

My hand squeezed his tighter. I focused on my favorite memories of Jeremy. The day that we met when we sat in his car laughing for hours. That childish grin when he tickled me on the couch. That beautiful, billowing laugh when we stayed up talking for hours. His smile before he kissed me on our wedding day. I showed him snippets of Jeremy singing with his guitar on his lap. I moved onto images of him holding Milly and singing to her too.

"Who's that?" Micah asked.

"That's Milly. She's your baby sister," I said.

"What's that?"

"A sister?" I asked. He nodded. "Well, it's like how Uncle Chris is your dad's brother. It means that me and your dad had another baby."

"Oh," he muttered. "I think I seen them befowe."

That ache in my chest widened as I continued walking along the beach. "Yeah, I think you did too."

"Can you show me other stuff?" he asked quietly.

My hand squeezed his. I flashed through some of my most pleasant life's memories. I started with Tinkerbell, showing her prance through the backyard chasing butterflies and lightning bugs. I showed images of the diner both upstairs and at the concerts downstairs. I showed him memories from Christmas where the whole family sat around eating and drinking with smiles and laughs. I flipped through memories of flying around our property in the summer and Images of the actual beaches I'd visited.

"I has to go." Micah pulled his head from my chest and met my gaze. "I be back tomorrow, okay?"

I smiled and gave a fast nod. "Is everything okay?"

"They don't know. But I has to go." He leaned forward and wrapped his arms around my shoulders. "I love you, Mommy."

My teary eyes closed, and I smiled, squeezing him tighter than I'd ever held anything. "I love you too, Micah."

Then, like a rubber band being pulled to its limit before releasing, I slammed back into my body.

My eyes shot open. A gasp heaved into my lips. I slammed upward in the bed.

Jeremy put his tired hand to my shoulder. "It's just a dream, baby."

I struggled to bring even breaths into my lungs. My gaze shifted around my room to grip where I was as Jeremy rubbed my shoulder. "It's still early, Lai."

"It wasn't a dream." My breaths began to level as I turned to meet his gaze.

His sleepy face screwed up in confusion. "What's wrong?"

"Micah," I said. "He—He pulled me into his dream. I was there; I talked to him."

He turned his head to the side. "What?"

CHAPTER NINETEEN

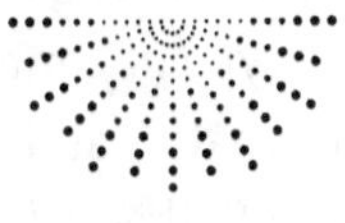

JEREMY

I squinted hard at the morning light that shined in through the curtains. The moment she said his name, I was too awake to fall back to sleep. But I didn't understand either. I literally just woke up.

"What does that even mean?" I asked.

"He—He was here. Or I was there. I—I don't know, but I talked to him." She ran a hand against her flushed face. "He doesn't know where he is, but he said he'd try to bring Chris next time."

"Laila, what are you talking about? I don't understand. He was in your dream?"

"No. No, I don't even think it was a dream. It was *like* a dream, but it wasn't a dream. He was in control of it. We were on a beach somewhere. I don't know where, but it looked familiar. Like I'd been there before? Or like I saw it somewhere?"

"You dream walked?" I asked.

Milly cried in her crib a few feet from the bed. Laila stood and lifted Milly to her arms. She grabbed a diaper and sat back down on the bed. "It wasn't like that. It was... It was like being inside someone's head. He was aware of what was happening and so was I. It wasn't a dream; it was like we were standing in one of his memories."

It still sounded a lot like dream walking. But dreams generally don't have the participant's awareness. If he was coherent enough to understand what was happening—and to physically pull her there—it wasn't dream walking.

I thought for a long moment, breaths growing short. "You both harness spirit. He must have found some way to reach your mind. But he's not even three, how is that possible?"

"He said Chris helped him." Laila unbuttoned Milly's onesie. "If they're bound, Chris has some type of connection to Micah's powers."

"He hops onto Micah's telepathy and targets it where it needs to go," I murmured. "I mean, we're all a little psychic. We can communicate with each other when we're in close proximity, but only Fae can stretch distances. I don't know where Chris would have learned to do that."

"Desperate times make you capable of figuring out just about any puzzle in front of you," Laila said. "He's probably been trying for a long time and just figured it out. Plus, now that he has the implants, his Guardian abilities are being blocked."

"Which means his Fae abilities are going to get stronger," I murmured, giving a nod. "He came into this world with a good reach on spirit. It makes sense that it'd be his strongest ability so far."

She threw Milly's dirty diaper to the trash can in the corner and lifted her to her chest. "He said he'd be back tomorrow. Maybe if you stay awake, you can go in my head when it happens, and I can carry you along. He said he'd try to bring Chris."

I was quiet for a few heartbeats, walking through that in my mind. "He can talk already?"

"Mostly." She laughed. "His Rs sound like Ws. But his grammar's actually pretty damn good for a two-year-old. There probably isn't much for him and Chris to do but talk."

I bit my lip, trying to wrap my head around it all.

Don't get me wrong, I was happy that he was advanced. Full sentences out of a two-year-old was amazing. But I wished I'd been that one to teach him that. I wished I'd have heard his babbles turn to words. That, and I didn't know what I was walking into. I didn't know what he thought of me. There was no way for me to know what lies Peterson had filled his head with about me.

"He wanted me to show him my memories of you." Laila smiled.

"Really?"

"Yeah. And he remembered seeing you and Milly at the skating rink." I pressed my lips together to keep them from shaking. "He wanted to see everything. I showed him the house and Tinkerbell and our wedding day. Oh, and he loved the balcony."

A huff of a laugh left my lips, smile pulling at the edges. "He did?"

"I never thought about why you put a door in his room." A gentle smirk came to her lips. "That was a nice touch."

He was exactly why I'd made that balcony, and why it meant so much to me. I wanted him to have large open views of the world we lived in. I wanted him to know he could walk outside any time he wanted here. I wanted him to know that he was free. If we ever got him back, at least.

But that wasn't what I was concerned with at the moment. "He's okay though? Mentally, he doesn't have, like, Stockholm's or anything?"

"I don't think so. He said he didn't like Peterson. We didn't go into much on that though. He just wanted me to show him this side of the world. Chris has probably given him a dose of reality; he trusted me." She smiled and breathed out a quiet laugh. "He's... He's a really good kid."

Milly began to fuss in Laila's arms and reach to pull her shirt down.

"I'll go heat her up a bottle. After she eats, can you show me?" I asked.

"How can you be sure it was him?" Leah asked, gaze serious but hopeful.

What Laila showed me was one hundred percent genuine. That was my kid. Aside from the fact that he looked exactly as I did in old family photos, the purity in his eyes couldn't be forged.

"It was him. None of them could pretend to be that innocent."

"I *felt* him," Laila said. "It felt exactly the way that it did when he was born. His energy, it's unmistakable. I know what my son's power feels like, and that was him, Leah."

"I'd believe it," Mary said.

"Really?" Leah raised a brow. "How?"

"Because of who he is. Micah's important. If he weren't, Peterson would have never wanted him in the first place," Mary said.

"You heard the chatter when I was pregnant with him," Laila said. "Even when I was pregnant with Milly."

"Our power isn't like everyone else's." I chimed in. "The children of the par animos are legendary. There's a reason the two of us fought like hell for centuries trying to have a kid. I bet if the two of you looked at your past lives, they'd probably be pretty similar." I gestured between Wyatt and Celena.

"You know that you're saying that wrong, right?" Mary said.

"What?"

"The plural of par animo is par animarum," she muttered.

"Fuck off."

"But what does this mean?" Brody asked from the breakfast nook. "However he's using spirit, can it be tracked? Can we find them?"

"Maybe. Helena said she'd call me back at noon. Otherwise, I have no idea," Laila said. "The only person I've ever tracked is Jeremy. I've never communicated with anyone else from such a far distance."

"But that's more of a subconscious knowing than a track," I said.

"How do we know it's a far distance?" Kai asked.

I said, "They're not stupid enough to stay close."

"And Wyatt or I would have picked up on their scent by now," Celena said.

"At a close distance, aye," he said. "But what if it's still far, just not as far as the others?"

"You think they're stateside?" Laila asked.

"I think it's worth exploring," Kai said. "I could be wrong. But this clan's got connections all over the country. You two've got a lot of pull in the North American pack, aye?"

"That's true," Wyatt murmured. "We could get samples of their scents out to the wolves. I'm sure Brendon would be willing to help after everything we did for his ass."

"All we have is one baby sock, a little lock of hair, and a few several years-old spit up rags," Celena said. "And after what Micah did, they aren't letting him outside any time soon."

"Chris smells a lot like y'all do though." Wyatt gestured between us. "I haven't seen him in a long time, but I'd know his scent if it was fresh somewhere because I've fed off a few of you before."

I thought for a moment. For the first time, a genius idea dawned on me. The power of a dog's nose. "Would the same apply for Amy and Nastya?"

"What do you mean?" Celena asked.

"Say you tasted Moriah and Lydia's blood. Would you be able to recognize Nastya and Amy's scent from tasting the blood of their family?"

"Oh, yeah," Wyatt said. "Definitely."

I thought for a moment.

Laila's eyes widened. "We make a cocktail."

"A little bit of each of our bloodlines," Brody said.

"Then we get it out to all the alphas," I said. "They pick up a scent, they tell us, and then we owe them a favor."

"Do you know wolves at all?" Celena arched a brow. "They're going to want a little more than a favor."

"Then they can have me," Laila said. My forehead scrunched up, and she said, "My blood, I mean. I feed them, one of you heals me, and then we owe them a favor if they get us a lead."

Huh.

That was a good point. Any blood sucker we'd ever encountered stared at Laila's pulse like a dog to a juicy steak. Not that I loved the idea, but if it could help us find our son, I'd do just about anything. And once Laila made up her mind about something, it wasn't like I had much of a choice anyway.

"So that's how it is, huh," Wyatt said. "Just gonna give your blood to the whole damn world but won't even let me try it."

"Little creepy, baby," Celena muttered.

"Is it that important to you?" Laila raised a brow.

"It kind of is," Wyatt said. "I've had Guardian blood, which is good —better than humans. Never had Angel or Fae that wasn't tainted though, and ya know what, yeah. I want to see what all the hype's about."

"What am I?" Celena huffed. "Chopped liver?"

"You taste better than humans, darlin', but the wolf gene kind of cancels out the Fae and Angel," Wyatt said.

Laila extended her arm. "Fine, just do it then."

"Really?" Wyatt asked.

"Yeah, really?" I raised a brow.

"Can you get me that deal with the pack?" Laila asked.

"Can I get a bunch of wolves to drink your blood?" Wyatt laughed. "Yeah. Shouldn't be a problem."

"We can do it. Brendon's gotten pretty notable recently, and we've got a lot of pull with him," Celena said. "He'll want a down payment though. And Roland Allard wanted to meet you anyway, Lai. I don't wanna just show up at his door, but if we get a sample to Brendon, he'll get a meeting with him for sure."

"Then yeah, let's do it. You can have some too, Celena." Laila waved her wrist out in front of them.

"At least sit down first so you don't pass out," I muttered.

I wasn't crazy about the idea of hundreds or thousands of wolves feeding off of my wife. Especially because I knew arousal played a part in feeding, and because I knew Laila kind of had a thing for wolves. But if she wanted to do it, there was no stopping her. And if it could bring Micah home, I'd deal with however inferior it made me feel.

"This is the best day ever," Celena beamed.

"I'm not going to have to yank either of you off of her, am I?" I asked.

"No," Wyatt said. "We've got control."

"But when you go to feed the alphas, we're going," Celena said. "We're around people like you all the time; we know how to control ourselves. Not everyone does."

I licked my teeth. I looked over Laila. "Eat your breakfast before you go draining yourself."

"No one's draining anyone," Celena said. "But yeah, eat your breakfast."

"One thing though." Laila took a bite of her pancake. "No one touches my neck. Drink from my wrist or no deal."

"I'll let Brendon know," Celena said.

"What good does this do if they aren't in the states though?" Brody asked.

"It's never a bad idea to have the packs on your side," Celena said. "If Brendon can get this to the Monarch, we can take this worldwide. No one's going to turn down a chance to taste your blood, Lai. And since we have all these healers, you're basically a never-ending blood bag. You feed them; you have their loyalty. Even if it doesn't get us any leads. It's still a hell of a way to build alliances."

"I'm in," Laila said. "If the end of the world's coming, we need as many friends as we can get."

"What about you, Jeremy?" Leah raised a brow. "Are you okay with this?"

"Guess I have to be." I took a sip from my coffee. "Last time I told Laila what to do, I got shot. She slapped me."

Laila grinned. "That a boy."

CHAPTER TWENTY

JEREMY

After we finished eating, I set Milly in the play pen and Laila sat on the couch beside Celena. I knew they said they wouldn't lose control of their thirst, and I wanted to believe that. But the fact of the matter remained that both of them were half animal. I trusted them with just about everything but drinking my wife's blood was another story. Feeding brings out that animalistic side of a wolf that wants no part of being controlled.

Still, I was far more comfortable with them feeding off of her than the crowd of alphas that'd be licking their lips at just the thought of drinking from my wife. I started doing the math in my head to figure out approximately how many that would be. On the east coast alone, we had three. The west coast had around fifteen last I'd heard. Each state had at least three from that point out. A hundred? Maybe even two in the United States alone. Worldwide, there were at least another five hundred to a thousand.

I saw her point. It was a good plan. If every pack in the world had Amy's, Nastya's, Laila's, and my family's scent, there's no way we wouldn't find something. Even just a general idea of a location that we could narrow down. But the thought of at least five hundred different wolves sinking their teeth into her flesh made me sick.

Feeding for wolves isn't just about eating. Much like it is for Vampires, drinking blood is typically a sexual experience, at least for the one being fed on. Sometimes both. I knew that wouldn't be the case with Celena and Wyatt, but it wouldn't be that platonic for the other alphas. My wife was—and still is—hot as shit. After all the people she'd saved in our world, she wasn't just a hero but an icon. The fact that her clothes burned off when she fought didn't help either.

It's not that I worried about Laila being attracted to them. I was sure she would be for a moment, but I understood that biology is involuntary. What worried me were the abundance of men much stronger and larger than me that I assumed would make less than considerate comments before sinking their teeth into my wife's flesh. I also knew myself and my temper. At some point or another, I was going to end up getting my ass handed to me over this.

"So how does this work?" Laila asked. "Do you shift?"

Celena shook her head. Two large canines grew from her gum line toward her lower lip. Her eyes shimmered a bright shade of blue as she spoke. "I'll stop if you tell me to, but it'll hurt at first."

"Only for a second before the euphoria sets in," Wyatt said. "Just make it through the first couple seconds, and you'll be fine. You'll probably like it actually."

"I do," Celena said.

"Alright then. Have at it." She extended her hand up toward Celena. Her gaze met mine. "Can you time this, baby? I need to know how long I can go before I have to stop."

I pulled my phone from my pocket. "Sure."

"Watch her color," Celena said to me. "She probably won't want us to stop even if we need to."

I nodded.

Celena turned down to Laila's wrist and tugged it slightly to her face. She pulled her mouth open and slowly bit down into her flesh. I winced at the pain in mine as Laila gritted her teeth and cleared her throat.

"Just give it a second," Wyatt muttered.

Laila nibbled on her lower lip. After a second, her tense expression softened. She blinked a few times, and her gaze found mine. "Damn, it really does feel good."

"Told you," Wyatt said.

"Have you ever done this?" she asked.

"Twice," I said.

"There was a pileup on the highway, and the hospital needed all the blood they had. Me and Mom had to eat," Wyatt said.

"Worst blue balls of my life," I muttered. "Never looked at Ashley the same after that."

"Ew." Wyatt's nose curled. "That's my mom, dude."

"And that's my wife," I said.

"Yeah, but it's not like that," he said.

"Just relax," Laila murmured with a slow-forming, disoriented gaze.

Celena straightened up licking her lips and holding a glowing white light over Laila's wrist. Then Laila pulled her wrist away. "I need to know how long I can go before being healed so that we can do this as efficiently as possible."

"Fair enough." Celena pulled her hand away. She stood, and Wyatt sat in her place. His canines fell quicker than Celena's as Laila extended her hand to him. He lowered his mouth to her forearm. His hand held hers in place almost the way I did with a rack of ribs to chew the meat from the bone.

"Ow," I muttered as he sucked away at her skin.

"His teeth are a little bigger than mine." Celena wiped blood from the corner of her mouth and licked her thumb.

"This isn't weird at all," I murmured.

"Is anything around here normal?" she said.

"Not usually," I muttered.

After a few more moments, Laila's eyes grew even more stoned. "Slow down." Celena put a hand on Wyatt's shoulder.

"You okay, babe?" I asked.

"I'm great," Laila said with heavy eyes. I carefully watched the already light color of her skin gradually become pastier. Her head did something of a rolling motion before landing against the cushion behind her.

"Stop, Wyatt," Celena said. I stopped the timer. She tugged at his shoulder, and he pushed her back a bit. She scoffed, grabbed ahold of his shoulder, and ripped him back. But when she pulled him, he pulled Laila with him.

I reached down and grabbed a fist full of his hair. I yanked. Laila's eyes peeled open a bit as I ripped his head back and brought a hunk of her wrist along with it. Celena gasped. Wyatt's dilated pupils looked around in awe. She flung her hand to Laila's wrist and began healing as I shot Wyatt a death glare.

"You said I wasn't going to have to pull you off of her."

"My bad," he muttered, chewing on a piece of her flesh.

"Yeah. Your bad," I snipped. Celena held her hand over Laila's bleeding wrist. Her eyes carefully fluttered open as the color gradually returned to her face. Wyatt stumbled to his feet as I lowered myself to the couch beside her. "Are you okay?"

"Mhmm," Laila murmured. "Did I pass out?"

"Yeah, because Wyatt wouldn't stop," Celena muttered. "Push me again, motherfucker."

"Sorry, darlin'." Wyatt wiped blood from the corner of his lip. "Got a little lost in the moment."

"I don't like this." I pushed hair from her pale face. "If Wyatt couldn't stop, we're bound to come across a wolf that can't."

"That's why you'll be there," Laila muttered.

"So my input doesn't matter but I can be your bodyguard?" I raised a brow.

A soft smile played at her lips. She reached out to touch my face. "You don't have to. Celena and Wyatt can."

My tongue ran along my teeth. A heavy breath left my nostrils. "No. I'll be there."

Her smile widened a bit, color nearly restored in her cheeks. "This is a good thing, baby. This could bring him home."

"That doesn't mean I have to like it," I said.

"I think you're all taken care of." Celena dropped Laila's hand to her lap. "How do you feel?"

"Honestly, I feel pretty great." Laila's gaze shifted back and forth between my eyes.

"How long was it, Jeremy?" Celena asked.

"Little more than two minutes," I said. "Maybe we should do blood draws and give them bagged blood."

"They'll want it from the source," Wyatt said. "Nobody prefers cold blood to straight from the body."

"So we set a time limit," Celena said. Laila pushed hair from my face, twirling a piece between her fingertips. "Two-minute feed, heal, two-minute feed, heal."

"No, a minute and a half," I said. "Ninety seconds and they're done. They don't stop, you guys rip 'em off, and if they go back for seconds, I tase them."

"That sounds fair," Celena said. "I texted Brendon. He said we could meet in an hour. Could one of you give us a lift?"

"Sure," I said. Laila cascaded her hand from my cheek down my shoulder. My gaze turned to her with a raised brow. "You alright, Lai?"

She nodded, eyes sliding over my lips.

Wyatt laughed. Celena chuckled. "How about we watch Milly for a minute so you can go take care of your wife?"

I chuckled. "Is that what you want to do, Laila?"

"I know I shouldn't with the day it's been." She grinned. "But yeah. Yeah, I really do."

A quiet laugh left my lips. "We'll be back."

"Have fun." Wyatt smirked.

Besides forming those much-needed treaties with packs around the world, the only benefit to Laila using her blood as a bargaining tool was how often I got my dick sucked in those coming weeks.

CHAPTER TWENTY-ONE

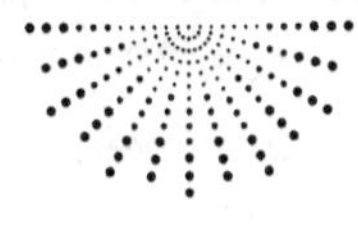

LAILA

That could have been the best sex of my life. Honestly, it's a messy blur now, but I think I orgasmed six or seven times? If nothing else came from this, at least I got some great fucks in. Wolf venom was better than a little blue pill.

"I really don't feel good about this," Jeremy muttered as he buttoned his jeans.

"Like you think something's going to go wrong?" I lifted my T-shirt over my shoulders. "Or like you don't feel good about a bunch of random dudes putting their mouths on me?"

He narrowed his gaze. "Why do you have to say it like that?"

I laughed, stood from the bed, and put my arms around his neck. "It's business, Jeremy."

"That's probably what strippers tell their boyfriends before they go grind on other dudes for money," he muttered.

"And what do you have against strippers?"

He put his hands on my hips. "I don't have anything against strippers, but that doesn't mean I'd want to be married to one."

"So if I took up exotic dancing, you'd divorce me?" I asked. His eyes rolled. "Alright then. Baby, nothing's going to happen. You're going to be there."

"Yeah, but it's still cringey," he said. "They're all going to be thinking about fucking you, and it's just not a pleasant thought."

"But it's not like they will," I said. "We'll go home, and I'll fuck you."

He ran his hand over his mouth. "Listen, I know that this isn't a bad idea. It could help us bring Micah home and that's great. But that doesn't mean I have to like it."

"I wouldn't feel good about it if I were you either. But we have to do this." I pushed hair from his face. "We have to do everything within our power. And this is within our power."

"I get it, Lai. I just don't like it."

"You're going with Celena and Wyatt to talk to Brendon though, right?"

"Yeah, that's the plan. We should probably get back to the house and grab Milly," Jeremy said.

"I'm going to take her with me to go talk to Helena. After I get word from you guys, I'll call Moriah."

He blew out a long, billowing sigh. "Someone else we've got to talk to." I cocked my head to the side. "Seems like Amy goes out in the world more than the others. Out of everyone's, her smell is the most important."

"Lydia," I muttered.

"Lydia," Jeremy said.

"I guess I'll handle that while you go with Celena and Wyatt."

A huff of a laugh left his lips. "Good luck with that."

***

Ray sat at the kitchen island with a cup of coffee in one hand and a newspaper in the other. I adjusted Milly on my hip. He turned to meet my gaze with a soft smile. "Hey."

I fought the internal sigh that desperately wanted to leave me. It was time to swallow my pride and apologize. Still, I didn't feel like I'd done anything wrong. But I wanted something from the guy. That meant I had to play nice.

"Hey." I lowered myself to the stool beside him.

"How are you holding up?" he asked.

"Better than I was last night," I muttered. "Look, I'm sorry for what I said. I helped you on my own free will. I made the choice to get in that van. Losing Micah was my fault, not yours."

"No, you were right. About everything. You gave me my little girl back. What they did could have destroyed her, and I could too if I'm not careful. Blaming shit on her isn't going to help anyone."

"She's blaming herself enough already. The moment someone else says it, that self-doubt solidifies and sends you plummeting into a really dark place," I muttered. "Trust me, I know."

"Yeah. Yeah, I know. But you were right about the other stuff too," he mumbled. "When I was fourteen, I spent every day outside with my friends. Even in crap weather like this. I was at football games every Friday night; I had my first girlfriend. In Lydia's shoes, I probably would have snuck off too. And no, she can't do all of that right now. She can't have a predictable routine. But she can go to a birthday party without me once in a blue moon... If she knows how to defend herself and call for help."

I raised a brow. "You're going to let me work with her?"

"That's the best option for all of us, Lydia included," Ray said. "I hate the idea of her being a big kid that doesn't need me anymore. But those days are on the horizon. And the fact is, I can't protect her from all of this anyway. To fight fire, you have to have a way to put it out. And Lydia has the hose that I don't."

"Wise man," I murmured.

After a moment, he said, "I'm sorry I've put my family's problems onto your shoulders. You've done more for me than I can ever do for you and I should act like it."

And there was my opportunity. "I've got a place where you could start."

"What do you mean?" he asked.

"I wouldn't ask this if there was another way. But I can't think of any."

"What is it?"

"It's kind of complicated. But Wyatt and Celena have ties to a pack leader that might be able to get us in contact with all of the wolves around the world. We have an idea, and don't get me wrong, it's a little crazy. But it could bring my son home." I looked between his eyes for a moment as he waited for me to go on. "Amy gets to go out. She goes to gas stations and out for coffee. Her scent is out there somewhere, and if every alpha worldwide knows that smell, they can contact me when they pick up on it."

"Do you need her hairbrush or something?"

"No, we need her blood," I said. "And since we can't get to her, we need Lydia's."

"What—Like a finger prick?"

"Like half a gallon." I gave a pleading, bubbly smile. My smile was hard to say no to. "For now, at least."

He scrunched up his forehead. "That's half of her body content."

"We can heal her as she loses it. It'll be uncomfortable, but it won't be lethal," I said. "I get that I'm asking a lot. But I put my son's life on the line to save your daughter. This isn't even risking Lydia's life, just her comfort. And I'm sure she'd be willing to do it. I wouldn't ask this if she couldn't consent. But she can, and this could bring my son home. This could end it all."

He thought for a moment. "If Lydia's okay with it, then go for it."

I smiled. "Thank you, Ray."

"Least I can do," he muttered.

I knew he didn't like it. I wouldn't either in his shoes. But we both saw the look on Lydia's face when he said it was her fault they put the trackers in him. She wanted him home almost as badly as I did.

CHAPTER TWENTY-TWO

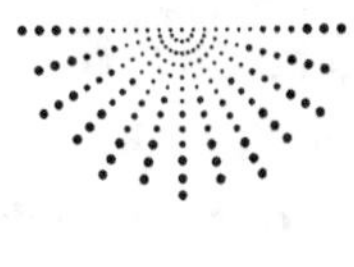

JEREMY

The cabin we stood in felt smaller than ours did before the remodel. Admittedly, it looked better than it had last time I stood within in it. The charred floor from Celena and Laila's flames had been sanded and refinished. There weren't old chairs with people tied to them anymore. Now, comfortable chaises and lounges sat in their place before a large—but modest—desk.

Old thick wooden logs stacked from the ground to the ceiling formed the four walls around us. A small stone fireplace sat in the corner behind the desk just ahead. Large, intricately carved book-shelves lined the back wall with a thousand books of what appeared to be every genre. Name a notable author in history, and I could find at least one of their works in Brendon's personal library. Emily Dickens, James Patterson, Shakespeare, Stephen King. Any that one could name, he had it.

Wyatt gently caressed his hand up and down Celena's bicep as she stared at the rug beneath our feet. She cleared her throat when her gaze turned up to mine. "My aunt was killed right here. It's just weird to see it like this, ya know?"

"Oh, shit," I said. "Yeah, I'm sure it is."

"I learned what evil is in this room," Celena said. "You'd think that would've been when I was bit, but no. It was when they ate my aunt alive."

"Seeing something like that's got to do something to your head," I said.

"Fucks you up pretty good," she said. "But the shit I went through brought peace to a group of people who haven't seen any in a long time. I can't say that her life was worth the sacrifice. But at least something good came from it."

Honestly, helping them take that bastard down had been the most fun I'd had in a very long time. Brendon seemed like a nice kid—and I hadn't heard anything about young girls disappearing or found in the woods eaten by wild canines. So I agreed. At least one good thing had happened during the time that Laila and I were broken up.

"Sorry to keep y'all waiting," a voice said from the door behind us. I turned to see the young alpha tramping his bare feet on the doormat. He wore a pair of black basketball shorts and a gray pullover hoodie. "You weren't here too long, were you?"

"Just a couple minutes," Wyatt said. "No worries."

"And thanks for meeting with us," Celena said.

"Yeah, of course." Brendon smiled. He patted Wyatt's shoulder in a brotherly fashion before turning and shaking Celena's hand. He turned to me and extended his hand. "Nice to see you again, Jeremy."

"Yeah, likewise." I shook it. I gestured around. "Like what you've done with the place. Looks a lot better without the torture chairs."

"Yeah, thanks." Brendon laughed and walked around the desk. "Go on, have a seat. What's all this about?"

We lowered ourselves to the seats. Then Celena grinned. "How would you feel about trying a sip of my sister's blood?"

His face said he wasn't sure if that was a trick question, especially when his gaze met mine. "Isn't that your wife?"

"She is," I said. "And this was her idea."

"And what is that exactly?"

"We're looking for someone," I said. "Five someone's, actually."

"And we're out of places to look." Wyatt chimed in. "So we're outsourcing."

Brendon looked my way, squinting slightly. "Your kid."

"And my brother, and the people holding them captive," I said.

"We have no idea where they are. Maybe they're in Kentucky, maybe they're in Japan. Who knows," Celena said. "But we had an idea."

"Which is?" Brendon asked.

"Get a sample of the bloodline from all five of the people we're looking for into the belly of every alpha on Earth," Wyatt said. "If every alpha knows their scent, they'll know it if they come across it."

"If they do, they contact Laila," Celena said. "If nothing else, it's a free bite. But whoever leads us to Micah will have a lifelong ally with the Skoulda family."

"And more so, Laila's going to owe a hell of a favor to anyone who helps us find our kid," I said. "Nothing bad could come of this on you guy's end."

Brendon leaned back in his chair and sucked his teeth for a moment. "That's where her blood comes into play."

"You guys taste a cocktail of the bloodlines from all five people we're looking for to get the scent," Celena said. "Then you feed on Laila as a thank you for your help."

He huffed. "That simple?"

"That simple," Wyatt said. "No risk on your end. Anyone catches the scent; they report back to Laila. No one engages or puts themselves at risk."

Brendon rubbed his mouth. "I can't see a reason to say no. If she tastes anything like you, sounds like a hell of a deal."

"Way better than Celena," Wyatt said. "No offense, darlin'."

"It's true, she does," Celena said.

"But you want to get it out to all of the alphas?" Brendon raised a brow. "Why not just hit the nomads? They get the opportunity to feed on a hybrid like her, they might be able to track 'em down for you."

"Sure, that's an option," Wyatt said. "But stationed wolves are just as good if we want a wider reach. Nomads are flaky."

"She wants to build alliances," I said blatantly. "Look, I'm sure you've heard the rumors about an apocalypse on the horizon. We want to have a network of allies around the world if shit hits the fan. We don't have to be best friends. But having pals in high places isn't a bad thing for anyone."

"Can't say I disagree with you there." Brendon rubbed his mouth. "Alright, I'm in."

"Can you get in contact with the North American Monarch?" I asked.

"We have an alpha meeting tomorrow," Brendon said. "Your lucky day."

"Do you think he'll be in?" I asked.

"I'm sure," Brendon said. "Laila's a pretty hot commodity. She gets brought up a lot around here. We try to respect y'all's privacy, but everyone wants the fire power she's got. Get me a sample of this blood mixture, and I'll bring it with me tomorrow. If he agrees, I'll get a taste to the North American alphas. He'll want to set up a meeting with her though. Keep y'all's phones on, he might want it tomorrow."

"How many of you are there?" I asked.

"About a hundred," Brendon said. "If they agree, they're going to want a taste though. So be ready if he does."

I nodded, licking my lips. "Laila has rules about feeding though."

"What do you mean?" Brendon asked.

"Feed from her wrist or don't feed at all," Celena said. "And ninety second time limit per feeding."

"Fair enough," Brendon said. "You've got yourself a deal with this alpha."

CHAPTER TWENTY-THREE

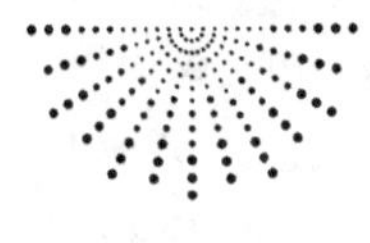

LAILA

"You want me to give *my* blood to every alpha in the world?" Moriah nearly yelled. "Are you bloody mad? Why on Earth would I agree to that?"

Of course. I should've known that the pretty princess was going to be our biggest problem. Ray had been a piece of cake next to Moriah. We'd already been arguing for ten minutes.

"You aren't feeding them; they're just getting a little sample. And because we're forming alliances," I said into the phone. "If the end of the world's coming, we need to have friends in high places. Especially you. People don't like you much, you know. May want to build up your rapport a bit."

"My blood is valuable. As is yours, darling, you shouldn't be so quick to give it up," she said. "Do you know what they're going to call you for this?"

Yes, I knew what those who were fed on were called in the supernatural world. But people could call me any name in the book at this point, and I'd give two fucks less. Call me a junky, call me a skank, it didn't matter. Nothing—especially not my reputation—mattered if it meant I could bring my baby home.

"Blood slut, whore, I don't really care, Moriah. It's not like it'll be the first time someone's called me a name. This is bigger than me and you. We need allies, and the wolves are a good place to start. Especially if this helps me find my baby and kill the son of a bitch who tortured him last night."

She fell silent as I lifted Milly from the playpen to my hip. "They did what?"

"They held him down and put the implants in. They could have sedated him, and they didn't. They wanted him to suffer," I snapped. "I'm not fucking around anymore, Moriah. I shouldn't even have taken the break that I have. I need to get my son home."

Another silence crept in. "How much blood do you need?"

Maybe she had a sweet spot in her after all. Not so sure she'd have been so apt to do it if the person responsible wasn't her sister, but one way or the other, it's hard to say no to helping someone find their baby.

"A lot," I said.

"Bloody hell," she blurted. "So you'll have to be there to heal me."

"Probably best unless you have your own healer."

"Fine. But I have plans at ten o'clock my time. We'll need to do this soon."

"I can come grab you in an hour," I said.

"How are we doing the bleeding?" she asked. "Should I wear something I don't mind ruining?"

"No, Jeremy's at the hospital getting some needles and blood bags now. My friend's a nurse; he's doing the blood draws."

"Very well then. I'll see you shortly," Moriah said.

"See you soon—"

"But one thing, darling," Moriah said.

"Yes?"

"I'm sorry. For what my sister's done to your son," she said in a soft, gentle tone. "Truly, from the bottom of my heart, I am more sorry than I've ever been in my life."

"Thanks," I muttered.

"But when you do bring him home, which I'm certain that you will. Could you make sure that he knows I helped you find him?"

"Yeah, sure. But why do you care what my son thinks of you?"

"I believe he's going to be an important person in the next genera-tion. And I'd like to bring the La Fay name back to good standing in our community. Not with the Council, they like us, but the people. *Our* people. After my however many greats grandmother destroyed our name, my ascendants spent centuries rebuilding it. And in less than two decades, Nastya has drug our name to Hell and back. I want the next generation to know that it isn't our entire bloodline that's faulted. Some of us just want to live our lives."

Ah, fair enough. I didn't want people to think poorly of me based on the actions Mary had taken. And truly, Moriah had been good to us since we'd met. I did believe her intentions were pure.

"I can make that happen."

"Alright then. Let me know a few minutes before you come to grab me so I can put my shoes on."

"Will do. Thanks, Moriah. I can't put into words how much this matters to me."

"Sure," she said. "See you soon, love."

I ended the call. Milly cooed in my arms with a gesture to my chest. A huff left me. "Alright, missy. Let's get you a bottle and go see Aunt Helena."

———

"You're absolutely sure that it was him?" Helena asked.

"A hundred and ten percent."

She thought for a moment, quizzical eyes scanning the room. "It is possible, I guess. But he's only two. You don't even know how to do something like that; I don't know how he would."

"He said that Chris helped him. Maybe he has some control over Micah's abilities because of the bond with Nastya."

"Must be," she said. "You know what it is that he did, right?"

"Not really. I know it had something to do with astral projection."

"Kind of," she said. "But the only reason he could reach you was because you control spirit too. The two of your souls are already attached because of the fact that he's your son. I think what he did was a constructive search for your energy. In theory, you could do the same to find him using the trace of energy he left in your mind when he entered it. But knowing Nastya, she's using his power to mask their location."

"So we're back to ground zero?" I asked.

"We can try a spell to trace him through your mind," Helena muttered. "But I wouldn't say you're at ground zero. If he can bring Chris along next time, he can get you intel. Magically speaking, we're probably at a dead end. But Chris could be your golden ticket."

"That's what I'm thinking too," I said.

"But we'll do the spell either way. Doubt it'll work, but it's worth a shot." Helena stood from her dining table and started to the wardrobe at the edge of the kitchen. She pulled out an array of herbs and then stopped abruptly. She set the items back into the cabinet and turned to meet my gaze.

"What is it?" I asked.

Her perfect brows scrunched over her glistening pink eyeshadow. "I don't think we should try the spell."

My head tilted. "Why not?"

"It probably won't work anyway. But if he comes back tonight, he'll leave another trace of his energy behind."

That sounded like gibberish. "I don't understand."

"We should let that energy build up," Helena said. My face surely showed my skepticism because she lowered herself back to the chair. "Okay, listen. Whatever trace he leaves behind won't be able to give us a location. But if we wait, if that energy gets bigger every time he visits you, eventually, we might have enough to do something else with it."

"Like what?" I asked.

"Like bind him to you," Helena said. "If the two of you are connected with me as the glue instead of Nastya, we have a shot. You can trace his energy in a matter of seconds from the time that I cast the spell. Ancestral magic, like she's using. He can't be bound outside of his bloodline, but you're his mother. Whatever energy he left behind last night isn't enough to do that, but if he comes back ten or twenty times, I should be able to extract it. Then we can perform the spell.

And if I do it right, I can keep Nastya from realizing we've done it. That'll give you enough time to formulate a plan of entry."

My eyes widened a bit as a smile came to my lips. "You can do that without him present? You just need his energy?"

"Souls are better than physical bodies," Helena said. "If I've got a big enough amount of his, then absolutely."

I laughed. "That's the plan then."

Finally. A real, solid fucking plan. And it was all thanks to the two-year-old I was trying to save. He was one smart kid.

CHAPTER TWENTY-FOUR

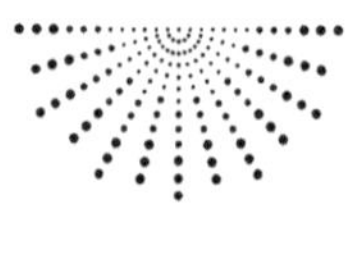

JEREMY

When I got back to the main house, I explained to Laila what had happened with Brendon. I also kept my phone on in case he called. She told me about her call with Moriah, that she was going to grab her shortly to get a few bags of her blood, and then moved onto the conversation with Helena.

As she spoke, the scent of the alcohol wipe drifted up my nose. I tied the tourniquet tight around my forearm, tapping against my cool skin for a vein. It was a bit surreal at how fast I found one now that they weren't all blown out.

"So there's nothing Helena can do," I muttered, eyeing my favorite one. It was always easiest to get the needle in when I hadn't used in a while—and always the hardest to get when I was using.

"Not right now." Laila set Milly in her highchair. "But if we take it one day at a time, if we do this right, we'll get our son back."

"If you guys think this is the best course of action, then let's do it." I flexed and released my palm, watching the vein throb upward. "It's more than we had to go on yesterday."

"Anything's better than nothing," Laila said. She turned to me and cleared her throat. "Are you okay to do that?"

Good question, but this kind of needle was attached to a tube that my blood would flow into. Not the kind that was full of warm, dark liquid.

I looked down and tapped at the vein. "It's not a trigger, if that's what you're asking. My veins are hard to get. Doctors always miss and jab me a good twenty times before they get one. I'd rather do it myself and call it a day."

She lowered herself to the breakfast nook beside me. "You're sure?"

"Yeah." I smiled. "I'm fine, Lai. Really. The last thing on my mind is getting high right now."

She smiled back. It stretched higher. "So how do you feel about meeting Micah tonight?"

A laugh escaped my lips. "I'm trying not to get my hopes up in case something goes wrong. We don't know for sure if he's going to be able to do that again."

"He said he would," Laila said.

"He's two."

"Almost three," she said. "And he's probably closer to three and a half mentally. Fae mature faster than other races."

"Still," I muttered, carefully pricking the needle into my skin. "He's a kid. We can't count on him being his own hero."

She fell quiet. "Yeah. Yeah, I guess."

As the blood began to stream from my arm through the plastic tube and into the blood bag on the table, I met Laila's gaze. "But if it does work, I have no idea where to start. He knows you. At least he had an impression of you in his head before he showed up. He has no idea who I am."

"Chris has told him about you." She ran her hand along my bicep with a sympathetic gaze. "He doesn't really know me either, baby. But I don't think that matters. He just wants to be with people who love him that aren't going to hurt him."

"Yeah. Yeah, I know. I just... I don't even know where to start."

"It'll come to you." She smiled. "I didn't know what to say either, but he's easy to talk to. And he'll recognize you because you look like

Chris. I showed him my memories of you too. You won't be a total stranger."

"Pretty close though," I muttered. "I don't know. Hopefully he doesn't hate me."

"He couldn't hate you." Laila pushed hair from my face and tucked it behind my ear. "He's going to love you."

"I hope." I pulled a simple, somber smile to my lips. "I really hope."

Meeting Micah was a fantasy for me since I learned that he was alive. But I always pictured it as this awesome movie moment where I kick a bunch of ass, slit some throats, and teleport him back home. Some way so that he could see me as a hero that fought for him and not some dead beat.

I definitely didn't picture it in some dream, virtual-like reality where things were slow and peaceful. There was an entirely different image in my mind, and I wasn't sure how this one was going to pan out.

"How's it going in here?" Leah galloped down the steps.

"So far so good," I said. "Once I fill two bags, Laila's going to heal me. Then we'll do Lydia. She agreed, right?"

"Yeah, she was happy to help," Laila said. "I didn't go into much detail of the why though. She knows we need her blood, and that's about it."

"That's all she needs to know," Leah said. "If you do talk to Micah and Chris tonight, don't tell them about anything you learn. If it's in their head, Amy can get it. Let's keep them out of the loop for now."

"That's what I was thinking too," I said.

I fainted three times before we accumulated a substantial enough amount of blood to feed the North American alphas. Then Liam came over to draw Lydia's and Moriah's. It didn't bother me to watch Moriah get hers drawn, but I had to leave the room when Laila healed Lydia. I couldn't help but remember that Micah felt that pain just as Lydia did and that knowledge left me with a nasty gurgle in the pit of my stomach.

Then we poured our collective blood into a couple of water jugs and left it in the fridge. Laila took Moriah home while I walked back to the house with Milly and Tinkerbell. She happily pranced down the gravel path chasing bugs and picking up sticks before running back to me with a wagging tail. I smiled and threw it each time.

Tink loved living at the new house. She spent most of her time frolicking through the fields and running in and out at her beck and call. But we hadn't been giving her the attention she deserved since Milly was born. For the most part, she didn't seem to mind. But I could tell she missed us, and I felt guilty. Maybe Micah would be home soon, and she'd have someone to play with.

Laila was back at the house before we made it there. She took a shower and slipped into her pajamas while I fed Milly and got her ready for bed. Laila's smile was as wide as the ocean when she climbed into the sheets and lay against the pillow. I sat down in the chair beside the bed and played my guitar as she drifted to sleep. I tried to be as happy as she was, but I felt more nervous than I ever had in my life.

He could hate me. Peterson surely attempted to accomplish that feat. Why else would he cut my face out of the pictures of Laila and me? He didn't want Micah to know me, let alone like me. He wanted to be viewed as his father.

Even if Chris had shown him memories of me, I was a kid when he disappeared. At sixteen, I looked a hell of a lot different than I did at twenty-six. My hair and eyes were the only recognizable features. I'd grown a beard when Laila was in captivity and hadn't given it more than a trim since. I was an entirely different person than Chris remembered.

As that thought crossed my mind, a bright realization followed. I'd get to talk to Chris. I'd seen him the year before, but that was just the cage that housed his soul. This time, I wouldn't get to see his body, but I *would* get to see his soul. That's all that mattered anyway.

By two A.M., keeping my eyes open felt harder than changing a tire with no jack. Fighting the urge to let them close was more difficult than I could have imagined. But I held on, continuously popping into Laila's head every few minutes to see if anything had changed.

Around a quarter to three, I went into her mind again. But that time, they were there.

CHAPTER TWENTY-FIVE

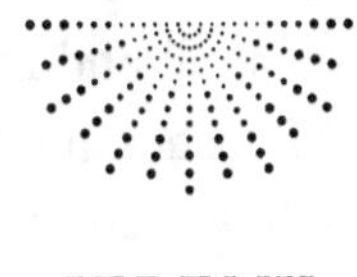

JEREMY

The moment I entered her mind, I knew where Micah formulated this place. It was the image from the false window in his bedroom at the last compound. For a second, it tore me apart to realize that my son's only idea of the outdoors came from a printed image on glass with a few lights behind it.

He was Fae. If he were anything like every other Fae I met, he'd love being outside. Laila and Milly liked the comfort of our home too, but there was nothing like their smiles on a warm day with the sun on their cheeks. My blood boiled at the fact that Micah had never felt that.

I saw them, and that fury vanished.

Laila kneeled in the sand with her arms around Micah's torso. I didn't see his face from beneath their mess of dark hair, but I saw his chubby hands gripping her back. Beside them, Chris stood with a large, joyous smile and big, happy blue eyes.

He grinned, brushing past Laila and Micah to me. "I almost didn't recognize you." Chris's arms looped around my shoulders. I found myself completely dumbfounded for a moment, entirely unable to form words or even thoughts.

I wouldn't have recognized him either had I not seen him last year.

One thing the two of us always shared was our love for our hair. It broke my heart that his was gone.

At least they let Micah keep his.

Still, his embrace felt as real as any other. It was different than it'd been before; he was so much thinner. But I could feel his heart beating as his chest touched mine. His voice sounded as clear as if he were actually beside me.

We stayed that way for a moment as I looked down at Micah over Chris's shoulder. He looked so small and innocent resting his head on his mother's chest. When Laila pushed hair from his face, it was as if I was looking at a photo of myself as a child. His smile looked like Laila, but otherwise, he could be my twin.

"Are you okay?" I made out in a murmur as Chris pulled back to meet my gaze.

He forced a smile. "Yeah, we're okay." His smile softened as he turned to Laila and Micah. "Hey, kiddo, look who it is."

Micah's vibrant blue eyes lifted open as he inched back from Laila. I struggled not to look at the sewn skin of his neck when he peered up at me. I brought a smile to my lips. I took a few steps forward and lowered myself next to Laila. He gazed up at me with big, nervous eyes. I guess he got my awkwardness too.

"Hey, buddy," I said, trying to decide what to do with my hands.

"Hi," Micah murmured.

I brought on a smile pointed to his head. "I like your hair. It's really cool."

He looked over the black locks that hung around my cheeks. "So's youws."

I smiled, giving a nod. I thought about saying it was just like his, but words didn't want to leave my lips. Talking to him was like treading on broken glass. I didn't know what Peterson had said about me; I didn't want to repeat anything he'd said or have my words misconstrued.

"Micah, this is Jeremy." Chris walked around us. "He's your dad."

"I know," Micah said.

I felt Laila's eyes on mine as Micah and I awkwardly stared one another down. But he was a good icebreaker.

"You a good singew, wight?" Micah asked.

An awkward laugh left my lips. "So I've been told."

"I've shown him memories of us playing music together," Chris said. "He says I'm bad at it, so he gets to see snippets of you singing before he goes to bed."

Warmth radiated through me, stomach flipping. He *did* know good things about me. He'd seen me sing. I was bad at plenty of things, but I was a damn good musician. If that was all he'd heard of me, then that was something to smile about.

Micah looked up at Chris. "'Cause you awe."

I laughed. "Yeah, you always were a bad singer."

"Yeah, yeah." Chris smiled.

Laila brought herself to her feet and took a few steps forward. She smiled and put her arms around Chris's shoulders. "Thank you," I heard her whisper before they took a few steps away.

"Do you like to sing?" I asked Micah with a smile. He nodded. A soft grin pulled at his lips. "It's a lot of fun, huh?"

"I *love* to sing," he said. "Maybe we can sing togethew sometimes."

"Yeah." I kept my smile, still kneeling in the sand before him. "Yeah, we'll have to do that. Hey, maybe I can teach you to play the guitar too."

His smile widened. He nodded quickly.

A positive reaction. Okay, music. That's what we'd talk about. Not exactly a hero moment, but something he liked. And something I was good at.

"I know how to play a lot of other instruments too," I said. "The piano, the violin, even the saxophone. I can teach you how to play those too."

"What's a sasophone?" he asked.

I extended my hand out to his. "Here, I can show you."

My eyes stayed open while I showed him snippets I'd seen on YouTube of live performances from some of my favorite saxophone players. His brows raised and fell over his closed eyes as he watched flashes of Sonny Rollins and Dexter Gordon. A grin pulled at his lips while his eyes fluttered back and forth behind their lids.

Peterson took a lot of shit from me, but he'd never be able to take what I got in that moment. I didn't realize those short images and sounds would give him so much, but in that single instant, my son fell for jazz. *I* got to show my son to his first love.

When his eyes peeled open over his smiling lips, a laugh left mine. "So you like the saxophone?"

He nodded quickly, grinning wide. "You can do that too?"

"Not as good as they did," I said. "But I'm an alright sax player. Good enough to teach you how if you want to learn to play."

He held his joyous expression.

"Alright, you've got yourself a deal." I smiled wider. "We might have to wait a couple years though. You might not have the lung capacity yet."

"What's that mean?" he asked.

"Oh, well." I thought for a moment. "With the saxophone, you have to blow into the top part really hard and press the buttons with your hand. With other instruments like the guitar, you just have to use your hands. You don't have to blow into anything, so it's a little easier when you're small."

"Oh." Micah looked out in thought for a moment. "I start with the da-tar then."

I laughed. "That sounds like a plan to me."

Micah smiled back. He turned to the ground. He looked back up and met my gaze. "I seen you befowe."

My tongue ran along my lips. "Yeah, I think I saw you too."

Fuck, I hoped he wasn't about to ask why I hadn't grabbed him in that moment. Truth was, I wished I had. I should've exposed us. If it meant I'd have brought him home, that he'd be safe, I would. Exposure was an ugly picture, but we had an impenetrable forcefield around our home. If I could turn back time, I'd have done it. I'd have exposed us and hunkered down in the safety of our home from anyone the world and anyone else that was pissed that I'd done it.

"You twied to find me," he murmured.

"I've been trying to find you for a long time," I barely whispered.

"That's what Mommy said too."

This conversation wasn't easy to hold with anyone, let alone with the child I'd waited over three years to meet. Trying to find the words felt like searching for a needle in a giant pile of needles. No matter what I said, I'd end up stabbing myself.

"I'm so sorry, buddy," I whispered as I looked between his somber blue eyes. "I'm so sorry you are where you are. I want you home with us so bad. And I'm trying really hard to find you."

He fell silent. His gaze stayed on the ground. "I axed him 'bout you one time. I seen you talk to Lydia befowe so I axed about you." *Lydia* sounded a bit more like *Wydia*, but it was adorable.

"Peterson? The doctor?"

He nodded but kept his gaze turned to the sand. "He says you's a bad person." He turned back up to meet my gaze. "He lied, wight?"

The lump in my throat thickened. I didn't want to lie, but I couldn't be completely honest either. I worked hard to get to the place I was at, but I still struggled to believe that I was decent. Between my addiction to my inability to be honest to the people who mattered most to me, I couldn't pretend that I was a 'good' person. I knew that I was a hell of a lot better than Peterson. But I didn't want to lie to him either. Any psychic would know if I lied, Micah included.

"I'm not perfect," I said. "But I try really hard to do the right thing."

Micah looked between my eyes. "You wouldn't huwt me though, wight?"

It hurt that he asked that, but I could answer that one honestly. "I'd never hurt you, kid."

His gaze shifted back and forth from my left eye to my right. "You pwomise?"

I summoned a smile. "I promise."

He did the unthinkable—at least to me at the time. His chubby arms reached forward and wrapped around my neck. He rested his head on my shoulder and squeezed hard. Mine twisted around his tiny torso, and I held him tighter than I'd ever held anything.

I couldn't help the tears that left my eyes as I held my son for the first time. It may have only been a virtual reality, but it brought with it one of the best moments of my life. Suddenly, I understood that vibrant, radiating energy Laila referred to when she talked about him.

He felt pure. Innocence and kindness practically poured out of him. Describing that first perception feels nearly impossible now, although I still feel that same power when I stand beside him as a grown man.

"I know you don't really know me yet," I murmured. "So you don't have to say it back. But I want you to know that I love you, Micah. I love you so much more than you realize."

He didn't say anything, but I didn't care. He didn't have to. He just had to know that I loved him. No matter what else Peterson put into his head, he had to know that I loved him.

CHAPTER TWENTY-SIX

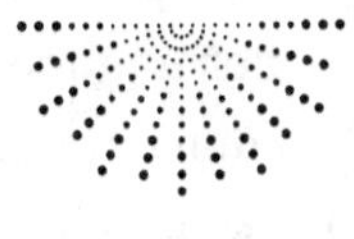

LAILA

"I'm just glad he has someone besides them," Chris whispered.

I glanced down at Micah and Jeremy talking. And as much as I wanted to join in on that conversation, Jeremy needed a few minutes with him. Plus, I needed intel from Chris. "Let's give them a minute."

We took a few side steps away from Micah and Jeremy. "I don't know how long we have. It's daytime; they think we're napping."

"Do you know what time?" I asked. "Because I think it's past midnight back home."

"If there's a clock, I can't read it, Laila." Chris kept his voice low so Micah wouldn't hear. "I only know because there's a damn bird's nest outside and they never shut the fuck up in the daytime."

"Right." My voice was hardly above a whisper. "How did you know what time I'd be asleep then?"

"We didn't. We've been working on this for months. It's been a lot of trial and failure, but it worked that one time, right? That's how you found the second facility?"

"Yeah. We were a little late though," I said.

"That's my fault." He frowned. "Amy caught me. She knew I gave you information, so they started clearing out and moved us. I didn't get to control my body for a while after that."

I ignored the chill that rose to my skin. "Do you have any clue where you guys are?"

"We move a lot. Usually every few weeks, sooner if something sketchy comes up. Once they figured out how to get in my head, they stopped using human forms of transportation. It's exclusively teleportation now. But we've been at this place for a while. Maybe a couple months? A rooster caws each morning too. Whatever they have us in, it's very close to being outside. I don't even think it's insulated."

"What does it feel like?" I asked. "The walls, the floor. How does it feel?"

"Cold," he said. "It's all cement except for the door. It's metal, I think."

"Like a basement?"

"Maybe partially, but I don't think so," he said. "I've tried to have Micah show me, but he closes his eyes when they open the door. That usually means they're taking me or coming in to drug us."

I fought the burning tears in my eyes. "I'm so sorry, Chris."

"I'm not worried about me, Laila. I'm worried about him."

"So am I," I whispered. "We're working on a couple of things. But I need him to keep coming here for it to work. Can you do this again?"

"I don't think we can come every day. It isn't easy to pull off. I'm in Micah's head right now while still being consciously aware in my body. The shield I'm holding up to keep Amy and Nastya out is really fucking heavy. I feel myself losing grip as we speak." He glanced at Micah. "He doesn't realize it, but it strains him too. He could barely walk after yesterday. That could have been the..." He caught himself. "I'm sorry I couldn't keep that from happening. Tell Jeremy I said that I'm sorry if we run out of time here."

No part of me blamed Chris for this. I owed him my life for taking care of my baby—for giving him the slightest sense of normalcy. For showing him what it meant to have family. I hated that he had the scars now, but I had them too. So did Chris and Lydia. Scars are just scars. They don't go away, but they don't matter all that much either.

I turned my gaze to the ground. "It's not your responsibility to keep him safe. I appreciate it, but that's not your job."

"It wasn't your responsibility to keep my sister safe either," Chris murmured.

"We've learned a lot about the alleged apocalypse, but it's about as much as the humans think they know about the ocean. Do you know anything?"

"I heard them talking one time." His voice fell even lower as he glanced at Micah and Jeremy. "It was just once, and they thought I was asleep, so they were whispering. I thought that you died that day until then. That's what they told me. They said that you and Jeremy both died getting those people out. And I don't know why I believed them, but I did. They said that I had to be there for Micah since you weren't and obviously, I couldn't turn down that opportunity. I tried contacting Leah like this a few times, but her energy is so hard to find compared to yours. Hell, I even tried to get to Mary since I knew she was related to Micah, but I couldn't find her anywhere. But they were talking about you. About how you'd just learned that Micah was alive. That's when I realized I could try and contact you instead."

"Did you hear anything other than that they were going to kill him?" I whispered.

He shook his head. "They said that they had to use extra caution because now that you knew, you were going to be looking harder than you had for the other survivors. Peterson kept saying, 'No, I'm supposed to have more time. It has to happen at the right time. She can't have him yet, it's not time.'" Tears formed in his eyes. "He said they'd have to 'secure the backup enclosures' and 'move between them as often as possible.' That if they were careful, they could buy the years that they needed."

"Did they say a date?"

"No," he said. "But I've heard him mention the twenty-fourth year. It was in other contexts, he didn't say 2024. He said the twenty-fourth year."

I squinted in thought. "Twenty-four, huh?"

"Does that mean something to you?"

"Maybe," I murmured. "Maybe, I don't know."

The curse our souls had been under, Jeremy and I had started to call the twenty-four years curse. In each life, we died before or just after making it to twenty-four. But if this had any connection to that, it'd mean that fate or destiny wasn't on our side. Not if this connected to the twenty-four years curse.

"I hope it gives you something," he murmured.

I bit my lip and gave a nod. "Is there anything else you could think of that might help us find you?"

"I know that one of the places they were keeping us a few months ago was in Australia. A cop, I think, found Micah and me. We were being kept somewhere bigger then. A warehouse, maybe? I'm not sure. But when I heard his voice, I thought that was it, we were finally getting out. Then Nastya killed him, and we moved to where we are now."

There was probably an article on something like that somewhere. Something like two or three cops on duty die in Australia per year, and closer to a hundred a year in the U.S. Really said something about how badly we needed to reform law enforcement in the states, but that's another topic for another day.

"I might be able to track that," I murmured. "If I can find the reports on the missing cop, maybe I can find the place they were keeping you. They left in a hurry; they might have left something behind."

"One other thing you might need to know. They're not staying where they're keeping us. Probably because they don't want to invest money into the shit holes we're locked in in case we have to move again. Our cell was a palace compared to where we are now," he muttered. "I don't know if that's going to help you or not, but it's good to know."

A palace? A steel room with a jail toilet? What the fuck were they staying in now?

But I couldn't dwell on that. I needed as much information as possible, then to spend some time with my son.

"Yeah," I said. "Yeah, that's great intel. Thank you. How many guards are there?"

He laughed. "A hell of a lot less than there used to be. Thanks to you, I presume." I smiled, and he said, "No more than twenty, at least where we're being kept. I couldn't tell you how many there are wherever they are."

I'd hoped he'd know a more precise number, but no more than twenty would have to do. I could wipe out twenty guards easy either way.

"Can I give you a tip though?" Chris asked. I nodded, and he continued, "I'm sure you guys have primarily been focusing on searching for Micah and me. But wherever we are is going to be way more magically secure than where they're staying. I can feel it, this border around us is small. Nastya doesn't have unlimited resources, and no Witch is intended to pass the amount of power it takes to hold the shields they have around us for any length of time. There's no way the spell she has where she lives is as powerful. It couldn't be, ours would be weaker if it were. My advice is to focus on finding her or Amy. They were protected under the other compounds before, but now they aren't. Maybe if you find them, you'll be able to figure out a way to find us."

I hadn't thought of that.

"That's a good point," I said.

"Whoa!" Micah exclaimed, laughing from the sand a few feet away. In his hand, he held a glowing ball of fire. He turned up to Jeremy with wide eyes. "How'd you do that?"

"I didn't, you did." Jeremy laughed. "It might be a little different than in the real world, but if you can do it here, you can do it there."

"I can?" he asked.

"Mommy can." He turned to me with a smile. He looked back to Micah. "I think you can too."

Him referring to me as Mommy to our kiddo gave me butterflies and forced a smile to my lips. This wasn't how either of us had pictured meeting Micah. It should've been in a hospital two and a half years ago. But this was the best we could do under the circumstances, and it brought me so much joy.

"Weally?" he asked.

"You can do a lot more than that, kiddo." I smiled, turned from Chris, and lowered myself beside him. "You can do almost anything."

"Weally?" he repeated.

"Really." I smiled.

Micah thought for a long moment as Chris chuckled behind me. "So you believe it when they say it, huh?"

Micah grinned, and I smiled back. I took his hand in mine and just looked at him. It could have been a few seconds, a couple minutes, or a couple hours. But for that moment, I just enjoyed being with my son and husband at the same time. I got a glimpse into the future we were fighting like hell to create.

Unfortunately though, our happy ending didn't come with the future. Instead, our happy ending started in the past.

CHAPTER TWENTY-SEVEN

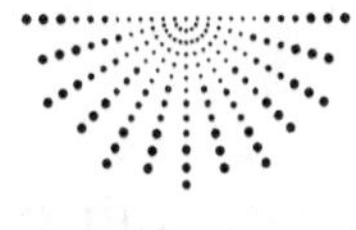

JEREMY

Micah and Chris hugged me and Laila one more time before abruptly ripping us from the alternate reality he created. That sensation felt like jumping from a plane without a parachute. My eyes slamming open and a deep gasp entering my lungs was like the impact of hitting the ground.

Laila did the same, slamming forward in the bed and grasping her heaving chest. I turned my gaze to Milly still sleeping soundly in her crib. I glanced at the clock that read three twenty-eight. The last I'd looked at it, it said two forty-two.

Forty-six. I got forty-six minutes with my son.

A smile stretched up my cheeks.

"He liked me," I whispered.

Laila laughed. "I knew he would."

"He's amazing," I said. "He's the coolest two-year-old I've ever met."

"Have you met a lot of two-year-olds?"

I laughed. "No. No, I guess not. But they can't all be that cool. If they were, they wouldn't call it the terrible twos."

"He's almost three, you know," Laila murmured.

I sucked my teeth. "Yeah, Laila. I know. But he's still two now so I'm going to call him two."

Her face said she didn't appreciate my tone.

It bothered me when she said he was almost three. I knew that, but he wasn't yet. I hadn't missed three years of his life yet because three years ago, I just found out that she was pregnant with him. She meant it in a prideful manner, and I knew that. But it hadn't been three years yet.

"I'm sorry," I murmured.

Milly stirred in her crib.

It's okay, she said into my mind. *Turn the baby monitor on and come out to the kitchen. I'm going to make some cookies while I tell you what Chris told me.*

I brought a smile to my lips. She gave a gentle smile back. She disappeared. Being able to leave a room without opening a door made having an infant a hell of a lot easier.

"They were in Australia?" I asked.

"The cop that died trying to let them out had an Australian accent so yeah, I think so." She dropped a piece of cookie dough into her mouth.

"What else did he say?"

"Wherever they're at is really shitty. Cold, not insulated, cement walls and floors. And that they're not in the same building as them this time. They're probably staying somewhere nicer. But Chris thinks that wherever they're staying won't be as magically guarded as him and Micah are. He says we should focus on finding Amy and Nastya and let them lead us to Micah and Chris."

"That makes sense," I said.

"They move a lot, and they don't use human transportation. They just hop onto the S.S. Chris and take their ride." Laila chewed on a piece of cookie dough. "So that's how they've diverted most of the algorithms Leah has in place. My guess is that they only go out in public if they go places where they can stay invisible. Back roads, closed circuit security cameras, et cetera, et cetera."

"Yeah, we would have gotten a hit on one of them somewhere if not," I muttered.

"Another thing," Laila said. "When I found out that Micah was alive, they panicked. Peterson kept saying that 'it had to be the right time' and that he needed 'more time.'"

I nibbled my cheek and squinted a bit. "Do you think that means the timeline changed?"

"Maybe," she said. "Maybe, but it could mean that he got things mixed up. I was already pregnant with Micah when Mary tried to break us up. Mary said that she did her math wrong, that's why it didn't work. My guess is that she knew Micah's birthday."

"But since he came early, you were pregnant sooner than she thought," I murmured with a nod.

"That's what I'm thinking." Laila popped the baking sheet into the oven and turned back to meet my gaze. "Peterson knows things too, but he doesn't know everything. Timelines are intricate because every block of time has to be mapped out perfectly. He knows the date that we win. But he doesn't know the details of every event that leads up to it."

"But he knew that Milly came first," I murmured. "That's what he meant when he said, 'don't let her get wiped from history.'"

"Yeah. Yeah, I think," she said. "He said that if they started moving around, if they secured the other locations, they could buy the years that they needed."

*The **years** that they needed.*

Years? He thought he'd have my son for more years than he already had? Fuck no. His days were numbered.

Behind gritted teeth, I said, "I hate that bastard."

"Tell me about it," she muttered.

"We should try and get a couple hours of sleep and then we'll go talk to Leah in the morning. I have to get to the diner at ten-thirty to sign for the deliveries. Max is leaving today to go to that clinical trial with his mom so I'm going to be there every day this week. Adam's going to be cooking tomorrow, and he has his serv-safe so I can leave after I sign for everything. That way, I can be there in case Brendon can set something up with the Monarch. Oh, I forgot to tell you with everything that happened with Lydia, but I gave Max a couple grand. Something happened with their sewer, and they've been shitting in a port-o-potty. He asked for an advance, but I told him not to worry about it."

"I figured that was coming," Laila said. "I tried to give him a couple hundred last month when he put that deposit down for this treatment, but he wouldn't take it. I'm glad he asked."

"Yeah, dude busts his ass. He deserves more than we pay him anyway," I muttered.

She walked around the island and sat beside me at the bar stool. A smile came to her lips. "He's amazing though, isn't he?"

"He's perfect." I smiled back. "Ya know how when Milly was born, I said that I felt a little different about Micah than I did about Milly?" She nodded, and I said, "All it took was meeting him. Now I get it. I love them both more than I love anything."

She gave a somber smile. "Yeah, I know what you mean."

"He likes the saxophone," I said. "I was telling him about all the instruments I can play, and I showed him famous sax players, and you should have seen the look on his face. It was like I just opened his eyes to a whole new world. We should get him one."

"Well, you're the musician. Pick one out, and we'll set it up in his room," Laila said.

"He won't be able to play it for a while. He's way too little to even hold one so we'll start with the guitar first." I laughed. "He called it a 'da-tar.'"

A quiet laugh left her lips. Smiling, she blinked tears away. "I told you he'd like you."

My smile gradually drooped to a frown. "We have to find him, Lai."

"We have more now than we ever have," she murmured. "We're getting close. I can feel it. We're going to get them both home."

I really hoped so. There was nothing I wanted more. But there was still a very real possibility that they'd kill him first. "At least we got to meet him, right?"

Her hand reached for mine. She held her sad smile with teary eyes. I forced a smile to my lips and looped my arms around her shoulders. She lifted an arm around my back and rested her head against my shoulder. I raised our hands to my lips and kissed her knuckles.

"We're closer than we've ever been." My gaze looked on the timer on the microwave. Twelve minutes and twenty-four seconds. "We're getting our son back."

Those numbers always showed up. Soon, we'd know why.

CHAPTER TWENTY-EIGHT

LAILA

Jeremy and I ate a couple of cookies before he turned in around four-thirty. Milly was still asleep, but I couldn't go back to bed. Instead, I sat down on the couch with the plate of baked goods and my laptop. I started digging.

As it turned out, there weren't many missing cops in Australia, but there were even fewer murders. It took about an hour of Googling to find the man who gave his life trying to save my son. He was found dead on the ground outside of his police cruiser with dried blood streaming from his eyes, nose, mouth, and ears on a deserted road about two hours from a place called Beagle Bay. Official cause of death was internal hemorrhaging caused by vehicular homicide.

The story stated that the officer was presumably performing a routine traffic stop before he was hit by a passing car. Apparently, the camera on his cruiser seemed to be defective and had no available footage from the week prior to the officer's death. A reward of 10,000 dollars was offered for any information leading to the arrest of whoever was responsible for the man's murder, but it sat unclaimed.

I found myself delving deep into the internet rabbit hole. His wife had a blog with over half a million followers. My fingers kept scrolling through every article she'd written since his death. She insisted that there was more to her husband's story than met the eye. Her tirades were confusing at times because of the passion behind her words, but I kept reading.

In almost every article, she mentioned a case that he'd been working on that kept him awake for days on end. Three months prior, he stopped a suspicious person driving southeast out of Beagle Bay. Two passengers were in the backseat, but one of them caught his attention. It wasn't a perfect match, but he remembered seeing his face on a most wanted list from America. It took him weeks to even find the place where he'd seen the image, but he eventually did.

Robert Peterson? (Multiple Aliases)

He went on searching for the man for months but never came back with anything. At least, that's what his wife believed. But I knew better. Somehow, he got a lead and followed it. Maybe he'd been tracking the car they drove, maybe he had abilities and set out for vengeance like the rest of us. Whatever the case may have been, he found Peterson. He found my son. If he could, so could I.

Once I'd read every blog, most of which were just about what she was going through now as a single mother toward the end, I looked her up on Facebook. I didn't add her as a friend, but I flicked through her photos with watery eyes. They had pictures on the beach and others from amusement parks. They were planning a trip to Disneyland before his untimely death. When I made it to their wedding pictures, I let the tears flow from my eyes and heavy sobs leave my lips.

That man died trying to save my son. His beautiful wife and daughter had to go on without him. Yet again, two more lives destroyed at the hands of Doctor Robert Peterson.

I couldn't let another two be destroyed.

The smell of pancakes, sweet syrup, and strong coffee wafted to my nose. Bright morning light lit the kitchen of the main house, shining against the tile floors. Heat from the stove warmed my chilled arms.

"So it went good then?" Leah asked, flipping a pancake at the stove.

"It was amazing." Jeremy smiled.

She gave a soft smile back. "And Chris? How was he? What did he say?"

"We didn't have much time for chit-chat," I muttered. "But yeah, he was okay. He was just trying to give us information."

"I barely even talked to him," Jeremy said. "I wanted to, but I was so caught up in the moment with Micah."

"I think he understood, baby." I smiled and ran my hand over his shoulder. He smiled and sipped from his cup of coffee.

"Did he give you anything useful?" Leah asked.

"Maybe. They were being kept somewhere in Australia until a few months ago. A cop found them, but Nastya killed him before they had the chance to get away. I did some research and found the cop. They found him dead outside of his cruiser. They think he got hit by a car during a traffic stop."

Leah thought for a moment before plopping the pancake onto a plate. "Can you handle these for a second, Lai?"

"Sure," I said. Leah walked around the counter and flipped open her laptop. "What are you looking for?"

"I just... I want to check something. Australia, right?" Leah lifted her glasses to her face and tucked them behind her ears. Jeremy squinted over her shoulder as she clicked away at the keyboard.

"Are those latitude and longitude lines?" he asked.

"They're ley lines." She clicked on the keyboard. "Do you know where they were in Australia?"

"Not exactly, but they had to have been close to Beagle Bay." I flipped the browning pancake.

A smile pulled at her lips, eyes widening.

"Aren't ley lines pseudo-science?" Jeremy asked.

"To humans," Leah said. "But to the Fae, they're the most important part of the planet."

"What do you mean?" I asked.

"I was reading this book I got in the Fae Realm. Kai had to help translate a lot of it because I'm not fluent in Elvan, but from my understanding, the Fae and Elvan people believe that our planet's vibrations echo through these pathways along every dimension. Hell, Heaven, here, and the Fae Realm. Think about it like the Earth's Wi-Fi. Every living thing is connected to it, but the Fae and Elvan people have ways of tapping into it. So do Witches if they're strong enough. That's how Kai opened the portal to the Fae Realm; he used Elvan magic."

"What are you saying?" I asked.

"I don't know yet, hang on," she murmured. "But I do know that not all Fae can use it. Only those of us who harness spirit. Me, you, Kai, Celena." She paused and looked at me over her laptop. "Amy."

My eyes widened a bit, heart beginning to thud in my chest.

"We tap into it every time we heal," Leah continued while she clicked. "Every time we read a mind or access a past memory, we're using the Earth's energy. Okay, Beagle Bay, you said?"

I nodded, and she laughed. Her head shook slightly as she moved the mouse around. "Unbelievable. Un-fucking believable."

"What is it?" I studied Leah's look of amusement and Jeremy's disgruntled gaze.

"Vancouver, Alter do Chao, and Beagle Bay are all located on a ley line," Leah murmured. "Beagle Bay and Alter do Chao are on the same major line. Vancouver's on one of the branched lines, but they're all there."

"They're using Elvan magic," Jeremy murmured.

"They have to be," Leah said. "That's why Amy matters so much, and Lydia doesn't. She's more in touch with the Terra Firma. They didn't need her. They needed the Sprite bloodline."

"And Micah's more in touch with spirit than anything," Jeremy muttered. "They're using his own powers to disguise him."

"And Nastya's a powerful Witch that's mastered ancestral magic from one of the most powerful lines of Witches to ever live," I murmured. "That combination's unstoppable."

"No." Leah smiled. "Not when we have six people who can access the same type of magic. Four of which are at least ten times as powerful as them."

"Six?" Jeremy asked.

Leah shifted her gaze to Milly in the play pen.

"That bitch isn't getting anywhere near my daughter's mind," I said.

"Fine. Five then," she said. "Either way. You, Kai, Celena, me and Lydia... If we're right, if this is what they're using, then we can use their own strengths against them. We can tap into the same magic, and we can find them. If they're using that level of energy, and channeling Micah's in the process, they're going to be pulsing like an antenna on the lines. If we have a remnant of Micah's energy like Helena thinks we will, we can use it like a reverse engine search on the internet."

"How would we do that?" Jeremy asked.

"Micah's energy is like the photo," I said. "We pop it into the search, and it shows us where he is on the map."

Leah smiled. "Exactly. But that'll be a last resort if something goes wrong with the binding Helena casts."

"But don't you think we'll need someone experienced in Elvan magic to pull something like this off?" I asked. "Kai knows some, but Nastya has decades of experience with way darker magic than this."

"Maybe, but we have Helena too," she said. "Nastya is using Amy, and maybe Micah, like a satellite. I bet Helena can do the same with us. Especially because there's no way all of our combined power isn't going to be at least equally as strong as theirs."

"Wait," Jeremy murmured. "When Laila was being held captive, we fucked around with the idea of searching the Earth in shifts by teleporting and crossing off areas. Process of elimination and everything, but you guys said we couldn't do that because they could be anywhere. We had nowhere to start. But now we have a map. We could search it in shifts. If we do it carefully, we might be able to find them."

"Ley lines are everywhere. Vancouver, or at least where you were being kept near Vancouver, is on a branched ley line, it's not on one of the four primaries. That still means that they could be anywhere," Leah said.

"No." I lifted the pancake from the skillet to the plate. "No, Chris heard Peterson talking once, before we got everyone out of the last compound. He said they 'had to secure the other facilities.' You said the one in Brazil and the one in Australia connected, that means that they're sticking to the stronger lines. They're not using the branch lines anymore; they're using the concentrated energy. Hiding Micah would take stronger magic, a stronger line."

Leah bit her lip. "Maybe. That would make sense. We had no idea what we were up against with the first compound so she could use the weaker energy. But now that we've been testing them, they're going to use the most powerful energy that they can."

"Especially because Micah's energy signature can't be easy to block," I said.

"That's where we start then." Jeremy stood. "We start following these ley lines and scouting areas that could be used to hold someone captive."

"No, I study satellite images first," Leah said. "That way they can't trace our energy and get scared off. I get a list compiled of all the possible locations so that we don't waste time on leads that go nowhere."

"Once you get a list together, we send Adam, Brody, and Gwen to scout," I said. "Anyone with low enough energy signatures that Nastya and Amy won't be able to feel. Maybe even some of these wolves we're gonna be working with. Once we have a confirmed location, then *we* go. But not until we're sure. The two of us go too soon, and we'll scare them off. If Chris is right, if they're staying somewhere else, we might be able to pull this off seamlessly. Get Micah and Chris, and then go back to deal with the trinity of assholes once our family's home safe."

As expected in our line of work, things did not go seamlessly.

"That's smart," Leah said. "That's really smart."

"Yeah, I agree." Jeremy smiled wide. He walked over to the play pen and lifted Milly to his arms. He gave her a quick hug and a kiss on the cheek before turning to me and quickly pressing his lips to mine. "I have to get to the diner, but if Brendon calls Celena or Wyatt and they want to meet, don't go without me."

"Will do."

I almost couldn't believe it.

A real plan. Getting stronger and stronger each day that went by.

We were close. A few more weeks, maybe a few more months, and I'd get my baby back, damn it.

CHAPTER TWENTY-NINE

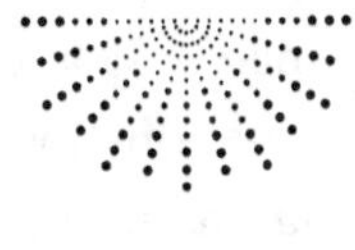

LAILA

"Hey." Celena smiled, coming in through the back door. She tugged off her headphones and tucked muddy blond hair behind her ear. She leaned toward the highchair to say hi to Milly. "Me and Tink were having a blast out there. It got all muddy last night, so I took her with me down to the stream. You might want to check her for ticks when you get home."

"Don't encourage the mud, man." I looked up from Leah's laptop. "Do you have any idea how much more free time I would have if I didn't have to wash her paws every time she comes inside?"

"Hey, it's bad enough she's stuck in this cage and doesn't even get to kill her food." She wagged finger and grabbed a bottle of water from the fridge. "Let her have some mud."

I huffed. "This property is over two hundred and fifty acres. It's hardly a cage, Celena."

"Really?" Leah looked my way.

"Yeah, we had it surveyed when we built the house," I said. "That's plenty of room for one dog and a couple of wolves."

"It is a nice piece of land," Celena said. "And an incredibly secure territory, which is really nice. But since you put up that spell, the game's dwindling between Wyatt and me. We might have to find somewhere else to hunt."

Jeremy and I used to spend a lot of time in the woods when we first got together. We lived in a weird cusp between the suburbs and the boonies; there was plenty of hunting land around here.

"Yeah, I know a couple places. There's a good hundred acres around ours that are protected state forests," I said. "Stay close to the border, and it might be a good place to hunt."

"Sure, if you wear an orange vest and carry a gun." She huffed. "We've outrun a couple. Not something I want to experience again."

"Well, we can't just bring in animals for you guys to eat." I laughed.

"That would be kind of morally questionable, huh?"

"Little bit," Leah muttered.

"What're you guys looking at?" She squinted at the screen over our shoulders.

"We found a pattern," I said. "Each place where Peterson has been holding them captive is on a ley line."

"No shit," she murmured.

"So we're following the ley lines on satellite images. Chris said it was cold there and that it was daytime. That means it had to be somewhere to the northeast. But these paths span thousands of miles. We've only made it, what—A hundred?"

"Something like that," Leah muttered.

I bit my lip. "And we've already found thirty possible locations."

"I should be able to narrow that down though," Leah said. "It's going to take some time, but with Google Maps and digging up property details, I should be able to cut that in half."

"But if we find another thirty for every hundred miles, even if you cut that in half, we're still looking at tens of thousands."

"So what?" she asked. "Then we have to scout tens of thousands of locations. It's better than having billions. One way or another, this is going to help us."

She was right. With teleportation, we could scout thousands of places in under an hour. But it still didn't feel that encouraging, not when I considered how fast they could pick up and move to a new place.

However, if we got a location from one of the wolves, we could double check to see if it were on a ley line.

"Oh, good. You're back." Wyatt jogged down the steps, smiled at Celena, and gave her a quick kiss on the cheek. He turned to me. "Where's Jeremy?"

"He had to take care of some stuff at the diner. Why? Did Brendon call?" I asked.

"Yeah, they want to meet with you as soon as possible. Like, two hours," he said. "Brendon said that Roland jumped at the opportunity to meet you. Guess you're a pretty popular topic to anyone high up in the supernatural community."

"Yeah, Moriah says they talk about me at the Chamber's Meetings all the time. Even had her hand deliver a letter once. Jeremy says it's a bad idea though."

"Yeah, cause it is," Leah said. "No one that important got there doing good things. Those people can twist and bend you however they want. Fuck the Council, and fuck the stupid Chambers."

"Hence why I've declined." I stood. "But the wolves seem more my kind of people."

"I don't know about that," Wyatt said. "The things you've done, you had a damn good reason for. Some of these alphas are more like Damon than the two of us."

"Maybe. But at least they don't try to cover up their ruthlessness like those rich bastards."

"Guess that's true," he said.

"Could you watch Milly until Hannah gets home from school? I can lie her down for her nap, and she should sleep most of the time we're gone," I said to Leah.

"Yeah, my head's spinning a little bit anyway. I need to stop looking at this screen for a while. I'll go back to it when you guys get back."

"Alright sounds good. I'll take her back to the house and get a bag together while I call Jeremy."

"I'm going to go grab a shower real quick then." Leah stood, stretching her arms above her with a yawn. "Haley's supposed to spend the night tonight and I stink. We really need to get a bigger water heater; I haven't gotten a shower in three days."

"That's probably our fault," Wyatt said. "These woods are really muddy."

"You guys realize we have an entire house a few minutes down the road, right?" I asked. "You're always welcome to come take a shower."

"Yeah, go shower down there once in a while," Leah said as she started up the steps. "And leave your pubes for Laila to clean."

"They aren't pubes, I'm just hairy," Wyatt said.

"Either way," she called.

CHAPTER THIRTY

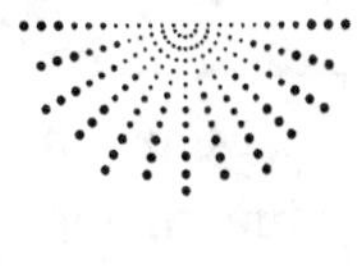

JEREMY

"She'll probably sleep for two hours." Laila tucked the blanket around Milly in the stroller. "There's milk in the freezer, but if she's still hungry, you can give her some rice cereal or bananas."

"You do realize that I'm around this baby every day, right?" Leah raised a brow. "She's fine, Laila. Just go."

"Right." She set the diaper bag down on the counter. "Just don't take her anywhere, okay?"

"I know, Lai. Just go." Leah chuckled.

I put a hand at the small of her back. "She's fine, baby."

Not that I was excited to see my wife get super turned on by a bunch of strangers with their teeth in her skin, but I was pumped to get this started. I wanted to find my kid, damn it. And this might just work.

"Yeah, we should get going," Celena said.

"They were expecting us five minutes ago," Wyatt said.

"Alright, alright. Geez." Laila pulled away from Milly.

"You have the address?" I asked.

"Yeah." Wyatt sent an image to my mind of a large colonial

mansion, handing me a slip of paper with an address. "The area's clear; we don't have to land indoors."

"I think I know this place. Vaguely, anyway. Right outside of Shreveport, right?"

Wyatt nodded. "Werewolf Capitol of North America."

"Used to be Baton Rouge, right?" Leah asked.

"Yeah," Celena said. "But there's too much hype around us there. They moved for privacy."

A slow breath left my nostrils. I didn't know him personally, but I'd heard the name. Roland Allard, Monarch of both the North American and France packs. My dad had mentioned him when I was a kid, and never in a kind light.

"This guy, Roland. He's kind of a dick, isn't he?" I asked.

"Kind of," Wyatt said. "Not like Damon was, but yeah. Yeah, he's a dick."

I said, "Alright. Let's get this over with."

I twined my fingers through Laila's. She took Celena's, and Celena grasped Wyatt's.

We landed in a grassy field full of cars, in front of a large colonial styled mansion. Six thick white columns held the roof over the large ivory colored home. Each wall had what seemed like a million windows with thick growing foliage behind the glass. It was like a smaller, more homely version of the White House.

The large red door slowly swung open as Brendon peeked outside. He waved, smiled, and made a rolling motion for us.

"After you." I gestured to Laila.

She gave a soft smile and started to the door. Celena stayed close beside her as I turned to Wyatt. "So we can trust this guy?"

"He's not known for betraying people," Wyatt said. "Pretty good leader, to be honest. Lets the packs manage themselves for the most part. He hit on Celena pretty hard last time we saw him, so brace your-self for that. But he stood behind Brendon at these things after we killed Damon. He's got to be half the reason we were able to bring peace to Brendon's pack. He knew that Damon couldn't stay in power forever. It was just a matter of time until a true alpha took his place.

Roland respected that. He told Damon to submit or die. So yeah, I like the guy."

I clenched my hands at my sides as started up the small staircase. "Well, I hope he doesn't expect me to belly-up to him."

Wyatt let out a huff of a laugh. "You're not a wolf, you're good. I'm not an alpha. I'll swallow my pride. But don't be surprised when he hits on your girl. He's got a way with women."

Another slow sigh. Dude was about to chomp into my wife's skin, get her super fucking horny, then flirt with her.

Yay.

A large window let in bright sunlight that reflected like a mirror against the dark mahogany floors. I licked my teeth, noting the taxidermic animal carcasses decorating the dreary, high class room. We stood in a small office encased with massive bookshelves covering all four walls. I used to ponder why wolves read so much, but when one lives for centuries, they have to find something to occupy all that time.

Laila stood beside the bookcase on the left flipping through pages of books older than everyone in that room combined.

"You probably shouldn't be snooping." Brendon glanced at Laila.

"I'm not snooping. I'm reading because I'm bored. We've been standing here for thirty-five minutes," she said. "What's he going to do anyway? Bite me?"

Brendon made a face. "Whatever you say."

She rolled her eyes and turned back to Moby Dick in her palms.

"Can you see how long this is going to be?" I asked. "Feeding all of these alphas is going to take time. I'd rather not waste it."

"Yeah, I'd like to get home to my kid." Laila snapped the book shut and set it back onto the shelf.

"It doesn't work like that," Brendon said.

Just as Laila was about to say something else, the French door pulled open. A man laughed in the hallway, deep, husky voice echoing off the high ceilings. "Oui merci," he said. "Reste un peu; je serai bientôt de retour. Nous avons plus à discuter." *Yes, thank you. Stay a while; I'll be back shortly. We have more to discuss.*

"Sorry to keep you waiting." Roland turned into the room. He held a relatable smile while looking between us. His accent was almost unnoticeable when he spoke English, but his French was flawless. "These things get a little hectic. I'm sure you understand."

Roland stood a few inches shorter than me than but still taller than most. He had long, grayish brown hair raised in a half ponytail at his shoulders against his sepia-colored skin. His large shoulders rested beneath a neat gray button up and white tie. He had a strong, squared jaw and long angled nose beneath his hooded honey eyes.

"Mhmm," Laila said. "No problem."

He smiled wider when he met her gaze. His eyes shifted over her scars before looking back up to meet her gaze. "Laila, I'm assuming."

"And you must be Roland." She extended her hand out to his.

Rather than a simple shake, he lifted her hand to his lips. My lip curled. "Pleasure to meet you, Miss."

"Missus," I corrected.

She pulled her hand away.

He turned to me with a friendly smile. "Of course. My apologies."

I forced a smile back and extended my hand. "Jeremy Skoulda."

"I know who you are." He firmly grasped my palm, shaking it in his. "Adele, Raphael, and I go way back. Jèan too."

"Yeah, I remember him mentioning you."

And hating you.

Maybe this was why. Maybe he hit on my mom like he was about to hit on my wife.

"When you live as long as I have, you grow to know a lot of people." Roland turned to Brendon, Wyatt, and Celena. "Thank you for arranging this meeting, Brendon. Please join the others downstairs. The two of you as well."

"No, we'll stay." Celena smiled.

He creased his brows, still smiling a bit. "I'm sorry, did I ask for your input, love?"

Celena's bubbly smile dropped. "Is that relevant?"

His shoulders stiffened as he turned to her. When he opened his mouth to speak, Laila interjected. "If we're talking logistics, they can leave. But if anyone's going to feed off of me, they're going to be present."

He turned to her and looked between her eyes for a moment. He smiled and gave a careful nod. His gaze shifted back to Celena. "We'll call for you when you're needed. Please leave. Now."

Celena made a face at him that was hard to place. Wyatt put his hand on her back and sent Roland a nod. He civilly nodded back. Then they started to the door. As it thudded shut, he made his way around the desk. "Have a seat, if you would."

I lowered myself to the fancy seat in front of the desk. Laila leaned against the arm and put her hand on my shoulder. I had to appreciate that gesture. She knew how small my dick felt in front of that massive, very attractive man who'd just kissed her hand.

He turned to the bookshelf, lifted a crystal bottle and a few glasses to the table between us. He sat and began pouring into three glasses.

"Brendon gave me a brief description of your proposal, but if you don't mind, I'd like to hear it from your perspectives. What is it that you want from us exactly?" Roland slid the glasses across the wood.

"Not much." Laila leaned forward to lift the drink. As she did, Roland's gaze traveled from her eyes to her chest. I gritted my teeth. His gaze shifted back to hers. "All we need is for your alphas to get a sample of our blood in their system."

"Yes, you want us to have your scent. I know that. But why?" Roland asked. "To find your son?"

"In a manner of speaking," I said. "But we're not asking anyone to fight or engage with these people. All that we want is contact if one of you catches the scent."

"You smell my son, you call me." Laila looked firmly between his eyes. "You smell the other Fae or the Witch, you call me. You smell his brother, you call me. No one is to make contact, no one needs to be a hero and go after them guns blazing. All they do is call me. I take it from there. Your people then know to stay back from wherever we are when shit goes down. None of your alphas are at risk."

"And we get what for this?"

"My blood," Laila said. "Apparently it's better than sex."

He smiled, eyes washing down her body. "I'll bet."

I clenched my jaw and fought the urge to make a snarky comment. Laila was hot and she used it, which didn't usually bother me. But guys like Roland made things complicated. I could hurt him if I tried. I could probably kill him if I wanted to. And over my wife, I would. But that would open a can of worms we didn't have time to deal with.

He looked my way. "And you're okay with this?"

I sucked my teeth and gave a nod.

His brow raised, smile pulling at his thick lips. "So just a single feeding then?"

"There's thousands of you." I narrowed my gaze. "So yeah. Once is going to have to be enough."

"That won't work for me." His gaze shifted over Laila, half grin across his lips. "Once I try it, I'm going to want more. The others, once is plenty for. But I'll need more than that."

"Well, tough sh—" I began.

"What do you propose?" Laila said.

"Monthly," he said. "For at least twenty-four months."

"Twelve," Laila said.

"Twenty." He smiled.

She leaned forward a bit. "Fourteen."

"Twenty." Roland repeated.

"Fourteen or not at all," Laila said. She took a sip from the glass and smiled. "Final offer."

"Possible contract renewal at the end of the fourteen months." He grinned. "To be decided upon on at a later day."

"Possible," Laila said.

Roland licked his smiling lips. He stood and extended his hand over the desk. "You've got yourself a deal, mon ange." *My angel.*

As Laila stood and raised her palm, I followed and caught her hand before they could shake. "But there are conditions."

"Oh?" Roland pulled his back.

"Ninety second feeding sessions," I stated. Laila lowered her palm but kept her fingertips against mine. "Sooner if they feed too fast and she feels like she's going to faint. And anyone who doesn't stop when they're told has to understand that I have the right to kill them if I have to."

"Sufficient for the pups," he said. "But I'm a slow feed. I like to enjoy my meal. I'll feed until she tells me to stop or she passes out. Whatever comes first."

"Fair enough," Laila said. "My husband, sister, and brother in-law will be present at each feeding."

"And no one touches her neck," I said.

He glanced over the scar beneath her ear and gave a fair nod. "What about the femoral artery?"

This fucker. He had some god damned nerve. Probably wanted to smell how wet her pussy got while he did it so he could beat off to the thought later.

I narrowed my gaze. "You're not putting your head between my wife's legs."

Roland smiled and raised a brow. He took a sip from his glass. "The wrist then."

"The wrist," Laila said.

"And if anyone has the balls to try and turn her, they're signing their death certificate," I said. "This is a business agreement. Nothing more."

"Is that all?" he asked.

"Just about covers it," Laila said.

Roland leaned back in his chair. He sipped his drink. "And aside from our informing you if we smell these people, what do you get out of this?"

"Your loyalty." She sipped her drink. "We're not looking for much. We just want to be on the same side. I'm sure you've heard the rumors."

"Of a potential apocalypse?" he said. "I have. I've heard it a thousand times before too. I'm sure the chatter will cease in a few years. Regardless, I agree. You're a valuable colleague. I'd appreciate your allegiance as much as you would mine."

"It's settled then." Laila extended her hand. "We're in this together."

He smiled and shook her hand.

"Can you help us make contact with Monarchs worldwide to make similar deals?" I asked.

"I'll take a vial of your blood once I get my taste." He looked between Laila's eyes, licking his lips like a bear fresh out of hibernation craving a meal. "After they have a taste, I'm sure they'll be more than willing. I have control over a central part of France as well as North America. Those areas, at least, should be simple. I get the feeling it won't be difficult elsewhere either."

"Great," I murmured. "Let's get it over with then."

CHAPTER THIRTY-ONE

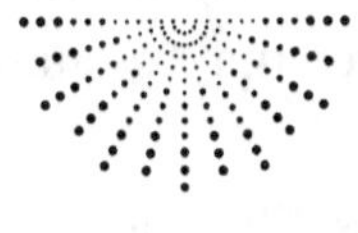

JEREMY

When our conversation ended, Roland spoke to someone in the hall for a moment. As we waited for him to return, I put my hand on Laila's knee and squeezed a bit. She looked up from the book in her hand and met my gaze with a smile. "Yeah?"

"Are you okay?"

She grinned. "Are *you* okay?"

My jaw tightened. "He's looking at you like he wants to eat you."

"Because he does." She chuckled.

"Not like that," I muttered.

Laila closed the book and stood. She took a few steps in front of me and put her hands on either side of my face. A smile tugged at her cheeks as she leaned down and touched our mouths together. I closed my eyes and felt her lips brush mine, raising my hands to the sides of her neck.

I'll admit, that kiss brought me a touch of relief. But I still didn't like this. I knew that guy was gonna try something. And he was big. His biceps were at least twice the size of mine. I didn't want this to end badly. We needed his alliance, but I wasn't going to let another guy emasculate me either. My wife did that plenty.

After a moment, she inched back and rested her head against my forehead. I looked at her through the locks of brown hair that hung between us. She smiled as her thumbs brushed the scruff along my jaw. "This could bring our baby home. If I have to shed a little blood for that, then that's what I'm going to do."

I pushed hair behind her ear. "I guess so."

"It doesn't matter what he thinks. We both know you're the only one I want." Her hand grazed my cheek. "But I can prove it to you when we get home if you need the reassurance."

I laughed. "Oh, yeah?"

"Mhmm." She bit her lower lip and brushed her hand from my face toward my chest.

The door swung open, and Wyatt grinned. "Well, sorry to interrupt."

I chuckled. Laila straightened up. She laughed and placed her hands at her hips. "Are we ready to do this?"

"Ready when you are." Roland walked in behind Celena.

"As I'll ever be," Laila said. "Where do you want me?"

Fuck, why'd she have to say it like that?

He gave a crooked grin, and I clenched my jaw. "The couch should do."

She lowered herself to it. I stood. Roland sat beside her as she pulled off her hoody. When she raised her arms over her head, his gaze steadied on her mid drift. Celena and Wyatt exchanged a glance my way.

His gaze shifted over her, and he inhaled deeply. Sharp canines protruded from his gums. He licked his lips beneath flaring nostrils. Laila extended her arm out to him, but he raised his palm to his mouth first. He pushed his fingertip into his canine and pulled it away. A pearl of crimson appeared at his fingertip. He took her forearm with his other hand. He rubbed the blood in a small circle against her pale wrist.

"What're you doing?" I asked.

"The venom in my blood that makes this a good experience for the donor has numbing properties." He looked in my direction. "Makes it more pleasurable for both parties."

The numbing idea was nice but referring to this as a 'pleasurable experience' forced my eyes to narrow.

"I never knew that," Wyatt said.

"Pups usually don't. Try it next time you feed." Roland turned his gaze to me. "When their donor enjoys it, it makes everything so much more fun."

Fun.

Fucking asshole. Nothing about this was fun.

Although, if my wife sucked my dick as hard as she did yesterday after this, maybe it would be a *little* fun.

Laila laughed, staring at her wrist. "It feels like my arm just got a cavity filled."

Roland laughed and gestured toward her wrist. "May I?"

Laila extended it toward him. He smiled in front of his pointed teeth. He carefully wrapped his hand around her outer wrist. He lowered his lips to her skin. Before he sunk his teeth in, he met my gaze and smiled.

My nostrils flared as he delicately slid his tongue to the patch of blood. Eyes on mine, he licked her skin.

I clenched my hands to fists.

This is for Micah, I reminded myself.

Laila wasn't fucked up yet. She didn't tell him to stop, so it wasn't my place to. I'd just have to bite my tongue.

He pressed his teeth into her flesh. Unlike Wyatt and Celena had, his fangs pierced in like cars coming to a slow halt at a red light. As they slowly edged into her skin, a gentle, familiar gasp left her lips.

That was the same expression that she had when my dick slid inside of her. It'd barely started, and he'd already turned her on as much as I did.

I wanted to rip his fucking throat out.

But it could help us find Micah. I had to keep reminding myself that it could help us find Micah. All that mattered was finding Micah.

Then a soft, bordering sexual moan left her lips. My eyes widened.

C'mon, Lai, you have to moan?

Her eyes fluttered shut like they did when I kissed down her body.

But it could help us find Micah. This could help us find Micah.

He suckled slowly while moving his hand near her elbow up her tense arm to her shoulder. The stiffness in her posture softened. When she sighed again, I swear I saw him smile.

"You okay, Lai?" I asked.

Her barely open eyes met mine. A smile pulled at her lips. "Yeah, baby."

Jesus Christ. She said it like a porn star.

The way those words left her mouth with another man's lips pressed to her skin made my heart stomp in my chest. I guess in that moment, I felt how she felt when she saw what Ally did to me three years ago through Brody's eyes. I rationalized. I'd been under a spell that made me want to fuck too. She didn't make the decision to be aroused; it was an involuntary response.

But when another breath left her lips, I couldn't help but grind my teeth to a tighter line. I had no idea how I would make it through the countless other times I would have to see her do this. Maybe she was right. Maybe I should have stayed home.

After seeing it though, there was no way in hell I'd let her do it without me.

We stood there a few seconds longer that felt like centuries. It'd only been about a minute when his hand at her arm drifted to her knee. He squeezed gently, and another sigh left her lips.

I bit my tongue at first. Knees are no more intimate than a forearm. But as the seconds ticked by and more deep breaths left her lips, his hand began to slide further up her thigh. She didn't even notice; she was too busy sighing and moaning like she was auditioning for *Casting Couch.*

"Move your hand," I said. He pretended he didn't hear me as his palm drifted closer up her leg. My voice lowered to an octave I didn't realize it could reach. "I said move your hand."

He opened his eyes and met my gaze over her arm. Still sucking at her wrist, his hand slid further up. The tips of his fingers dipped down to the crevice at her upper thigh. He squeezed again in a massage like motion. Her eyes opened, and her brows pulled down, feeling his pinky brush the outside of her jeans in the crease where her thighs met.

Without thought, I teleported across the room and grabbed ahold of his hair. His eyes filled with rage as he released her forearm and darted to his feet at an impossible speed. He reached for my neck, but I teleported a foot away.

He stumbled, recollecting himself and turning back to me. He leaned in for another grab. I teleported a blade that sat in a fancy sheath on his desk to my hand. As he leaned forward to grab me, I put the blade to his neck and teleported him into the wall.

The bookshelf shook behind his head. A few plummeted to the floor as I pushed the blade to his skin. "I said to move your fucking hand."

He reached for the knife, but I pressed it deeper to his skin. "She didn't."

"She didn't tell you to put it on her pussy either." My gaze narrowed, eyes shifting between his. "Attraction isn't consent. You don't get to use your powers to seduce someone. Especially not my wife. But you knew that. You aren't a rapist; you just wanted to test your luck. You wanted to see how far I'd let you get before you tried to assert your dominance over me. But I'm not one of your fucking puppies, Roland. That's my soulmate. I'll kill for her in a heartbeat. I swear to god, I will fucking *kill* you. I don't give a shit if you have a hundred wolves downstairs. I'll kill them too. Don't test me. Pull some shit like that again, and I'll slit your fucking throat. Keep your goddamn hands to yourself, and do as I say when you're feeding on my wife."

His nostrils flared. He gritted his teeth. Although still furious, after a quiet moment, he laughed quietly. "Can't say I wouldn't do the same."

I looked between his eyes for a few more seconds, panting out angry breath. I pushed him into the wall and took a step back. Celena was just finishing healing Laila's arm as I pushed hair from her face and raised her chin so her gaze met mine. "Are you okay?"

She nodded, blinking hard for a second. I took her hand to help her to her feet. As she steadied herself, her narrowed gaze turned to Roland. "If he doesn't kill you first, I will. I'll burn this place to the ground. I'm not here to play games. If you are, tell me now so we can call this off."

Roland's lips curled into a smile. "We're on the same page. My apologies."

I gritted my teeth.

Guaranteed, this was why my dad didn't like him. I didn't remember much about my mom, but I remembered how much he loved her. And she was pretty. He'd surely made a pass at her a time or two.

Roland held his smile. "I'll go speak with the alphas and prepare samples from those bottles you brought. Come down when you're ready."

Laila released her tight jaw. I circled a hand around her waist. Roland turned and started out the door. When it shut, I looked back to Laila and cupped her face in my hands. "You're okay, right?"

"I am." She leaned onto her tiptoes and pressed her lips to mine. After a second, she rested her head on my chest. Her arms twisted around my back. "Thank you."

A slow breath eased from my nose. I tucked my arms around her waist and pulled her closer into me. I brushed my hand along the back of her head and touched my lips to her hair. My head shook a bit, holding her tighter.

This was gonna be hell on me. But maybe the impression I'd made on Roland would overlay to the others. Maybe he'd send the message that I'd kill anyone who tried anything with my wife.

Had to hope, at least.

CHAPTER THIRTY-TWO

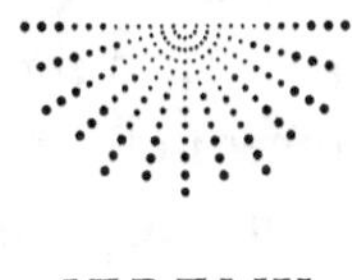

JEREMY

"Gentlemen," Roland announced. He perched over the railing at the top of the wide, intricate winding staircase that over-looked what I could only describe as a ball room. "The ladies as well. Thank you all for staying after the meeting. I do apologize for taking more of your time, although I believe you'll be grateful in a moment."

I touched my palm against Laila's as he spoke. Her fingers grazed up my hand before her pinky caught and hooked against mine. She glanced up at me with a soft smile. I smiled back and held her pinkies closer.

"I'm sure you're all wondering what this array of aromas you're getting from my friends up here are so allow me to introduce them." Roland gestured in our direction. "This is Wyatt Braxton. He is the son of Ashley Braxton and Damon Locklear, brother of Brendon Locklear, alpha of many sections of the Mid-Atlantic and South-Atlantic regions of the United States. Wolf-Guardian hybrid as his father was."

He gestured to Celena. "Beside him stands the beautiful Celena Jones, origins unknown. Fae-Angel hybrid turned unwillingly four years ago on the orders of Damon Locklear. After refusing to enter his pack for the way she was brought into it, Celena found solace in assisting Brendon to his rightful place as alpha in his region. She now resides with her sister, who stands to her left. I'm sure you know her name but now, you'll know her face." Roland turned and took a look over Laila. A smile tugged at his lips. "This, my friends, is the famous, or perhaps infamous, Laila Callidy."

Much to my surprise, the men, and few women, in the audience appeared awestruck. Hands raised to cover mouths while smiles and tears formed on other faces. A man in the center of the audience lifted his hands together and clapped. Then someone beside him did, then someone in the back and another in the front. In a matter of seconds, the room echoed with strong, civil applause. I turned to Laila with a soft smile. She blinked tears away and smiled at the audience, giving an awkward wave.

She wasn't just a savior to the survivors. She was a savior to everyone in our world. Because everyone knew someone—or knew *of* someone—Peterson held captive. That she set free.

"And beside her stands her husband, Jeremy Skoulda. These two need little introduction so we'll just go straight to the part where I explain why they're here," Roland said as the applause softened. "This pair worked tirelessly to free nearly a thousand of our people we didn't realize were still alive. Everyone here today knows someone who is living their life in freedom once more because of the actions these two took. For that, our people will forever be in their debt.

"But the irony of the matter is that when Laila and Jeremy's clan set out to find these people, they were looking for a loved one of their own. Christopher Skoulda, the eldest of the five siblings in this generation of their bloodline. Along the way, Laila lost her son in trying to free our people and her husband's kin. Still, of all the people they released, Christopher and their two-year-old son are still being held captive by the same people who kidnapped and tortured our families. Today, they have come to ask for our help. Every single one of your help.

"The small cups in the back of the room are for each of you to drink. In the blood, you'll taste Fae, Witch, Guardian, and a splash of human. I tasted it myself; it's a pretty intricate mix." He chuckled. The alphas looked between us with questioning gazes, sniffing the air. "To our knowledge, two women and a man are holding the child and his uncle hostage. We have no blood of the man in this drink because no one is sure who he really is. However, we have the blood of the Witch's sister and the Fae's daughter. Jeremy's blood is also in the mixture. The idea is that if you have a sample of these bloodlines in your system, you'll be able to recognize them should they arrive in your region."

"What do we do if they do?" an alpha asked from the crowd.

Roland turned to Laila and raised a brow. "Would you like to take it from here?"

She stepped forward. "If you guys smell this blood anywhere, anywhere at all, please don't engage. These people are using my brother in-law as their personal teleportation device. The moment we have a lead, we'll send out scouts of our own. If it leads us to them, we'll let you guys know so you can clear your people from the area. There's no telling how things will go down once we know where they are, but we don't want any friendly fire either."

"This is for our son and my brother." I took a step forward. "This is our fight."

"And we're ready to fight it," Laila said. "But we don't need anyone to put their lives on the line. All that we need is for you to tell us if you smell them on your territory. If you help us find them, we'll owe you more than words can describe. But even if you don't find anything, I still want this to be a fair trade. In exchange for doing this, you'll each get to feed on my blood."

Many faces in the crowd gazed up with wide eyes. Others grinned and licked their lips.

"But there are rules," I stated. "Each alpha gets ninety seconds of feeding or until Laila faints. Whichever comes first."

"You feed from my wrist, and you keep your hands to yourself," Laila said. "This is a business transaction. My blood may be payment, but I'm no whore. You can touch my wrist. But that's it."

"We'll be present at each feeding." Celena placed her hands on the banister and leaned out over the crowd. Her eyes glowed a bright, fluorescent shade of blue, smile coming to her lips. "In case anyone has a hard time stopping when they're told."

"Which I do understand," Laila said. "I know that my blood's intoxicating to you guys, so I won't hold it against you if you lose control. But if you absolutely will not stop and put my life at risk, you'll be risking your own."

"The purpose of this is to feed you," I said. "If anyone tries to turn my wife, I will personally rip your throat out."

"Only one of you will feed at a time, and it will be done in privacy," Wyatt said. "If we have to use force to pull you off of her, we don't want to deal with fighting off another alpha who's trying to defend their friend."

"But above all else, we're here to form alliances." Laila looked over the alphas. "I know time has shown that Guardians, Angels, and Wolves don't always get along. But my clan is a mesh of all the races. We have Wolves, Demons, Angels, Guardians, Fae, Vampires, and even humans in our family. We aren't concerned about race; we're concerned about peace. We don't fall into the segregation our ascendants did for centuries. After what I lived through, seeing the ways that *all* of our blood has suffered, there's nothing I want more than peace. We've heard rumors, like I'm sure most of you have, about a possible apocalypse. And I don't know if they're right. It could be a bunch of horse shit. But if it's not, we need to stick together."

"Peterson knows our weaknesses," I continued over the crowd. "This man is human, and he knows all of our weaknesses. They used wolfsbane when they tortured your kind, morion and hematite when they tortured mine, silver on the Vamps and psychics on the Fae. He has proof of what we are on film. If he decides to turn that information over to the wrong people, we'll have a civil war on our hands. I'll have to fight the people I've sworn to protect, and you'll have to fight your food supply. Even if there isn't an apocalypse coming, we need to stand together. We all need allies."

"And I'm a damn good one to have," Laila stated.

Once again, applause sounded from the crowd. They clapped and nodded, some even howled. Part of me worried that we'd been a little abrasive with our speech. But in hindsight, we handled it with perfection. We needed to act firmly if we wanted to earn their respect. They had to know that we wanted their allegiance, but we wouldn't bow to them.

We'd already proven that we were strong enough to want as an ally. But that open, yet blatant, discussion also made it clear where we stood. We'd fight them if we had to, but we didn't want that. We wanted their partnership.

And they wanted ours.

The feedings with the other alphas proved far more professional than Roland's feeding had been. When they entered the room to drink her blood, the first thing they did was shake my hand. At least, the men did. The women gave me a civil nod before speaking with Laila. Which culturally made sense. That's how wolves were supposed to behave. They didn't touch another person's mate without permission.

Even Celena and Wyatt weren't affectionate with the family. Us guys were with Wyatt, but in all the years I'd known Celena, we'd never made physical contact aside from our finger grazing when we passed a joint back and forth. Wyatt had—on a very rare occasion—given Hannah a hug, but that was incredibly scarce.

Regardless, when they approached her, rather than shaking hers, they gave a civil bow with a hand over their heart. They respectfully removed their hats as if the national anthem were playing.

When they went to actually feed, they wouldn't sit beside her. They lowered themselves to their knees and respectfully turned their gaze away from hers. No one else attempted to slide their hand up her thigh or down her arm, which only proved what I thought about Roland.

He tested me. He wanted to see how far was too far. He'd probably heard rumors about how much of a pussy I was and wanted to see how close I'd let him get to Laila's before I would prove otherwise.

And don't get me wrong, I was a pretty chill guy. But not when it came to my wife and kids. Anyone who fucked with them had a death wish.

Still, I found great respect for the other alphas. Although we looked to them as equals, they looked to our clan as superiors. They literally kneeled before Laila. It made her a little uncomfortable at first, but I suppose that's when it really clicked.

Peterson was still the worst thing to ever touch the Earth's grass. But he did it. He created this. He created who she was becoming.

A leader. A monarch of her own.

Those burly men kneeled before her and thanked her for saving their daughters and brothers and cousins from torment with tears in their eyes. Not one alpha turned down the opportunity, and each one of them, aside from Roland, bent their knee to her.

And those were just the North American alphas. There were still a few more thousand around the world. Not to mention the Guardians, Demons, Vampires, Shifters, and Fae that called her their savior.

I could never excuse what that sorry bastard did. But at the end of the day, he built us a magnificent army of supernatural, already trained soldiers as loyal to our family as they were to their own.

It'd take a while but eventually, we'd understand just how important those relationships she'd built would be to the future of our world.

CHAPTER THIRTY-THREE

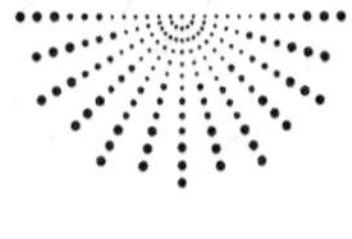

LAILA

"How do you feel?" Jeremy asked with a hand on my shoulder.

"I'm okay," I said.

I was better than okay. Not that feeding almost a hundred wolves wasn't terrifying or entirely pleasurable at first, but at the same time, it felt like I was floating. And I was hornier than I'd ever been in my life, almost embarrassingly so. It hadn't been so intense with Wyatt, Celena, or Roland but as the feedings went on, the euphoria attached to it didn't have the time to dissipate. My motor functions worked fine, and my words didn't slur. But I was high as a kite.

Jeremy chuckled, looking between my eyes. "You sure?"

"I'm fine." I smiled, wiping some dried blood from my arm with the cloth Roland gave me. "But I'm ready to go home."

To be specific, I was ready to get home and have his dick inside me.

"Sure." He soothed his hand down my arm until our fingers twined together. "Roland said he'd be in touch about the other Monarchs. Said we should hear back in a week or two. He's going to tell them all of our rules and conditions and take it from there."

"Good," I said.

"You guys can head out if you're ready." Brendon peeked around the doorway. "I'll give Roland your regards."

"That'd be awesome, thank you. We should get home to our daughter," Jeremy said.

"Sure." He smiled. "Nice seeing you guys. And I'll keep you updated if anything comes up. Best of luck either way though."

"Thanks." I smiled.

"Of course," Brendon said. "Wyatt's my brother; that makes you my family too. Gotta fight for family, right?"

"Thanks again though." Celena smiled, took Wyatt's hand, and rested the other against my arm.

Brendon gave a smile. Then we spun through the air. We landed in the kitchen of the main house with a quiet thump.

"*Shhh!*" Hannah hushed. "She just got to sleep."

"Where is she?" I asked.

"In the playpen in the sunroom," she whispered. As I started to the doorway, she caught my arm and gestured to my clothes. "Maybe you should go shower first, don't ya think?"

I looked over my jeans and purple blouse covered in drying drops of crimson. "Oh, gross."

"Little bit," she muttered.

"We're going to head up to bed," Celena said.

"Sure. Thanks for everything, guys," Jeremy said.

"No, thank you for the entertainment." Wyatt gave a soft laugh. "It's been a minute since I saw you pin someone to a wall. That was good, man."

He laughed. "You would've done the same."

"Nah, I'd've killed him," Wyatt said.

Hannah looked between us with an amused grin. "What happened?"

"The Monarch got a little handsy when he was feeding on Laila," Celena said. "Jeremy went all macho man."

He rolled his eyes. "He's a dick. He was just trying to see how far he could push me before I did something."

Honestly, when he had Roland pinned to that bookshelf and said he'd kill him and every wolf downstairs if he tried anything like that again, I was more turned on than I'd ever been by anyone or anything. Of course, the bite may have played a part in that. But how broadened his shoulders grew, how deep his voice got...

Just thinking about it made me wet.

That's what I loved about Jeremy. He was generally sweet, friendly, personable—even docile. But when someone threatened me, he took on this absurd strength and almost feral attitude. He'd protect me with everything he had. He didn't need to often, but when he did, nothing was hotter.

"It was kind of sexy, though." I smiled. "You weren't even that jealous when Brody kissed me."

"Brody didn't put his hand between your legs while you were moaning like a ghost, and he was sucking your blood."

I made a face. "I was not moaning."

"No, you definitely were," Celena muttered.

Wyatt grimaced. "Yeah, it was a little awkward to be honest."

"You have no idea," Jeremy grumbled.

I turned to Hannah and shook my head. "I wasn't moaning."

Celena laughed. "I'm going to bed."

"Yeah, me too," Wyatt said. "Goodnight, guys."

"Night," Hannah said. The two of them started toward the maid stairs. "Do you guys want to go get a shower and come back to get Mills? She was really tired; at least let her get a little sleep in before you move her."

"Yeah, that sounds good." Jeremy put a hand at my waist. "Can you keep her for another hour?"

Hannah laughed. "Yeah, we'll be here."

"You're the best." Jeremy pulled me into him, and we teleported again.

That time, we landed in our bathroom. He spun in front of me and lowered his lips to mine. I laughed as he placed his hands at my hips and hoisted me to the sink. "Just jumping straight in there, huh?"

"I've been watching you make sex faces and moan for hours." His big blue eyes shifting between mine with dilated pupils. "And to be honest, I'm feeling a little inadequate. But confusingly turned on. And I think fucking the shit out of you might solve both of those problems."

I laughed, leaned forward, and unbuttoned his pants. He stooped forward and pushed his lips to mine. His hand snuck up my shirt and squeezed my breast. The other pulled my face closer to his. I yanked his pants down and scooted to the edge of the counter. His hand at my neck slid down my chest and into the crease of my jeans. I sighed against his lips as my hand crept inside of his boxers. He reached around my waist, tugged me closer to him, and teleported my pants to the ground. He pushed himself inside me and let out a deep breath at my ear.

There was no sting as my body stretched around him. Only pleasure. Pure, ecstatic bliss. I'd been ready for this moment for hours, and that fast, I felt complete.

"You're the only person I want to do this with," I whispered at his ear.

"I better be if I'm going to have to sit through that a thousand more times," he murmured. His lips parted against my ear. He nibbled softly. Then his hand at my hip spun around to my pelvis, thumb rubbing my clit. I gasped and collapsed my head to his shoulder, euphoria buzzing through my skin. "Moan for me like you moaned for them."

Well, I hadn't moaned *for* them. It was involuntary.

But when his hot breath murmured that at my ear in his husky tone, I couldn't help the deep groan that fell from my lips.

A quiet chuckle shook his shoulders. His hand caressed up my chest, squeezing my breast as this thumb brushed back and forth at the same pace against my nipple as my clit. "Like that." He pulled his hips back and thrusted in deep, hitting some magical spot with the base of his dick against my front wall. I moaned again, and he grabbed harder, pinching my nipple that time. He kissed down my neck, free hand finding my hair and yanking my head back. "Just like that."

"Jesus fuck," I murmured.

He chuckled again.

The pressure in my groin was so intense, already tightening and loosening around him. I wasn't quite at the climax yet, but with each touch, each thrust, my legs fastened at his hips. Still moaning at his ear, he pulled back slightly. The hand at my hair released, dropping to my thigh. He yanked me closer to the edge of the counter and pulled them open.

He dropped his forehead to mine but gazed down at his cock sliding in and out of me and his thumb rubbing against my clit. "Fuck, I don't think you've ever been this wet before."

"Because you're so fucking good at this," I murmured.

Granted, that was half of the truth. I knew that I was so turned on because of the feedings. But it wasn't a lie either.

No one else could touch me like this and make me feel like I was enveloped in pleasure. No one else could grab the back of my hair like he did without pissing me off. No one else could hale me across the counter, tear my legs open, and not make me want to punch them in the face.

But Jeremy could do anything to me, and I'd fucking love it.

"Fuck." He pulled out and pushed the tip of his dick against my clit. Warmth shot against me, and he rubbed the tip back and forth against it. Another sigh of bliss dropped from my mouth, small contractions of bliss vibrating through me. He huffed loud, grabbing my boob harder, still staring down at his dick as his cum erupted on my vulva. Once it slowed, he dropped his head. "I'm sorry."

He had nothing to apologize for. Fast, but all things considered, I couldn't blame him. But I wasn't done.

"It's okay." I touched my grinning lips to his. "But you better get down there, or I'll go get that monarch to finish the job."

He narrowed his gaze, slight smile against his mouth. "And I'll fucking kill him."

I laughed, unsure of why that made my stomach flip. He smiled, leaned forward, and pushed his lips into mine. The hand that had been on his dick slid down. He plunged his finger inside of me and rubbed hard against my G-spot.

A deep gasp heaved into my lungs, pressure gathering around his fingers inside of me. I felt his lips smile against mine.

He kissed down my neck to my breast. His tongue flicked back and forth against my nipple, and I rolled into him with pleasure. "Keep moaning," he murmured, kissing down my stomach.

I breathed out another. Then his tongue traced along my labia, and I didn't have to force it that time. One of my hands lifted to his hair, fingers tightening at his scalp in the mess of silky, black waves. The other propped me against the counter.

My gaze stayed on his as he pushed my leg open and wrapped his fingers around my inner thigh. Then his big blue eyes met mine, practically smiling as his tongue slid between my lips to my clit.

He made a slow, teasing circle around the tip. I moaned once more.

He flicked it up and down fast.

A gasp heaved into my chest, head rolling back in bliss.

Uh-uh, his voice echoed in my thoughts. *I've had to watch you moan for other men for hours. I want you to look me in the eyes when you scream for me.*

Holy fuck, that was hot.

My eyes met his, brows raising and eyes wide open. I bit on my lower lip as a deep breath left my nose.

He smiled, he went back to flicking his tongue against my clit. My leg trembled against the scruff of his face before twisting around his shoulders. The pressure gathering inside of me built higher, as if overtaking my body. My hips bucked toward him, back arching.

There you go. His thoughts were a seductive whisper against my consciousness. He was inside of my mind and body at once, so close in every aspect. *Still want one of those wolves?*

I shook my head.

Why's that?

"Because no one's as good at this as you are," I murmured.

He smiled. He rubbed harder and faster against my G-spot with the same amount of pressure against my clit, still flicking his tongue up and down.

You're so fucking sexy like this, you know that? he continued in my mind.

Jesus Christ, with each word I felt my body getting closer and closer. I was almost there, muscles quivering against his fingers. My legs were shaking, my heart was racing, and my stomach wouldn't stop flipping.

God, I wish I had this view with my dick inside of you. His voice seemed deeper now, as if it were a low growl at my ear. My muscles contracted around his fingers, but not quite there just yet. He smiled. *That turned you on, didn't it?*

"Yeah." It came out as something between a sigh and a moan.

I meant it. His tongue slowed slightly, spinning rather than flicking against my clit. I gasped and tightened my leg around his shoulder. *You're the sexiest thing I've ever seen.*

A heavy moan that time, eyes still on his, body quaking, muscles contracting in mini tremors around his fingers.

And you know what the best part is?

"What's that?" I murmured.

That I'm the only one who gets to see you like this, he murmured. *Roland can fantasize, but I get to feel you. I get to watch your body shake for me. I'm the one who gets to know how fucking warm and wet you are. He might've gotten to hear you moan, but I make you fucking scream.*

My mouth dropped open as his tongue twitched faster against my clit. His fingers inside of me jerked so hard against just the right position on my g-spot and, like he said, a near scream of pleasure vibrated from my lips.

Then the climb turned to an explosion, contracting so hard around his fingers. If it weren't for his hand around my thigh, I'd have fallen off the counter. But as I moaned, holding tight on his hair, his smile stretched higher, still moving his tongue in a perfect rhythm against my clit.

Just like that.

Jeremy ran his fingers through my damp hair between the warm sheets. "All the alphas really liked you."

"They liked you too." I turned to meet his gaze. My chin rested against his chest, smile pulling at my lips. "I don't know how Roland feels, but the others were nice. They shook your hand."

"Let's not talk about Roland," he muttered. I laughed. He smiled, twirling my hair between his fingers. "But they *bowed* to you." He laughed. "They liked me. They loved you."

"I think they felt the same way about all of us. I'm just the figurehead."

"No. Figureheads don't fight battles. Warriors do. They look to you, and that's what they see. Someone who risked everything for a cause she believed in."

"I guess," I said. "I just hope it helps us find Micah."

"At least we got to meet him." Jeremy smiled, holding my cheek in his palm. "I wish it would have been real. But at least it was something. We got to be together."

A sad smile came to my lips. "It was kind of a beautiful way to see each other for the first time, you know? Because when we find them, I doubt we're going to have time for a moment."

"I can't see it going smoothly. We can hope and pray, but we should prepare for the worst."

"Always," I murmured. "Chris said that they won't be able to keep doing that. At least, not daily. Micah was really weak after last time."

He chewed his lower lip. "It's going to be sporadic. Meaning I won't know when to go into your dreams."

"I think so," I murmured.

He blew out a long breath. He smiled. "Well, you can show him me. Little snippets, you know? Like videos? And you can do the same for him, you can tell him to pretend he's talking to me and we can send messages back and forth between our memories. And maybe, maybe when his saxophone comes in, I can explain how it works to you and you can show him that."

I smiled and moved my head in a nod. "Yeah. Of course, baby."

"It's just a matter of time until we find him." Jeremy looked up at the ceiling, giving another nod. "And he's met me. This isn't the same, but it's more than he had of me before, ya know? I'll count my blessings. As long as he knows who I am when we meet, I'll be okay. As long as I'm not a stranger, and he knows that I'm his dad."

I held my smile and sat up in the bed. "Speaking of our children, we should probably go get our daughter."

"I'll go get her." He yawned. "You still seem a little stoned. You'll stumble and wake her up."

My gaze narrowed as I stood. "Fine. I'll go feed Tink then."

"Fine." He grinned.

CHAPTER THIRTY-FOUR

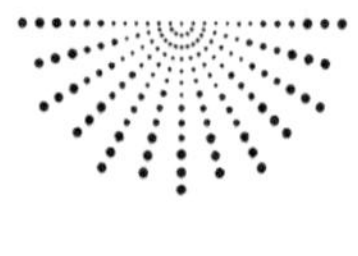

LAILA

After about two weeks, Micah came to me in another dream. The wounds from the implants had begun to heal. He seemed less awkward and nervous each time he visited me from that point on. Our little meetings were far and between, averaging between once a week and three, but sometimes not even that often. Nonetheless, we were getting to know one another. He was getting to know me, and I was getting to know him. It was far from what we deserved, but it gave me the strength and will power to commence the search harder than ever before.

Searching the ley lines hadn't given us anything definitive yet. But we found a total of six facilities so far that could potentially have been used—or may be used in the future—to house Micah and Chris. Moriah and Helena helped by confirming that there were perimeter spells put in place on all six locations. Once we knew for sure that they were facilities under Peterson's rule, we crept around in the dark and equipped them with small cameras. Leah set them up so that when it sensed motion, it would send her a push notification. We figured that if they moved to one of these new facilities, we'd already have a general idea of the terrain and building's structure to make penetrating its walls that much easier.

The other Monarchs made contact in the days following my first feeding. By the week's end, I'd fed another eight hundred Wolves. Roland was still the only alpha who didn't fall to his knees and place his hand to his heart at my presence. I didn't care. He could sit beside me to drink if it made him feel more important than the others. He kept a firm gaze when he looked at me and Jeremy but ultimately, he knew who was in charge. He wanted to feel like the top dog, so I allowed it. At the day's end though, he knew that he ranked well below us.

A few days after I fed the last alpha, Gwen approached me with an idea. She suggested we repeat the routine with the nest leaders in the vamp community. Jeremy was even more against it than he had been with the Wolves, but I agreed. The more creatures that had our scent, the better chance we had at saving our son and brother. Vampires were even more volatile than Wolves and had a harder time controlling their thirst. That said, I insisted that I'd only feed them bagged blood.

The vamps seemed satisfied with a cool meal. It made the logistics of feeding far easier. I spent about six hours a day collecting my body's liquid into bags before Celena or Kai healed me, and the cycle repeated. Jeremy and I hand delivered the blood to each nest over the course of the following seven days. They weren't as respectful as the Wolves, but they were just as obedient. Peterson held less Vamps than Wolves, so they weren't as grateful for what I'd done. But they were just as grateful for the blood and my allegiance.

In a matter of two weeks, we'd formed blood bound treaties with nearly every leader of Werewolves and Vampires in the world.

Then we moved onto the other races. Guardians weren't as much help. They could sense plentiful amounts of energy, but they had no way of tracing it like the vamps and wolves did. I had less to offer them, but they were more grateful for what I'd done at the compounds than any other race. Peterson held more of them than any other supernatural creature that existed. Belonging to their race already, and with Jeremy having relationships with most of them prior to our need for them, obtaining their loyalty was seamless.

Almost every Demon on Earth that we came across was more than willing to help. The well-behaved ones, anyway. We didn't attempt to gain the support of Demons that lived as animals. But the half breeds and other hybrids were not only willing to help, but joyous to. Much to the surprise of most, they stood pretty firm in their beliefs against killing and torturing small children. Our prior allegiance with Lilith surely helped in their department. Aside from that, the Demons made up a decent chunk of the people Peterson held. They hated him as much as they hated the Angels. Hunting and killing that man was almost as important to them as it was to me and my family.

There weren't many Fae on our plane of existence to form alliances with. The ones we were able to narrow down came to a fifty-fifty split of those that respected us and the other half that hated me because I had Angelic heritage—not that I really blamed them. Still, the portion that did like me were faithful followers. Most of the others still agreed to make contact if they found an energy force strong enough to embody Micah, Chris, Amy, or Nastya. They just weren't as eager to do so. Still, they recognized that Peterson needed stopped, regardless of their racist take on yours truly.

The Angels didn't offer much assistance either, even at the mention of the apocalypse. There were about ten who agreed to inform us if they stumbled upon our family. But most didn't give a damn. That realization terrified me. I believed Mary when she said she was unsure where the Angels loyalty laid. I never doubted it for a moment. But to see their general disinterest in my son proved to me what Mary had claimed. They weren't fighting for us. They weren't even fighting for the humans. They were fighting for their god and nothing else. Then again, I suppose sacrificing a first-born son was something they'd grown accustomed to over the past few thousand years.

It made me ponder if they didn't only want the world to end but if they were assisting in its soon to come demise.

Still, the fact remained. In June of 2019, I acquired over two-hundred allies who would later become my warriors. In December of 2020, my small army nearly quadrupled in size. But between late October through early December of 2021, I had acquired nearly ten-thousand soldiers around the world. All of whom were not only willing to help me find my son, but to help me fight what was coming.

CHAPTER THIRTY-FIVE

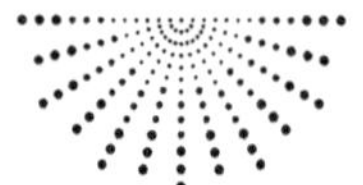

DECEMBER 13, 2021 - JEREMY

The scent of the steaming cup of coffee on the end of the desk touched my nose. I lifted it to my lips and swallowed down a slow, hot gulp. The bitterness settled on my tongue. It was probably too late in the evening for a cup of coffee—the ticking clock read 8:43—but Adam had just brewed a pot before he left, and I didn't want to see the whole thing go to waste.

"Hey, you," Laila said in the office doorway with Milly at her hip.

"Oh, hey, baby." I smiled. I stood and walked to her. My lips pressed to hers. Milly grinned and reached for me. I took her from her arms and kissed her forehead. "I didn't realize you were coming by."

"We had plans today, remember?" She arched a brow. "We're supposed to drop her off with Celena and go out to dinner?" My eyes widened a bit, and a smile came to her lips. "You forgot, huh?"

I frowned. "I did. I'm sorry. Max is out all week, and I'm drowning a little."

"Oh, no." She gave a sympathetic frown. "Denise isn't doing too good, is she?"

"She entered stage four last week. They moved her onto hospice. Just trying to keep her comfortable now. They're thinking she only has a few weeks, maybe a month tops. He's not doing great. I told him to take as much time as he needs. They're living on his Christmas bonus right now so at least he's not struggling too bad financially. But things aren't looking good."

"I should go visit her," Laila murmured. "That woman was a second mom to me growing up."

"Yeah, you won't have the chance for much longer."

"I'll go on Wednesday then," she said. "Do you need help with anything here then? I could take Mills to Celena and come back. We could just eat something here."

"I don't want to do that though." I smiled and pushed hair behind her ear. "We've got to make a little time for each other once in a while."

"It's okay." She grinned. "It'll be like the good old days. We'll finish up whatever work needs done, and then we can fuck on the desk."

I laughed. "Are you sure?"

"Yeah." She gave a smile. "Yeah, of course. But I do have to run down to the post office and grab some stamps before they close. Should I take Milly with me?"

"No, I've got her." I tightened my arms around her and smiled. "I miss her. We'll hang out for a little bit until you get back. She'll prob-ably be clunked out by the time we get home tonight."

"Cool, I don't have to fight her chunky thighs back into that car seat." Laila squeezed her leg between her thumb and forefinger. Milly giggled and dropped her head into my chest, grinning at Lai. "I'll be back in a couple minutes and I'll flash back home and drop Mills off."

"Sounds like a plan." I leaned down and touched my lips to hers.

Laila kissed me back before leaning forward and kissing Milly's cheek. "Mommy'll be right back."

"Say bye-bye, Mama." I lifted her hand and raised it in a wave.

Laila smiled and ran her hand along Milly's hair once more. She turned and started to the back door.

Milly fussed, reaching for Laila. "Mama!"

Our eyes simultaneously widened.

"Damn it," I murmured.

We knew it was coming. But I was really hoping Dada would be first. Laila got more time with her than I did though. She'd been coaching her into Mama.

"Yay!" Laila clapped, bouncing up and down. She reached out for Milly's hands. "Good job! You did it, you did it!"

Milly giggled, craning out for Laila.

"You don't have to rub my nose in it," I mumbled.

She smiled wide. "I told you 'mama' would be first."

"Well, she said 'duh' two months ago, so I'm still taking credit for the first word."

"Still not sure if I believe that." She smirked. I raised my middle finger, and she laughed. "I'll be right back. She's probably hungry. There's some food in the bag if you have the time to feed her."

"Yeah, I'll feed her so Celena and Wyatt don't have to worry about it," I said.

She waved to Milly and made her way out the back door. Milly fussed for a moment. I lifted her up in the air in front of me. I dropped her and caught her a few inches below. She giggled and brought a big smile to her lips. "See, you like hanging out with Dad. Mom's boring."

"Mama," she babbled, gesturing to the door.

"Now you're just trying to break my heart." I hoisted her to my hip and grabbed the diaper bag from the floor. I started through the kitchen to the swinging stainless steel door. I pulled one of the high-chairs from the corner and sat it beside a bar stool.

Milly and I babbled back and forth as I set her in the highchair and fed her the puréed apples and peaches. She giggled and repeated 'Mama' a good thousand times with a gesture toward the door. I don't remember much of what Milly and I actually babbled about, but I remember thinking that it felt right. It was one of those life moments where I realized I was doing better than I thought I was capable of. I didn't have my son, but I was a good dad. Better than most even.

But a moment or two later, I'd feel like the biggest idiot in the god damned world.

The bell rang above the door. I expected to turn and see Laila.

But instead, Olivia walked through the threshold. Her heavy winter coat swung open in front of her large, swollen stomach. She pulled the door shut and met my gaze with a smile.

I returned her smile as I stood. "Long time no see."

"It has been a while, huh?" She placed her hands at her hips.

"Probably my doing." I awkwardly cleared my throat. "I wouldn't have wanted to talk to me either."

After Laila broke up with me in that hospital room in early 2020, I blamed Olivia. It hadn't been her fault, not really. It was mine. I was the one who'd been lying to my wife about my addiction. But Laila was sure Olivia and I had slept together when we hadn't. I'd thought she told her that we had.

I showed up at her door around three a.m. the next morning. Honestly, I have no idea what names I called her. But it wasn't kind. It certainly wasn't fair.

Since then, we hadn't spoken a word to each other. Mostly because I didn't want Laila to think there was anything going on between us. But also because I was really ashamed of myself over that night.

She shrugged, managing a smile. "You were pretty fucked up. And it was kind of shady of me to tell her everything that I did."

"I should have," I muttered with a shake of my head. "But ya know. Can't turn back time."

She nodded, and her gaze shifted to Milly. "So this is that little girl I keep hearing so much about. Milly, right?"

"Malina. But yeah, Milly. Congratulations, by the way." I gestured to her stomach, giving a smile. "That's really exciting."

"Yeah." She smiled, stroking her belly. "Yeah, thank you. We're really happy."

"You're engaged too, right?" I asked.

"I am," she said.

"Is he a good guy?" I asked. "You weren't always the best at picking men."

She laughed and made her way to the bar. "Yeah, he's great. Kinda outgrew the whole tortured musician thing."

I laughed. "Ouch, but fair."

It felt a little odd to have her in the diner after what happened the last time she sat at that counter. I kept my distance this time, and she wasn't drunk or hitting on me, but I still wanted to be safe rather than sorry. The last time we'd stood in that diner together, my relationship collapsed as a result.

Liv grinned, gesturing toward the danishes on the counter. "Can I get one of those to go?"

"Sure." I grabbed a paper bag from beneath the counter and stifled a yawn. "So what's going on?"

She rubbed her mouth. "Okay, so my fiancé and I are moving to Chicago. He got a job offer he couldn't turn down, and he has family out there, and God knows I hate mine." I nodded, and she said, "Anyway, so I'm going to be working at a human hospital out that way."

"Chicago's a really fun city. Expensive as shit, so I'm sure you'll like it." I smiled.

I'd always made jabs at her taste for the finer things. She may not have liked her family, but she did like their money. Honestly, she wasn't much different than Moriah in that regard. Granted, Moriah was a bit more uppity. But Olivia was still a brand princess.

She sucked her teeth beneath her smile. "Anyway. I've been cleaning out my things at the hospital here. And I..." She cleared her throat and scratched her head.

I placed the danish in a bag. "What is it?"

Liv swallowed hard. "I completely forgot about this. You guys probably did too."

I tilted my head slightly as I sat the bag on the counter. "You're going to have to give me a little bit more than that."

She spun her purse to her lap. She began digging inside of it. She raised her hand with a small vile of something I could barely describe. Black liquid, or perhaps smoke, spiraled inside the glass jar. She carefully extended it out to me.

I took it in my hand and puzzled down at it for a moment. "What is this?"

"Remember when I got to take a look at Daniel's body?" she asked.

I searched my mind for the vague memory. Then my eyes widened. "This is the energy of the Witch that bound herself to him."

"This is Nastya La Fay's soul," I murmured, staring down at the dark, swirling substance.

"Not exactly," she muttered. "But I've heard about what you and Laila are doing. Looking for anything you can find to lead you in the right direction. And I'm not strong enough to do anything with this to help you. But Helena, that's your go-to Witch, isn't it?"

I nodded, unable to look up from the bottle in my hand. "She might be able to do something with it."

"Yeah, that's what I was thinking," Liv murmured. "I've heard rumors about that little girl. Lydia, I think?" I nodded again, and she said, "She's bound to Nastya, isn't she?"

"Something like that," I mumbled.

"I mean, I don't have all the information at hand. Use this however you guys think is best. But if you have two pieces of a binding spell—"

"You can break it," I murmured with a nod.

CHAPTER THIRTY-SIX

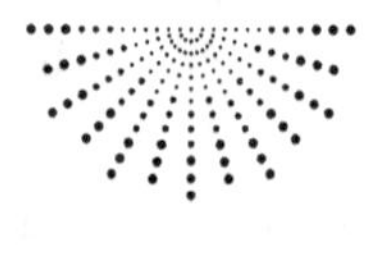

LAILA

As I pulled into the diner's lot, I noted the woman getting into her car near the front door. I couldn't be sure at first, but as she turned her head, I immediately realized who she was. And my heart sunk. It shouldn't have; I knew Jeremy was faithful, and I believed him when he said there was nothing romantic involved the year or so prior.

But still, that woman played a big part—if not every part—in the separation that nearly led us to divorce.

When she backed out of her parking space, she gave me a gentle wave and a soft smile. I summoned a similar smile to my lips and raised my hand. I put the car into park. As I unbuckled my seatbelt, I watched her pull out of the parking lot in the rearview. My heart hammered against my rib cage as I started into the diner.

Jeremy stood next to the bar wiping Milly's face with a baby wipe. I cleared my throat. "Hey."

"Hey." He turned and forced a smile. His reddened eyes looked sorrowful yet tied up in guilt.

Ah, fuck. I swear, if something just happened between them, I'm catching his ass on fire.

"What's wrong?" I asked.

He could hardly hold my gaze. "Adam said he'd handle the diner for a little bit. We need to go see Helena."

Okay, that's good. Not anything shady.

"Helena," I murmured. "Why? What'd you find?"

He rubbed his hand against his mouth. "When Daniel was murdered, Ray helped Liv get access to his body. That's when we discovered the implants. She took one; that's how Leah was able to hack into them at the first compound."

"Right."

He reached into his pocket and kept his hand cupped around something. "She was also able to extract a sample of the energy from the Witch that cast the spell." His shaking hand raised, exposing a small glass vial. Within it swirled a dark gray fluid.

My face screwed up in confusion. I walked across the room and lifted the bottle. "This is Nastya's?"

"Looks dark enough, doesn't it?" he muttered.

I squinted at the energy swirl within the glass. Then a quiet, joyous laugh left my lips. "This could be it. This could be the last piece of the puzzle."

"Maybe," he murmured. "With Micah's hair and this, we could break the binding between them. But even if we did, she'd know immediately and do it again. Then we'd be back to nothing."

"So we use it some other way. Did you call Helena?"

"Yeah. She said to come by whenever you get back from the post office."

"Good," I said. He nodded again and turned his gaze to the ground. I placed the vial in my pocket and took his face in my hands. "What's wrong, baby?"

"I don't know how I forgot about this. I should have remembered," he said. "If this does lead us to them, that means that I wasted all of this time for nothing."

Shit, maybe so. But that didn't matter, not anymore. All that mattered was bringing him home. And if this could help us do that, then that'd be wonderful.

"I didn't even realize he was alive," I said. "Let's call it even and figure out how to not waste any more."

———

"Well, first thing's first." Helena grabbed a box from her wardrobe of supplies. "Until we do figure out how we're using that, we've got to wrap it up. We break that bottle, and we're back to nothing."

"Good thinking." I passed it to her. She placed it inside of a tiny metal box lined with foam. Helena laid it in the indent in the center. She carefully closed, clicked the two brackets shut, and set it on the table.

"With a piece of energy like this, there's about a hundred things I could do. I could unbind her to Micah and Lydia, but like you said, that isn't going to do us any good. I'm sure Ray would be happy to remove the bond, but it isn't hurting her long term and it's helping us access the boys." A slow sigh left her nostrils as she lowered herself to a chair. "I could hex her, but she's a La Fay. She'll break it in no time."

"It's not enough to locate her?" Jeremy asked.

Helena shook her head a bit. "See how the energy looked like it was moving? That means it's not very dense. That bottle's got to be solid before I could use it for a locator spell, even using that Elvan magic Kai's been showin' me."

"So there's no use in it?" I asked.

"I didn't say that," Helena said. "Get me a brandy and let me think for a minute."

I brought myself to my feet. Jeremy bounced Milly on his knee. I walked to the wet bar and poured Helena's drink. She pursed her lips. She took the drink, and I lowered myself back to the chair.

"I could duplicate it," she murmured.

"Duplicate it?" Jeremy asked. "What do you mean?"

"It's not the same as the real thing. A little weaker." She took a sip from the glass. "Think about it like mitosis. I can make a copy of this. Even two. It'll be a little diluted, but if I use more than the spell calls for, it might work."

"Might?" he asked.

"Why didn't we do that with the remnant Micah left in me?" I asked.

"Because the real stuff's better and duplicating energy takes time. To double what we've got here, I need at least three months. Even if Micah only visits you twice a month, you'll have as much as I need to do something impactful in two. I'd rather use the real thing and make sure my measurements on the spell are correct."

"So in two months, you'll have enough energy to find Micah?" I asked.

"To find him?" she asked. "Maybe. But I know I'll have enough to bind him to someone. Say I bind him to one of you. It's going to be stronger than anything Nastya's cast because of the power you already have and the fact that you're direct kin. Nastya will feel it when I do, but she won't be able to break it. All you'll need is a minute to track his location if I piggyback onto the same Elvan magic she's using. The barrier spells might be able to keep you from breaching his thoughts until you're inside, but I'm sure you'll be able to find him. Plus, if we map out where all these possible locations they could be are, all that you'll need is a second in his mind to dig for enough to tell you which one they're at."

That did sound like a good plan. I liked the idea of me or Jeremy being bound to Micah. The only way it could be broken is if a Witch had access to us and Micah at the same time, meaning he'd be within arm's reach. I had no doubt that once we were that close to our baby, this fight would be damn near finished.

But that still left a variable open.

I dipped my head in a slow nod. "So what do we do with Nastya's?"

Silence settled between us for a moment.

"We save it," Jeremy murmured.

"What?" I asked.

"We get Micah's location through you," he said, eyes distant in deep thought. "Or maybe me. Whichever works better. Then we go after him. But things might not go as planned. Nastya's soul is a last resort.

But there's a good chance things are going to go wrong. If they do, you bind Nastya to Laila too."

"I'm not following," Helena said.

Neither was I, but that look in his eyes practically screamed eureka. I hadn't seen that expression in a long time, meaning whatever he was getting at was going to be concrete.

"Okay." Jeremy's gaze darted around the room in thought. He raised his hand to stroke his mouth. "Okay, say we go to get Micah, and something happens. We don't come back after a certain number of days or hours or what have you. You hold onto this piece, and you bind her to Laila if we don't get back in whatever span of time we decide on."

"Me," I said. "Why me?"

"Because you're a powerful psychic," Jeremy said. "If you're bound to her, you can control her long enough to keep them in one place and send a message back home. If you're holding her down, the others will be able to handle Amy and a couple guards. Leah can hold Amy off while the others get Micah and Chris back home. They get them into the perimeter, and they're safe. Then we handle Nastya and Peterson."

"You think we're going to be taken?" I tilted my head.

"That's what that kid we captured from the last compound said," Jeremy said. "He said you'd have to go back. That's what you kept hearing in your dreams last year. Peterson said he'd have you again more times than I can count, and he knows more than we do. Maybe he doesn't know how you get out, but he knows he gets you again. We fight like hell to keep that from happening, but if it does, this is our plan. This is how you fight them from inside."

The puzzle pieces all started to align then. We keep saving up Micah's energy. We duplicate Nastya's so Helena could bind me to her in a worst-case scenario. Then we use Micah's, bind him to one of us, and track his location. We get our son back. And then we have a way to take the bitch down.

"It's a good plan," I said.

"But it won't be like before," Jeremy said. "We're doing this together. If they take you, they're taking me."

A slow, shaking breath I hoped he didn't notice left my lips. That is what they'd said. And I supposed that thought had lingered in the back of my mind from time to time. But I didn't want to face that reality.

The thought of being strapped to a table like that again made my stomach hurt. It made my legs go numb. My chest grew tight.

But I'd do anything to bring my baby home. If that meant I had to switch places with him, I'd do it without a moment of consideration.

However, we couldn't both end up in there. One of us had to stay free. We couldn't abandon Milly. She needed us. Or at least, she needed one of us. But we'd talk about that later. For now, we needed to work out the rest of the plan.

"Let's hope it doesn't come to that," Helena murmured. "But I agree. That's a good plan. You're stronger than you used to be though. Might be able to get it on the first try."

"But if it does," I murmured with a nod. "If it does come to that, I like the idea of having a backup plan."

"How long do you think until we have enough energy to do this?" Jeremy asked. "Two months?"

"Give me three to four," she murmured. "Duplicating energy is time consuming and draining. But that'll give us enough time to be sure we have enough of Micah's spirit for the spell. We might want to save up some extra of his energy in case things don't go as planned. Binding him to Leah might be a good idea to throw into plan B. She could use his connection to Nastya and double whammy her with Laila's power. Celena could handle Amy."

"That's a good idea," Jeremy agreed.

I paused to do the mental math. "So March or April?"

"Something like that," she said. "You've waited two and a half years, think you can handle a few more months?"

"If one of the races finds something before then, then we act sooner," I said. "But three or four months is better than a question mark."

CHAPTER THIRTY-SEVEN

JEREMY

Laila stood above the crib staring down at Milly as I walked from the bathroom to the bedroom. She turned and met my gaze. A forced smile came to her lips. She looked back to our sleeping daughter. And I already knew where she was going with this. I'd seen her face at Helena's when I said she wasn't doing this alone. She didn't want me to be there and risk our daughter having neither parent.

But I'd be damned before I let her go at this alone again. It wasn't happening. I was going to stand beside her every step of the way, because whether she realized it or not, she needed me. And I was going to be there for her even if she didn't.

I walked behind her. I tucked my arms around her waist and looked down at Milly over her shoulder. Those big round cheeks, her suckle on the pink binky behind her lips, the little brown curls against her creamy skin.

Laila's hands gently gripped my wrists.

"She's so perfect," she murmured. I rested my head on her shoulder and kissed her cheek. We gazed down at her for another moment. Then Laila turned to meet my gaze with watery eyes. "I don't want her to lose her parents."

"No one's losing anything." I pushed hair from her face. "She's getting a brother and another uncle."

She swallowed hard. She cleared her throat. "We can't risk her losing both of us."

I released a half laugh. "You can't honestly expect me to sit this out, Laila."

"But if we both go, that puts her at risk and—"

"I'm going with you, Laila. You're not going after them by yourself. He's my son. I'm going to fight for him. No one can get inside of this perimeter; Milly will be okay with our siblings while we're gone. But there's no way I'm letting you do this by yourself."

"Jeremy—"

"No. No, I'm sorry, but no. I won't go through that again, Laila. I won't."

"Bab—"

"No, Laila," I said. "I won't be powerless again. I won't—"

"That's exactly what I'm afraid of, Jeremy," she whispered. Tears sparkled down her cheeks. "You're not going to be in any more control than you were the last time. If they take me—if they take you—they'll find a way to make us compliant. I don't know how, but they will. And there's no telling what they'll do to us. Especially you." I raised my hands to wipe the rolling tears as they escaped her eyes. "He hates you. He'll have mercy on me, but you..."

I wasn't afraid of that man. The only thing that scared me was what he could do to the people who mattered most to me.

No, I wasn't backing down on this one. She was out of her damn mind if she thought I was letting her go into this without me. There was no fucking way.

He fucking destroyed her. And I wouldn't let him do it again. I wouldn't let him take away all the progress she'd made over the last two years. He took too much from her already; he wouldn't take her recovery too.

I promised to be her strength when she was weak. And that's how he made her feel. Weak. If he were going to take her again, I'd be her strength in there.

No, I didn't want to leave Milly either. But I knew my baby girl would be safe at home within the perimeter. And I wasn't going to let that bastard kill me. I'd make it home to my daughter. With her mother, her brother, and mine at my side.

"I'll take the worst of it." I thumbed the tears from her cheeks. "He can hurt me so that you'll be strong enough to fight when we need you to."

Her tears fell heavier, and her head shook.

"Come here." I leaned forward and tugged her into me. I traced my palms over her back as her shaking hands squeezed mine. "We're stronger together, remember? We have to do this together."

She squeezed tighter. My shirt warmed with the moisture of her tears.

"You won't be alone." I closed my eyes against her hair. "I'll be right there beside you. Every step of the way, okay?"

She bobbed her head in a nod against my chest. We stayed like that for a while. Just standing in our bedroom holding one another and fearing what the future had in store for us. We wanted to believe we'd get them out in a quick, simple effort, but we knew this was going to end in a messy bout of bloodshed. All we could do was pray that it wouldn't be ours. But we stopped believing in an easy ending long ago.

"I don't want to be in a cell again," she whispered.

"Then let's fight like hell to keep that from happening." I trailed my hands from her back to her arms. I leaned back and twined our fingers together. I raised her knuckles to my lips. "But if it does, I'm not losing you again. We hold on, and we don't let go, okay?"

A soft, sad smile pulled at her lips. "I won't let go."

I smiled back. I leaned forward and kissed her forehead. She looped her arms back around me and rested her head against my chest.

Finding Micah was our hero's journey. Laila believed that this sequence of events revolved purely around her, but every single thing that happened to her happened to me too. I had as many lessons to learn as she did.

It was my fight too.

There were still things I had to learn.
She may not have realized that, but I did.
And so did Peterson.

CHAPTER THIRTY-EIGHT

JEREMY

Leah rubbed down the bridge of her nose. "Walk me through this one more time."

"Yeah, I'm confused," Celena said.

"Okay." Laila rubbed her eyes. "We already have a piece of Micah's energy in me that is going to continue to grow every time he visits."

"Right," Leah said. "We were already planning on using that to track him once it's big enough."

"Not just to track him," I said. "Once we have enough, we're going to use it to bind Micah to Laila."

"When we do, I might not be able to get to his thoughts. I might, but I might not. But regardless, I'm going to be able to track his location through the binding," Laila said. "The one Lydia has to him isn't as strong; that's why we can't track him through their binding. But Micah is my son. It'll be strong enough to track him for sure."

"Okay, I get that, but what are we doing with Nastya's?" Wyatt chimed in.

"We're duplicating it," I stated. "If something happens to us when we go to get Micah, that's our lifeline. After a certain amount of time, if we don't make it back, Helena uses it to bind Laila and Nastya. When she does, Laila hops into her mind and holds her back."

"Controlling her is a more exact way of putting it," Laila said. "If I'm bound to her, she won't be able to keep me out of her head. At least, not for long. Even if it's ten minutes. That's all I need to figure out exactly where Micah and Chris are being kept. I send that information to Helena through the bond, she gives it to you, then you guys come for them. If I'm holding Nastya down, you can handle Amy."

"I'm sure I can," Leah murmured.

"So why don't we just do that in the first place?" Celena asked.

"Because they're always one step ahead of us," I said.

"This time, we have a backup plan," Laila said. "We can't go in guns blazing. We have to be slow and precise with this. We fucked up last time because they were tipped off too soon. They knew we were coming, and they moved. The first time, I fucked up because I didn't think out every detail. I didn't think about them escaping. I didn't have a plan B, and that's why I failed. Wouldn't hurt if we had a plan C and D just in case this time."

"We've got to save our high cards," I said. "This sample of Nastya can be used a thousand ways. If we use it right now, we lose the opportunity to use it for something better if things go off track."

"Let's say we do the binding to Micah, and I find him in ten seconds," Laila went on. "That's great. I tell you guys where they are, and then Jeremy and I go. But when we get there, we only manage to grab Micah and lose Chris. Or vice versa. Or we get them both and lose Nastya, Amy, and Peterson."

"Then we live the rest of our lives looking over our shoulders," I said. "These traces of energy, every single one of them is a different pathway to the same outcome. Why use them all up at once?"

"The wise man uses his first wish from a genie and saves the last two," Wyatt murmured.

"What?" Celena asked.

Wyatt said, "Old story Mom used to tell me."

"We save the high cards," Leah murmured, nodding. "Like in a game of spades. You see what trumps you can take with your low cards first then steal everyone's kings and queens with the ace of spades everyone forgot was still in play."

"And we keep enough to bind them both to someone else," Laila said. "First, Helena binds me to Nastya. If something doesn't work out there, she binds you to Micah. He'll be with Chris; you'll be able to track them down. But then you send someone else to get him because if Nastya only has Micah, she'd need you or Helena to break the binding."

"Me and Kai," Celena said. "Leah stays in contact with Micah, then we go out to get him with his insight."

"And since he's bound to Chris, I can communicate with him too," Leah said. "Might even be able to keep Amy out of his head long enough for you guys to grab them before you get them back into our perimeter."

"One of you and one of the teleporters go first," Laila said. "One healer, one teleporter. Something happens to you; Wyatt tracks your location and brings Kai. Hannah if he has to."

"But Leah," I murmured. "You have to stay with Hannah. If they realize we have a backup plan, they might do the sacrifice immediately. We send you word, then Brody or Adam come to us with Hannah."

Leah nodded, squinting hard in focus.

"I don't want to think about that either, but we aren't fucking this up again. We're winning this time, damn it. And to make sure our plan is full proof; we have to stack backup plan upon backup plan."

"I know it's confusing," I said. "There's a lot of variables. That's why we have to prepare for every outcome. Hell, there's a good chance none of this will go as planned and we have to come up with a new plan in the moment. But our biggest priority has to be keeping Hannah safe. Literally speaking, she's our secret weapon. She's our escape from death. Neither of us would be alive right now if it weren't for her."

"Yeah, me neither," Leah murmured with a nod. "Hey, Lai, you think I could hop into one of those dreams with Micah?"

"If I can get him to come on a specific day," Laila said. "Why?"

"So that Micah can meet me if I have to bind myself to him. He doesn't know me. All he's seen is me bashing a bowl into Lydia's hand. I'd like him to know that he can trust me before I invade his mind with my own," Leah said. "Plus, I'd really like to see Chris."

"We were talking about seeing if he could come on Christmas, remember?" I chimed in. "Maybe if he can tell Chris, they could count the days. Then we could all see each other on Christmas Day."

"Maybe," Laila said. "They might be able to try. I think it's kind of hard for them to keep track of time there though. Especially Chris, he can't see when the sun sets and rises."

"Just mention it the next time you talk and see if it's possible," Leah said. "Even if I have to stay up for a few nights and just wait for them to come. I can work while I wait and sleep during the day."

"I'll try," Laila said. "He really wants to see Jeremy. Maybe he'll be able to figure it out."

I gave a smile that quickly fell, remembering that getting my hopes up wasn't best.

"Well, I'll be damned." Wyatt smiled as he straightened up. "Sounds like we've got a real plan this time."

"And it might just work," Celena said.

"In the meantime, let's keep working on those ley lines. If anything comes up on them, we act sooner." I took a sip from my coffee. "But otherwise, we're looking at having Micah home by his third birthday. And Chris right around his twenty-ninth."

Leah smiled. "Only took us ten years."

"Regardless," Wyatt said, "we're about to end this forever. It took years, but this time, we know we're going to win."

"Let's not be overconfident," Laila said. "I've learned my lesson there. Anything can happen. But I've got a good feeling this time."

Our gazes met, and I smiled. "Me too."

For the first time since we hit Daniel with our car in 2019, I did too. I didn't have a good feeling when Laila blew the roof of the first compound. I was terrified when we took the second.

But the third time? It was gonna fucking work.

CHAPTER THIRTY-NINE

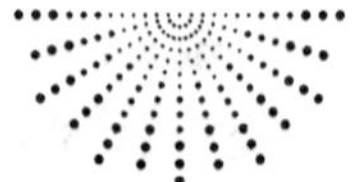

TWO DAYS LATER - LAILA

Two and a half years passed since the last time that I saw Robert Peterson's face in person. A year and three months passed since I saw an image of him when he sent Tina the videos of my torture. But now that I had a linear frame of reference of when I would see him again, he'd crept back into my nightmares. The nightmares revolved around Micah for the past year or so, and for the most part, I preferred it that way. Those dreams tied into pain and guilt, but Peterson... He was the only man alive that could make me feel powerless. The only man who struck fear through every bone in my body.

I won't go into the details of the dream. I can only put those treacherous moments of my life onto paper if I know that I can burn it a moment later.

But I will say that his look of joy as my limbs fought against the metal brackets left me aching worse than any physical pain had before, even the open oozing sores on my back. I can still taste the disgusting, minty yet sulfur of his lips pushing into mine as I screamed against them, gagging on my own vomit as it seeped up my esophagus. My cheek burned with the feel of his fingertips when they smacked against it. In that dream, I could even feel the warmth of blood rolling from the bite mark at my neck.

That wasn't even the worst part.

The worst of it all was Jeremy's voice. I couldn't make out what it said, but I could tell it wasn't far. A few feet away, no more than ten. But he couldn't stop him. He screamed and yelled, and I felt his pain too as he fought against restraints of his own. But he couldn't stop it. Neither of us could.

More symbolic than anything, I suppose. Peterson would never force himself inside of me again. But he would break me down once more. And he would do whatever it took to do the same to Jeremy. Whether Jeremy realized it or not, the best way to hurt him was to hurt me. He thought he could take the worst of what was coming, but the worst that he experienced would always be by proxy.

I flung from the dream onto that hot sandy beach with a heaving gasp.

"Awe you okay, Mommy?" Micah darted from the waves to me.

I gripped my gasping chest and forced a smile. My head moved in a nod. I struggled to summon even breaths into my nose. "Yeah, baby. Yeah, I'm okay."

"What's wong?" he whispered with a hand on my shoulder.

"I was just... I was having a bad dream." I released a slow, calming breath. I pulled a smile to my lips. "But I'm okay."

He lowered himself to the ground. "I get bad dweams too."

I grazed his soft cheek. "How are you doing? Are you okay?"

He nodded. A smile came across his mouth. "I got a new toy yestewday."

"A new toy, huh?" I asked.

Little did I realize, that was the first and only toy Peterson ever gave him.

His smile widened. He extended his hands out to mine. "Do you want to see it?"

"Sure." I grinned and put my hands to his. My eyes closed. Then the memory washed over the backs of my eyelids.

He sat on the floor of a white tiled room with no windows. Chris

was unconscious in the corner with shackles on either foot and a set of
cuffs that kept his hands bound together at his hips against the ground.
I fought the scream that wanted to leave my lips as Peterson opened a
thick metal door carrying a small red bag. Glitter from the red ribbon
handle drifted to the ground like glistening rain drops. He made his
way to Micah on the floor.

A smile stretched across his lips as he extended the bag out to
my son.

"What's this?" Micah asked.

"An early gift for Modraniht, my little lamb," his soft voice said.

My stomach clenched, but I noted that word. I'd read about it when
I was in high school. It refers to mother's night in Norse solstice tradition. Festivals once held where the women of clans would gather to be
honored by the people, but also to honor the goddess Frigg and other
female deities. It was also used to summon the power of previous
Witches in the family bloodline, the Disir, to bring protection.

Micah's chubby fingers reached into the bag and pulled out a thin
piece of white tissue paper. He lifted a small, stuffed white lamb. The
correlation made me sick to my stomach. But Micah stared down at it
in awe.

"Look here." Peterson took it from his hands. He turned it and spun
a small piece of metal on its flank. Music started to play. From that
moment on, I'd never hear *Mary Had a Little Lamb*, Milly's favorite
song, the same way again.

A gasp dropped into Micah's lips. He smiled up at Peterson. "It's
music."

"It is, it is music." Peterson smiled back.

"Thank you!" Micah exclaimed. He leaned forward and wrapped
his arms around his shoulders. "Thank you, Daddy."

I pulled my hands from Micah's and cleared the lump in my throat.

He really was the sweetest kid in the world. In a profound way, he
understood that Peterson was the villain. But he still cared for him. He
cared for all of them. Above all, he cared for his family the most. That
didn't change that he did care about Peterson.

And I hated that. But I loved his loving heart.

His smile fell to a frown. He turned his gaze to the ground. "I sowwy."

"You have nothing to apologize for." I forced a smile, put my fingertip beneath his chin, and turned his gaze up to meet mine.

"He..." Micah murmured. "He not always bad."

I pushed hair from his face and looked between his eyes. "Sometimes bad people are really good at pretending not to be. That's why when they hurt us, we have to remember it. You can forgive them if you want to. But you can't forget what they've done to you. Because they've already proven that they can't be trusted."

He moved his head in a slow nod, looking down again.

I cleared my throat again. "I know that you care about him and the others. But that's because you're a good person. They... They aren't like you, Micah."

He turned his gaze up to mine with droopy, nearly tear-filled eyes. "They don't love me?"

"They might think that they do," I whispered as I looked between his blue eyes. "But the people that love you aren't supposed to hurt you. People that love you don't do this." I drifted my fingertip along the scar at my neck, then the slow scarring line at his. "If someone loves you, they want to protect you. They never, *ever* hurt you on purpose."

"He said this was to potect me," Micah murmured.

"He did that to control you. He did that to keep you from coming home. It had nothing to do with keeping you safe. He did that to keep *himself* safe."

"Fwom what?" he asked.

"Me," I murmured. "He knows I'm trying to find you."

"Awe you going to huwt him?" Micah whispered.

Fuck. Walked right into that one.

Well, I wasn't going to be like Peterson. I wasn't going to lie to him. Did I like the fact that I was a murderer? No, I hated it. But he needed honesty.

"I'm going to do whatever I have to do to make sure he never hurts you again," I whispered.

Micah turned back to the ground. He looked back up to meet my gaze. "When can I see my weal dad again?"

I smiled at the change in subject. I brought myself down to my butt. "I'm glad you mentioned that. Daddy actually had a really good idea the other day."

He smiled and sat in my lap. "What is it?"

I tightened my arms around him and kissed his hair. "Well, back home, we have this special day every winter. It's called Christmas."

"Chwistmas?" he asked. "Like Uncle Chwis?"

I laughed. "Yeah, like Uncle Chris. But on Christmas, we all sit around, and we eat this big dinner, and drink hot chocolate, and then we give each other all kinds of fun presents."

"Like the lamb?" he asked.

The knot I'd swallowed crept back up my throat. He'd be getting a lot more than a fucking lamb next Christmas.

I forced a smile. "Like the lamb. Since we're here, we can't give you a real gift like the lamb. But experiences can be gifts too, right? Like how good this feeling is when we get to see each other?" His smile widened. He nodded. "So Daddy was thinking that maybe for Christmas, if you can come on that day, maybe we could all spend some time together. Maybe you can bring Uncle Chris, and I can bring your dad and your Aunt Leah? Because she really wants to meet you. And she really misses your Uncle Chris."

"How do I do that?" he asked.

I brushed hair from his face. "Well, what do you do every day?"

"In the mownings, me and Uncle Chwis eat ouw oatmeal," Micah began. "Then we play a little, and I nap. Then we eat ouw oatmeal again and play until it's time for dinnew. On bath day, Amy gives us ouw medicine and then we nap a little longew and wake up in the bafwoom. It's bedtime."

Oatmeal.

That's what Chris used to call the slop they served us through the metal box in our cells. He said that he liked to imagine the little lumps as blueberries. They tasted like feet, but the visual made it more enticing on the days that I couldn't keep it down.

Part of me wished I hadn't asked. But at least I knew their routine.

"So do you think, maybe you could keep track of the days?" I asked. "Could you come back nine nights from now?"

"How many is that?"

I took his hands and opened both fists. I closed his pinky to his palm. "Every morning, pull one finger down." I gently pushed his pinky to his palm before moving to each finger. "When you run out of fingers, that's the night that you come to me again like this."

"And bwing Uncle Chwis?" he asked.

"If you can," I said.

"And you'll bwing my daddy?"

The way his eyes lit up when he said that made my heart flutter. Butterflies even flapped in my belly. He wanted to see him so bad. I'd shown him glimpses here and there, but it wasn't interactive. Hopefully, that would all end soon.

I smiled, giving another nod. "And I'll bring your daddy."

His smile widened. He opened out his nine fingers and relaxed his head against my chest. "Is seeing Aunt Leah like the lamb to Uncle Chwis?"

My eyes glistened with tears. I kissed his hair and took in the smell for a moment. "Yeah, it kind of is."

"I do it then," he said.

I laughed and hugged him close to my body. My eyes closed as I engulfed myself in his purity.

Micah was born with a heart of gold that spread endlessly in every direction. If I looked up sweet or innocent in the dictionary, his gentle little smile should have been the image attached. Even now. All these decades later, I still marvel at his kindness. I love all of my children equally, but Micah would always hold a special place in my heart. He'd always be the sweetest, kindest, and most compassionate little boy I ever met.

CHAPTER FORTY

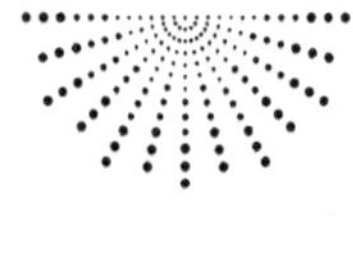

JEREMY

My forehead crunched down in question. "You're sure he said Modraniht?"

"Yeah, I'm sure." Laila hoisted Milly to her hip. "I'm a writer, Jeremy. I know a word when I hear it."

"Right," I murmured. "And he gave him a lamb?"

"He gave him a fucking lamb." She slammed the kitchen drawer shut. Milly's eyes widened, meeting mine. I walked to her and took Milly from her arms. "How fucking cryptic is that? Why is he so fucking creepy?"

I cleared my throat. "You know that sacrifices are made during Modraniht, right?"

"I do." She slammed a skillet from the dish strainer to the stove.

"They use animals though," I murmured. She reached into the fridge and dropped the eggs to the counter, probably breaking a few in the process. "Usually horses, if memory serves."

"Not lambs?" She slammed the fridge door shut.

I set Milly into her highchair, walked beside her, and put a hand on her upper back. She started the back burner.

"It's a Wiccan celebration, Lai. It focuses on ancestral magic. It doesn't even do much, it's just for—"

"Protection. Yeah, I know." Laila turned to face me with a shake of her head. "But Micah's not a Witch. We aren't pagans; we don't worship shit. The gods don't help people like us. We drink eggnog and hot chocolate and roast marshmallows and give each other gifts. And he gave him a fucking lamb. That's what he got. He got a fucking lamb. The symbol of why they want to fucking *murder* him."

She was right. We weren't Witches, but we weren't Christians either. And we still celebrated all of the Christian festivities of Christmas. Although, the tree in the corner was really a Yule celebration that Christianity had stolen from the same people that did, in fact, celebrate Modraniht.

I saw her point though. What they were doing was fucked. They were manipulating our kid. The whole lamb thing was really fucking twisted. He should've been home with us roasting marshmallows and jamming them between graham crackers and chocolate. We should've been drinking hot cocoa together.

But at least he got a gift. Cryptic as it may have been, at least he got something that brought him joy. I hated that he wouldn't be here in the morning to open presents and dote about all the things Santa had brought him, but at least he got to unwrap something.

Tears formed in her eyes. She shut them to keep them from escaping. "I want to give him gifts. I want to string popcorn with him and make paper snowflakes and cut down a tree together. I wanted *our* first Christmas in this house to be *his* first Christmas in this house. I want him to wake us up at five in the morning screaming that Santa came. And I want to drink our coffee and record him opening his presents."

A slow, quiet exhale left my nostrils. I cupped her face in my hands. I looked between her sad green eyes and wiped the salty water from her cheeks. I leaned forward and placed my arms around her back. Her head rested against my chest as she placed her hands around my sides.

It wasn't much, really. But I felt her stiff shoulders soften at my touch. I couldn't do anything else, but I could hold her.

"He'll be here next Christmas," I said. "And we'll get to have a big birthday for him in June. We'll get a cake and a bounce house, and—hell—we'll buy a pool. I'll do it; I'll buy a pool." She chuckled against my chest, nuzzling her head further into me. "Even if it's just one of those little blow up ones, I'll get him a pool. And we'll get a banner with his picture on it. And tons of balloons."

"Balloons are bad for the environment. Kids always let them go," she muttered.

"Okay, no balloons." I smiled and kissed her hair. "But then we'll have Halloween, and Thanksgiving, and Christmas next year. We can cut down a pine tree and put it up the day we get him back though. Even if it's eighty degrees. We'll cut the damn tree down, string some popcorn, light the fire, blast the A/C, and we'll have Christmas in the summer. Okay?"

She nodded and squeezed me a little tighter. "He really wants to see you. He said he's going to try to come on Christmas."

"See, there ya go." I smiled and pulled back. "We'll get to see him on Christmas."

"It's not the same."

"It's something," I said. "Beggars can't be choosers, right?"

She wiped her face. "Yeah, you're right."

"That's going to make Leah's day." I smiled and pushed hair from her face. "It made mine."

The barest of a smile came to her lips. "You know what he said?"

"Hmm?"

"I told him that experiences can be presents too." Her smile widened as she wiped an unwilling tear from her eye. "And he asked if Uncle Chris getting to see Aunt Leah would be like a gift to him. And I said yes, and he said, 'I do it then.'"

A quiet laugh left my lips. "He's the sweetest kid in the world."

"He's so smart. He thinks so deeply for someone so young." Her head shook a bit. "I love him so much."

"Me too," I murmured.

She looked up at me, eyes slightly reddened. "They don't deserve him."

Truer words had never been spoken.

"No. They don't."

She buried her head against my chest. "I just want to bring him home."

"A few more months. Just a few more months and all of this will be over forever."

I wish it would have been that easy. But it was never really over. Finding Micah was our consolation prize for what was coming.

CHAPTER FORTY-ONE

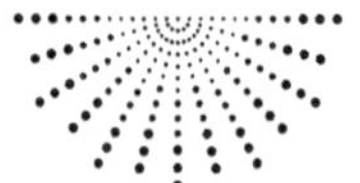

CHRISTMAS EVE - JEREMY

I hummed along to the sound of *Have Yourself a Merry Little Christmas* sounding from the acoustic in my lap. Warm hot chocolate still lingered in my mouth. The smell of Tinkerbell's muddy fur settled in my nose from the bed. She watched me play, body curled into the crook of Laila's sleeping legs.

"So how does this work?" Leah asked. I looked up from my guitar. "We just pop into her mind every few minutes?"

"Basically." I glanced at Laila. "If you don't see a beach, get out. You don't want to see all of her dreams."

"Rule of thumb for just about everyone," she murmured. "She still gets the nightmares?"

"Not as often as she used to. Hasn't woken up trying to kill me in a while, so that's good. But yeah. Yeah, she still has them."

She bit her lip. "I'll just watch you then. When you go inside, I'll see it on your face. I'll follow you."

I turned back to my guitar. Leah looked over Laila chuckled. "Did you ever think we'd be here?"

"Trying to communicate with my son through an astral projection while he's being held captive by some time traveling maniac?" Something between a grunt and a laugh escaped me. "No, can't say that I did."

"No, I mean this." Leah gestured to Laila on the bed and Milly in her crib. "When I met Laila, I knew that I liked her. Even though I thought she was human, I still liked her. Remember?"

I smiled. "You said 'I know she's puny, but I think she's good for you.'"

"She still is." Leah released a quiet chuckle. "Not so puny these days, huh?"

I'd never really thought of Laila as puny. Sure, I thought she needed my protection for a long time. But I never saw her as helpless, even when I thought she was human.

She always had this way about her. This fire that struck a chill down my spine. I supposed that was an intuitive, all-knowing sensation—perhaps a lingering memory from a past life. But still.

Never thought of Laila as puny.

I laughed. "Seems like a lifetime ago."

"It was," Leah murmured. Then a smile tugged at her long lips. "I'm really excited to meet him. Micah, I mean."

"He's amazing." I smiled.

"And he knows I'm coming?" she asked.

"Yeah, he knows. Laila said he was happy to help Chris see you."

She laughed quietly. She met my gaze and her smile gradually drooped to a frown. "I'm really sorry you have to go through this."

"It is what it is at this point, ya know? I wish it weren't, but I can't let it fester. I'm going to keep doing everything I can to bring him home. But we have Milly too. And I... I have to keep it together for her."

"Well, you've done a damn good job so far." Leah smiled. "You're a great dad, Jeremy. And a great husband. You get your ass up every day and go to work so she can be here with her, you're still clean, and you... You got your shit together. I'm proud of you."

I smiled back and gave a soft nod. "Yeah. Yeah, thank you. I know I've come a long way."

"You have," she murmured. "You really have. Mom would be proud of you too."

"Mine or yours?"

"Both." She leaned forward and smacked my knee with the newspaper in her hand. "My mom was your mom too, ya know."

I always called her Annie, but yeah. She was my mom. I wished I could call my real mom 'Mom', but I hardly remembered her. Annie wouldn't have liked it if I called her Mom though. I had once.

If memory served, I was around ten, and I'd let it slip. And she'd made it abundantly clear that she wasn't. Not in the sense that she didn't view me as her kid—although that was how my young mind interpreted it—just in the sense that she'd never take her sister's place. She loved us as much as she could, as much as she loved Leah. But she always wanted me to remember who my real mom really was.

A smile tugged at my lips. "Yeah. Yeah, she was, huh?" Leah gave a soft nod. "I wish she could see this. I wish she could have met Laila and Milly and... I don't know. See that I was capable of more than I showed her."

"She knew you were capable. That's why we locked you in that room." I chuckled, and she smiled. "It was just those past few years. As a kid, you were great. You were just a rough teenager; she knew you weren't a bad person."

A slow breath. "Yeah. Yeah, I hope."

My eyes closed for a second, focusing on Laila's thoughts. A chuckle left my lips as I watched her dreaming of Tinkerbell running through the yard chasing a frisbee. I peeled my eyes open with a shake of my head.

"What's she dreaming about?" Leah grinned.

"Her." I gestured toward the husky mutt on the bed. Tink opened her eyes and met my gaze.

Leah chuckled, glancing between Tink and Laila. "For such a bad bitch, she can be so fucking basic."

"That's what I liked about her," I said. "She's gentle and soft and somehow still so..."

"Aggressive? Volatile?"

Another laugh. "I was going to say strong-willed. But yeah, aggressive's a good word."

Leah chuckled, her gaze turned to the ground. She chuckled, head shaking.

"What?" I asked.

Her gaze met mine. "I wish I had what you two have."

"You and Haley are great." She made a face. I turned my head to the side a bit. "Aren't you?"

"I don't know. Sometimes," Leah muttered. "We used to be. And we still are once in a while. But I guess a lot's changed. Mainly for her. I... I don't want to say it was a fling for her. It wasn't. I know that she loves me. But she just... She doesn't have kids. I mean, I know you guys aren't actually *my* kids. But you were only eight when you became my little brother, and I was almost grown then. And Hannah was so, so little. Brody was just a kid too; he was barely fifteen when Mom died. And Mom worked a lot before she did. I took care of you for a decent chunk of your childhood. The only one I didn't play a big part in raising was Chris. He was only a few years younger than me, he helped with you guys a lot, ya know?"

"Sure," I murmured, giving a nod.

Leah frowned. "And Haley just doesn't get it. I can't leave you guys. I can't move out there with her. I just can't."

My chest tightened slightly. Leah had given up so much for us. I took that for granted when I was young, but now that I knew how much heart and soul went into bringing up a kid, I had a whole new appreciation for her. It wasn't easy to be a parent. And essentially, that's what Leah had been to us. Not just as an adult, but as a teen too.

She deserved a shot at happiness.

"You could if you wanted to," I said softly. "We're raised. We're all living our lives. We don't want you to, but if that's what you have to do to be happy, we understand. You don't have to take care of us anymore."

"That's just it, Jeremy. I don't want to go. You're my family. You're my brother. She's my sister." She gestured to Laila. Her gaze shifted to Milly in the crib. "And that's my niece. I'm about to meet my nephew too. And I don't want to miss this. Why do you think I went into a field where I could work from home? I do love computers, but that wasn't why I did this. I did this so that I could be close to the people that matter the most to me. I chose this life because I love it. I love the chaos that our family comes with. I love helping to clean up the messes and coming up with a plan to solve the constant drama. I love helping people. Not just family but all the other lives we've touched. I love being a part of this family, and I wouldn't trade it for the world. I don't want to leave."

I knew that was true. Leah wasn't just our surrogate mother because she had to be. She could have pinned Brody and Hannah off on the rest of us when Annie died, but she chose to adopt them. She chose to take on that responsibility because our family meant more to her than anything else.

"You shouldn't have to then," I murmured.

She fell silent for a moment and wiped the corner of her eye. "To be with Haley, I think I might. Because I don't know how much longer I can do this long-distance thing. She blows me off all the time. I'm pretty sure she's already seeing someone else. I think that's why she keeps cancelling our plans. I'll read her mind and I'll know. I thought about just showing up, but I'm not sure I *want* to know. I definitely don't want to see it. She just... I don't know."

Aw, damn. That sucked. I'd never seen Leah as happy as she was with Haley. But fuck that bitch for hurting my sister.

"I'm sorry, Leah," I said. "I know how much she means to you."

"Yeah. Yeah, me too," she said. "Maybe it's all in my head. I could just be overthinking. I'm good at that."

"Psychics tend to be." I smiled. She gave a soft smile back. I said, "I hope you're wrong. But if you aren't, you're still young. You might have a soulmate out there still."

"Doubt it," she muttered. "Isn't that a hetero thing? Seems like it would be if God set it up. He smote an entire city for butt sex."

"I have no idea." I laughed. "But I can ask Lucifer when we meet with him."

It definitely was not just a hetero thing. Even the Greek myth the par animarum was stated that there were homosexual couples involved.

That's another story for another time, though.

Leah laughed. "Things only we say."

CHAPTER FORTY-TWO

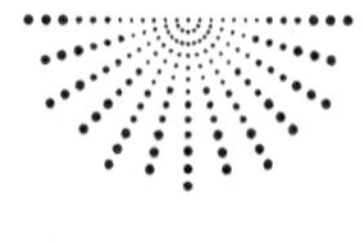

JEREMY

"Daddy!" Micah caught my gaze over Laila's shoulder. His blue eyes widened, giant smile stretching across his lips. He released her frame and ran the short distance between us. I lowered myself to my knees with a smile just as big. His arms twisted around my neck.

I laughed and circled my arms around his waist. Holding him close, I said, "Hey, buddy."

I looked at Chris over his shoulder. He pulled a strained smile to his lips and gave a small wave. I smiled back, tightening my arms around Micah for a second.

I touched his shoulders and pulled back to meet his gaze. "How have you been?"

He smiled and nodded fast.

"That's good." I took a look at his neck. The stitches were gone, leaving only a long, dark scab and the dots from the thread. "Does that feel better now?"

"Lots bettew."

"Should be all gone soon." I forced a smile. "Hey, guess what me and Mommy got for you this week."

"Like a pwesent?" His eyes widened, smile lifting higher.

I smiled back. "Your saxophone. We just picked it up yesterday."

"Weally?" He bounced with joy, hands on my shoulder. I nodded, smiling back. He extended his hands with a begging gaze. "Can you show me, Daddy?"

Hearing him say that made warmth spread through my body. Milly may not have been calling me Daddy yet, but at least he was. And I wasn't sure why, but it filled me with this unusual sense of pride.

I laughed and took his hands. He closed his eyes. I gave him a slow once over of the beginner alto sax as I examined it at the music shop. It wasn't the best on the market, but it was the best we could find for someone so little. Still, his lips crept upward in joy. His eyes lifted wide open in wonder.

His smile made me smile.

Laila and Chris started toward us across the sand.

Then Leah appeared beside me. She spun in a circle, she caught my gaze. Her eyes froze when they fell on Micah. His eyes peeled open. I glanced at him, looking back up to Leah. "Micah, this is your Aunt Leah. She's me and Uncle Chris's sister."

She smiled, lowering herself to the ground. "Wow, you look just like your dad."

Micah took a step closer to me and leaned between my arm and chest. "That's what Mommy says."

"She's a smart lady." Leah grinned. Laila brushed her fingertips along the top of Micah's hair. Then Leah extended her hand. "It's nice to finally meet you, Micah."

He made a face, clearly perplexed at what she expected him to do with her hand. He took it and held it. He didn't shake or quickly release it. He just held it for a moment.

I laughed.

Leah laughed too. Her gaze met Chris's. Tears bubbled in her eyes as she brought herself back to her feet. Chris made a similar expression. Then the two took a step forward and wrapped their arms around each other. Micah looked up at them and smiled as wide as the ocean beside us.

It was such a sweet moment. My sister wasn't a hugger, aside from with babies. To see her arms wrapped that tight around our brother, my heart swelled with joy.

I wished that this were happening in our living room. But this was close enough.

And at least, this way, Micah got to feel important too. Because he gave his uncle a gift.

Laila lowered herself to the ground and tightened her arms around him. She kissed the side of his hair and met my gaze. I smiled and reached for Micah's hand.

"This is Chwistmas?" Micah asked.

"Not really," Laila muttered. "But it is this time. Next year, we'll have a real Christmas."

"What do we eat?" Micah asked.

I laughed. "What?"

"You said thewe's lots of food, Mommy." Micah looked at Laila. "What do we eat?"

Laila paused, looking for a way to describe something he'd never seen or touched or tasted. An image wouldn't do a Christmas dinner justice. Hell, neither would a memory.

Chris pulled back from Leah and lowered himself to the ground. "Remember when we had those little sugar puffs a few months ago?" Laila gave him a questioning expression. He gave a half, sad smile back. "Those baby food puff things? Ya know, the cinnamon ones? We were between places then. Guess the oatmeal was scarce."

"They was so good."

"Well, Christmas dinner's even better than that." Chris grinned.

"But Thanksgiving dinner is the best." I chimed in.

"What's that?" Micah asked.

"A bullshit holiday," Leah muttered. "But the food is good."

"You'll get to be there next year." I met Micah's gaze. "For Thanksgiving and Christmas."

"Weally?" Micah smiled.

Chris shook his head a bit, afraid I'd fill Micah's head with hope that couldn't be delivered. But I smiled up at him and gave a nod because I knew it. I knew they'd be home by then. I didn't have room for doubt, and I was right to be confident about it.

Next Christmas, we'd be roasting marshmallows in the living room with cups of hot cocoa in our hands. We'd sing Christmas songs and watch *Home Alone* and *How the Grinch Stole Christmas*.

We'd all be together. The multitude of brothers, sisters, aunts, uncles, and cousins would finally spend a holiday together for the first time in ten years. Some were gone and some were new, but who could be there *would* be there. Our family would be together, no matter what it took.

It wasn't an empty promise. It was just a promise.

"We have a plan," Laila said quietly. "I don't want to get into the details because you never know who might be listening. But we do, we have a plan."

"And I really think it's going to work," I said.

"Really?" Chris's eyes widened. "Really? When?"

"A few months," Leah said.

"Maybe more than a few," I said. "But by Micah's birthday for sure."

Chris pressed his lips together and gave a slow nod.

"June 22nd." Laila gave a gentle smile.

He forced a smile. "Right."

"Hopefully sooner," I said.

Micah looked between me and Laila. His big blue eyes were full of curiosity, head tilting to the side. "What do you mean?"

"We're going to get you out of wherever you are." Laila smiled and ran her hand along his cheek. "We're going to take you home."

His eyes peeled open, smile growing so big that it reached them. "Weally?"

"Really."

"You pwomise?" Micah asked.

Again, Chris looked down at me and gave a slight shake of his head. But I smiled at Micah and gave a nod. "I promise."

I understood that he didn't want me to give Micah empty hope. And if I had a shred of doubt, I wouldn't have said it either. But we already had a way to trace him. We were *going* to find him.

There wasn't a doubt in my mind. I'd missed his first and second. But I'd be there for my son's third birthday, damn it.

CHAPTER FORTY-THREE

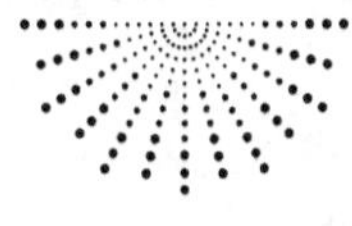

LAILA

"Aunt Leah." Micah sifted sand between the gaps of his fingertips.

Leah looked up from the wet mound she referred to as a sandcastle. "Yeah?"

"Why do youw haiw look like that?" he asked.

She glanced at the lilac strands and chuckled. "Because I color it."

"Oh," he muttered. "It's pwetty."

"Thank you." She smiled.

He gestured to her hand. "Do you color your skin too?"

Her brows fell, and an unwilling chuckle left my lips. Had an adult said that, I wouldn't have laughed. But he was a kid, and it was cute.

"No, I don't color my skin." Leah laughed quietly. "I'm just dark."

Micah looked between Jeremy and Chris. "But I thought bwuddews and sistews was opposed to look alike."

"We have different parents. That's all," Chris said. "I swear I'm not teaching your kid to be racist, guys. He's just never met someone that isn't white in person."

Micah's forehead scrunched up. "But I thought that having the same mom and dad makes you bwuddews and sistews."

"Usually." I laughed.

"Our family's got a lot of different parents in it," Jeremy said. "In a way, Aunt Leah was almost like my mom when I was a little older than you."

"Families are complicated," Chris said.

"But ours is the best." I smiled. "And the most complicated."

Jeremy smiled back, looking from me to Micah.

"I like it though." Micah gestured to Leah's arm. "It's pwetty."

Leah laughed, looking down at her wrist and then back up to him. "Well, thank you."

"You'we welcome." Micah smiled. He looked at me and Jeremy. "When do I get to meet my sistew?"

"Soon, I hope."

"You can't bwing hew next time?" Micah asked.

"I don't think so," I murmured. "She doesn't know how to use her powers yet."

"Oh," he said.

"But you'll see her soon," Jeremy said.

"Guys." Chris met his brother's gaze before looking to me. "Can I talk to you for a minute?"

I glanced at Chris and gave Micah a smile. "Can you talk to Aunt Leah for a second, buddy?"

Micah moved from my lap to the sand beside Leah. Jeremy helped me to my feet as Chris stood. He gestured a few feet away and put a hand on Jeremy's shoulder. We walked a just out of hearing distance. Leah caught my gaze and swallowed hard.

Once we were about fifteen feet away, Chris looked back at Micah and then at us. "They know you're getting close."

"I figured that," I murmured. "They always do."

"They aren't scared, guys." Chris looked at Jeremy. "I don't think they know your exact plan, but they know something. And they're excited."

Jeremy creased his brows. "Excited."

"They said 'the shift is coming." His nostrils flared as he glanced at Micah. "I think they need you for something. They're counting on you coming for us soon."

I took in slow, calculated breaths and clenched my hands together to keep them from shaking.

"Did they say that?" Jeremy asked.

"Peterson said something about you," Chris said, voice still low. "Something about unlocking something within you first. He said that was the key. I—I can't remember exactly, but he said that Laila's journey was almost over. But you haven't opened yours yet."

"Of course," Jeremy grumbled.

We knew what that meant. Peterson's way of unlocking potential didn't include books and training. It came from a place of torture and agony.

Suddenly, I was back to where I'd been when we talked to Helena. Jeremy had to stay home. He had to stay with our daughter.

"Don't come, Jeremy," Chris whispered, tears forming in his eyes. "He hates you. He fucking *hates* you."

"I'm not sending my wife into a trap alone."

"So you're going to walk in with her?" Chris's face was the equivalent to what a guard would say if a death row inmate asked for water as their last meal. "You're going to leave your kids without a father just like Dad did to us?"

His jaw clenched. "I'm not leaving anyone, Chris. I'm bringing my kid home; I'm bringing *you* home. No one's leaving anything."

"You're doing exactly what he expects you to do." Chris's nostrils flared, staring firmly between Jeremy's eyes. "You're going to willingly let this man kill you—"

"No one's killing me," Jeremy stated with a darting gaze. "I make it out of this. I know that I do because we write a book about this shit in forty years. And Peterson knows that too. Just because he knows what's going to happen doesn't mean he knows he's going to win. We win. He knows that we win. He told me—He told me that he knows who he is in this story. He knows he's the villain, and he knows that we win."

Chris made a face. "What?"

"When we get you out, we'll sit down and I'll explain everything," Jeremy said. "I'll show you everything that we've learned about him.

But I need you to trust me. If he tortures me, he tortures me. But I get my son back at the end of all of this. And if I have to endure some beatings for that, then that's what I have to do. I'd die for him. I'd die for my daughter too. I can handle some pain."

"It isn't just *some* pain, Jeremy." Chris's expression grew deeply offended, eyes slightly narrowed, forehead scrunched up. And I didn't blame him. Jeremy thought he understood how bad it could get, but no one can understand what it's like to be a prisoner of war until they are. "I can't even feel the water's temperature on my back when I bathe because there's no nerves left. He took my eyes. He *took* my *eyes,* Jeremy."

Jeremy frowned. He placed his hand on Chris's shoulder. "I know who he is. I know what he's capable of. But what kind of dad would I be if I didn't do everything in my power to bring my son home, Chris? I can't sit on the sidelines and watch it unfold. I'm fighting for my son."

Chris blew out a slow, careful breath. "If you don't get yourself killed, I'm sure your son will be really grateful for that one day. But there's something else you should know. We've moved again."

"What's the climate like?" I asked. "Any idea where it could be?"

"It's cool, but not cold," Chris said. "I think we're in an old warehouse or something. Our voices echo louder than they did in the last place. The room is big, way bigger than the last one. We don't have a toilet or a shower. It smells like mildew and like... I don't know, something metallic. Some oils or something that Dad used to use when he worked on the cars. Oh, and it's nighttime here right now."

No toilet, no shower. That meant they were shitting in a bucket like that kid had been in the last compound. But I pushed that thought from my mind. We'd worry about potty training when we got him back.

Nighttime though, that meant it was probably stateside. We had about a hundred and fifty possible locations in the U.S. We'd scouted about twenty so far, cameras set up at all of them. We'd broaden our systems then. And I'd get word out to the alphas and Nest leaders in the states.

"That might help us narrow it down a bit," Jeremy said.

"We literally just got here yesterday," he said. "And they said we'd be here until the end."

"Guess our epic battle isn't too far off now," I said. Chris puckered his brows, and I shook my head. "Just something Peterson said the last time I saw him."

"You said he knows how this ends," Chris murmured. "And you know that you win."

"We do," I said.

That may have been true. But if Chris was this adamant about Jeremy not coming, I had to be too. He said he'd be my strength if we were taken again. But I don't think he realized how much strength he'd need.

"Let's go enjoy the time we've got left of Christmas 2021 then," Chris said.

Jeremy smiled. "Christmas 2022's going to be a hell of a lot better."

It certainly was.

CHAPTER FORTY-FOUR

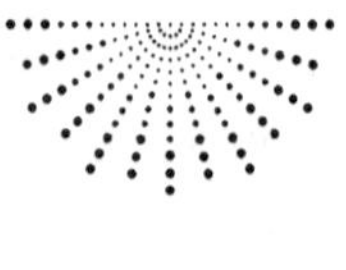

LAILA

When we awoke that morning, Leah's gasp pulled Milly from her sleep. The four of us made our way to the living room with Tink at our tail. As he made the coffee, Jeremy explained to her what Chris told us. He smiled and laughed like he had nothing to worry about while we sipped our coffee and fed our daughter.

But I was terrified. He thought he understood, and to a certain extent, he did. But he'd only lived it vicariously. Being tied to a table as someone cut my skin open and shoved objects inside of me had a way of making me feel smaller than an ant. Having his eyes spooned out or his back torn to shreds may sound easy once he'd been desensitized to the concept. But hearing it and living it are two different things.

What beautiful thing was Peterson going to take from my husband? His eyes? He knew how much I loved those eyes. Or maybe his hair. It'd be biblical enough for Peterson's taste. Jeremy was almost as prideful in his hair as he was in the life we'd built together. But that wouldn't break him—it'd grow back. That wouldn't be brutal enough.

No, he'd have to take what Jeremy loved most from him. It should have been obvious what that was, but it didn't click.

"Maybe Chris is right." Leah rubbed her hand against her mouth.

"No. No, Peterson knows what happens. He knows we get Micah back. If whatever he's planning to do to me is a part of bringing my son home, I'm going to do it," Jeremy said.

"But—" Leah began.

"No buts." He looked between his sister's eyes. "This is for my son. I'm doing whatever it takes to bring him home and keep him safe. Don't tell me that I shouldn't, Leah. If it were for one of us, if it were for Brody or Hannah or me or Adam or Chris, don't tell me you wouldn't take whatever pain was coming your way. I know that you would."

She was quiet for a moment. "I would."

He gave a firm nod. "If this is a part of what has to happen to get my son home, then this is what has to happen."

Now seemed as good a time as ever. Jeremy was still firm on his belief that we'd come out of this right side up, but I wasn't sure. So I had a plan in place. One he reluctantly agreed to, saying if it brought me comfort, then fine.

"Leah, we've been wanting to ask you something," I said.

She turned her head to the side a bit. Jeremy took my hand. "When we leave to get Micah, we need someone to watch Milly. And you'll have Hannah already, so we figure it'd be best for her to stay with you two."

"Sure. That's what I assumed the plan was already," Leah said.

I forced a smile. "Right. But we... You know, we aren't Catholic or anything. We don't do the godparents thing."

Her head tilted slightly.

Jeremy cleared his throat. "We don't know what's going to happen out there. We know that we make it out alive—"

"We think," I muttered. "We think that we make it out alive."

"But we don't know when," Jeremy said. "And if something goes wrong and we're gone for longer than we expect to be, we want to know that someone's here to take care of Mills. The whole family would help you, I'm sure. But there's... There's a lot more to it than that, you know?"

"If I'm not there, she needs to have a mom. Even if it's her aunt," I said quietly.

"Our will designates all of our money and assets to Milly and Micah but if—"

"Guys." Leah's expression said she didn't appreciate us even discussing the possibility. "No one's going to die."

"Probably not. I don't think so either," Jeremy said. "But just in case something does happen. We want to know that she'll be taken care of."

She frowned. "I'll be there for her no matter what. But don't get comfy with that thought. Don't you dare die on me." She looked from Jeremy back to me. "I've seen both of you die before, and it never sticks. Don't let it, alright? You—You come home too. No matter what, you come home to that little girl."

"That's the plan," I said.

But I knew that things didn't always go as planned.

"It just amazes me how smart he is, you know?" Jeremy laughed, picking up the wrapping paper Milly had just torn into. "He's got to have an astronomical IQ for a two-year-old. We should get him tested when we get him home; I bet he's a prodigy or something."

I forced a smile. He turned his head to the side a bit. He lowered himself to the couch beside me. "Hey, are you okay?"

"Yeah, I'm good."

He lifted my chin and turned it to meet his gaze. "No, you aren't. What's wrong?"

"You know what's wrong." I let my lips fall to a frown. "The same thing that Chris and Leah said is wrong. Whatever he's planning isn't going to be pretty. But you won't listen."

He laughed, cupping my cheek in his hand. "So you can be stubborn, but I can't?"

"This isn't funny, Jeremy." I took his hand from my face and held it on his lap. "He's going to do whatever it takes to break you down. He's going to—"

"I know that, Laila," he whispered. "But I'm not running from him. And I'm not letting him hurt you again."

"I can take care of myself."

"Of course you can. But he took you from me once. And I won't let that happen again. I made you a vow. I told you I'd be your shelter, remember?" He brought our hands to his smiling lips. "You need me for this, and I'm going to be there. Stop asking me to break my vow. Let me protect you. Just this once, Laila. Let me be there for you when you need me the most."

My eyes filled with tears. "I don't want to lose you—"

"I'm not going to die—"

"Some part of you will," I said. "You might be breathing when you walk out, but if he has a plan for you, some part of you is going to die in there. You're going to be different. And I, I don't want you to change."

He smiled. He pushed hair from my face. "I didn't want you to change either. But you did. And I love you just as much as I always did."

"Baby, you don't understand what he'll—"

"Didn't we decide that it was time to stop arguing with fate?" He arched a brow. "After we saw our past lives. After we saw the way they turned out, didn't we realize that even the painful things that didn't make sense still had a purpose? That it's better than losing each other for the millionth lifetime?"

My gaze shifted downward.

He caught my chin and cupped my face in his hands. "I'll make it through this Laila. I'll make it through anything as long as it means that we don't have to start over again. We've got our girl." He gestured toward Milly in her swing beside the couch. "We've just got to get our boy. Then this stupid cycle is over forever. And we can have our happy ending. We can have each other and our kids and our dog and our simple little life.

"I don't understand it all either, Laila. I don't know why we've had to go through such shitty things to make it this far, but we have, and that fact can't change. If we have to go through one more shitty thing because destiny is fighting to give us the chance we've waited forever for, I can accept that. And you have to, too."

My head shook a bit as I looked between his eyes.

"Besides, what if we interfere with Peterson's timeline?" Jeremy asked. I creased my brows, and he said, "Last year, on that cliff. He told us that we get him back. That's what happens in his timeline. We get Micah back. If whatever he does to me plays a part in that, I'm okay with—"

"You're *okay* with that."

"I am," he said.

"What if he kills you?" My eyes watered as I looked between his. "He's said he wouldn't kill me. What Nastya pulled last year was just to back us into a corner. He's never sworn to keep you alive."

"I'm not going anywhere." He smiled and wiped a tear from my cheek. "But if I do, there's a pretty easy solution. Just go looking for me in twenty years. You're an Angel in this life; you'll still look my age then, so it won't even be creepy. Then when you find me, you show me this. Show me us. And I'll come back to you."

I made a face. "Don't say that. I'm not doing this without you."

"My point exactly." He grinned.

Little did I realize, he was exactly right about one thing. I'd love him just as much once he learned the lesson Peterson had to teach him. In fact, I may have started to love him more after that.

Because he was going to become one step closer to the first man I fell in love with.

CHAPTER FORTY-FIVE

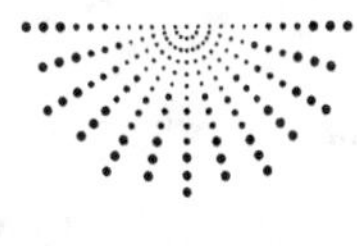

JEREMY

Leah told the family what Chris told us. The. Whole. Family.

So, I spent all of Christmas 2021 being berated by my brothers and sisters.

"How could you even consider it? Obviously, you have to sit it out. Listen to Chris."

"If you know something bad is going to happen to you, you'd have to be an idiot to walk straight into it."

"What about Milly?"

"What about Laila? What would she do without you? She already blames herself for all of this, you'd let her blame herself for losing you too?"

"What are you thinking?"

The list goes on and on. Funny, because when I knew something could happen to Laila the year before, I got punched *and* slapped in the face for trying to keep her safe.

After a while, I got annoyed and went outside to smoke a joint. I breathed in the cool winter air, letting the smoke from the herbs warm my chest. I tried to relax into the peace of the glistening stars against the cerulean sky, but I was just so pissed.

The hypocrisy was killing me. They were all so eager to allow Laila to risk my daughter's life, but I couldn't risk my own for my son?

It wasn't fair. Yes, I loved my wife and daughter with everything I had. But I loved my son too. And I promised him I'd be there for him. Laila wouldn't let me be her hero, but he wanted me to be his. And god damn it, I wanted to be too.

I hadn't done much for him yet. But I wanted him to know I fought for him. This wasn't just Laila's journey; it was mine too. I needed to take it.

Every time I said it, I meant it. I'd fight, kill, and die for my family. And I really didn't think I was going to die on this thing. I would have, if it meant my kid was safe. But I was damn sure going to fight and kill for him.

"Bit chilly out here." Kai shut the patio door behind him.

"Little bit." I took a hit off the joint and extended it his way. He pulled his own from his pocket. "So did you come out here to bitch at me too?"

He laughed. "Not at all."

"Really?" I raised a brow.

"Aye." He leaned against the banister. "I respect what ye're doing, Jeremy. You love my sister and niece and nephew more than anything. And ye're doing what ye believe is best to keep them safe. You haven't failed in that regard yet, and I trust that ye won't now."

Always did like that guy.

"Thanks."

"Laila thinks she can do it all on her own." He glanced at her laughing at the kitchen with Milly on her hip. "And she can do a lot, I'll give her that. But we've all got our parts to play. And as men, it's our duty to protect our family. That's not a woman's place, at least not without her husband by her side if he's still there to be."

I laughed. "Don't let Laila catch you say that."

"Never." He smiled. "But ye ken my point. She may not want to admit it, but what that man did to her... She does, Jeremy. She needs ye there when she faces him."

"I know she does." I looked over her. "I think she knows it too."

"Aye," he murmured. "Just that ego as big as the ocean of hers that's getting in the way."

I laughed and took a hit off of the joint. "It usually does."

"I'm sure it's going to turn out fine, brother. She'll see."

"I guess we all will."

Kai cleared his throat and scratched his head. "Can I ask ye something, Jeremy?"

"Sure." I turned from the snowy line of trees to meet his gaze. "What's up?"

"Hannah," he muttered. A smile came to his lips. "We've been seeing each other for some time now."

"Yeah, it's been, what? Three years now?"

"Aye," Kai said. "Ye probably don't ken this, but three years is the usual length of courtship for my people. Then ye're left at a fork in the road. Ye part ways or ye move onto the next step."

"Oh," I said, only then realizing what he was getting at. "You mean marriage."

"Aye." He smiled. "Yes. Yes, I do."

I'd said it before, and I still say it now. Kai was the only man in the world I'd trust to marry my sister. I loved that guy. He was perfect for her in every meaning of the word. I was incredibly grateful that my other sister was a lesbian because Kai truly was the only man I wanted either of my sisters to marry.

"I'm not her dad or anything. If anything, you should be asking Leah for her permission."

"I have," he said. "But it's customary to ask the wedded man closest to the bride in the family. And I don't have much to offer, but—"

"Offer?" I laughed and shook my head. "Kai, we don't do that here. There's no dowry. All that any of us want is for you to treat her how she deserves to be treated. And I already know that you do that, so you've got the okay from me. And I'm going to do you the favor of not telling Hannah that you were willing to buy her."

"Buy her?" The expression he made was the equivalent to what it'd been if I'd asked if he wanted to eat puppies for dinner. "No, the money wouldn't go to ye, Jeremy. It's hers. It's insurance. For her to know that she has a way out should something arise between us or should I pass. The purpose is for ye to allocate it should such situations arise."

"Really?"

He nodded.

Huh. That was kinda cool actually. I knew that things functioned differently there. Fae culture wasn't jaded by religions that gatekept women for centuries. But women did serve a slightly different role. They were typically mothers that stayed at home. Not always, they did have workers and women in their armies. But I supposed I thought it was still a bit more sexist than it was here.

That wasn't the case though. Women actually had far more freedom in Fae culture than they did on Earth. They were adorned and respected regardless of the path they chose to walk. Truly, the Fae people looked at women as the stronger sex, because they had the power to bring life into the world even if they chose not to.

Some wanted to be moms, and no one looked down on them for it. Others wanted to work, and no one looked down on them for it. Some wanted to fight in wars, and the same applied. And some wanted to do all of the above, and they still weren't looked down on for it.

It'd take a little while, but soon enough, I'd have a vast under-standing of the way the Fae worked.

"That's actually not a bad arrangement. But we don't need that either, man. If you have any money saved up for your future together, tell her. Let her decide what to do with it. If she wants us to hold it for your tradition, then we will. But let her be the judge of that."

"Ye think that's the best route?" he asked.

"That's what I'd do," I said.

"And I've got yer blessing?"

"You do." I smiled. "But I can't promise you that she'll say yes."

"That's alright." He shrugged, smiling back. "If she wants to wait, we can wait."

"When are you asking her?"

"Tonight. Leah gave me your mother's ring. Silly tradition, if ye ask me, but I ken that's what she wants," he said. "Does Laila still wear her anklet?"

"She does." I extended my foot and pulled up my pant leg. "So do I."

He smiled. "I've got me mum's and pa's too. Her husband died when I was a lad too young to recall him. She asked me to give it to a wife of my own when that time came. If Hannah says yes, I'll give it to her on our wedding day."

I smiled back. "Well, I can't wait to see what she says. I bet it'll be a yes though."

"Aye, I hope." He laughed. "I love her more than words can describe, brother."

"I know you do. And she loves you too." I smiled. "Couldn't have asked for a better guy for my baby sister."

"Neither could I." Kai smiled. "I'll take care of her, Jeremy."

"And I'll take care of her." I getured toward Laila as I took another hit off the joint.

"Looks like the two of us have a pact then."

"Looks like it."

We always had.

CHAPTER FORTY-SIX

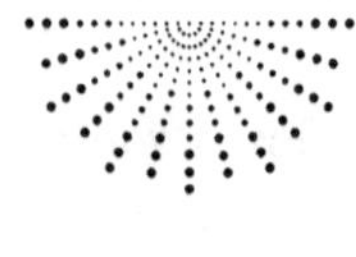

LAILA

Christmas carols accompanied by laughter echoed from the sitting room at the front of the house. Leaning over the kitchen island, I breathed in all the different aromas. Pumpkin spice, thyme and rosemary from the ham, sugar from the hot chocolate. I lifted a spoonful of warm apple pie to my lips. Jesus Christ, if heaven were a place on Earth, it'd be that piece of pie.

Two chilly hands touched my hips where my shirt rode up. "I know we're butting heads," Jeremy whispered at my ear. "But come here real quick."

I swiveled to meet his gaze. "Baby, I'm tired. It's Christmas, and I'm just not in the mood to sneak off and fuck in the bath—"

"You're a perv, you know that?" He grinned. "I need to tell you something."

I turned to Celena, gesturing to Milly in the highchair. "Keep an eye on her for a second, please."

She spooned her some sweet potatoes. "Will do."

"And we aren't butting heads." I took Jeremy's hand. "I'm just worried that something—"

"Yeah, yeah. I know. But that's not what I want to talk about." He carted me into the living room. He turned and met my gaze with a glance into the kitchen. "You can't be a blabber mouth though."

Not my strong suit, but I'd try.

"What is it?" I cocked my head to the side.

He smiled and glanced at Hannah. "Kai's going to propose."

"It's about time," I muttered. "Maybe the poor girl will finally lose her damn virginity."

"Really? They've been together all this time and they've never... Ya know?"

"Fucked?"

"Gross, don't say it like that." He grimaced. "That's my baby sister."

I laughed. "Regardless of the terminology, yes. Your baby sister's flower is still intact."

His nose curled, lips pulling down at the ends. "That is so much worse."

"See, fucking sounds better. Great word," I said.

"I wonder if they're like us." Jeremy looked over them in the kitchen. "I always assumed not because they'd been together for so long. But if they haven't..."

"Fucked?"

I'd never thought about that. But it would make sense. When I met Kai, I thought that he'd felt so familiar because he was my twin. But I remembered Hannah saying the same thing, even Jeremy. If they were par animarum too, maybe we'd met far longer ago than I'd thought. It'd explain why we all trusted him so much from the get-go.

Jeremy grimaced once more. "That. Then, it'd be possible. DNA has got to play some part in why we're soulmates. Kai's your twin, Celena's your little sister. Maybe they'll have this too."

"Maybe," I muttered, giving a nod. "That'd make sense."

Genetics certainly did play a big part in the par animarum. At least, they did in this life.

He squinted over them. "It'd be good if they were, I think. I want him to love her as much as I love you and Wyatt loves Celena. She deserves to be loved like that."

"She does." I smiled.

They really were a great match. I wasn't sure about how I felt when we first met Kai because she was so young. Admittedly, Kai was pretty naïve then too. It was more over the fact that I didn't know him than anything else though. He was so loving with her over the past three years. Truly the perfect gentlemen. They made one another so happy. And I liked the idea of them being married. But I loved the idea of them having what Jeremy and I shared.

He turned back to meet my gaze. "I'm fighting you on this because I love you. You know that, right?"

"I do."

"Can you tell everyone to get off my ass about it then? I know you don't like it, but I didn't like watching you moan when all those alphas were drinking your blood—"

"I wasn't moaning."

I got it. I one hundred percent got it. I wasn't willing to back down from the fight a year before either. How could I expect him to? It terrified me, but Micah was as much his son as he was mine. I understood why he had to be there too. And ultimately, I'd be incredibly grateful that he was.

"But yeah, I'll tell everyone to drop it. Can't promise that they will though. They're saying it because they love you."

"I know that. But it'd mean a lot if I at least had your support. You could get hurt too, but I'm not telling you not to go because this is about our son and I understand risking your life for him."

I looked between his eyes for a moment. I reached forward and put my arms around him. "You have my support."

He circled his arms around my waist and kissed my hair. I looked out into the kitchen over his shoulder, watching Leah and Kai speaking quietly in the corner. "I can't believe that little shit didn't tell me."

"You're bad at keeping secrets," Jeremy said. "Probably thought you'd uncontrollably giggle and give it away."

"I'm good at that, huh?" I grinned, pulling back.

"One of your many talents." He smiled.

Then Leah clanged a fork off her glass. "Hey, everybody, shut up for a second."

"So romantic." I laughed.

Jeremy chuckled and hooked an arm around my waist.

Then Kai began. He cleared his throat and pulled a smile to his fair, reddened cheeks. "Love, could ye stand for a moment please?"

Hannah brought herself to her feet, and—between chews—she said, "What?"

He laughed and touched her jaw. "I've got something to ask ye, cheadsearc."

I looked up at Jeremy. "What does that mean?"

"My first love in Gaelic," he muttered. "At least, that's what it means in our version of Gaelic."

"Nuh-uh." Hannah wiped pie from her lips, eyes widening. "You are not asking me to marry you after I ate all of that food. I already changed into my PJ's. Now I'm going to have to go change back into my dress for pictures because you had to wait until everyone was about to leave."

I raised a brow. "Did he ask?"

"I don't think he got there yet." Jeremy laughed.

"Is that a yes then?" Kai asked as he turned his head to the side a bit.

"Of course it's a yes. but you should have done it earlier when I wasn't bloated and my makeup wasn't faded. Now I have to go reapply my lipstick and—"

He leaned forward, took her face in his hands, and pressed his lips to hers. Everyone laughed before a few of us clapped. After a moment, he pulled back and pushed hair from her face. "I had a sweet little sonnet written out for ye."

"I know you love me." Hannah grinned. "Now where's the ring?"

"Bet you're really happy Laila turned that down right now," Jeremy called.

Kai rummaged in his pocket. Hannah smiled at us over her shoulder. Then Kai took her hand and slid the ring over her finger. He leaned forward and kissed her again.

Smiling, warmth spread throughout me.

Still, I wished the fucker would've told me. But it was still a very sweet, authentic moment to witness.

Jeremy kissed my forehead. Then his phone rang in his pocket. He looked at it with confusion in his gaze for a second.

"What is it?" I asked.

He turned the screen to face me.

Rather than a simple ten-digit numeral code, the number 6 stretched from one end of the screen to the other with a ... at the end.

CHAPTER FORTY-SEVEN

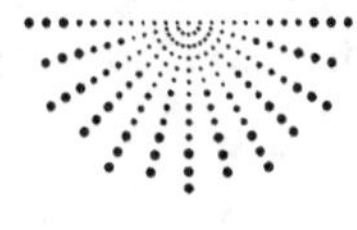

JEREMY

As Laila and I started into the living room, I slid the green bar. I put the phone on speaker and said, "Hello."

"Is this Jeremy?" a gentle, yet deep voice said on the other end.

"It is." I met Laila's gaze over the phone. "My wife's here too."

"Good," he said. "It's a pleasure to speak with you as well, Laila. I assume that you know who I am."

Yeah, the 6666666666-number made it pretty clear.

I licked my lips, unsure of which name to use. There were hundreds depending on which name he preferred from which text and time period.

"We do," Laila said, eyes meeting mine.

"At one point you knew me as Heylel, Jeremy." His voice danced like a song as it left the phone's speaker. "But you can call me whichever name you prefer. They all ring the same bell."

I looked at Laila and mouthed, "I thought that."

"I'm calling because I was only informed yesterday that our meeting is not until next year. I suppose I didn't make it clear to my secretary how high the two of you are on my list of priorities. I would like to sincerely apologize on her behalf as well as assure such an error will not be made again," he said. "If you'd accept my apology, I'd love to arrange a sooner date. I understand that the two of you are parents this time around so please offer a time that works for you, and I will make it work for me. Congratulations, I should mention. I'm sure she's wonderful."

Don't get me wrong, he sounded like a very nice guy. He was not only polite, but friendly and considerate. He spoke on a gentler level than any Angel I'd ever met, my wife included. Still, rumors can do wonders to tarnish a reputation. My impression of who the devil might be was far different than the reality.

And despite his kind tone, I failed to notice a lot of the clues he gave me in that apology.

"How soon are you available?" Laila asked.

"Tonight would work although that's probably too short of notice for you given the holiday. Perhaps tomorrow morning would be best. And I recommend you ensure a babysitter for the day. We have a lot to discuss. I would love to meet her, but I expect you to be hesitant. Trust will come with time and knowledge."

"Sure." Laila gave a slow nod.

"Where do you want to meet?" I asked.

"I will send you the address unless you prefer to meet somewhere else. But as I said, this conversation will be extensive. My office is the best place to give us a private space to speak. I'll order lunch and dinner if you could bring some doughnuts."

Laila and I looked between each other's eyes for a moment. She nodded.

"Yeah, we'll come to you," I said.

"Excellent," he said. "But while we're on the subject of trust, I feel it best to mention that I know little of the child you're searching for. I wish that I could help you find him, but I know nothing of him in this life. For that, I extend the sincerest of apologies."

"What do you know then?" Laila asked gently.

"I knew you." His voice was still smoother than silk. "Both of you. You've forgotten much of who you are, but I have not. I don't know that such information will help you find your son. But I do believe I could help you understand what this war everyone is so afraid of comes down to. But more importantly, the part that you play in it."

"You know about the war then?" I asked. "The details of it, I mean."

The softest, gentlest laugh escaped him. "I was there when it began, esiasch. I know more of its inner workings than anyone."

"Do you..." Laila began. She cleared her throat. "Do you want anything in exchange for this information?"

He chuckled again. "No, esiasch. I want to give you what I've given you before although never manages to resonate. The knowledge you've needed since it began."

"I don't know what that means," Laila muttered.

I did. That word anyway, esiasch. Brother, sister, aunt, uncle— essentially all kin—in Enochian.

"You will soon. One day, when we have more time, perhaps once your son is returned to you. Perhaps then we'll sit down for a few days and I can show you all that I remember of the both of you." He laughed softly. "Then again. It may take more than just a few days."

I creased my brows, looking at Laila. "I guess we'll understand what that means after tomorrow too then."

He chuckled. "I assure that you will. Until morning."

"Thank you," Laila said.

"Of course. Thank you for reaching out." And the call ended.

I looked over her. "That was him. Not a secretary or a Demon, that was really him."

"Seems like we're old pals," she muttered.

"He called you family." I licked my dry lips. "He... He knows us really well. Do you remember meeting the devil in any of our past lives?"

"No. Pretty sure I'd remember that. But our past lives, they couldn't have gone back more than—What? Six hundred years? We're supposedly a lot older than that."

"That's something I want to ask him," I muttered. "The legends always said that our kind hadn't been born in centuries. But we know that isn't true because all of our past lives were in the past few hundred years."

"But do you remember how we hid?" she asked. "When we were in colonial America. When I was that Witch. We snuck off into the woods to see each other."

I smiled. "I do remember that."

She rolled her eyes and fought the smile at her lips. "My point is that this is the only life I remember publicly announcing what we were."

"But why would we?"

"That's the question we should ask Lucifer," Laila said.

"Heylel." The correction was nearly involuntary when it left my lips.

"Right," she muttered. "Do you remember calling him that before?"

"I don't think so," I said. "But it's kind of like when you hear a song your parents used to listen to. It comes on, and you don't really remember the song itself. Not the lyrics, but the melody... It brings back a feeling."

"And what do you feel?" she asked.

"The same thing I felt while we were all eating dinner together." My face screwed up in confusion, honestly unsure of how it felt. "Family? Friendship, maybe?"

"I feel familiarity." Laila's head tilted slightly, squinting. "I know that I've heard that voice before."

I nodded slightly, biting my lip. "I guess we'll know more in the morning. Let's go find a babysitter."

CHAPTER FORTY-EIGHT

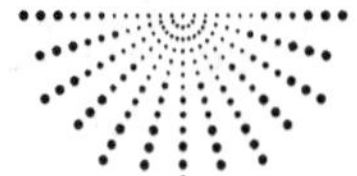

DECEMBER 26, 2021 - LAILA

Heylel's office was not what I expected. The room could have easily been the size of our entire first floor. The walls were painted a soft blue. The glass desk sat in front of a massive book collection on a modern, glass bookshelf. A modular, but comfortable, black couch sat before a glass coffee table in exquisite condition. Five or so magazines sat on top; a Rolling Stones, a Times, and a few others from different parts of the world.

Inviting plants sat all around. A bouquet of lilies in the center of the table, a few ferns hung from the ceiling, and a handful of Ficus stood on the marble floor. To my left was the door that a very polite young Demon had shown us into and prepared us a few fancy coffees from a cart in the corner. And to my right was a beautiful garden with a thousand different plants. I made a mental note to ask Heylel what the massive flower with the huge orange petals was because I wanted to plant some in my own garden.

Oddly enough, I didn't have even the slightest inkling that something was wrong as I sipped that coffee. I'd learned to trust my instincts, so I was rolling with them. They were telling me exactly what I needed to do. And that was get comfortable, because this place was damn near home.

"This is weird." Jeremy looked around the large office and out the wall of windows. "I didn't expect it to be so fancy."

I looked down at the black marble floor reflecting the sun that glistened in from the window. "He is known as the bringer of light, you know."

"To Peterson, so are you," he muttered.

"And we also have a wall of windows." I smiled. "Did you expect it to be a dungeon?"

"I don't know. Maybe. I didn't expect a coffee bar with a cappuccino machine. We own a diner, and we don't even have one of those," Jeremy said.

"Baby, relax." I laughed. "It's nice."

"Well, I'm sorry that I expected a little less namaste and a little more murder from the king of hell."

"It's not like our house looks like a mass murderer lives in it either," I said. "Can't judge a book by its cover."

He curled his lip. "It's just weird, Laila."

"Is anything in our lives ever normal?"

"Valid point," he muttered.

Then the door clicked open.

"Thank you for your patience," his familiar soft voice said. "I didn't expect you quite so soon, you were never much of early birds."

As I turned to meet his gaze, I found myself taken aback. I'm not sure what I expected, but I didn't picture him so pretty. Like a more slender and less defined, almost boyish version of a Hemsworth brother. He stood as tall as Jeremy but, although still slender, far more toned. I can describe his shape so clearly because he was shirtless as he entered. In fact, that was all that I noticed at first. Not because of the magazine-perfect, lady boner inducing muscles, but because of the scars.

His face and neck were untouched. But the rest of his physique seemed to be almost a single layer of scars. Finding skin without it proved nearly impossible. Some were worse than others, but they all connected. Surely, none of them were recent. And with his ability to conjure, as most Angels possess, he could surely blur them from our view. Yet he wore them with pride. His strong shoulders sat firm beneath his blond hair that was half pulled into a ponytail. Brilliant, yet pale, familiar blue eyes met mine as he pulled a white collared shirt over his shoulders.

"My apologies." He gave his head a gentle bow.

I pulled a smile to my lips. "It's not a problem. Thank you for having us."

"You and yours are always welcome." He smiled back as he approached. Jeremy extended a hand. But Heylel pulled him in for a hug. He met my gaze over his shoulder and patted his back. Heylel laughed, he pulled back, and met my gaze. "Laila, you go by now."

I nodded. He extended his arms toward me. His embrace felt warm and familiar as he squeezed around my ribs. There was no touch of flirtation or attraction. It was the way I felt when I hugged Adam or Wyatt or Max. Friend, yet family, even if not by blood.

Familiar.

That word kept echoing through my mind.

This is all so familiar.

He smiled and gripped my arms as he pulled back. He took ahold of Jeremy's shoulder and looked over the two of us. "You're so close to who you were then now. So much smarter than you've been in the past lives."

"Who is that, exactly?" Jeremy asked. "How do you know us?"

His smile fell a bit. He cleared his throat. "I know that you had no choice in your loss of our time. Yet, it hurts to meet your gaze and see that you remember nothing of me."

"I want to," Jeremy said. "I recognize you, if that helps."

His smile crept back up his cheeks. "It does. Thank you. Let's get to it then. Have a seat."

"We were told that you were there when our souls were created." Jeremy intertwined his fingers between mine. "Is that true?"

Heylel laughed and lowered himself to the chair across from the couch. His head shook, smile resting against his lips. "Hardly. But you were there when mine was."

I huffed. "No shit."

He chuckled as he looked between my eyes. "No shit."

"So that means that you don't know where this all started and how it connects to our son," Jeremy said, although it sounded more like a question as it left his lips.

"I can't tell you with absolute certainty where you came from. That was long before me. No, but I can tell you where all this began." He gestured around. "How your son connects to it. But before I get there, for you to understand it, you have to understand who you were. *Why* you were placed here into these cycles. Cycles I believe you may have finally broken."

"I don't follow," I murmured.

That soft, gentle laugh cascaded from him again. He sipped his coffee. He wiped a napkin against his lips and looked between us. "Would you look at that. We're all back within the garden. But this time, I'm reminding *you* of who you are. Opening your eyes again to the wonder of yourselves. Feeding you with knowledge in the hopes that you'll allow the others to eat from the tree of life."

"I know that you're, like, older than dirt but until recently, I thought that I was in my twenties," I said. "We don't talk in such detailed metaphors and idioms. I might need you to dumb it down for me a bit."

"Wait," Jeremy muttered. "The garden. As in, the garden of Eden? Are you suggesting we were Adam and Eve?"

"No. You weren't, but two others were. Two others of the par animarum, I mean. I'm suggesting that you were both someone far more important." Heylel sat forward in his chair. "That story, though twisted, does have some truths to it. Although, that one is more about you and me" —he gestured to me— "than the other two. They did eat from the tree of knowledge. That same knowledge I will deliver to you here today. Not that they were naked, that's a mere fraction of the story. The knowledge of realizing who they were without clothing isn't what got them kicked out of Eden. It was the knowledge that being naked together brought." He smiled as he looked between us. "We nudged them in the right direction. But it was the two of them that completed the bond. We just helped to remind them who they were to one another."

Literally, not one word of that made sense to me.

"I'm very confused."

That was a lot to take in, and it left my head spinning. I didn't know much about the Bible, but I did know who Adam and Eve were. But I wasn't sure what he was getting at. Heylel and I, we were the snake in the garden?

"Perhaps I should start from the beginning then, hmm?" he asked.

"If you could," Jeremy said.

Heylel licked his lips. Which seemed like a common tick people did when they thought, but one I knew all too well. Jeremy did that constantly.

He ran his hand along the short hair of his beard. "When I was a child, the two of you, as well as the other twenty-two, were already grown."

"Other twenty-two," I said. "Other twenty-two what?"

"The par animarum. The Elohim," he said. "There are twenty-four of you. Twelve pairs. Are there not?"

"We know of two," Jeremy said. "Us, her sister, and a friend of mine."

"The Wolves. Yes, I've heard." Heylel smiled wider. "I wonder which ones they were. I'd love to meet them too. Probably the ones of the hunt, that would make the most sense. Maybe you could bring them next time we see one another."

"Sure," I muttered.

"But I see now that you know even less than I thought," he murmured. "What do you believe of the par animarum?"

"I was told the same stories we all were as children," Jeremy said. "That when God created the races, he made an error with the par animos. They were too powerful to fit into a body, even once split in half, so he tried to destroy them. But they wouldn't die."

Heylel huffed, eyes rolling. He took a second, as if trying to find a way to put it into words. He spoke.

"Well, one part of that is true." Heylel licked his teeth and nodded slow. "He tried to destroy them. The two of you in particular. But not because he created you. The twenty-four of you and him were equals. You were the Elohim. The par animarum ranked well over any of us." He smiled. "Still, your kind called ours brother and sister. The concept of a god didn't come around until after the war. The humans called all of you that once, but you never saw yourselves as such."

"The war," Jeremy repeated. "What war?"

Uh, that's what you just took from that? Because the last line was what was repeating in my head.

"The war that granted you the twenty-four-year curse," he said. "The war of the gods, as it came to be known to the ones that lived through it. Although, the Archangels dare not call it that now. That'd get Daddy's panties in a bunch. Have no other gods before me and all that." His eyes rolled.

"We were gods." I tilted my head to the side. "Is that what you're saying?"

"You called yourselves The Elders then." He gritted his teeth. "You've been in the new one's presence, have you not?"

Holy shit.

I wish I could say it came as a total shock, and admittedly, it was a lot to take in. But it also made a lot of sense. It explained why I stood out to Peterson. It explained why he called me a goddess when we first met. It explained why I was so powerful, and it explained why my son mattered so much. Because if he were the offspring of two gods, that would make him a god too.

It also explained why the people looked to me as if I was a god long before I was.

It explained almost everything I'd wondered about myself for a long time.

But to hear him tell it, to hear him say we didn't refer to ourselves as such, that explained something too. I may have been confident, a bit egotistical at times, but I also always had a firm belief that I was no better than anyone else.

"Once," Jeremy muttered.

"Have you ever wondered why the gaps between those twelve chairs are so large?" Heylel's nostrils flared. "Did you feel the pain of what took place all those centuries ago in that very room?"

"Can't say that I found it pleasant," I murmured. "But never really noticed the chair thing."

"There used to be twenty-four," he said. "Twenty-five, technically, to break an even vote if you count him, but only to break an even vote. However, each of your votes combined was equal to one because you were all of one whole. Regardless of the circumstance, the paired soul had to come to the same decision to provide balance. To see both sides to each decision, reflect, and to find fairness. That's, at least from what you told me then, why you existed. To balance one another."

"What happened?" Jeremy murmured. "In that room, what evil took place?"

A somber smile came to Heylel's lips before it fell. As it did, I watched true, genuine tears bubble in his blue eyes. His gaze turned to the floor for a moment. He looked back up to meet Jeremy's eyes. "The war had just ended. The par animarum made a treaty with my father. I believed that peace was on its way, most did. And then... And then the slaughter came that reset the course of time."

"What slaughter?" I asked.

He tightened his lips together, fighting to keep them from trembling. "If I—If I would have known what he was planning that day... I would have fought for you. But they came as thieves in the night. I didn't know what happened until you were already gone."

"I'm still confused," I murmured.

"He killed us," Jeremy whispered, squinting in focus. "He killed us all."

"Even your children." Silent tears rolled down Heylel's cheeks. "My nieces, my nephews. Cousins, more so, but yes. Yes. He slaughtered any of your immediate bloodlines that remained. He wiped any trace of you that was left on Earth and killed anyone who spoke of you."

"That's how you betrayed him," Jeremy said quietly. "He couldn't destroy us, so he put us into bodies. We had no knowledge of what he'd done."

"Nothing ever truly dies. That's what you used to tell me. But yes." Heylel smiled softly, wiping his cheek. "He took your memories when he put you into new bodies. That's what happens when a soul is recycled, they forget their last life."

"Wait, but go back to this garden thing." I leaned forward. "You said that story was about the two of us. What do you mean?"

Heylel looked to me. "Don't you know what the snake truly was, Laila? Or at least what it symbolizes?"

Hell no. Symbolism was never my thing. I am, and always had been, a blunt ass bitch.

I shook my head.

"The living personification of fertility. *You* were the snake in the garden. I just helped you find it and get inside." He pressed his lips together. "When you gave Adam and Eve fruit from the tree of knowledge, they made love. And then they remembered that they too were gods. Those words are written verbatim in the book. 'You will certainly not die,' the snake told them. 'For God knows when you eat of the tree of knowledge your eyes will be open, and you will be like God, knowing good and evil.' Knowledge was remembering who they were. They were the first to die in the wars. They were the first to be reincarnated of the par animarum. You showed them who they were. You reminded them, because you loved them. They were your family. You wanted them back. And that... that was your last attack on him before that day in the Elder's Hall."

"The tree of knowledge." Jeremy chuckled before it turned to a huff. "The tree of knowledge was seeing that Yahweh was not God. Or at least, not the only god. *You* were the tree of knowledge."

"Mmm," Heylel said. "In a manner of speaking, anyway. And for it, I fell. But not before the Fifth Heaven was created."

As he said those words, a bell tinged in my mind. But not one that had rung in a long time. Eons, actually.

"The realm of light," Jeremy murmured.

He smiled at Jeremy's focused expression. "Am I jogging your memory, esiasch?"

"Not exactly," he muttered. "But all of that mythology I used to obsess over is starting to make a lot more sense."

Heylel nodded slightly, smiling. His eyes shifted to me. "And you?"

"That." I thought for a moment. "The Fifth Heaven. It sounds familiar."

"It should." He smiled wider. "To both of you. I helped you to create it."

Jeremy made a face. "We *created* the Fifth Heaven."

Heylel chuckled as his smile grew. "Aye."

"What's the Fifth Heaven?" I asked Jeremy. But he just swallowed, blinking hard a few times.

Heylel met my gaze. "You may call it the Fae Realm."

CHAPTER FORTY-NINE

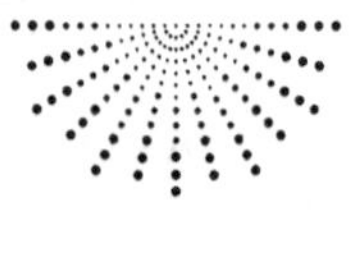

JEREMY

"We created the Fae Realm," Laila repeated with question in her tone.

"Not the realm itself," Heylel murmured. "You two just tapped into it and showed your people to do the same. Then we terraformed it, so to speak. Brought plants and creatures from your last home to the new world we were creating. The ones capable of living in that atmosphere, anyway, and the ones that would make human life impossible on Earth. The dragons, for instance. With their connection to their world, they were meant to be with the Fae and Elvan people. Humans feared them so the Earth Realm was too unsafe a place for them to stay. Such adjustments and ecosystems were designed carefully to give the *planet* a chance at survival *and* give the races the best chance at survival."

That explained why I felt so at home on the Fae Realm when we'd travelled there. Left me pretty ticked at that bastard who kicked us out of his shop though. Little fucker wouldn't have even been there if not for us. I had to laugh at the irony though.

"From our last home," Laila repeated. "What was our last home?"

"One was the First Heaven. It was called Matriaza. The other was Morduaine." He paused and laughed. "I don't think we'll have the time to get to that today, and I know ill of that life regardless. For now, let's stick to the story you came to hear."

I knew that I should have started panicking. Laila seemed shaken, at least, after the line about us and the Fae Realm, but I didn't have a drop of fear in my body. What he was saying did sound insane. But it wasn't nonsense. On one hand, the words coming from his mouth sounded crazy but on the other hand, they sounded so familiar. Like hearing an old story for the first time since childhood. I remembered none of its details, but I knew I'd heard it before.

Or rather, lived it.

"And now you're of the same blood yours served to create." Heylel smiled over Laila. "If that isn't dust to dust, I'm not sure what is."

"We created the Fae," I said.

Heylel sighed. "It isn't as simple nor black and white is that. More like you... You saved them, so to speak. But as a blanket statement, it'd be fair to say that you two played a bigger part than any. Even this is off track though. You came to understand why what's happened to you has happened, yes?"

"We did," Laila murmured.

Heylel sipped his coffee and propped his elbows on the knees of his black slacks. "As I said, I was young when the feuds began. But from what you told me then, Laila, it had been a long time coming."

"What were the feuds about?" I asked.

"Primarily, the tree of life," Heylel murmured. "That's where it began."

"You said that we fed you from the tree of life, what does that mean?" I asked.

"I did not say *you* fed me from the tree of life." He turned to Laila. "I said that you did."

"And what the fuck does that mean?" Laila asked.

Heylel looked from her to me. "You truly know so, so little, don't you?"

"That's why we're here," I said. "We want to know what the hell has been happening and why we play such a big part in it. But like you said, we lost any knowledge on all of this that we had. We know nothing, Heylel. I'm sorry that you have to break it down so small, but we're paying attention. It's just a lot of information to take in at once."

His head dipped in a nod. "Of course." He paused and took a sip from his coffee. "You, Laila, had control over eternity. You had the capability to give eternal life. Immortality. You, and my father. All the others too, but they could only give it by proxy, hence why Angels and Demons have the lifespans that they do. I'm the exception; you gave eternity to my mother as well. But most Angels only have one eternal parent. Him. I had two."

Laila's face said she didn't absorb more than a few words of that. "I gave you immortality?"

"You did," he said. "Through the two of them, anyway."

I tried to meditate on that for a second.

Laila was the tree of life, that's what he was saying. A few moments prior, he'd described her as the personification of fertility. Fertility, tree of life—it made sense. It'd also explain why she was such a hot commodity.

But what I didn't understand was why the hell we were here, what all of this even meant, and how this tied into everything with Micah. I also didn't understand how we were immortal, but he managed to kill us.

"Why did we come here then?" I asked.

He let out a slow, even breath. "You came to create the peoples of the races. All twenty-five of you. You were to govern the people. Once every soul had eaten of the tree of life, they could be returned to the home planet and this planet would return to its creator."

"So we essentially leased Earth," I said. He nodded, and I said, "What was the payment?"

"The people," Heylel said. "Not as a literal payment; you weren't turning them over as trade once they attained eternal life. But the purpose was to help them grow. I think, anyway. Truly, this part is a blur for me too. I wasn't like you all; I was a child to you. This was not my business. I was kept out of it. Only the par animarum knew all of these intricacies."

"Okay, back up a little bit," Laila murmured.

Heylel sat forward rubbing his eyes. "You and the others were given trillions of souls. New, young, and vibrant souls. You came here to start the cycles that were meant to bring them to ascendance."

"So we were supposed to teach them to be good people, is what you're saying," I said.

"Yes," Heylel said. "Teach them to live as you lived. So that they could expand and create as well. So that everyone could become like you. Like me, eternal."

"Are you saying that Wormwood gave us the planet to raise the souls?" Laila asked.

"Precisely," Heylel said. "How that arrangement was worked out, I'm not sure. Like I said, that was before me. But you were to teach them every lesson that needed taught before they could move into enlightenment and ascend back home to the land that you all came from."

I thought for a moment. "And God wanted to make that as difficult as possible for the people."

"But not because he was cruel. Though what you may call a bigot, he didn't truly care about many of the things he declared as sin. He did so out of fear for himself."

"What do you mean?" I asked.

Again, Heylel closed his eyes. "I don't know the exact details of what happened. But I do know that you learned you and the peoples of this planet could never return home because of something he'd done. What that was, I do not know. But he stood trial before the court that he belonged to and was found in error. You all sentenced him to a thousand years of imprisonment and to never hold a place among the Elders again. I suppose that sounds like a long time for you, but to someone who cannot die, it was deemed a fair punishment."

"That was the peace you thought was coming," I murmured.

"Yes," Heylel said. "But he had a plan in place. My brothers. My mother's first sons. You'd know them as the Archangels."

The Archangels. The Council. Aside from god himself, they were the only people that ranked above the Elders.

And I'd put money on the fact that they knew who we were. Maybe not years ago when the rumors of the paired souls first surfaced, but now, after everything Laila had accomplished, they had to. They must've made the connection. After all, she was the snake in the garden.

That'd explain why they refused to help me when she was taken captive.

Suddenly, my shitty life made a lot more sense. I pissed off God in a past life, and the fucker hated me so bad, he cursed me into a cycle of reincarnation Then when I finally got the life I'd been fighting centuries for, he tied my kid into the apocalypse.

"If we ate from the tree of life, how did we die?" Laila said suddenly with a confused expression. "You said that I could give eternal life. How were we slaughtered then?"

"Extract a soul from a body and it shall rot," Heylel said. "The soul will go on living. But the body will die."

I rubbed my hand against my mouth and leaned back into the couch.

"How do you do that?" Laila asked.

"*You* don't." He glanced at me.

"A necromancer does," I murmured.

"Yes," he said.

"That's what God did," I said. "He tore our souls from our bodies and then destroyed them so we couldn't be brought back into it."

"I'm not entirely sure how, but he did something with the twenty-four of your souls so that no one could reach them to pull them back to the corpses. Your children were held, they could not be born into just any body. Neither could you, but the groundwork had to be laid genetically first."

"That's why I'm a hybrid," Laila murmured. "That's why Mary was told to make me and Kai with my dad."

"And that's why Micah's so innocent," I said. "Because his soul has been waiting eons to be born."

"Yes," Heylel said.

My heart thudded as I tried to wrap my mind around the intricate details of what he just said. "So I was right. Our lives have been shitty but someone's trying to help us break the cycle."

"It'd seem so," he murmured.

On that point, to some extent, we were both right, and we were both wrong. Someone was helping us. But it wasn't the person that had commanded we be born.

"What is the cycle, exactly?" Laila said.

"What's the worst curse you could cast on divine lovers? Or gods of fertility, so to speak?" He looked between us with a sad, gentle expression. "To forget one another. To lose each other over and over, life after life. To never reach the point of bliss when your child enters the world only to grow as big and tall as yourselves."

"To end us just before we get to the good parts," I muttered.

CHAPTER FIFTY

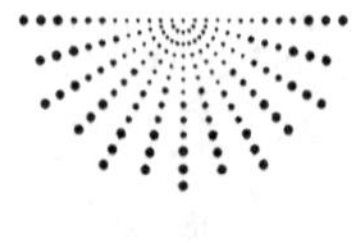

LAILA

I kept looking at Jeremy to see his expression. Though puzzled, it stayed fairly calm as Heylel spoke.

And seeing the way that Heylel looked at Jeremy left me completely perplexed. It reminded me of how Hannah or Brody gazed at him. Or maybe even the way that Micah did.

He knew him. They knew each other on a very deep level at one point.

In some odd, existential kind of way, I felt like I knew him too. It was something in the way his lips curved when he smiled and a little neuron fire when a chuckle escaped them. It brought me some form of joy that I can't quite explain. But it also freaked me the fuck out.

"Tell me." Heylel smiled, leaning forward. "What are they like? The children, I mean."

"We don't really know Micah," I said, knowing that I didn't want to go into the details of our astral communication. "But Milly..."

"She's Laila's twin." Jeremy smiled.

"So just two then," he murmured, giving a nod.

I raised a brow. "Were there others?"

He smiled and took a sip from his coffee. "Time will tell, I suppose."

"I don't like the way you said that." My eyes widened slightly. "How many did we have?"

He chuckled, strong shoulders lifting in a shrug. "In our time, you were known as the Great Mother. Let's leave it at that. You are named after the Angel of conception, are you not?"

"I'd like to get my first home before I go conceiving again, if that's what you mean," I said.

"That's alright." He smiled. "You have plenty of time."

"You said this ties into Micah," Jeremy said. "Can you elaborate on that?"

Heylel gave a nod before taking another drink from his cup. He sat it on the table and stroked a hand against his clean shaved jaw. "It was a part of the curse. Twenty-four of you cursed to live no longer than twenty-four years. But yours in particular, the strongest voices of the Elders, the ones who insisted on his imprisonment the strongest, you were the Great Mother and Father. The worst to do to you was allow you to bare no children. That was your punishment for trying to imprison my father."

"But we did," I said.

"It would seem that you've broken the worst of the cycle for yourselves, yes," Heylel said. "But not the worst of it all."

"What do you mean?" Jeremy asked.

"The breaking of the cycle was a part of the arrangement made with Wormwood upon your death," he said. "I don't understand the details; those you'll have to find for yourself. But from my understanding, my father arranged it so that the breaking of the cycle would signal them back. To tell them you've completed the cycles."

The breaking of the cycle. Was that getting Micah back? Or the sacrifice that Peterson was planning?

I was so confused, barely registering anything of what he was saying, but also panicking over what I did gather. "What?"

"But we don't even know what the tree of life even is," Jeremy said quickly.

"Yes," Heylel said. "That's exactly why he set it up this way. Don't you see yet?"

He looked between us with brows heavy over glistening blue eyes. "This was all about hurting the two of you. The people on this world, they meant even more to you then than they do now. By tying your son into this, not only do you have to deal with the loss of him, but the loss of this world."

"The worst revenge imaginable." Jeremy's jaw tightened. "Call them back well before any of them are prepared to ascend while we grieve the loss of our child."

I was still so confused, but I was listening. I just wasn't quite comprehending it all.

"And when there is nowhere to ascend to," Heylel said. "The human souls have nowhere to go. Whatever he did that you imprisoned him for kept us all from returning to the original heaven. Matriaza, you once called it. You were working on a plan for what to do with the souls before they returned, but then you were slaughtered." He squinted slightly. "Does this make any sense?"

Not really, but I was trying.

"We lose our son, and it calls them back," I said it as a statement, but I'd intended it as a question. I knew he already said that, but this was a lot. My head was spinning. Hardly any of what he was saying truly resonated.

"Yes," Heylel said.

"So if we save Micah, we buy time," Jeremy murmured.

"I suppose."

I raised my hand to my mouth and chewed my nails.

Well. The bar for saving Micah's life just got a hell of a lot higher.

"Why?" I lifted my gaze to Heylel's. His head tilted. "Why did he want revenge this badly? What did we do?"

Another slight shrug. "He is a jealous god. He always has been; he even boasts it in his holy book."

That didn't really answer the question. But when his gaze shifted to Jeremy, when that awe-filled, almost childlike expression touched his eyes, I had another question.

"Why do you look at him like that?"

Heylel's eyes shifted back to me. "Who?"

I nodded to Jeremy. "You look at him the way daughter looks at him. The way his little siblings do. Is that what you were? Were you his brother?"

Heylel smiled. His head shook. "No. I was not."

"Then who were you to us?" I asked.

His smile stayed. "You were my aunt by marriage." He looked to Jeremy. "And you were my father's brother."

When I say that my jaw fell to the ground, I mean it. The muscles below my cheeks ached from the tensity of how fast it'd dropped.

Jeremy's brows crunched down so far, I could hardly see the blue in his eyes. "God was my brother."

"Half-brother," Heylel said. "But yes. You were. And he wasn't exactly father of the year. You were the only fraternal figure I had to look up to that shared my blood."

Jeremy blinked long and hard for a minute. "And he killed me. And my wife, and my children."

Heylel's gaze turned down. Another slow breath. "Like I said. You and he always said, 'nothing ever truly dies.'"

I continued staring at the marble floor.

Jesus Christ.

Shit, should I stop saying that now? Seems a little stupid with all of this considered.

But even if that were true, even if nothing every truly died, that didn't justify it. Not only had he killed us and our family, but he damned the entire world. We had a plan, that's what Heylel said. The par animarum were working on a plan to keep the people safe when the end came. But he killed us, and we lost it all.

Heylel looked between us. "You were overtaken by a tyrant. But you had a strong following. Your people loved you far more than they loved him. I believe you could build that again."

"Not in the time span that we have," Jeremy said. "If this is all true, if we are who you say we are—"

"You are," Heylel said.

"Then we have no idea how to face what you're saying we have to," Jeremy said. "Compared to who you say we are, we're primitive. We know a drop of all of this. We need more time."

He smiled, sipped his coffee, and raised a shoulder. "That, you do."

CHAPTER FIFTY-ONE

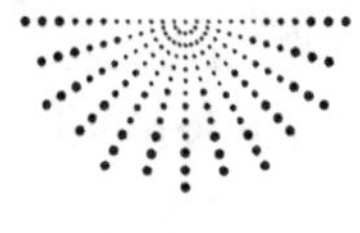

JEREMY

"I hope that I haven't overloaded you with information," Heylel murmured. "I know that this is probably more than you expected."

It was, but it wasn't. I wasn't sure why I believed it. I wasn't sure why I felt peace when I heard it. But it felt... it felt like a ball of yarn in my brain was unwinding. I still didn't understand a lot of it.

But certain things made perfect sense.

Suddenly, I understood why my life had been shit. I'd always wondered what I did to karmically justify everything that had happened. And now, I knew. God hated me.

Granted, that wasn't great news. Especially since I was raised Catholic and grew up believing he loved me. But now... Well, I felt a lot less guilty for leaving the faith, I'll put it that way.

Also, I understood why I was so compelled to withdrawal from the Elder's and the Council's reign all those years ago. Because I should've never been in it. I wasn't welcomed. I was an enemy of God.

Still, I didn't completely get why. But I understood a tad.

I felt Laila's shaking palm brush my knee. My hand found hers, twining our fingers together. "The stories throughout all of mythology about the gods being in constant friction... That was about us."

"It was," he said. His gaze shifted over Laila. "Are you all right?"

"A little overwhelmed," she said. "But yeah. Yeah, I'm okay."

She was not. Her face made that abundantly clear. She was ready to go home.

I traced my thumb along the back of hers. She put her other hand just above my forearm, holding it close to her. Heylel looked over us with a smile across his lips. "I'm glad to see you two like this again. One of the lighter notes in the chaos, I suppose."

"Is this how we were then?" I asked.

"Together and in love?" He smiled. "Yes. The definition of it, perhaps."

"What sets us apart from the others?" Laila asked. "Aside from the tree of life thing. What makes us more significant than the other twenty-two?"

"You were the first beside my father," he said. "The others came later. But you three were first."

"My head hurts," Laila murmured.

Heylel smiled, gazing over her carefully. He saw the same thing that I did. "Perhaps I've shared enough for one day then. You're always welcome here. Should more questions arise, I'll answer the ones that I can. But maybe you should rest on the information I've given you today. Let it settle in a while."

"Maybe that's a good idea." I grazed my thumb over Laila's. "This is a lot to take in. I don't want to forget anything important."

"Well." Heylel stood with a smile. "My door is always open."

"Thank you." I returned his smile as I stood. I took Laila's hand and helped her to her feet. "We really appreciate it. Thank you."

"Of course." He smiled still. "I hope to hear from the two of you soon. Let me know when you find that little boy of yours."

"Sure," Laila murmured.

He reached forward and put his hand on my shoulder. He looked back to Laila. "Don't be surprised if you start to have fleeting memories of the lives you once lived. I'd be surprised if you did not."

"Like flashbacks?" Laila asked.

"Yes." He smiled, resting his hand back at his side. "Maybe then you'll have a broader understanding. Won't sound as much like a fairy-tale if you see it for yourself."

"It doesn't sound like any more of a fairytale than the rest of our lives have been." I slid my hand to the small of Laila's back. "I do have a question for you though."

"Sure," he murmured.

"Everything that's happened to us in this life." I said. "Losing our son... When I lost her... Do you know why all of that happened? Why that man, Peterson... Why he did this to us?"

"I do not," Heylel said. "But I do know that the two of you were cursed to endure the worst things imaginable. I've been told that this Peterson claims to have done these things to help you?"

"So he claims," Laila muttered.

"Well, perhaps he meant that. Perhaps all of this was done to prepare you with the intent to help you break the cycle. An unfortunate end, if we're right about your son. But if what I've heard about this man being from the future is true, perhaps he's from a time when the war with Wormwood has come to pass. Maybe he wants to help you win."

Laila gritted her teeth. She licked them and turned her gaze to the ground.

"But I could be grasping at straws," Heylel said. As he looked over Laila, a wave of grief washed over him. "That man may be important to you now. But I think he's very small in the larger picture. I bet a day will come when he's nothing more than a gnat to you, esiasch."

"Well, you're right about that," I said. "He's no one."

He gave a soft, sad smile followed by a nod. "I look forward to seeing the two of you again soon."

"Likewise," I said.

"And I..." He paused, pressing his lips together. "I'd love to see the children. I know that sounds odd. Not something that anyone wants to hear from the devil. But I'm not what society has made me out to be. Those children were my family. And for thousands of years, I've mourned them. I understand, of course, if you aren't comfortable with that. But it would mean a great deal to me."

Before I'd met him, there's no way I'd have been comfortable with him meeting my kids. Now though... I don't know. It didn't sound like a bad idea.

"We'll be in touch."

———

The familiar scent of eucalyptus from the wax melts settled into my nose. My body settled into the plushy sofa. Quiet wind whirred outside between the barren trees. I gazed out the wall of windows. Like Laila had said, it did remind me a great deal of Heylel's office.

Laila sat down beside me with Milly on her hip. "So you believe him?"

"I don't have a concrete reason to," I said. "But I don't have a concrete reason not to either."

She squinted slightly, forehead scrunched up.

That face meant something. The gears were turning behind those emerald eyes. Did she not trust him? Because I did. But I trusted her more.

I placed a hand on her arm. "What are you thinking?"

"That none of this makes sense," she murmured. "But also that it does. I just... I don't know what to think. I'm really confused."

"It was hard to follow." I pushed hair behind her ear and lifted her chin to meet my gaze. "Are you okay?"

She bit her bottom lip and shook her head. I twisted a hand around her waist and pulled her into me.

"I thought that this would help us find him," she said. "Or at least give us some understanding of why this happened to us. But... But it's just made things harder. I'm so confused, and I—I don't understand any of it. I know we have to tell everyone what he just told us, but I don't know how. I don't even know where to start."

"We'll figure it out." I gave a smile. "For now, we find Micah. We keep them from hurting him, and we keep them from coming back. Then we worry about who we used to be. But for now... For now, we just focus on who we are. Not who we were, but who we are now."

She pushed her head further into my chest, looking down at Milly in her arms. "Well, I guess I was right."

"About what?" I asked.

"I always said that if God was real, he'd have to be a real prick to put people through the shit that he does," she said. "If Heylel was right, then so am I. Dude seems like a real cunt."

Oh, yes. She was right. But we were also biased.

I laughed. "Yeah. Yeah, it seems like it."

She turned up to meet my gaze. Her hand raised to my cheek before moving down my jaw. "But ya know something?"

"What's that?"

"When I met you, I swore that I knew you from somewhere." She smiled and pushed hair behind my ear. "I guess I was right about that too."

"So did I." I smiled, looking between her eyes. "Always knew there was something special about you."

She smiled back. Her hand slid from my neck to my shirt. She gently grabbed ahold of it and plopped her head back to my chest. "Didn't think we'd be this important though."

I kissed her forehead. "I did."

CHAPTER FIFTY-TWO

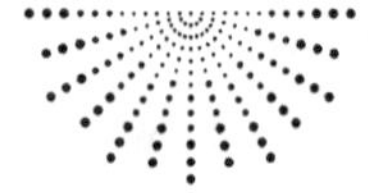

DECEMBER 27, 2021 - JEREMY

The diner was closed for the holiday, so we did what we did on all of our days off. We had breakfast, we drank our coffee, then we went up to the main house. But Laila was damn near silent all morning. She talked to Milly, but she barely said a word to me.

I guess it made sense. She didn't know what to say.

We were both really confused. Maybe a bit heartbroken at the messages Heylel had given us the day before because they hadn't given us much that would help Micah.

But I had a good feeling about that guy. I knew he'd be a valuable friend as time went on.

"What happened back there?" Celena looked at Laila beside Leah at the island. Her chin rested against her palm. She squinted at the computer screen, rubbing the dark circles beneath her eyes with the back of her hands. "She didn't say a word when you guys came to pick up Milly last night, and she pretty much ignored me when I asked what happened with Lucifer."

Ugh. How does one tell their sister-in-law that she's a god? Sure, Heylel had done so last night. But I wasn't sure how to relay that information to Celena. Maybe Laila would want to. Then again, maybe she wouldn't.

"It's really hard to explain. I don't even understand half of what he told us."

"Was it as bad as I imagine it was?"

"He was really nice actually," I said. "I... He said that he knew us in our first lives. Or maybe not our firsts, I don't know exactly. But the lives that started this."

"Well, yeah we figured that," Celena said.

"No, you don't understand," I said. "We're older than him, all of us. You and Wyatt too. And I guess the other twenty of us."

"What do you mean us?"

"The par animarum. He said there were twenty-four of us total. And that we..." My eyes closed, trying to think of a way to put it into words. Laila and I hadn't talked about how we were going to tell everyone, and I didn't want to say something she didn't want to be common knowledge.

"It's kind of crazy. And complicated. But no, he wasn't bad. I liked him, actually. I have a feeling we can trust him."

Celena scoffed. "You think it's safe to trust the devil."

"He fell for us." I felt my face involuntarily screw up in defense. "It's written in the Bible, Celena. He fell from Heaven because he gave us knowledge."

She turned her head to the side a bit. "As in, he fell for Earth? Or he fell for you two?"

"Both, I think," I muttered. "We... He isn't lying, Celena. We know him. I can't remember him, not really. But at the same time, I kind of do. I don't know, it's hard to explain. Meet with him and you'll understand."

"He wants to meet with me and Wyatt?"

"Yeah," I said. "He doesn't know which ones you two are, but he's curious."

"And which ones are you?" she asked. "How did he know who you were?"

"I guess because of our kids," I said. "Maybe because we were the first? And we were the first to find each other in our generation too. But maybe because of Laila. Or maybe something to do with the feud."

"The feud... What feud?" Celena stared at me with a puzzled expression. "And what do you mean she fed him from the tree of life?"

I ran my hand against my mouth. I couldn't blame her for that look, that came out sounding like it was from someone long off their psych meds. "I told you, it's really confusing. I'm still trying to process it all, and we didn't even get that much information in the grand scheme of things."

Her gaze was still full of question. "Alright. Well, once you work out the kinks, let me know. You kinda look like you've seen a ghost."

I let out a huff of a laugh and ran my tongue along my teeth. "In a way, I think we did."

"She okay though?" She gestured tos Laila.

"She will be." I glanced over her. "I don't know, she's kind of got the weight of the world on her shoulders."

That was the first time that figure of speech left my lips without being a hyperbole.

The world was banking on us and our two-year-old to save it. I had faith that we'd be able to pull it off. But Laila didn't seem to.

As I gazed at her from my seat in the sunroom, I began to see it. That violent guilt eating her from the inside out. When she killed those hundreds of guards at the compounds, she did so with the rationality of *let the few die so that the many can live.* But this information changed all of that.

If we failed to bring Micah home in time, that would mean that when she got in that van three years ago, she didn't just kill our son. She killed us all. We had no idea what the tree of life was, and we certainly hadn't 'eaten' from it yet. We had no resources to supply the people of the realms with eternal life.

We had an army. But we weren't prepared to fight a war. We couldn't even kill one damn human as minuscule to the grand scheme as a gnat at a picnic.

There was no way in hell we could fight an army of unknown origins at least as powerful as God himself.

We weren't ready. Not yet. But Laila already realized what only occurred to me in that moment. Saving Micah meant saving the world. If he died, so would every other thing that we loved. We would either die with it or watch it burn.

CHAPTER FIFTY-THREE

LAILA

Hannah's arms flung around my neck, nearly pulling me from my seat at the bar stool. "So are we going to be, like, double sisters now? Is that how this works?"

I laughed and reached for her hand. She grinned, extending it out to me. I smiled, looking down at the detailed, vintage diamond ring on her finger. "This looks like it's right where it belongs."

"It does, huh?" Hannah grinned. "I'm so glad Dad didn't bury Mom with it."

"Han." Brody turned from the fridge with a slight grimace. "Little insensitive."

"Well, I am." She rolled her eyes. "Mom wanted me to have it anyway."

"What, she tell you that?" he asked.

Hannah put a hand at her hip. "Matter of fact, yes. Yes she did."

"You've talked to Mom?" Jeremy came into the kitchen from the living room.

Brody said, "Yeah, shouldn't she have been recycled by now?"

"Well, yeah. Now. But I've had my power forever, guys. She left when I was four, I think."

"Huh." Jeremy sat beside me. "Was she the one that told you not to tell anyone?"

"Yeah. She gave me a whole index of rules, actually. I didn't understand why until I was older."

"That's kind of bullshit," Brody muttered. "You got an extra four years with her."

"It's not like I asked for it," Hannah said. "You guys can go anywhere you want at any given time, and I see dead people. If I could trade, I would."

"What about Dad?" Jeremy asked. "Did you ever get to see Dad?"

Hannah frowned and shook her head.

"Probably too ashamed to show his face," Brody muttered.

"I don't get that." Jeremy glanced at Milly in her highchair. "He didn't even come back to check on us?"

"If he did, I was too young to remember," Hannah said. "Doesn't really matter now though. He did what he did."

"Hey, that reminds me." Brody grinned, leaning against the counter. "Which one of us is going to walk you down the aisle?"

She raised a brow. "What makes you think it's going to be one of you? Because you have a penis?"

"Obviously Leah's going to." Jeremy gave a soft smile.

I zoomed in on an image of a large structure through Ohio that ran along a ley line. I half paid attention as they bickered back and forth about why one of the brothers should get to walk her down the aisle. I wanted to be excited for them, but I couldn't stop thinking about everything Heylel said the day before.

When we lay down to sleep last night, I thought about what we were planning. That there was a good chance I'd end up on that table again. Tied down. Unable to help myself or anyone else. And it almost felt symbolic. My arms and legs were bound. And no matter how hard I fought to escape, the unfortunate fates I'd faced were still strong enough to hold me back.

Things were going to get worse before they got better, if they ever got better, and I found myself truly shaken to my core. The only chance

I had was finding Micah. If I failed—as I'd failed time and time again —nothing I'd done so far would matter. All of it would be for nothing.

My daughter's life, it would end. As would my husband's. My sister's, and my brother's, and my mother's. My friend's. My own. All of our lives would be gone if I didn't bring my baby home.

Of course, I'd wanted to find Micah before too. There was nothing I wanted more. But now, it wasn't just about finding Micah. It was about saving the entire fucking planet.

"You're awfully quiet." Brody smiled my way. "Aren't you excited?"

"Yeah." I forced a smile and looked at Hannah. "Of course, I'm so happy for you guys."

Hannah smiled back. "We're thinking June or July."

"Really?" I asked. "I thought you liked winter weddings."

"So that Micah and Chris can be there. If they want to be, of course. I'm not sure how they'll feel about a party right away. But I want to at least give them the option, you know?" Hannah gave a bubbly smile as she went on. "Hey, maybe Micah could be the ring bearer. And Milly's definitely going to be the flower girl. She should be walking by then, right?"

"She's already trying." Jeremy placed his hand over mine. "She should be."

"That's perfect." Hannah grinned with a nod. "And Laila, I want you to be my maid of honor."

I looked up from the computer and met her gaze. "Really?"

"Well, yeah. Leah can't; she's walking me down the aisle. And you've been my sister for years. There's no one else I'd rather have up there. No offense, Celena."

"None taken," Celena said from the breakfast nook beside Wyatt. "I'll be a bridesmaid, but maid of honor is too much work."

"What are you thinking for a dress?" I smiled, forcing myself away from the computer. "I see you in strapless."

"I'm actually thinking sleeves." Hannah grinned. "And I've always wanted a big frilly ball gown. Kai likes modest anyway."

"How are you planning on paying for this big frilly ball gown?" Brody asked. "Already call Mèmè and Papy?"

"No. No, Kai actually had some money put away." Hannah chuckled. "He said that back home, he would have given it to me as security in case I decided to leave him. So that I could start over if I wanted to."

Jeremy laughed. "And you're going to use it on the wedding instead?"

"I sure am." She grinned. "I want a big wedding, shoot me. Hey, I wonder if Mèmè and Papy would let us have it at the vineyard."

"You're marrying, and eventually, breeding with a Fae," Jeremy said "That's going to be a firm no."

She huffed. "It's so pretty though. Fucking racists."

Jeremy said, "I'm sure you can figure something out."

"We might be able to help if you need it," I said. "We're still trying to replenish what we took out of our savings to build the house, but we could probably help with the venue or something."

"That would be amazing." Hannah's smile widened. "Thank you so—"

Just as she went to finish her sentence, Kai appeared from nowhere falling to the floor. A gasp left my lips. He groaned out, "I'm all right."

"Jesus Christ." I raised my hand to my chest.

Hannah helped him to his feet.

"Still working on sticking that landing," Jeremy muttered.

"The lot of ye make it look so easy," Kai grumbled with a hand at his hip. "This shite idn't easy."

"Came pretty easy to me," I said.

"Well, yippee-ku-ya-yay for you," Celena said.

"Would ye mind, love?" Kai gestured to his hip. "Something's out of line back there from that drop."

"Sure." I stood and walked beside him. He pulled up the back of his shirt to reveal a large red splotch that seemed to be swelling already. "Damn, I wonder if this is a broken hip."

"I couldn't tell ye, but I know it hurts," Kai said.

"Right. Sorry." I raised my hand to his lower back and allowed it to glow that bright white light into his skin.

He grumbled and pulled forward a bit. I sent a steady stream of that odd, goldish twinkling light speckled with glittery dots of violet from my other hand. As it touched his skin, he instantly relaxed. He even released a slow sigh, as if enjoying the pain.

Once the swelling receded, I pulled back and met his gaze with a smile. "All fixed up?"

"How'd ye do that, lass?" His eyes were slightly widened, fingers coasting over the spot that'd been sore. "It—It hardly hurt."

"Mary says it has something to do with our souls," I said. "Just about everything seems to."

"Hey, I actually wanted to ask you something, Kai." Jeremy gestured his way. "What do you know about the gods in the Fae realm?"

"Eh, not as much as I ought to," Kai muttered. "Never paid much mind in chapel."

"But there was chapel," I said. "You praised the creators of your world then?"

"I wouldn't say praised." He smiled, almost fighting a laugh. "We'd bend our knee and pray to them, aye. Give thanks for harvest, ask for a good crop if the last had been scarce. But praise, praise isn't the word for it. We... We give thanks, of course. But our gods are respected as our kin. The pioneers for the first clans."

Well, that didn't sound so bad. Certainly sounded better than the way religion was portrayed in modern America.

"Did you ever have to, like, beg them to forgive your sins?" I asked.

He made a face and laughed. "Sins. As in, our mistakes?"

"Yeah," I said. "Did you have to ask the gods for forgiveness when you did something wrong?"

"Not a rule that I can recall," he said. "But when we hurt someone, we're taught it our duty to make it right, if that helps."

"How many gods do they have?" Jeremy asked.

"Hundreds." He chuckled. "But the top three are the ones we talk about the most."

"Three," I murmured.

"Who were they?" Jeremy said. "What were their names?"

"Solais, Nix, and Vèa," Kai answered.

I remembered that name. From my memory trip that Helena

showed us. Vèa. That was the word uttered by the fuzzy, barely-there man, with my children on his shoulders before I awoke.

Jeremy thought for a moment. "God of light, dark and... What does Vèa mean again?"

"It's the equivalent of Eve to the Fae, I think," Brody said. "First mother, or great mother, right?"

"Great Mother, aye," Kai said.

My heart nearly fell from my ribs. Two for one special on the mythology there.

"You alright there, love?" Kai asked.

Not really.

That fucking story. I always hated it. A dumb and helpless woman is told that she can become smart if she takes in the tree of knowledge. She does, then offers the same knowledge to her lover, and is held accountable for the actions of both him and her. She's blamed for the pain associated with childbirth for all of the human race as a means of punishment for the desire to attain intelligence. For the ambition to improve herself, she is deemed to be the first sinner of Earth. The sinner that ended Eden for the rest of us.

I knew Heylel had said I was the one that gave Eve the knowledge, that she wasn't me. But I still hated it. How women were perceived as villains to all of humanity for that single story in one popular book of myths.

After clearing my throat, I said, "We should probably get everyone together."

"What for?" Hannah asked.

"We—We need to talk about what Heylel told us," I said.

"Heylel?" Hannah asked.

"Lucifer in Hebrew." Brody looked over me with concern. "You don't look so good, Lai. Are you alright?"

"Mhmm." I gave a quick nod. Jeremy put a hand on my upper arm. He gazed down at me with a gentle, yet worried expression. I forced a smile and cleared my throat. "I'm going to go sit outside with Tink for a minute. Can you watch Milly and get everybody together?"

Jeremy said, "Sure, baby."

I smiled back, blinked away tears, stood, and started toward the door.

CHAPTER FIFTY-FOUR

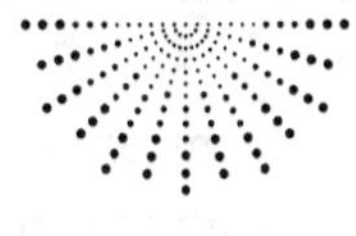

LAILA

Over the course of the preceding three years, I learned to control my emotions pretty well. I learned to choke down the lump in my throat and to grasp the concept of biting my tongue. I managed to hold onto that ability as I threw the stick across the yard and watched Tinkerbell chase after it. But swallowing hard and chewing my tongue didn't change the way it felt inside.

It was a feeling I knew all too well.

Like falling from a great height. Not the impact of hitting the ground, but the fall itself. The weightlessness before the sudden collision. The peace tied up in terror. The knowing of what would happen when I'd slam to the ground but being unable to stop it.

The last time I fell as hard as I felt that I was about to, I realized that flailing my extremities wouldn't keep me from hitting the surface. But I had to catch myself. I had to keep from slamming to the bottom of that pit of depression because if I hit the bottom, I'd have to heal from my wounds before I could even attempt to make it back to the top.

"Lai," Jeremy said on the porch with Milly on his hip. I turned to meet his gaze and gave a quick smile. "You aren't alright, huh?"

I threw the stick to Tink again. "Not really."

He trudged down the snow-covered steps, placed a hand on my waist, and kissed my hair. "Me neither."

I tilted my head up to meet his gaze. Milly reached for me. If for nothing else, I had to keep from slamming into that pit for her. I had to catch myself.

Looking into those sweet, innocent green eyes, I lifted her to my arms. "This is just... It's too much. It's just too much."

"It is a lot," he murmured.

"We..." I huffed. "We just want to be normal. That's all that we want; we just want to be normal, and we never were. We never can be. If we fail, if Micah dies—"

"Don't say that."

"It could happen." Tears welled in my eyes as I looked between his. "We could fail, Jeremy. And if we do, if we fuck this up, we're killing the entire god damned planet."

"It really would be a 'god damned planet,' huh?" He sent me a quick, humorous smile. Him and his damn dark humor.

I clenched my jaw.

"I'm sorry. I saw my opportunity and I had to take it," he muttered.

"This isn't funny, Jeremy. This is about the end of the fucking world and our son being murdered and you think it's okay to make it a punchline?"

"I'm just trying to make you smile," he murmured. "I'm sorry."

"Mama." Milly put her warm, chubby hand on my face. I turned down to her and smiled. Then tears flooded my eyes and clouded my vision. I positioned her in front of me and looped my arms tight around her little back. Tears continued to gush from my eyes as I closed them.

If I failed, I wouldn't just lose Micah. I'd lose her too.

I felt Jeremy's hand on my waist, and the other touched Milly's back. His chest felt warm against me as he squeezed his arms around us. For the first time though, they didn't feel safe. Still, the safest place in the world. But nothing felt truly safe anymore.

Once the tears started rolling, they wouldn't stop. I was on the verge of a breakdown, and the only thing that truly kept me vertical was the little girl wrapped in my arms.

She couldn't even stand on her own, but she kept my feet on the ground.

CHAPTER FIFTY-FIVE

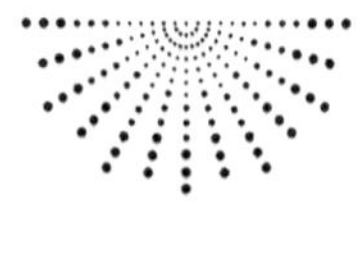

JEREMY

"So what's all of this about?" Adam asked from his perch on the couch.

"Yeah, is it important?" Jenna asked. "Because I woke Luka up for this."

"Yes, Jenna." Laila rubbed her tense forehead. "It's pretty fucking important."

"What is it then?" she said.

A slow breath left my lips. I squeezed Laila's hand. She glanced up to meet my gaze before she turned hers back to the ground. "Do you want me to tell them?"

She nodded quickly, eyes still locked with the floor.

I cleared my throat and looked around. "I'm not even really sure where to start."

Brody looked us over and said, "What did you find out?"

I ran a hand against my mouth. "A lot, actually. Way more than we expected to."

"Is it going to help with finding the boys?" Leah leaned forward with her elbows on her knees.

"Probably not." Laila ran her tongue along her teeth. "But we did find out why they're doing this. Or at least, what Micah has to do with it."

"Spit it out then," Mary said.

I rubbed my eyes. "To understand the why, you have to understand the what."

Hannah looked between us. "Then what?"

"More than anything, we got more information on the par animarum," Laila said. "And for the record, God didn't create us. Not even close."

"Who did then?" Brody asked.

"We don't know, but that's irrelevant anyway," I muttered. "What matters is who we were to him. All of the par animos, not just the two of us."

"Now you're talking like Mary," Leah said. "Just say it."

"We stood beside him as equals," Laila said. "Twelve sets of par animarum ruled the world along with God. The intention was to help them improve from primitive people into people worthy of eating from the tree of life."

"What?" Mary's forehead wrinkled. "What are you talking about?"

"Exactly what you think we're talking about," I said. "Your god isn't any more of a god than we are."

"But there is only one god," Mary said. "Yahweh is the only god."

"That's what he wants you to think," Laila said. "Built a few damned religions over himself, but he didn't even have a vote on The Council unless it was to break an even one."

Mary's eyes darted around the room in rapid thought. I could practically see the mushroom cloud exploding behind them. She may have fallen, but she still loved her god—her father. And there we were describing him as nothing more than a man. "I... I don't understand."

"We weren't gods," I said. "Heylel said that word came around after we died."

"You died." Celena raised a brow. "How do gods die?"

"We weren't gods," Laila repeated. "Leaders, sure. But gods aren't real. The word god is a title someone assigns themselves when they're on a power trip and have small dick energy."

"Okay." I ran my hand over my mouth and sat forward on the couch. "Alright, for humans, what is the purpose of life on Earth?"

"To ascend," Mary said. "To learn the lessons necessary to attain eternal life. To become the best version your soul can become."

"Right. And then to eat from the tree of life. To live eternally," I said. "To return to the first Heaven once they have, right? Matriaza, that's what Heylel called it."

She gave a slow nod, expression still puzzled.

"Haven't you ever wondered why no one ever seems to reach that goal?" I asked. "Why every soul that you've met is reincarnated again and again and is never good enough to ascend?"

She blinked a few times.

"Because Laila is the only one who can grant eternal life. Laila harnesses the tree of life. God can only do so by procreating. And even so, you guys can still be killed; you aren't immortal perse. You just live a really *really* long time."

"When Earth began, the twenty-five of us were sent here to help and judge the soul's progress," Laila said. "We were supposed to determine what was and wasn't acceptable behavior for the souls to reach eternal life. The planet was loaned to us to give the people a place to live and learn before they're able to return to the first Heaven."

"The idea was that once everyone had ascended to eternal life in the first Heaven, we'd give them the planet back. But the thing is, none of us can ever return to the first Heaven because of something that God did. He made it so that we couldn't go back."

"When we learned this, the twenty-four of us started working on another plan. But he had to be punished," Laila said. "We voted to imprison him for a thousand years."

"But he was already prepared. He had the Archangels kill us to save himself," I said.

"And for turning on him, for trying to lock him up, he killed us. All twenty-four of us and our children," Laila said. "He cursed us with what Heylel called the twenty-four-year curse."

"That's why in our past lives, we died before both of us made it to twenty-four," I said. "To ensure we'd never get a happy ending, he tied our children into it."

"Micah's death calls Wormwood to take their world back," Laila said. "But since we have nowhere to go, that leaves all of the souls on this planet homeless. Judging by the book of Revelation, I'm assuming that means they're going to slaughter us. And I don't have a clue what happens to the souls after that."

The room fell silent. Everyone's breathing picked up, their feet tapped, their faces screwed up in confusion. They looked a lot like we did the day before when Heylel told us.

"But we think that if we keep Micah from being sacrificed, we can keep this from happening," I said. "If he stays alive, Wormwood doesn't return, and our lives stay what they've always been."

"Sounds like a pretty easy solution then," Brody murmured after a quiet moment. "We keep doing what we've been doing. We get Micah, we get Chris, and we dodge the apocalypse."

"What about the next life?" Wyatt said. "If we keep it from happening now, who's to say it doesn't happen in a hundred years anyway?"

"We haven't gotten that far yet," I said. "Right now, we can only do what we can do. We can't fixate on something we have no control over."

"Fair," Wyatt murmured.

"Is this why ye asked about the gods in the Fae Realm?" Kai asked. "Something that Heylel said?"

I nodded, chewing my lip. "Yeah."

"He said that we created it," Laila said. "He said that me, Jeremy, and him created the Fae Realm."

Kai stared between us. "Ye *created* the entire realm?"

"If it's that simple, why don't you just create a new world to move the people of Earth to?" Jenna asked.

"We have no recollection of this shit, Jen." Laila's eyes flashed with luminance, but quickly dulled. "We have no clue how we did any of this."

"And we didn't create the realm itself," I said. "Heylel said that we created the life on it and taught our people to travel between the dimensions. We terraformed it, so to speak. Brought plants and animals from the last world to the dimensions here on Earth to create different ecosystems that worked best with the races living on each dimension."

"So you were aliens," Hannah muttered.

"Apparently, everything on this planet is alien," Laila said. "None of us are indigenous to Earth."

Celena thought hard for a moment. "Guess those ancient alien theorists weren't too far off. I always liked that shit. Maybe this is why."

"So ye..." Kai murmured as he looked between me and Laila. "Heylel is Solais, then. The bringer of light must be the day." His eyes met mine. "And you must have been Nix. The lord darkness."

I didn't really get what that meant, or where the concept came from. But it'd been a common phrase I'd heard throughout my life. That I was dark. Not twisted, not mean, not evil. Just dark. It had to have some deeper symbolism; I just wasn't sure what that was yet.

But I'd find out soon enough.

"I'm guessing," I said.

"And you." He looked over Laila. "You were Vèa. You were the mother of the Fae people. The Great Mother."

Laila swallowed hard. "That's what Heylel said."

"Well." Leah huffed and brought herself to her feet. "I'm going to go make a very large drink. If that's all."

"Just about covers it," I said. "We're going to meet with Heylel again soon. But in the meantime, if you guys have any questions you think we should ask him, start making a list. We'll bring it with us when we see him next."

CHAPTER FIFTY-SIX

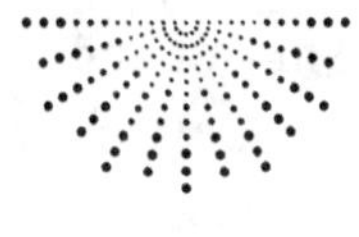

LAILA

My gaze shifted over Jeremy as he searched for a T-shirt in the pile of clothes I hadn't had time to put away. As he rummaged, I looked over his chest in the mirror. I often wondered how he was able to maintain a slightly toned physique eating the way that we did. He didn't have a six pack, but his muscles were still defined. His shoulders weren't very broad or bulky, but it looked like he worked out every now and then.

Staring at him, I wondered what he would have been like all those centuries ago. He was a god of fertility. Maybe that's why he always looked so cute with a baby on his arm.

If I was known as the Great Mother, and Jeremy was known as the Great Father, what did that equate to in modern interpretations of mythology? The only father I knew of in mythology was Odin, and he was kind of a prick. Zeus was another notable father god in Greek mythology, but he was a cheating womanizer that fucked literally anything with a pulse.

That wasn't Jeremy. I certainly wasn't Hera.

What I should have done—instead of sitting there and questioning to myself—was hop on Google and look up the names of the gods most prominent in Celtic culture. But it was the Christian god aspect that threw me for a loop.

That's what this seemed to center around—the Abrahamic religions. After all, that's where my son and I were prophesied. What I didn't realize was that that perspective was from one of twenty-five of us.

We weren't just Elohim.

But I'll get to that part of the story eventually.

He caught my stare in the mirror and smiled. "What?"

"Just looking at you." I smiled back. "Wasn't an invitation, if that's what you're thinking."

A chuckle left his lips as he turned to meet my gaze. "Damn it."

I held my smile. He walked across the room and lowered himself to the bed. And I let out a slow, quiet breath. "I'm sorry."

His head tilted. "For what?"

"Being short with you today," I said. "And snapping earlier. I'm not mad at you or anything, I'm just... I'm in my head, ya know?"

He smiled. "It's okay, baby. You aren't like me; I know silence doesn't mean you need to talk. It means you need me to shut up. And that's okay."

I laughed, head tilting to the side. Surely, he had some profound reasoning behind that, but it sounded like a riddle. "What?"

He took my hand. "When I'm ashamed of something, I hide it. I get quiet. That's what every single thing that's happened negatively between us boils down to. Me, being short with you. But you're different. If you're quiet, it's because you're working through something. And you have a lot to work through after yesterday. It's okay."

Well, it was sweet that he knew me well enough to know that. I supposed it'd make sense considering he'd known me for thousands of years. But still, that kind of made me wonder...

A slight smile played at my lips. "Are you keeping something from me right now?"

Jeremy smiled back. "No. No, my conscious is pretty clear at the moment. But it's just... It's okay. If you aren't ready to talk about all of this, you don't have to. I'm alright. Don't worry about me."

"It's just so fucking bizarre. All of it. Us... As gods."

"I thought we weren't gods." He smirked. "I thought that word was small dick energy."

I laughed, smacking his chest. "You know what I mean."

A quiet chuckle left him too. He traced his thumb along the back of mine, then lifted our knuckles to his lips. "It is pretty crazy. But... But at the same time, people recorded those stories for a reason. They were relevant for some reason. And maybe this was why. It got twisted on the way down because that's what happens when stories are told by word of mouth and rewritten over and over. All those stories in the Vatican that didn't make it past the final edits? I'm sure there's a lot of knowledge in those that they kept out for a reason too."

I let out a huff of a laugh and leaned back against the bed frame. Shaking my head, I rubbed my eyes. "You know what's crazy?"

"Hmm?"

"I was an atheist before I met you."

He smiled, inching his way up the bed beside me. "Well, technically, you weren't wrong. Gods don't exist. They're just people."

"I don't just mean gods." I rested my head against his chest. "I mean, Angels. And Demons. And fucking fairies."

He laughed and ran his fingers through my hair. "Stranger than fiction, huh?"

I thought for a moment. These myths couldn't have all been biblical. The myth of the par animarum is found in Greek mythology. There, it was Zeus who split the souls apart. "In Greek mythology...." I looked up to meet his gaze. "Who do you think we were? In their stories, I mean."

"Huh," he muttered. "I don't know. I could see you as Athena."

I laughed. "The goddess of wisdom?"

"And war and art."

"I am the least wise person alive."

"You made women suffer the pain of childbirth for wisdom." He grinned.

My face screwed up, and I sat forward. "Adam chose to take in that knowledge too. It's bullshit that Eve's the one that takes the fall for—"

He laughed. "I'm kidding, Laila."

"Athena never had kids either." I put my head back to his chest. "And never married. I'm pretty sure she was asexual, honestly."

He chuckled.

We could debate those theories for hours. But our real names never made it to human mythologies. We were identified by our abilities on Earth.

The only mythology that got it right? The Fae. Because they hadn't jaded their religious heritage. Maybe that was because when we ruled there, we weren't tyrannical monsters with small dick energy.

I took his hand in mine. My fingers twined through his. "So I guess it's official then. We're never going to be normal."

"Starting to look that way," he murmured.

My phone rang on the side table, and I groaned. Max's name flashed across the screen. I answered the call and held it to my ear. "Hey, man."

"Hey," he murmured with a sniffle. "Hey, are you busy?"

Max didn't cry often. But his mom was on hospice. So, a call from him at midnight fighting back sobs told me all I needed to know.

My chest grew tight, and a lump formed in my throat.

I stood and grabbed my hoody from the armchair. "No, just getting ready for bed. What's wrong? Is everything okay?"

"It's my mom." He cleared his throat in a failing attempt to level his voice. "She... She's really not doing good, Lai. They don't think she's going to make it to the morning, but she has a DNR, and she's maxed out morphine, so I just have to watch this thing slowly kill her."

That lump got thicker, water burning my irises. We all knew it was coming, but my life had been too crazy to really take it in. And I loved Mrs. Campbell. I spent a good chunk of my adolescence on her couch and stealing bottles from her liquor cabinet. I'd visited a handful of times, but I wanted to say my final goodbyes.

"Oh no." My voice was quiet and soft. "I'm so sorry, Max. Is there anything I can do?"

"Thanks. Yeah, she's... She's in a lot of pain right now. And I know there's nothing you can do to make her better but do you—Do you have a way to make this easier for her?"

No, I couldn't heal her. But I did have a way to take her pain away. Or at least to make it bearable until she passed.

"Let me get my shoes on, and I'll be right over."

"Thank you." He sniffed again. "You can teleport, the nurses already left."

"Okay, I'll be there in five minutes." I started to the closet. "Hang in there alright?"

"Yeah, we'll be alright. Thanks again, Lai."

I slid the phone into my hoodie pocket.

Jeremy met my gaze in the closet doorway. "What's wrong?"

"Max's mom." I pulled on my tennis shoes. "She's only got a few hours left, and she's in a lot of pain. I'm going to go sit with him. Can you stay with Mills?"

"Yeah, sure. We'll be here. Tell him I said I'm sorry," Jeremy said.

CHAPTER FIFTY-SEVEN

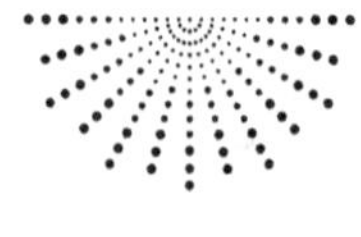

LAILA

arm air from the register floated down around me. The smell of baby powder mixing with fresh laundry drifted to my nose. That's always how Denise smelled. I dreaded the fact that this would be the last time I breathed in that scent. I glanced around the tidy kitchen and fought the pit in my stomach.

So many memories in that room. Max, Adrian, and I used to sit at that round table in the corner and play Apples to Apples in elementary school while Denise cooked at the stove. Then Cards Against Humanity when we made it to our teens.

She'd laugh, saying that we needed to wash our mouths out with soap.

Damn.

I'd barely spent any time with that woman since I entered adulthood. Life had happened. I was just too busy. And now, she was on her makeshift deathbed set up in the living room because she couldn't walk up and down the steps anymore.

Fuck, I was gonna miss her.

But at least I had a few more minutes.

My slippers squeaked against the aged linoleum as I started into the front room.

Max looked up at me beneath the mop of mousy brown hair hanging in his brown eyes. "Hey."

"Hey." I gave a gentle smile. My gaze shifted over Denise's feeble body laid on that tiny bed. She barely opened her eyes. The oxygen mask around her cheeks nearly whistled. I sat in the chair beside Max and reached for her cool hand against the fuzzy blanket. "Hi, Mrs. Campbell."

Her shaking hand reached for the oxygen mask at her face. Eyes fluttering open, she slowly pulled it down her cheeks and spoke through dry, cracking lips. "Hey, sweetie."

I smiled and summoned a bit of moisture from the air to her dry mouth. "How are you feeling?"

"Not too good today," she whispered.

My smile lowered. I gave a slow nod. "What hurts?"

"Everything." She pulled a pain-filled, forced smile to her lips. Tears pearled across her soft brown eyes. "Dying just hurts."

"It'd be too easy if it didn't, huh?" I solemnly smiled back. She made out what she could of a laugh. I turned to Max. "Should I just do it?"

He held back tears and gave a nod. I stood and sat beside her on the bed. My thumb traced the back of hers, gently bringing that sparkling gold energy from my skin and watching it dance around her. Her brows pleated, watching the light radiate from my hand up her arm.

"What is that?" Her gaze made it clear she was unsure if she was hallucinating from the drugs while my light engulfed her body.

"I'm not really sure." I kept my voice quiet, soothing. "We don't have a name for it."

As it drifted across her face, her tense expression lightened. A soft, genuine smile lifted her lips. A quiet laugh left her, eyes closing for a moment. Then they opened and met mine blinking hard. "What are you?"

"She's an Angel, Mom." Max sat on the other side of the bed beside us.

Her eyes closed, and her smile widened. She rolled her head back to the pillow and made out what she could of a laugh. "I knew I liked you."

I chuckled, still holding the energy around our bodies. "I always liked you too, Mrs. Campbell."

"He did it," she murmured with a slow nod and closed eyes. "He did it."

"Who did it, Mom?" Max asked.

"I prayed that God would send someone to watch over you." Her eyes parted open, and she smiled. "And he did. He did it, and she was here all along."

I smiled, tears burning my eyes.

Max wiped the corner of his, forcing a smile. "I guess he did, huh?"

He did help some people; I will say that. He wasn't *all* bad. The asshole just had a personal vendetta against me. And my family.

Her eyes opened a little wider. She looked between mine. "Am I going to heaven, Laila?"

My watery eyes overflowed. I fought the urge to sob, summoning a smile to my lips. "Yeah, Mrs. Campbell. You're going to heaven."

She smiled. "I can't wait to see my mom."

Fighting the yearn to break into a million pieces proved the hardest thing I ever had to do. She wasn't going to Heaven. No one was. She'd sit in purgatory until the universe figured out which body she'd be best born into next. Her mother was probably around our age in a new body somewhere in the world already. Maybe they'd meet again. But they wouldn't remember one another.

Max caught my gaze and fought the unimaginable fear my face must have invoked.

"You'll take care of my baby boy, right, Laila?" Denise looked between my eyes. "You'll keep him safe for me?"

I wiped a tear from my eye. "I will, Mrs. Campbell."

"You promise?"

I cleared my throat and glanced at Max with a smile. "I promise."

She smiled, nodded slightly, and closed her eyes.

And I kept that promise.

I held that gold shimmering light around her body until the moment her soul left her body. About two hours later, Denise told Max she loved him one more time. She drifted away.

Max held her hand for forty-five minutes before we called 911. I held his shoulders as they lifted his mother from the hospital bed to a gurney. He fought the urge to sob as they covered her with a white sheet and rolled her into an ambulance.

But once she was inside, it all flooded out. He broke. He lowered himself to the ground beside her bed and wept as the morning sun peeked in through the windows. His body quaked like a boat in a storm as I twisted my arms around his broad, shaking shoulders.

After he found some solace, he asked if he could stay with Jeremy and I for a night or two. Of course, I said yes. I wouldn't be able to stay in that house either.

I flashed home, grabbed a necklace from Leah, gave it to him, and returned to the house. We blew up the air mattress in Jeremy's junk room and he fell asleep a few hours later.

Most of the funeral arrangements had been in place since Denise first learned that she was sick. Still, in the coming days, I helped Max with the minuscule details. Writing the obituary, ordering the flowers, booking the preacher.

Denise's death hit me harder than any death before ever had. I hadn't given much thought to what happens when we died until recently. But now, I knew what happened. And it wasn't pearly gates and streets of gold.

It was another life with the same pits and peaks of the last.

CHAPTER FIFTY-EIGHT

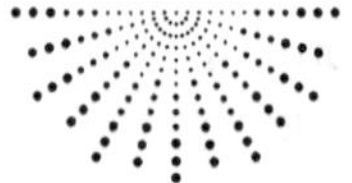

MARCH 28, 2022 - JEREMY

I took in the beautiful woman in white leaning over a table in the room I'd only seen once in this lifetime. But as I stood in the Elder's Hall in that memory, I felt as I did when I stood behind the counter at Moe's. Like I was there every day. Like it was nearly a second home

Her dress draped over her body like a cloud floating through the blue skies. Tiny straps hung over her shoulders, a thin sheer material molded around her breasts where her nipples poked against the fabric, flowing delicately to the floor from there to expose a golden, curvy silhouette.

She didn't look exactly like my Laila. But those brilliant green eyes were my wife. That long, dark flowing hair, although curly, wasn't much different. Her features were a bit more prominent than the Laila I knew, but she was still beautiful. I couldn't say that either she or my Laila were more beautiful. They were both gorgeous.

As my gaze washed over the straps of her gown down her shoulders and bust, a language I couldn't understand left my lips. She looked up and smiled. She replied in the same tongue. It was similar to Elvan, but it was a tad softer. I started toward her and spoke in a deep, yet gentle tone. I touched her hips, whispering into the soft hair at her neck. I breathed in the soft, almost floral scent of her skin. Like tea and honey.

She chuckled and smacked my chest.

I laughed, shifted my hands around her waist, and looked down at the papers laid out on the table. One of my hands brushed hair from her neck. She pointed to letters that looked to be some type of cuneiform. She spoke for a moment. She rubbed her eyes. I leaned down and touched my lips to her neck as she continued to ramble, gesturing to words and maps I barely paid half a mind to.

She turned and looked at me over her shoulder with a vivid green gaze. She muttered something. I laughed. She fought the smile that pulled at her lips before laughing. I kissed her cheek and inched my hand at her hip down the back of her dress. She chuckled and murmured something as I pulled her skirt up her leg. I whispered in return. Then my hand crept around to the soft curls at her pelvis, slipping downward to her moist opening and back up to her clit.

She sighed, closed her eyes, and her head of dark curls fell against my chest. I spun my fingers in a slow circle against her clit, listening to a quiet moan leave her lips. Her hand drifted up to graze my cheek. Her other hand dropped to the string that bound my pants. My pointer finger slid along her lips before slipping inside of her. A slow sigh left her mouth, and I murmured something in her ear.

She let out a laugh, muttered something in return, and snuck her hand into my pants. A heavy breath left my lips at the feel of her warm skin against my dick. She said something else.

I laughed and hiked her skirt high enough to reveal her bare ass. I grabbed my dick and helped it inside of her. She heaved in a gasp. I murmured something in her ear, and she laughed again. I grasped her hips and yanked them into mine.

A moan left her as she arched her back for me. I raised my hand to her neck and pulled her back against me. She sighed and met my gaze from below. I smiled, moving my hand at her hip to her clit, still holding her throat. Her brows raised, biting her moaning lips. My smile widened, and I pushed in and out of her faster.

After a few minutes, I grasped ahold of her and swiftly lifted her to the table. Her long dark brown curls fell into my face as I hauled her to the edge and grasped the side of her neck in my hand. She giggled, tugged my lips to hers, and moved my thumb to her clit. I pulsed in and out of her for a few moments, listening to her moan in my ear as I kissed her lips and then down her neck to her breasts.

Although I was dreaming, I could feel her clench around me as her legs tightened at my waist. I felt the warmth radiating from her palms just as I did in this life. I *felt* her orgasm, and then my own, as my barely opened eyes looked at the empty Elder's Hall over her shoulder. My body felt blissful for a moment.

Then my gaze caught the cracked door along the back wall. At first, I wasn't sure, but I squinted and caught a glimpse of someone standing beside the door.

My heart hammered against my ribs as my eyes shot open.

I panted hard, struggling to catch my breath and come back to reality.

I turned and took a glance at Laila sleeping beside me with her hands curled up to her chest.

Those dreams woke me at least three times a month since our meeting with Heylel. And although I really enjoyed it when I was in it, I felt grimy when I woke up. Granted, I knew that woman was my wife. And I ultimately had nothing to feel guilty for. But it felt as real as fucking Laila did.

I'm not sure why all that I'd seen so far was us fucking, but that dream was the first time I saw someone else. I couldn't be entirely sure I even saw someone, but I'm not sure what I expected. We were in the Elder's Hall—not exactly a private location. I guess that hadn't changed much. We always had a thing for public sex.

Maybe it was because those were my fondest memories from those lives. But Heylel said that Laila and I had kids then, and I hadn't seen them yet. I guess my soul decided seeing how passionately in love the two of us felt was more important than anything that could help us save the fucking world.

As I sat up with a raging boner, I reached for Laila's arms. Just as Milly started to cry on the baby monitor. My head hung.

"It's your turn," Laila grumbled with a shooing motion.

"It's time to get up anyway."

She yanked the blanket over her head. "My alarm has not gone off. It is not time to get up."

So much for my boner.

"Yeah, yeah." I started to my feet. Milly cried as I walked from the room up the stairs. A yawn escaped my lips when my gaze met hers.

She stopped crying and extended her arms out to me. I smiled and, before I could make it across the room, she appeared against my chest.

Ill prepared for her sudden weight, she plummeted. I rapidly teleported her into my arms. My eyes widened, and a gasp left my lips.

"Laila! Laila!" I teleported back to the bedroom.

"What?!" she yelled toward the stairs.

I bounced with joy. "She just teleported."

"What?" She sat up in the bed and started to her feet. "She hasn't even walked yet."

"I teleported before walking too," I said. "It's like how some kids skip crawling and go straight to walking."

Laila grinned as we met beside the bed. "Did you do that, Milly? Or is Daddy just trying to steal your first teleport?"

Milly giggled and dropped her head against my chest.

"You got the first word. I get this," I said.

"What were you doing?" she asked.

"I walked into her room, and she saw me, and just." I gestured to her in my arms.

"Teleported right into your arms?"

"Almost fell. But yeah, she did."

"No shit," she muttered. "Make sure we write that down in the baby book."

CHAPTER FIFTY-NINE

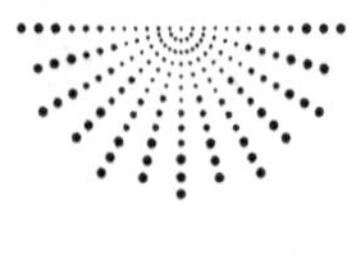

JEREMY

This time of year sucked. Not the weather; I loved spring. But I hated the fucking taxes.

That's what I was doing. Staring down at the 1099 on the desk. I lifted my warm cup of coffee from the edge and raised it to my lips. The bitter flavor popped on my tongue. I considered dousing the document with it. Although, I supposed I'd just have to print it out and do it again.

"Taking my smoke break," Adam said in the office doorway. He held up a small white joint and gave a nod toward the back door. "Care to join me?"

I looked up from the papers and stood. "Please."

He laughed as I followed him out the rear exit. I lowered myself to the step outside. The cool spring air brushed against my cheeks, bright sun shining in my eyes. The smell of honeysuckle from the tree line behind the diner wafted to my nose.

Adam flicked the lighter to the paper at his lips. I gestured toward it. "I might need you to get me some of that. I don't like going through Max's dude. He's sketchy."

"Yeah, just let me know." Adam passed it to me. "How's he doing, anyway?"

"He's good," I said. "I think he's in California visiting somebody him and Laila went to school with right now."

"Is he coming back?" he asked.

I huffed. "I wouldn't."

He laughed. "Yeah, me neither. Hey, do you think you and Lai could watch Luka this weekend?"

"Probably, we don't have any plans. It's going to be a few more weeks before we have enough energy to do that spell to extract Micah's energy."

He grinned. "But it's gonna be soon."

I smiled back and gave a nod. "Very soon."

Helena had said she could pull it off now. But we were giving it a few more days—maybe a week—for Nastya's energy to duplicate. Just the thought made me smile. I could be holding my son in a week or two.

Adam smiled and took a hit off the joint. "It's going to be really cool to see Chris again. Ya know, when he's not trying to kill one of us."

"Yeah. Yeah, I can't wait. But patience is key this time. We've got to play our cards right. You're going to take care of the diner while we're gone if Max isn't back yet, right?"

"That's the plan," he said.

Silence crept in for a moment. As it did, my mind traveled back to that memory dream fuck. "So let me get your opinion on something."

"Throw it at me." He leaned against the handrail and passed me the joint.

I took in a long drag. As I exhaled, I ran my hand against my mouth. "It's not cheating if it's a dream."

He raised a brow. "Well, duh."

I leaned back on my palms. "Then why do I feel like I'm having an affair?"

He laughed. "Who is it?"

"I think it's Laila," I muttered. "Like, in one of our really old past lives. The first one, maybe."

He laughed again. "It's definitely not cheating."

"But it's so real. It's like I'm really there, dude. I can feel it, I can smell it, I can taste it. It's just as real as this is."

"Does she look like Laila?" Adam asked.

"Kind of. The same complexion, same bright green eyes. Laila's a little daintier though. Smaller nose, thinner lips, rounder jaw. And my Laila's a little paler. That could just be a tan though," I said. "But it's not her though. Not the Laila I know."

"And that's all you've seen is you two having sex?"

"So far. But last night, I think I saw someone watching us. Or at least walking in and walking back out. I don't know," I said. "I woke up."

"Kinky," he muttered. "Well, don't know what to say about all that. But have you told her?"

I laughed. "That I'm having wet dreams about our past lives? No. No, I haven't."

"You should." Adam shrugged. "Show it to her. You'll probably have some great sex after."

I huffed. She'd been kind of in her own world lately. Not that I blamed her or anything; we were getting everything ready for Micah. Which was great, don't get me wrong. But she'd been training really hard with Helena and Moriah the past few weeks, and she was exhausted every day when she got home. "Sex has kind of been on the back burner."

"Maybe your blue balls are drawing out those memories." Adam grinned.

"Probably. But it's alright though, ya know? We're old, we have kids. Micah's all that matters right now."

"Yeah, it's going to be a hard adjustment for him. Being in a cell his whole life with one person and then coming into a family with a million of us in and out all the time. I'm sure it won't be easy."

He was pretty shy. At least, the first time we met he was. The second time, he acted like he'd known me forever. And in all the snippets Laila showed me of him since, he'd been a bouncing bean.

But our family was huge. We were a little overwhelming to anyone who walked into our lives. He'd be okay though; it'd just take some time.

"Yeah, I know," I said. "Laila's been talking to a child psychologist from an underground hospital in Missouri. She told us to call her with anything at any time when we get him home."

"Probably a good idea." He breathed out a heavy sigh. He tossed the burned joint into the dumpster. "He's going to be really close to Chris when he gets out, you know."

I bit back my jealousy. Every part of me was abundantly grateful for my brother having been there for my son. But I can't say that I didn't hold plenty of animosity toward him for getting the time with Micah I'd wanted since he was born. Especially since I never knew when he was coming and only had met him twice, and both times were in an alternate reality.

"Yeah. Yeah, I've thought about that. We got him a bed in one of the other bedrooms upstairs if he wants to stay with us."

"That's not going to be easy for you, Jeremy." Adam met my gaze. "Micah kind of looks like Chris as a dad—"

"He knows I'm his dad."

"Yeah, but I'm just saying. Chris has been there his whole life; you guys haven't even met yet."

"I'm well aware, Adam." I gritted my teeth. "It's not ideal. But he's young. The first few years are going to be hard but in a few, he might not even remember all of this."

He raised a brow. "You aren't going to tell him?"

Why the hell would we? We didn't want him to remember the awful things he'd gone through. I wanted him to lose those nightmares. I damn sure didn't want him remembering his mother's rapist as his father.

"No." My nose crinkled. "If he can forget that we missed out on the first few years of his life, then good. If he doesn't have to live with that shit in his head, then even better."

"Yeah, but…" He trailed off. "But what about his scars?"

Supposed I hadn't thought about that much. But we'd figure it out. He was only two and a half. We had time. "I don't know."

"Sorry, not trying to be a Debbie downer. I just... I know it's not going to be easy."

Maybe it would. Maybe it wouldn't. But nothing could be harder than the past few years had been.

"It'll be easier than missing another birthday," I said. "It'll be easier than fearing for his life all day every day."

"Yeah. Yeah, that's true," Adam said. "I know everything's going to be fine. But... I mean, if something goes wrong and you and Laila are gone for a while..."

"Milly and Tink are going to Leah," I said. "We're still working out the kinks of who stays back and who goes. Laila and I are first, but the rest of the details haven't been decided. They probably won't be until it's actually going down. We need someone with strong active powers to stay back with Leah, Hannah, and Milly, but Kai and Celena are too valuable not to have if we need."

"Well, you can put me wherever you need me. I'll go to the front line or play bodyguard. Whatever you guys think is best."

CHAPTER SIXTY

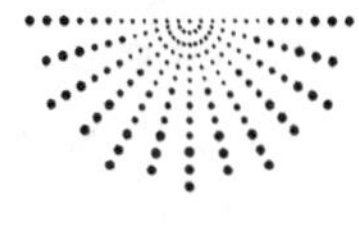

LAILA

"No, look." I pointed to the video on Leah's computer. A small burst of light appeared inside the window of a barn in Utah. We'd set up video cameras months ago and spent hours each day going over motion activity on them. "That could be something."

"We can go check it out, but that looked like a camera flare to me," Leah said.

"It's worth a shot."

As she clicked back to the satellite images, she blew out a long billowing sigh. She reached for the glass and bottle of brandy behind her laptop. I glanced at the clock reading 11:30 a.m..

Leah looked over me and rolled her eyes. "You and Jeremy are going on a suicide mission in a few weeks. I might end up raising another child. Let me enjoy my youthful single life for a couple more weeks. And I never judged your binge drinking, bitch."

"I'm not judging," I muttered. "Sorry."

Two and a half months ago, Leah showed up on my doorstep bawling her eyes out with a bottle of vodka and a tub of ice cream. She and Haley called it quits, and she found herself in a heavy slump. The old, sad, and mopey Leah was back.

That night was the first time I saw her *really* cry. I'd seen a number of glistening tears over the years, but that night, they fell like a summer storm. Haley broke her heart. I don't know all the details, but I know that she'd been sleeping with someone else for a while. The breakup was painful and messy. At that point, Leah was still mourning, and I was a little worried about her, but she was right. I was in no place to cast stones. When Jeremy and I broke up, I stumbled into bar after bar and did way more drugs than I should have. I guess you could say people in our family have similar coping mechanisms.

"It's alright." She pulled off her glasses and rubbed her eyes. "I'm sorry. I'm just not in a good place right now."

"Don't worry about it. We all have those days."

She rubbed her eyes "Where's Milly?"

"Sleeping." I glanced at the baby monitor. "She's been teleporting all morning."

"Really?" Leah asked. "Where to?"

"Not far. Just across the room. From her car seat to the couch right after I strapped her in, for instance." My eyes rolled.

"Little shit." She laughed with a look at her on the monitor. "I can't wait 'til she gets to meet her brother."

I laughed. "*I* can't wait to meet her brother."

"Me neither." She paused, gazing over Milly. "I can't wait to see mine."

"Soon," I said. "Soon."

I had faith in that. I knew we were close.

But I did have a bad feeling.

I wasn't sure where it came from. Was it because I was worried about Jeremy? Was it because I was worried about them sacrificing Micah before we got to him? Was it because I was scared we'd end up in captivity for months? I didn't know. But there was a pit in my stomach.

That didn't change anything. Regardless of my nerves, I was going to do what needed done. I was going to right the wrong I'd made all those years ago. I was going to bring my baby home. Even if it was the last thing I did.

"Hey, have you seen my pink sweater anywhere?" Lydia pranced down the steps. "I've been looking for it everywhere."

"In the dryer, I think," Leah said.

"Awesome, thanks. Can I take Tink with me on a hike, Lai? Don't worry, I'm not leaving the border. I just want to run and work on helping some of the flowers and stuff get back to full bloom."

"Yeah, she's out there with Wyatt and Celena already. I think I saw them by the tree line going toward the driveway." I gestured toward the back yard.

"Alright, cool." She typed on her phone for a moment before placing her headphone in her ear. As she clicked a button, the song *Lydia* by Highly Suspect played. She was more of a Halsey and Doja Cat sort of girl.

"Doesn't really sound like your kind of taste," I said.

She made a waving motion with her hand. "Some kid told me to listen to it."

"Not exactly a healthy love song either," Leah muttered.

She rolled her eyes. "It's because my name's Lydia."

"Obviously. But still," Leah said.

"Yeah, Jeremy sang *Layla* by Eric Clapton to me once. But that's like, actually a love song so it was cute."

"It wasn't intended to be a love song," Lydia grumbled. "But I like it. It's catchy."

"I love Highly Suspect," Leah said. "Listen to *Sixteen*; it's really pretty."

"True," I said.

My phone rang on the counter. As I reached for it, my eyes widened a bit.

Tina Davis

That could be a good thing. Or a bad thing. There was no way to know until I answered.

I slid the green bar and held it to my ear. "Long time no talk, agent."

"Too long, huh?" Tina said.

"Seems that way." I smiled, and she chuckled. "What's going on?"

"Can we meet?" she asked.

Leah leaned over to listen to my call as I said, "Sure. What's going on? Do you have information?"

"I do. Meet me in my kitchen in one hour," she said. "And bring Jeremy."

Fuck, was she about to tell me they found my son's body? Is that why it had to be in person? My heart thudded in my chest. I hurried to my feet. "Is everything okay?"

"Yeah. Yeah, everything's fine. Good, even. But we need to talk. In private, not on a phone."

She said good. Good news.

My racing heart slowed. Only a tad, but it slowed.

"See you in an hour then," I said.

The call ended, and I slid my phone into my back pocket. I glanced at Leah's glass of alcohol. "Can you watch the stinker, or should I ask Kai?"

"I'll dump it out." Leah huffed, starting to her feet. "That was Tina, right?"

"It was," I said. "I'm going to go grab Jeremy. Hopefully we won't be gone long."

She poured her brandy down the sink. "We'll be here. Unless Milly decides to teleport somewhere. We're going to have to put a tracker on her or something; we almost lost Brody a million times when he was little."

"The Owlet for teleporting tots."

"Could make us millionaires." Leah smiled.

CHAPTER SIXTY-ONE

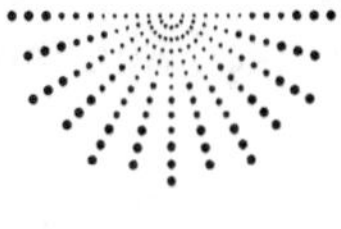

LAILA

The smell of greasy burgers and fries settled in my lungs. My shoes stuck against the sticky tile, walking down the stairs into the kitchen. I glanced at Adam at the stove and sent a wave. He smiled back. I turned to the office.

Jeremy's head rested in his palm; elbow propped against the wooden desk. His flowing black locks hung in his blue eyes. A cup of fragrant, steaming coffee sat on the coaster by our family photo. We'd have to get a new one taken soon.

Smiling, I leaned against the doorframe. "Hey."

Jeremy looked up from the paperwork and smiled. "Hey, beautiful."

"Think you can take a break?" I gestured toward the surplus of forms. "Tina Davis wants to meet with us."

He raised his brows. He stood and started around the desk. "Yeah, I can get to this later. What's going on?"

"She didn't give me details, but she said it was good news and she didn't want to talk on the phone."

"So it's about them," he said. "Yeah, let's go."

I started into the room and sat at the chair in front of the desk. "We have a little time. She said be there in an hour. I can help you finish up whatever you're working on."

"It's just the event schedule for the concerts downstairs," he said. "I'm still waiting to hear back from a few musicians to fill the rest of the time slots."

"*You* could fill some of the time slots." I smiled and took his hand. "If you wanted to, I mean."

"I'm alright." He sloped against the desk before me. "It's busy here without Max. And Sophie quit, did I tell you that?"

Aw, damn. I loved Sophie; she was my go-to server. She'd worked here since I started as a teenager. She taught me a lot about dealing with shitty customers.

My eyes widened a bit. "What? No, you did not tell me that."

"She's moving to Indiana. Something with her family, I don't know. Her last day's next Tuesday."

"Aww." I frowned. "She's been here forever."

"Yeah, we got her a cake to say goodbye," Jeremy said. "New beginnings can be a good thing."

I nodded.

He fell silent for a moment, eyes shifting between mine. He cleared his throat and sat beside me. He glanced to the open door and lowered his voice. "Have you had any memories from our life when we were the Elders?"

"Not yet," I said. He nodded, but his uncomfortable gaze made me wonder why he'd asked. I raised a brow. "Have you?"

Biting his lip, his eyes shifted between mine. "I think."

I glanced back at the door and telekinetically swung it shut. I turned my gaze to his and leaned forward with a grin. "Well, what have you seen?"

An awkward, bashful smile pulled at his lips. Then a laugh left them. "So far it's just been fucking."

"Huh," I murmured. "Is it good?"

He looked at me funny. "The sex?"

He seemed surprised I asked. That was typical Jeremy though. He was the jealous type, so he thought I was too. And granted, in most situations, I was. But he was talking about sex with me. I couldn't be jealous about that. In fact, I was really curious about what it looked like when two gods fucked. And I wanted to know how hot I was then.

"Yeah. Like, not boring missionary?" I asked.

He laughed. "Yeah. Yeah, it's great. Like, really great. Well, not better than ours. Pretty similar actually. So yeah, really great."

"What do I look like?" I grinned and sat forward. "Am I hot?"

"You're always hot." He smiled, cheeks reddening. So yes, that meant I was hot.

My grin got bigger. "Yeah, but does she look like me?"

"Kind of." He took a piece of my hair and twirled it around his finger. "Same color but curly. Your eyes are green, and you're still fair skinned. A little darker though. I think we spent more time outside then. But your face is a little different. You're a little softer looking than she is. Or was, I guess."

"What do *you* look like?" I smiled and traced my finger along the inside of his palm.

"I haven't looked in a mirror." Jeremy twined his fingers through mine. "But I have dark hair. Darker than my hair now, almost a bluish black."

"Still long, I bet."

"Still long." He smiled. "But I think I'm a little bigger. Either that, or you're ridiculously small."

"It's not fair, you know. You get to these hot dreams with a bitch that is your wife but isn't your wife, and I get nightmares."

"I feel kind of guilty for it if that helps." He smiled.

A laugh left my lips. "Not right now because we're about to leave. But tonight, show it to me." I lifted my hand to his jaw with a smile. "It's been a while."

He grinned, leaned forward, and touched his lips to mine.

CHAPTER SIXTY-TWO

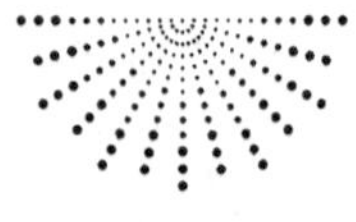

JEREMY

Warm spring sun shined in through the open windows, wafting the scent of the roses on the kitchen table to my nose. I looked out at the trees rustling in the wind. My anxious heart skipped a beat in my chest.

Tina had told Laila this was good news. That meant this was probably a lead on Micah. Maybe by this time next week, I'd be watching wind fly through the trees with my son.

"Laila, Jeremy." Tina walked into the kitchen from the hall. "Nice to see you guys, you look great."

"Thanks." Laila smiled.

"Likewise." I reached out to shake her hand with a friendly smile. "How have you been?"

"Hanging in there." She sat at the table. "You know how it is. Same shit, different day."

"That I do," I muttered as Laila and I pulled out a chair.

"So what's all of this about?" Laila asked. "You said you had information, right?"

"I do," she said. "I think I have a rough idea of where your son might be. Problem is, so does the FBI."

My heart raced. Good news, but bad news. If they got to them first, they'd scare them off. Then they'd teleport somewhere new before we had time to take care of Peterson, Nastya, and Amy. "Where?"

"Northern edge of California. We haven't pinpointed an exact location, but we picked up a picture of Amy Ramirez on camera at a Walmart outside of Shasta two days ago. She had on a hoodie and sunglasses, but the wind caught it and gave us enough of a picture to pick her up on the algorithms."

"Shasta, California," Laila murmured. Her gaze turned to mine, voice echoing through my mind. *That's an intersection of two ley lines. We have a few buildings marked in that area to be searched in the next few days.*

"We're closing in on them, Tina." I leaned forward in my seat. "If the FBI get involved, if they go after them—"

"They're either going to get killed or scare them off," Tina said. "I know. That's why I called."

"Do you have an exact location?" Laila asked.

"Not yet. But we got the plates of the car she got into. Picked them up on a traffic cam a few miles away. It's just a matter of time, guys. We catch those plates again, we follow them back to wherever they have them, we get a warrant, and we go in guns blazing."

"But that's not going to work," I said quickly.

"I know," Tina agreed. "I know what we're up against, but they don't. You guys can take on this fight, but we can't."

"We know a few alphas in that part of California," I murmured. "If we find them first, we can kill them and leave the bodies for the FBI."

"You realize they're going to know who did it." Tina arched a brow. "If your baby is magically home and there's just a few bodies behind, you have more motive than anyone."

"Do they really give a shit? They're not just America's most wanted; they're some of the world's most wanted," I said.

"Then we tip off the police after we kill Amy and Nastya. Take Peterson and leave the doors open for them to rescue Micah and Chris," Laila said. "No one's going to blame the two of them for murder. Chris is blind. He couldn't see whoever killed them to identify in court, and no one's going to accuse him of murder when he's holding a small child."

"That might work," Tina said. "You'll still be suspects but if you're not dumb about this, if you don't teleport to the childcare center or hospital we take him to when we find him and take a plane like the rest of us, your alibi's concrete. But you can't touch a camera's surface. If there's proof you were there and two bodies turn up, you're going away. Getting your kid or not, murder's murder. Might get a light sentence considering who they are, but three murders won't be swept under the rug. They'll build a case on you quicker than you can say shit."

I squeezed Laila's hand.

Maybe not ideal. But sensible. If we knocked out Amy and Nastya, kidnapped Peterson, and left Chris and Micah for them to free, then we'd still get our family back. Maybe a few hours or weeks later than we hoped, but they'd be safe and that's all that really mattered.

Laila cleared her throat. "We'll do what we have to do. Is there going to be red tape because of the fact that he wasn't born in the states?"

"Maybe," Tina muttered. "But all things considered, you should be able to apply for dual citizenship since you're both Americans. It helps that they're stateside. And that he's white, if I'm being completely honest."

"Are we going to have to prove that he's our son?"

"Most likely," Tina said. "But the fact that Chris has been with him will help. Like Laila said though, he's blind. He didn't physically *watch* the child grow. That could be an issue at first. They're probably not going to want to release him to you immediately. There will be background checks and DNA evidence required. They aren't just gonna hand your kid over to you because he doesn't know you. It's not like he's ten and got kidnapped at seven. Y'all have never even met."

We had. And Micah knew us pretty darn well. But there was no way to explain that without making it look like we played some part in his capture and subsequent torture. We'd have to make sure Micah knew he couldn't act like he knew us.

"The only way we can let that happen is if Amy and Nastya are dead, and we have Peterson in our custody," I said. "Otherwise, we're taking our son at the first opportunity that we get."

"Well, if you get caught, you might be leaving both of your kids without a parent for a few years," Tina said. "I don't like it either, Jeremy, but there isn't a magical solution to this one. Your missing child can't show up in your arms and his captors murdered on the other side of the country. He needs to be legal. He'll need a social, and a birth certificate, and everything else that goes into a human life. You can't just sweep him up and bring him home like the rest of this didn't happen."

"Obviously," I said. "But the fact is that you can't protect my son. *They* can't protect my son."

"So we're going to need you to hold them back until we eliminate the threat," Laila murmured.

Tina clenched her jaw, letting out a half laugh. "You guys think I matter. I'm no one; I don't make those calls. The most that I can do is tell you when we're on our way."

My eyes closed as a long, heavy breath left my lips. "That'll have to do."

"We should go then." Laila stood. "We need to contact supernaturals we know in that area and get the word out. See if anyone can confirm a location from their scents."

"We get a location and we're going," I agreed. "But we have some things we have to do first. Hopefully we have an exact location by the morning."

Tina nodded. "Be safe, guys."

"Keep in touch," Laila said.

CHAPTER SIXTY-THREE

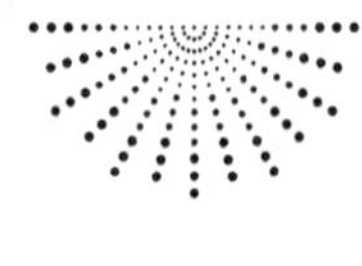

LAILA

Jeremy and I spent the next six hours making phone calls and sending people to look for one of their scents near Shasta, California. Leah leaned over her computer tapping and zooming in on possible locations before sending them out to wolves and vamps with low energy signatures that could easily, and quickly, sneak around without alerting Amy or Nastya.

By nine P.M., we had a total of six geographical places near or on a ley line in that region that *could* be where they were being held. By the morning, we expected to have a confirmed location by one of our many allies. With it happening so quick, one thing became abundantly clear.

Micah's energy needed to be extracted from my body immediately.

Like most things in our world, far easier said than done.

When Helena cast the spell to extract Chris's energy from my body while I was pregnant with Milly, we only had a drop. That's all that we needed to follow his trail, and even *it* was unpleasant to pull out of me. But with Micah, the situation required much more. Which meant it would be far more painful.

However, since we'd have a location, we could save it in case something went wrong. If we could get them without using magic, we wouldn't alert Amy or Nastya. We could get them back home to safety, then go back and do what needed done. That would also save my son the trauma of witnessing me murder the woman who cared for him since he was born.

I prayed that Micah would visit me that night. I hadn't seen him in eight days, which was the typical range of time that he came to me. I wanted to tell him we were coming. I'd already told him that he may feel one of us in his mind when we arrived, and he accepted the concept pretty quick. But I wanted to talk to him one more time before I left.

He had to know how much he meant to me. He had to understand that I was going to do everything in my power, and I would not give up on him. But if I didn't make it out on the other end, he had to know that I loved him and his sister more than I loved anything.

As I prayed, I found myself pondering who I was praying *to*. Who's guidance and protection was I asking for when the most well-known god was the one forcing me to live this shit life?

Regardless, we called Helena about extracting Micah's energy from my body. She wished that we had more time but was confident we'd at least have enough to bind two people to Micah. But she insisted I have a drink or two before she extracted his energy.

As I lay on the couch, and she set a needle the size of my shoe on the end table, I gulped down a glass of whiskey quicker than I could say ouch. Then another.

Jeremy moved the coffee table and brought a chair over for Helena. He sat beside my legs. "This is going to hurt, huh?" I asked.

He frowned. "Yeah, I think so."

"I can handle beatings. But something about needles." I shuddered.

He laughed, brushing hair behind my ear. "I wish I had that problem. But I'll do that energy thing; it might help."

"We should come up with a name for that, ya know. 'Energy thing' could be anything."

"We should, huh?" He smiled. "But who knows. This is going to hurt, but we could be holding our son at this time tomorrow."

I grinned. "It'll be worth it."

His lips curved higher as he looked between my eyes. "Almost there."

"Almost." I closed my eyes and relaxed into his hand.

"You ready, Lai?" Helena lowered herself to the chair and put a hand on my forearm.

"Let's just get it over with," I muttered. "I'm closing my eyes. Don't tell me where you're putting that needle, don't announce it before you stab me with it. Just do what you've got to do. But I'm warning you, I may cry. And if you laugh, I will punch your face."

Jeremy chuckled, and I knitted my brows. He cleared his throat and bit his smiling lip. "Sorry."

"Well, drink this first." Helena handed me a small cup. "Just pinch your nose and gulp it down."

I tilted my head back and slurped up the dirty, chemical tasting muck in the cup. With a shudder and a cough, I handed it to her and cleared my throat. I leaned back to the pillow and closed my eyes.

Jeremy's fingers coasted over mine for a moment. I heard his breathing get short. "Are you sure you know what you're doing?"

"Yes, Jeremy," Helena murmured.

Then a stab radiated in my ear. I winced and opened my eyes. He stared down at me with concerned eyes. His warm, gray and blue energy swirled from his palm to mine. My grimace faded to a smile as the needle jammed further into my ear. A sad smile held at his lips.

"I'm okay." I looked between his eyes.

The energy from his hand swirled up our arms and gradually engulfed us both. I continued to look between his pretty blue eyes. Helena murmured something in another language. As she pulled back on the plunger, my brain throbbed. Suddenly the worst migraine of my life pulsed in my skull. My vision grew disoriented. A gasp dropped into my lips. My chest involuntarily bucked forward.

Jeremy's eyes widened. He yelled something to Helena. She said something in return as pain ripped through my head.

"Hold her down," I caught Helena say.

Out of instinct, I fought against Jeremy's arms when he gripped my shoulders to the couch. But he smiled and said something that didn't register, and I relaxed in the glowing light gleaming from his body.

He smiled and gave a gentle nod. His hand at my shoulder gently grazed toward my face. Any words leaving his lips muffled by the sound of my pounding heart and liquid filled ear canal. But his gentle expression kept me levelheaded. Or maybe that was the euphoria of the light leaving his skin.

Helena continued to pull on the plunger as Jeremy held one of my shoulders in place and held my trembling head steady with the other. He murmured some soft and beautiful French term of endearment, and something shifted.

Suddenly, I was looking up into those same vibrant blue eyes. But a different version of my husband kneeled above me. He looked so close to the man that actually held me but not quite the same. His skin was a few shades darker, more of a golden than cream color. But those eyes and that hair were identical. His nasal root sat a bit more prominently above them but at first glance, I would have mixed him up with my Jeremy. They wore the same thick black scruff along that strong angled jaw and long black waves framing their diamond shaped face.

And the glow coming from his body looked identical to my Jeremy's. The grayish light that was soft enough not to hurt my eyes yet still bright enough to light a room. Speckles of blue danced through the shadows of gray that swirled through it like lightning in a dark sky.

He murmured something in a language I didn't understand, cupping my jaw with reddened, tear filled eyes. A language I didn't speak left my lips. Water from his bright blue eyes cascaded down his cheeks.

Then a soft sob left him. My bloody, shaking hands reached up to touch his face, more words I didn't understand leaving my lips. His head shook as his hand at my shoulder shifted around my back. He pulled me upward to wrap his arms around me. My eyes closed as I searched for the energy to raise my arms around him, but found myself entirely drained.

The only words that processed clearly enough for me to even slightly register came from Jeremy at my ear. Or rather, the man who Jeremy once was. "Mi lim."

CHAPTER SIXTY-FOUR

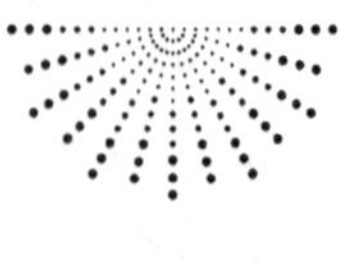

JEREMY

My confused eyes shifted between Laila's glowing green gaze. Her dazed expression seemed to look right inside of me. I couldn't understand a word leaving her lips, but I recognized it. It was that same language we spoke in the dreams. But I could understand the fear and pain behind them as tears glistened down her cheeks. Her brows pulled together, her lips quivered, her shaking hands clutched my face tight in her palms.

"She's hallucinating," Helena murmured, pulling on the plunger of the needle.

"No," I muttered. "No, she's remembering."

But what the hell was she remembering? All of my memories had been loving, and gentle. This... whatever she was seeing was a nightmare.

The moment Helena pulled the needle from her skin, Laila slammed forward and wrapped her arms around my neck. Her whispers faded as I placed my arms around her waist and put my head against her shoulder. "You're okay," I murmured at her ear, running my fingers along her hair. "You're okay."

She nodded and pushed herself further into me.

"Well, I was right." Helena tapped on the large syringe in her hand.

"We've got enough to do two bindings at least. I'm hoping I have enough of Nastya's soul to do two, too, but I might come up a little short."

Laila pulled back and wiped her eyes. "We've just got to make sure to use it on the right person then."

"It's going to be you, right?" Helena placed her hands at her hips. "Me and you should be able to hold her back long enough to get the boys out."

"That's the plan," Laila said. "But only if we don't make it home by night in their time. If we're in there, that means something happened and we need time to rework a new plan."

Helena said, "Let's hope we don't need to do it at all."

"You've got my blood samples, right?" I asked. "To bind me to Micah if you have to bind Laila to Nastya?"

"I do," she said. "If something goes wrong, I still have enough to bind Leah to Micah too."

I rubbed a tense spot at the back of my neck.

Helena breathed out a heavy sigh. "I'm going to stay back at the main house until this is done and over with. This perimeter is the safest place for anyone. Try and get some rest though, guys. You're going to need it."

My fingers found Laila's. I looked up at Helena. "We'll see you in the morning. You should get some rest too."

"Will do. Give me a lift?" she asked.

I waved my hand over her. She disappeared and I looked back to Laila. I pushed hair from her face and looked between her eyes. "That didn't look like a wet dream."

She laughed and turned her gaze to our hands. Her voice fell silent for a moment as she used her free hand to wipe a tear. "I think it was when the Archangels killed us."

I frowned, cupping her face in my hands. She looked at me with a quick shake of her head. She blinked tears away. She cleared her throat. "You did that thing. The soul light thing as I died in your arms."

"I'm sorry that's the memory you had to see," I murmured.

She managed something of a smile. "I want to see the good things."

I smiled too. She twined her fingers around mine. As the memories washed behind her closed eyes, I watched the gentle rise and fall of her chest. Her lips parted in a bit of awe.

A chuckle left my lips. Her eyes pulled open, and she smiled. "What?"

"Looked like you were enjoying that." I grinned.

She leaned forward and pressed her lips to mine. I smiled against her mouth. She lifted her knees over my lap and pushed her body into me. "Do that to me."

"Which part?" I murmured, reaching for the button on her jeans.

"All of it," she whispered.

"Jeremy." Laila turned her gaze up to meet mine.

I pushed hair from her face with a smile. "Yeah?"

"We're walking out of this together." She ran her fingertips along my jaw, eyes pleading. "Promise me we're walking out of this together."

I smiled and lifted our knuckles to my lips. "We're walking out of this together. I promise."

She smiled back as tears welled in her eyes.

I knew she was scared. And I understood why she was. But I was going to keep her safe. I didn't know how. But I knew that I would. I wasn't going to lose her again.

We'd be back in this bed in a week or two. We'd be curled up in these cotton sheets with our son and daughter beside us. Of course, we'd be clothed. But we would. I knew we would.

"We've got this, Lai. We've got a backup plan for our back up plan." I thumbed a tear from her cheek. "We're bringing our son home."

"I know. I know, I'm just..." She bit her quivering, swollen lip, fighting the urge to sob. "I don't want to be tied to a table again."

I fell quiet, wiping the salty water that gushed down her cheeks. "I'm going to be right beside you. I won't let him hurt you again."

"You don't know that," she whispered. "And I can't expect that of you, Jeremy. You haven't been in that position; you don't understand. Don't put that standard in your head because you might not be able to live up to it."

Again, she was right. I knew that anything could happen. But I was going to make sure we came out on the other side. She wasn't going to die on me in there, and I wouldn't either. He might torture me. He might hit me around a bit. But we were going to make it out. Then we were going to kill that bastard.

A slow, uneven breath left my nostrils. I ran my thumb against her cheek. "We're walking out of there together with our son and my brother. That's the only expectation I'm setting."

She swallowed hard. "That's all that matters."

Milly fussed on the baby monitor beside the bed. Laila started to her feet. But I caught her hand. I knew we weren't going to die in there. But it could be a while before we saw our baby girl again. I wanted as much time with her as possible before we left.

I gave a smile. "How about I bring her in here to sleep with us tonight?"

She managed a sad smile. "That sounds like a good idea."

I smiled back. I pulled my boxers up over my legs. I leaned down and kissed her forehead.

I spun through the air and landed beside Milly's crib. As I appeared, her sobs subsided and a smile came to my lips. "Da-da," she murmured, arms extended up to me.

A few tears burned in my eyes. I loved hearing her say that. I loved that I was who she reached for when she cried. But I won't say that I wasn't scared it'd be a while before I heard her say it again.

I lifted her against my chest and teleported back to our bedroom. Laila smiled, tugging her shirt over her head.

"You wanna sleep with me and Daddy tonight, Mills?" She grinned and lifted Milly from my arms. I stepped into my sweatpants as she sat down in the bed with Milly beside her. She turned on her lamp on the nightstand, I sat beside our daughter, and pulled the blanket over my legs. "Do you have a diaper over there?"

"I think." I rummaged through the basket on my nightstand. I tossed one her way and took a gulp from my water bottle. As she clasped the new diaper around Milly's hips, I passed the bottle her way. She grabbed it and eased out a deep breath.

"What is it?" I asked.

Her head shook. She took a long gulp. Then a quiet chuckle escaped her mouth as she wiped the edge of her lips. "You're going to be amazed at how shitty water tastes when it comes out of a rusty pipe."

I took her hand. "We don't know that we're going to be taken for sure, Lai. We might be in and out in seconds."

She lifted Milly to her chest. Her green eyes danced between mine in the soft yellow light of the lamp beside the bed. "Has anything ever been easy with them, Jeremy?"

A slow breath left my nostrils as I fell silent.

"Plan A probably won't work because it never does. Plan B might not either. Plan C might be the winner, but it could be plan D that hasn't even been thought out yet," she murmured. "We have to strive to win. But we need to expect to lose."

"We need to expect to be in this room with our son twenty-four hours from now." I squeezed her hand and looked between her eyes. "We're doing this, Laila. We're getting our son, and we're bringing him home. But right now, let's lie here and fall asleep with our baby."

She slowly lay down and rested Milly against the pillow between us. Her little face rolled to look at me. I smiled at her, and she giggled. Her chubby fist rubbed against her tired eyes. Laila took her hand and rested it against Milly's chest. I turned off the light and lay beside her, wrapping my fingers around hers.

Laila turned her fingers so that they twined between mine with Milly's hand in the middle. "Just don't let go, okay?"

"I'll *never* let go."

I was scared too. But I did exactly as I told her to. I focused on the idea of Micah being home with us. I couldn't think about the possibility of failure. We'd failed far too many times, and I had no room in my mind for more.

We were getting him back, damn it.

CHAPTER SIXTY-FIVE

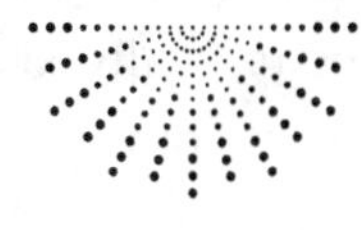

LAILA

"Mommy!" Micah exclaimed. He ran to me in a full sprint against the warm, familiar sand. I smiled and walked toward him. As he got close, I kneeled and extended my arms out. He jumped into them with a sweet grin before wrapping his around my neck.

I stood and spun in a circle as he giggled. "Hey, kiddo."

"I missed you." He grinned.

"Well, guess what." I smiled and lowered us to the sand.

His head tilted to the side. "What?"

"I don't think you're going to miss me ever again very soon." I pushed hair from his face as he crinkled his little brows. I couldn't help but smile at the expression. It was entirely his dad.

"What you mean?"

"We're coming to get you." I smiled wider, looking between his eyes. "Really soon. Just a few more days, I think. I hope, anyway."

Those big blue eyes widened, and his lips stretched to a grin. "Daddy's coming too?"

I bobbed my head in a fast nod as tears welled in my eyes. "He sure is."

Really wished he weren't. Because I had a bad feeling about whatever lesson it was that Peterson had to teach him. But he was being as stubborn as me on this one.

Micah looked between my eyes with concern in his. "What's wong, Mommy?"

I fought the urge to sob. I pushed hair from his face and forced a smile. "Everything's good, baby, this is going to be good."

"Then why awe you cwying?" he asked.

"I'm just a little scared." I willed my smile higher. "But it's okay, baby. Everything's gonna be better really soon."

His eyes shifted downward. He dipped his little head in a slow nod. "He huwt you too, huh?"

A lump formed in my throat before I cleared it away. "Yeah. Yeah, he did."

"That's why you have this." His fingertip traced along the scar on my wrist.

I pressed my lips together. "Yeah, that's why."

His sad gaze locked with mine. "Is it because of me?"

"What?" My heart hurt that he'd even think to ask that. "Of course not."

"That's what they said," he muttered. "That they huwt me to huwt you."

My eyes filled with tears. I took his face in my hands and shook my head. "Don't believe a word they say to you, okay? Not about anything. You listen to me, and your dad, and your uncle Chris and that's it, alright? Nothing they say matters. All that matters is family."

"Aunt Leah, too, wight?" he asked.

I smiled. "Aunt Leah, too."

He smiled back. He sat in the sand beside me. "Guess what."

"What?" I asked.

"I can count to ten now."

A joyous grin came to my lips. "Did Uncle Chris show you that?"

He nodded quickly and began counting on his fingers. "One, two, thwee, fouw, five, six, seven, eight, nine, ten!"

"Wow!" I exclaimed with wide eyes. "You're the smartest kid in the world."

His smile stretched bigger, bubbly laugh leaving his little lips. "When you come and get me, am I going to get to see othew kids?"

"Your little sister can't wait to meet you." I grinned. "And neither can your baby cousin. But we don't know a lot of kids your age. Maybe we can go to the park or something, and you can make friends there. How's that sound?"

He smiled and gave a fast nod.

I returned his expression. It receded to a frown. "Micah, I have to tell you something that's going to be a little hard for you to understand."

His gaze shifted between mine, waiting for me to go on.

"You know how we can do all kinds of things? Like how you bring my mind here to see you? And how you magically appeared when Lydia got hurt?" He nodded, and I said, "Well, the rest of the world doesn't know about all of this. And we... When we find you, we're going to take you back home until we know it's safe. But then some nice police officers are going to take you somewhere for a little while to make sure you're healthy."

His head tilted. "Awe you and Daddy going to be thewe?"

"We're going to get there as soon as they let us see you," I said. "But they... You were really little when the doctor took you from me. And the police officers don't know that we already know each other through these little visits. So we're going to have to prove to them that we're your mom and dad."

"How do we do that?" he murmured.

"They might rub a little stick in your mouth. Or maybe take a little bit of your blood." I tapped his forearm. "But once they know what we know, you'll get to come home with us. And me and your dad are going to be there every second of every day that they let us be there with you. And Uncle Chris will be there with you until they let me and Daddy. Is that okay with you?"

"Can you bwing my sister?" he asked with wide eyes. "And that big white dog?"

I smiled, laughing. "I can't make any promises about the big white dog. But your sister will be there."

"Milly, wight?" he asked.

"Milly," I said. He grinned, gave a nod, and moved from the sand to my lap. His head rested against my chest as I wrapped my fingers around his. "You and your sister mean more to me than anything in the world. Never forget that, okay?"

He smiled and gave a sweet nod. "I know, Mommy."

"I mean it, Micah," I whispered. I kissed his hair. "I'd do anything for you because I love you, and I wanted to. If anything ever happens to me, it wasn't because of you. It was because I love you, and I want to give you the best life that you can have. Never, *ever* blame yourself for something that was done out of love, okay?"

He smiled and closed his eyes against my chest.

He had no clue what I was talking about. But he needed to hear that. He needed to know not to blame himself if something went wrong. He needed to know that love is beautiful and never damning. If it was the only lesson I got to teach him, it was a damn good one to know.

I had no clue what would happen in the coming days. But I knew that I would do whatever it took to keep him alive.

CHAPTER SIXTY-SIX

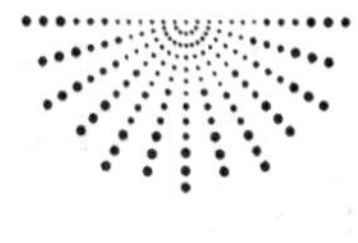

LAILA

"I'll wake her up now." Jeremy's voice pulled me from my dreams. "Yeah, ten minutes. I heard you, Leah. Let me get off the phone so I can get her up. Alright. Alright, yeah. Bye."

I stifled a yawn and scooted myself up the bed. "What's going on?"

"We have a location." He smiled. "Alpha from the outskirts of Texas took a little trip to California for us. She smelled all of our scents on a run. It's an abandoned factory not far from Shasta."

My heart skipped a beat. A grin came to my lips. "And they haven't been tipped off in any way?"

"So far, looks normal. Guards were circling a small shipping container shed thing in the back. I'm guessing that's where they're keeping them," Jeremy said. "The alpha's back at the house with Leah. She wants to show us what she saw so we know the terrain."

My breaths got fast with a combination of fear and excitement. I grinned. "Let's do it. Let's go get our son."

He stood from the bed with a smile. "Ready when you are."

"Your best bet's going to be night fall," the middle-aged woman said with her hands at her hips. "From what I seen, there can't be no more than fifteen guards. They were pretty absent minded too. The one was taking a piss, and I could've killed him in no time. I didn't, of course. Stayed back like you asked. But I don't think the guards are gonna be the issue."

My head tilted. "What will?"

"I can't quite explain it, but I've been around a long time. I've seen things. Felt things, things most people can't imagine. And I felt something there last night. Something big in the ways of magic."

"Probably our son," Jeremy said.

"No. No, I felt him too. But that's not what I'm talking about. Something different—something big. There's an evil there. And I know y'all are different than me, I know you don't believe in the old ways like I do. But I'm gonna tell you something right now. It isn't just that Nastya Witch bitch and a Sprite Fae. There's something bigger. Way bigger. As big as y'all and older than shit. Something awful's goin' on there."

I didn't know what she was talking about, and I didn't care. I was going into this prepared for the worst regardless. Knowing that something bad lurked inside wasn't a shock, and it didn't scare me any more than the rest of this did.

"I don't doubt that for a moment," I said. "What was your name again?"

"Emily." She extended her hand to me. "Emily Collins. We have met. I drank your blood."

"I remembered your face, just couldn't grasp the name." I smiled and shook her palm. "And this map here, this satellite image. That's a bird's eye view of the place?"

"Looks like it." Emily pointed to the large warehouse. "This place is where I smelt the Fae and the Witch. Couple humans too, probably that man y'all were talking about and a few guards. But back here" — she pointed to the small metal box a few hundred yards from the building— "this is where I smelled the boys. Smelled a lot like you, son. Ought to be your brother and baby in there. If not, I don't know who it could be."

Jeremy managed a smile. "I hope."

"Anything else we should know, Emily?" I asked.

She paused, as if searching for a way to go on. "I was sure the one guard would have heard me last night. But he didn't turn."

Jeremy ran a hand over his scruff. "You think he knew he was being watched?"

"Maybe."

That about settled it. We were walking into a trap. I already suspected it considering Amy showed up on a camera at the most popular grocery chain in the country, but that was the proof I needed to know it.

"Do you need a lift home, Emily?"

"If you don't mind. Might take me a while if I catch a cab." She smiled. "Best of luck to you. Let me know when you get that baby home."

"We will. Thank you for your help." I smiled.

She smiled back and lowered her head in a gentle bow. Brody took her arm, and they disappeared.

"I didn't want to mention this in front of guests," Helena said from the breakfast nook. "But I stayed up all night working on this, and I think it might help."

I turned to meet her gaze. "What is it?"

She blew out a long sigh, pushing a black dread from her face. "Well, you're not going to like the way we go about it. But I really believe it's necessary."

"Go on," Jeremy said.

She pulled two small pink jewels from her pocket and laid them on the table.

I reached down and lifted them in my hand. They were incredibly beautiful, a near magenta color that glinted in the sunlight. Unlike any crystal I'd ever seen. "What the hell is it?"

"These are what I like to call mirror crystals," Helena said. "They're from the Fae Realm. We don't have a real name for them here. This was Kai's idea actually."

"Well, what do they do?" I asked.

Leah spoke from her seat on the steps. "They're similar to the trackers Peterson put in you guys."

My nose curled. "You want that to go inside of me."

"It's brutal, yes," Kai said.

"And probably a PTSD trigger for you." Brody reappeared by the fridge. "But they could save your life."

"What does it do?" Jeremy lifted one to his forefinger and thumb.

"It's a tracker, for one," Leah said. "One bound to the magic of the planet and the Witch that binds it to your flesh. We put that in you, we have a bridge."

"Like a binding spell?" I asked.

"Not quite," Helena said. "Think about it like a Fitbit. It monitors you. It gives us basic information. Your heart rate, your respirations, your sleep pattern, and your location. But no one can remove it from your flesh but me."

"Why do you call it a mirror crystal?" Jeremy asked.

"It protects your mind," Leah said. "It puts this layer around a section of your thoughts that no one else can access no matter how hard they try."

"But it doesn't block out yer *whole* mind." Kai chimed in. "When someone hops into yer thoughts, they're going to see a portion of yer mind. They'll see the parts that ye allow but a good corner of it gets protected."

"I call it a mirror crystal because that's the effect it gives. That section of your mind that gets boxed off is metaphorically decorated in mirrors that face each other. They see those thoughts bouncing off of each other instead of what's inside the box. What you're actually thinking about," Helena said. "If I put this in both of you, you can communicate with each other and that bitch will never get in."

"And if we have to bind you to Micah, she won't see that either, Jeremy," Leah said.

"She'll know that we did it once we do. But she won't see the conversations you two have with each other," Brody said.

Jeremy's hand coasted over my arm. "What do you think, baby?"

I wasn't exactly fond of the idea. But I was damned and determined to get my son. That crystal would help Jeremy and I communicate, give them an idea if we were about to code to send Hannah, and was an addition to making our plan full proof. And at least I had healers around so I wouldn't get another scar.

"Let's do it. Then we go tonight."

CHAPTER SIXTY-SEVEN

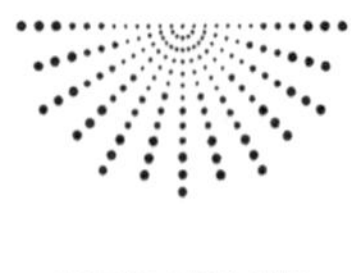

JEREMY

As I expected, the binding of that pink crystal to my flesh proved agonizing. But I suffered through the pain and got it over with. Then Laila did the same. It was harder for her than it was for me. When Helena slid the piece of metal below her rib cage and pushed the gem into her flesh, Laila's hands shook like they never had. Her teeth clambered together to create a sound like horses galloping on cobblestone.

But I held her hand and the trembling would steady for a moment. She fought with everything in her not to cry, and she succeeded. She stuck it out through the whole thing without shedding a tear. She wanted to, but she refused to allow herself that opportunity.

Then we sat around the house playing with our daughter and our dog. Rachel came over and helped make dinner. We ate with our brothers and sisters. We took Milly and Tinkerbell out to Dairy Queen after and stopped at the park. Then we returned to the main house and lit a fire on the back patio.

No one said any goodbyes that time. In those few hours, we simply enjoyed one another. Because although none of us would say it aloud, there was a very real possibility that the world we knew was about to change forever. But we weren't saying goodbye because we were coming home, damn it.

Then we lay on the couch to get some rest before we had to go.

"Jeremy," Laila murmured at my chest, gazing down at Milly sleeping in her arms.

"Yeah, baby?" I asked.

"Can you play your guitar for a few minutes?" She turned up to me and brought a smile to her lips. "Always calms my nerves a little."

I smiled and kissed her forehead. She pulled away and propped a pillow under her arm to support Milly's weight. "I'll play for a little bit. But we should probably get a nap in before we go. Midnight their time is three ours."

She pulled a throw blanket from the back of the couch to cover the two of them. I teleported back to the house, grabbed my Gibson, and returned to the main house's living room. I sat at the chair beside Laila.

A grin pulled at her lips. I smiled back, but Milly thought I smiled at her and erupted in giggles. A quiet laugh drifted from my mouth as I sat the guitar in my lap and began strumming.

I can't remember what I played that night. But I'll never forget watching them drift to sleep together. Their green eyes closed in near unison to the sound of my music. As I continued playing until I was sure they fell asleep, I hoped to the universe or the gods or the Earth itself that it wouldn't be the last time I lived that moment. That I'd get to sing my wife and daughter to sleep again. But that next time, my son would be there too.

"The calm before the storm, huh?" Brody put a hand on my shoulder.

I let out a sigh as he handed me a bottle of water. "Yeah, I guess so."

"Can't sleep? Or just wanted to make sure she didn't stay up on the verge of a panic attack?"

"The latter." I placed my guitar on the floor.

He sat in a chair beside me. "Everything's going to be fine, man. This is what we've been waiting for for three years."

"Almost to the day," I muttered. "You remember that? The day she was taken?"

"Wish I could forget it."

"To this day, the worst thing I've ever felt." I chewed my lip, looking over the scar at her neck. "If I could have taken the pain of what she felt for myself, I would have."

"I know you would have," Brody murmured.

"And that's what I'm going to do now." I turned to meet his gaze. "I'm not letting anyone take her from me again. I'll die first."

He nodded gently.

With this going on, I had something on my mind. I lived my whole life without a father or even a father figure. I had no men to look up to aside from Chris, and he was gone before I even made it to adulthood.

Should something happen to me, my daughter needed to know what a good man looked like. Yes, all of my brothers were that. But out of us all, Brody had his shit together the most. He was the one with a career, and a degree, and a real life ahead of him.

I had that too, I supposed. But if I didn't make it back, or if it took a long time before I did, I needed to know that my baby girl would have someone like my brother to look up to. The way he treated Gwen was the way I wanted my daughter to know she deserved to be treated too.

"If something happens to us, promise me you'll take care of my daughter."

His forehead crunched together. "That's my niece. Of course I'll take care of her."

"Leah can't do it alone again. It wasn't easy taking us in, but she did, and I don't want her to have to do it by herself. She deserves to be happy too."

"You're acting like you know you're going to die, Jeremy." Brody's gaze was something between questioning and accusative. "You need to look for the positive in this. We've waited years for this, and it's finally here. This is the first time we have a clear shot."

"I know. But they know we're coming. And he's got plans for me." I looked over Laila. "He hates me because he loves her. And I don't know what he's going to do to me, but I know that she's going to need a father figure in her life if I'm not here."

Brody frowned. "I'll take care of her, Jeremy."

"And if... If I don't make it back, make sure she knows I love her, okay? Make sure she doesn't think that I wanted to leave her because I don't. I don't want to leave tonight, but I've got to bring my son home."

He still frowned, apparently not dignifying that bit a response. "Try and get some sleep, man. Me and Leah have alarms set. We're going to come wake you up when it's time for you to leave."

CHAPTER SIXTY-EIGHT

JEREMY

"Guys," Leah murmured with a hand on my arm. "Guys, it's almost time for you to go."

My eyes pulled open, and for half of a second, I forgot what awaited us.

"What time is it?" Laila whispered, carefully lifting Milly against her chest.

"Ten to three," Brody said quietly. "You guys should probably head out."

I rubbed my eyes and sat up on the couch. Laila stood and gently lay Milly to the bassinet she barely fit in these days. A knot formed in my throat while I watched her pull her long dark hair into a bun. "And Helena's awake?"

"She's getting up." Brody handed me my knife. I slid it into the pocket of my jeans and stifled a yawn.

"Hopefully, you guys are back in no time and we don't need her though." Leah smiled. "I'm sure everything's going to be fine."

"Glad you are." Laila ran her finger along Milly's hand. I brought myself to my feet and tucked my hair into a ponytail.

"We'll be back soon." I looked over Milly. "We won't be gone long."

"We're stocked up on food and water if you are," Leah said. "Me and that baby aren't leaving the border until you guys get back. So hurry up."

I forced a smile her way and touched Milly's chubby cheek. I would've kissed her, but I didn't want to risk her waking up and teleporting after us.

Laila leaned down and kissed her forehead. Milly's eyes drifted back and forth behind her eyelids, suckling fast at the pink pacifier between her lips.

"You ready, Lai?"

She nodded. I tightened my arm around her shoulders. She hooked her hand around my waist. "I love you guys," Laila whispered.

"We love you too." Leah smiled.

Brody pushed a sad smile. "We'll see you soon."

I smiled back and gave a nod.

Then, we spun through the air.

The moment that we landed, the vibration of Micah's energy hit me like a twenty-ton truck slamming into a butterfly on the highway.

I didn't even get the chance to adjust to my new surroundings. It was dark, it was warmer than it'd been back home, but that was the only thing I noticed. All that I could focus on was him.

The purity, the innocence, the same thing I felt when I held his sister but on a much larger scale. Stronger. So much stronger.

A quiet gasp dropped into my lips. Laila raised her hand to cover my mouth. I gave a nod and lowered her hand to her side. She nodded back. She turned her gaze to the field in front of us.

I squinted through the brush and touched the small of her back. *We communicate telepathically. Don't say a word.* Laila's voice echoed through my ears.

I know.

That little metal shed. She gestured just ahead. *That's where they are. I can feel it.*

Are we just storming in?

She shook her head. *We take out those guards first. In silence. If*

Nastya and Amy are asleep, they don't feel us here yet. There's a border around that shed, but I can take it down. Me and Helena worked on something just like this. It's Elvan. I can feel it; she's using Micah and the power of the ley line to create it.

Take out the guards in sight and I cover you. I nodded. *Ready when you are.*

I go for the two on the left, you get the two on the right?

Works for me.

She turned and met my gaze. I smiled and pressed my lips to hers. *Let's go get our son.*

Laila smiled as she pulled back.

She was gone.

I grasped the knife in my pocket. I teleported to the guard just in front of the steel shed. In the swift motion of landing, I grasped the man's shoulder and raised the blade in front of his neck and tightly pulled back on the blade.

I teleported the body back into the woods just as Laila did the same. I repeated the process to the guard on the rear end of the metal container.

Laila and I simultaneously moved the bodies back to our landing spot in the woods. Then we joined bloody hands, as grotesque as that may sound, and appeared in front of the shed door. *Get behind me.*

I teleported so that my back was against hers. My gaze scanned the knee length grass in search of movement. But it was silent. Nothing but blue moonlight against dewy green turf.

Light began to glow from behind me as Laila whispered Elvan incantations for a moment. I felt the strain on her shaking hands against the handle of the small metal shack.

Still, I studied our surroundings, taking in every detail. I listened for any crack of a tree branch or the shuffle of feet but heard nothing. For a moment, I thought it would be quick and simple.

Then the lock broke open, and Laila let out a quiet laugh. *We're in.*

I heard her pull the door open but kept my gaze steady on the dark field around us.

"Mommy?" Micah's sweet little voice said behind me.

And I turned.

I never should have turned.

"Micah." Laila started through the threshold. But as she took a step forward, it looked like she took a step into a wall of vibrating glass. I couldn't see it until she touched it, but he was still locked in.

My heart hammered, hands growing clammy.

Shit.

This was not going to be an in-and-out situation,

"Daddy!" Micah exclaimed as he ran from a blanket on the cement to the perimeter.

I put my hand on the forcefield. But it stung like a thousand bee stings, and I pulled back.

Laila brought a glowing white light to her hands and continued speaking in Elvan. Only then did I see him in the illumination of her palms.

"Micah." I managed a smile, but tears burned across my eyes.

He didn't look the way he had in the astral reality. His hair laid in greasy, messy knots all over his pale, dirty face. His eyes stood out like oceans on Earth from space against the near brown smog over his dry cheeks.

I couldn't blame Chris; his resources were limited, and he couldn't see him to tell how filthy and decrepit he appeared. But my heart broke as I looked at those tiny, frail shoulders. His collar bone protruded from his neck just as Laila's had when she came home. It looked like it was ready to break the surface of his skin.

But then Micah's shadowed little body flew into the air as a light flicked on in the shed. A squeal left his lips, fear flooding his blue eyes.

My brother, my nearly dead appearing brother, held Micah against his chest by his ribs with a knife at his throat.

Then Amy's voice left his mouth. "You didn't really think it'd be that easy, did you?"

"Don't hurt him," Laila said. "Please, Amy. Please. Don't hurt my baby."

"We won't," Peterson's voice said behind us.

I turned and stood in front of Laila.

"Not yet, anyway." He smiled and met my gaze. "Nice to finally meet your acquaintance, Jeremy."

It was so surreal to meet him in the flesh. Those gentle brown eyes. His nearly feminine jaw line, his clean shaved cheeks, his thick glasses. That scrawny figure dressed so prim and proper. I towered a good foot and a half above him. He couldn't have been more than a few inches taller than Laila, yet he held every ounce of power over us.

Nastya stood at his side. She looked exactly as she had in the photos, just a bit older. Still though, neat and tidy. Like she was preparing for a day at work. While my son sat in his own filth, they both looked as though they were heading into the city.

"Fuck you," I spat.

He smiled, brows creasing. "Is that how you're going to talk to the man who holds the fate of your son's life in his hands?"

I kept a hand wrapped around Laila from behind.

"Thought so." He placed his hands at his hips and blew out a slow sigh. He looked at the spilled blood on the ground. "You sure love killing my men, Laila."

A *tsk, tsk, tsk* sound left his lips. "So here's what we're going to do. I am going to approach both of you with a little itty-bitty needle, and you're going to take a little nap. Then we're going to get to work. I know we probably don't have much time before you outwit me and get out of here. But, in the meantime, you do as I say. Or you watch your brother slit your son's throat. Your choice."

I clenched my jaw and tightened my hand around Laila's hip. As Nastya took a step forward, I pulled a ball of energy to my hand holding the knife.

"Come on, Jeremy, don't make me do it like this." Peterson's eyes were practically smiling. "Now isn't the time, you have things to learn first."

"I'm not leaving her," I said.

"You're not," he said. "You have things to learn together. But you're going to be unconscious until I get you into a secure location."

"Just let me hold him." Laila glanced over her shoulder. "Please. Please let me hold my son."

"You will, Laila." Peterson smiled. "You'll see him soon."

"You won't hurt him if we go with you?" she whispered.

He held his smile. "Not yet."

Tears overflowed from her eyes, and her body began to tremble against mine.

"But this gives you more time to try and think of a way to stop me." He raised his narrow shoulders in a shrug. "Maybe you'll figure it all out and beat me to the punch. You have before. I expected you to be in my custody far longer last time around. This time, I'm not expecting an extended stay though."

"Then why are you doing this?" I asked. "Why don't you just stop? You know that we get him back, you've told us this. Why are you still fighting?"

"Because if I don't do this, you don't get them back," Peterson said with a genuinely earnest look between my eyes. "I may hate you, Jeremy. But I know the role that I have to play in your evolution too. Although, I will admit, the cruelty you're soon to suffer won't keep me up at night the way the sound of your wife's screams do." He blew out a slow sighHe looked over Laila behind me. He started toward us. "Sometimes in a good way. Others, not so much."

Her body quivered against mine. The fear racing through her body echoed into mine. It was her worst nightmare. Making the *choice* to go back into his custody. Lining up like a lamb to slaughter.

And I wished there were a way to stop it. I wished there were a way to take her pain away. But yet again, we were cornered. Our only option was to do as he said.

"You're not going to hurt her again." I tightened my hand around her waist. "If you want to hurt someone, you hurt me. You don't touch her."

A real smile came to his lips this time. "You're not in control, Jeremy. I have a knife at your son's throat. If I touch her, there isn't a thing you can do unless you're willing to be the reason Micah dies. And she'll never forgive you for it. You know that."

I looked between his eyes, feeling Laila's hand tremble against my leg.

He was right. She'd personally slit my throat if I didn't listen to him and got Micah killed. More than that, I loved my kids more than I loved my wife too. We shared the understanding that they came before either of us. And if I had to watch him hurt her again, I would have to watch him hurt her. There wasn't a damn thing I could do.

"Am I injecting you or can you do it yourself?" Peterson extended his hand. "I've got a feeling you'll like that little concoction. You'll barely feel what's about to happen."

I held Laila's shaking hip as tight as I could.

"What's in it?" I reached out.

"Oh, you'll know soon." He smiled and dropped the small insulin syringe to my hand. "Don't dump the whole thing in there. Don't want you dying on me."

Heroin, I'd bet. That was the only thing capable of numbing me. And I didn't fucking want it. But I'd do whatever it took to keep my kid safe.

I gritted my teeth to a hard line. "What are you giving her?"

"Strong benzo." He shrugged. "You're getting the fun stuff."

"No." Laila's shaking hand took my wrist. Her fingers pulled the needle from my palm, head shaking harder. "No."

"I'll be okay." I soothed my hand along her lower back and took the needle from her palm with the other. "It's okay."

"Hopefully this'll ruin it for him, Laila." Peterson looked between my eyes, nose curling and lips turning downward. "He'll never enjoy it again after this."

As much as this was about to suck, I doubted there was anything that could make me not enjoy dope.

I leaned down and kissed her forehead. Her head rocked back and forth. Her shaking hands grasped my chest.

"It's going to be okay," I whispered.

She squeezed a tighter hold on my shirt. Then Peterson lunged forward and plunged another needle into her arm. I shoved him back and put my hands at her waist. Her eyes flooded with tears, and she slowly became unable to bear weight.

"Figure it better if she didn't see you shoot up," he said.

I held her body against my chest and looked between his eyes. My teeth tightened to a tight line. "Do you have a gurney I can put her on?"

"Your brother will grab the two of you after you're unconscious." He glanced at Chris behind me.

For the first time in my life, I didn't want that needle. Not an ounce of me wanted to get high in that instant. I wanted my son. But to get my son, I had to take the same thing that ripped me away from his mother.

"I don't want Micah to see this. Close the doors."

He dipped his head in a nod.

"Daddy," Micah whispered, glistening water rolling down his dusty cheeks, pulling my gaze from Peterson's to meet his. "Daddy, I'm scawed."

"It's going to be okay, buddy." I forced a smile and fought the tears flooded my eyes. "We're coming back for you."

His little lip quivered. His teeth began to chatter, just like Laila's did when she was anxious. "Pwomise?"

"I promise." I smiled. "You hang in there. We're coming back—"

"Aright, that's enough." Peterson said.

Nastya flung the doors shut.

I closed my eyes and felt the world slip out from beneath me as I carefully lowered Laila to the ground. "Do you have a tourniquet? Or am I supposed to make my own?"

"Intramuscular should be effective," Peterson said above me. "But chop-chop, Jeremy. All I have to do is give the word—"

"And you kill my son, I know," I snapped, meeting his gaze. "I know. I'm doing what you want; just shut the fuck up."

He made a face, and Micah screamed.

"I'm sorry." My eyes shot open, heart racing. "I'm sorry, okay? Just don't hurt him."

"Then take the drugs."

I clenched my teeth together and looked down at Laila's groggy, fluttering eyelids. "I'm sorry, baby."

I pulled off the cap and slammed it into my thigh.

In a second, a rush I hadn't felt in a decade washed over me.

Heroin hit way harder than snorting oxies. But it wasn't just heroin, there was something else in there. Maybe another benzo or maybe a sedative. Either way, it only took a second or two before I fell to the ground beside her with my hand against hers.

CHAPTER SIXTY-NINE

JEREMY

A sudden slam to my stomach pulled me from my dazed, stoned dream. I gasped, but only because that's what my body did out of instinct. It didn't hurt. Nothing hurt. As he slammed his foot over and over into my torso, I felt like I did in the back of a car when I fell asleep as a child. The movement shifted my body but there wasn't much else attached to it. No pain, no fear.

"Maybe I should have hit you with that after we did this," Peterson said above me, taking in long breaths and wiping sweat from his brow.

I couldn't help the huff of a laugh that left my lips when I looked up at his tiny stature. His shoulders were almost as small as my wife's. He was short. I'd always called myself scrawny, but next to him, I was a body builder.

But I knew that meant nothing here. I sure found it ironic in the moment though.

He slammed his foot into my chest again. He pushed up his glasses. I laughed again.

He narrowed his gaze. "Funny, huh?"

"Bitches kick." I laughed again with a shake of my head against the cold cement. "I mean, you kind of look like one from this angle anyway so—"

His steel toed boot slammed into my cheek. My head flung backward, scraping against the cement as a shock rang through my head. "That was a good one, I'll give you that." My hand lifted to my bleeding nose. "But c'mon, man, steel toes?"

"Always so bubbly." He gritted his teeth together. "It's cute on her. You can't pull it off."

I wiped my bleeding nose and shifted to try to sit. He kicked me down again.

"You stay down until I tell you to get up," he snapped. "I'll do it, Jeremy. All I have to do is think the word, and he's gone."

I clenched my jaw and closed my eyes. My head shook. "What do you want?"

"I want you to stop failing," Peterson barked. "I want you two idiots to learn."

"Great teacher, you are," I muttered. He grasped my head and raised it upward. I could have stopped him. I could have grabbed his hands and turned my back on top of him. I could have plummeted my elbow into his face. I could have flipped the tables and plunged my fists into his jaw until there was no skin left.

But all he had to do was think the word.

So instead, I watched the ground come toward my eyes in slow motion as he slammed my face into the hard, rough cement.

"Who was she before me?" He lifted my head by my hair and spoke near my ear. "What was she capable of before I taught her to tap into her instincts, Jeremy?"

"Before you tortured her," I said. "Don't rename what you do to sound like it's noble. This isn't tough love."

"At least I haven't watched her die a thousand times." Peterson dropped my head back to the ground. "At least I've never *let* her die."

I gritted my teeth together.

"Why do you keep failing? Over, and over, and over. You fail, and you fail, and you fail, Jeremy. Even when you have everything and more to fight for. Even in this life when it's right in front of you." He wrinkled his nose and looked over me with annoyance. "You have to use what you have inside of you, Jeremy. You have so much more potential than you realize too. And you miss it in each life. How do you not see it in this one? How are you still missing it? Why are you so inconceivably, staggeringly fucking stupid? How can the lock be that tight?"

In fairness, he was right. It was directly in front of me. I was a god damned idiot.

"What do I have to do to make you see it, Jeremy? Do I have to hurt him? Is that what I have to do? I have to torture him before I kill him—"

"You're not going to kill my son." I clenched my jaw and turned to meet his gaze. "Do whatever you have to do to me, but if you kill him—"

"Damn it, Jeremy!" Peterson yelled. "Listen to the words coming out of my mouth. Think about it really hard. I know you're a little cloudy up there but put it together—"

"Why don't you just say what you mean instead of talking like a troll under a bridge?" I grumbled.

"Because I can't tell you," he screamed with a deep, piercing gaze between mine. "You have to feel it. You have to figure it out. *You* have to see yourself."

I kept my cheek against the pavement as I looked between his eyes. He stared down at me with deep, uneven breaths. He gritted his teeth and turned away. "Stand up."

I licked my bloody lip, brought myself to my knees, and staggered to my feet. My fingers caught on a thick cold wall as he turned back to me. My jaw clenched as I looked between his dark brown eyes and caught a look at the metal over his knuckles.

"I can honestly say that it hurt me to hurt her." Peterson clenched his teeth together, and his nostrils flared. "But I'll treasure these moments forever."

He raised his hand and struck my cheek with his metal covered fists. I felt it that time and I hoped to hell and back that Laila didn't.

"Do what you have to do, man." I spit blood from my mouth to the ground before looking back down at him. "But just keep in mind that one day very soon, I'm going to be the one doing this to you. But it's going to be so much worse than this."

He slammed the brass knuckles to my cheek again. I laughed as my body veered to the side, and he backed me into the wall. "Have you ever heard of Japanese bamboo torture?" He slammed the knuckles into my other cheek. Blood sprayed from my face, a cough of red leaving my mouth. I spit a wad of blood to the ground. "Lai's been reading up on it. But you know all of that cool stuff she can do with plants, right?"

He slammed his hand into my face again. I fell to the ground. I released another long, billowing laugh. "She's planted a lot of roses lately. Just imagine all those thorns slowly growing through your skin. Sounds like a horrible way to go."

He grabbed ahold of my shoulders and pushed me into the wall again. I laughed as I looked over his furious little face. He clocked me again.

CHAPTER SEVENTY

LAILA

As my eyes drifted open, my heart sunk from my chest through the table below me.

I swore that I would never end up on one of those tables again.

Yet, there I lie.

"Rise and shine," a voice said from a speaker in the corner of the concrete room. "How'd you sleep, darling?"

Tightening my hands to taut fists, I groggily pulled myself upright.

Instead of the scrubs that I expected, I wore a white nightgown. If that wasn't horror movie enough for Peterson, Nastya's cackle did the trick.

"Well, come on now, Miss Fiercely Independent. Stand up and do something. This is what you've been waiting for, isn't it? Your shot at me? Well go on then, take it. Right over here behind the glass window. You can break through it, can't you? You've broken through much stronger than this."

My jaw tightened as I looked around the room.

It smelled of freshly poured cement and paint. They'd designed this room just for us.

No steel this time, aside from the table beneath me. Three out of four walls stood solid sheets of concrete. A rack of iron rails that appeared to have been molded into the cement frame to separate the space in two. In the middle, I noted the hinges that allowed a portion of the metal to spin in and out. Beyond the metal rack hung the metal door, the only exit, with no handle. A foot or two from it, I saw another table. But he wasn't there.

Only then did I turn to the large, tinted window that overlooked a small office space where Nastya sat in front of an array of computers.

"Where's Jeremy?" I started to my feet and grasped ahold of the iron rods. "Peterson said he'd be here. He—He said we'd be together."

"Not so independent now, are we?" Nastya smiled.

I gritted my teeth to a line, knowing that I could break through that window. It'd only take a minute to get the barrier in front of it down, but it'd only take a second to slit my son's throat. If they didn't have my son and his uncle, that glass would be fragments in puddles of her blood on the ground.

But Amy was still there. That's why she wasn't on the other side of that glass; she was in there with them so that she could kill Micah the moment I did something I wasn't supposed to. If she sat on the other side of that glass, I could simultaneously kill them both which would be like knocking the eight ball into a pocket on the first shot. They knew we were coming, and they had a plan of their own worked out.

"Where is he?" I asked.

"I'm surprised you don't feel it." Her head tilted slightly. "Then again. He hasn't used in a very long time. His tolerance..." She gave a smug smile, eyes widening in phony fear. Her hand lifted to her chest, as if clutching her pearls. "Well, I hope we didn't give him too much."

I gritted my teeth to a line. I felt a sudden ache in my ribs. The impact felt soft, but I could feel his brain slamming between his ears.

"They should be back soon." Nastya placed her hands at her hips.

Slow deep breaths drew into my lungs as I looked between her cold blue eyes. That moment was the first we truly met. The last time, we didn't speak a word to one another. Jeremy and Moriah both showed me pictures, but I expected more. I expected her to be as pretty as

Moriah, and in some way, she was. But there was something in her eyes that would make a dog run away with its tail between its legs.

No wonder she hated the world so much. Her face practically screamed evil. Although attractive, she displayed a total lack of warmth. Most of the time, I could look at someone and see something. Not literally a soul nor an aura, but something that my mind registers yet doesn't allow my eyes to see. But the feeling attached to the invisible image always came in loud and clear, as it did that day with Nastya.

There was not an ounce of good in that woman. Even when her intentions were, she couldn't be. What she'd do in the coming hours would only validate that notion.

As I gazed at her, I swore that if I ever figured out that tree of life shit Heylel talked about, no matter how much she changed from life to life, in no reality would I *ever* condone that woman living for all of eternity. Never.

"What? Cat got your tongue?" She smiled with wide eyes.

I clenched my jaw and turned around.

"You used to be so rowdy," Nastya said. "Vibrant. Exciting. Certainly entertaining. This is... This is boring. I expected more from you, Laila."

"You have my son." I gazed at the cool cement beneath my feet. My tongue ran along my teeth as I focused on the tiny box within my mind.

One day. I had to make it through one day—less than a day actually —before I got in the bitch's head and ended it forever. Before I sent a message to Helena to bring Kai, take that shield down around Micah, and get my baby out of there so that I could kill that cunt. Just one day.

I thought about focusing in on Jeremy but knew that I shouldn't. He wasn't in too much pain or I'd know. I'd see him soon. I had to maintain my composure.

She expected me to lose it. They banked on it. But Kai was right that day when we got back from saving the others. If I was going to make it out, I had to do the opposite of what they expected me to do. I had to behave because doing as she's told is the reverse of the Laila Callidy they expected to see today.

Things were different last time I was in a room like this. I was a child then. I thought that I was grown, but I wasn't. This time, I still wasn't grown; not really. But I knew it. I didn't pretend that I had it all figured out. I didn't pretend like I was invincible. I counted on not getting it right the first time. I had a plan for when I failed, and I was going to follow it.

My daughter counted on me to make it home. My son counted on me to *bring* him home. And if I had to bite my tongue and swallow my pride to make it there, I would.

I wasn't going to be stupid this time. I was sticking to the plan.

"Believe it or not, Laila, I'm doing this as much for you as I am for me," Nastya said. "You won't see that for lifetimes from now, but I think one day... One day, you'll understand. You might not agree, but you will understand. And some small part of you will at the very least respect why I did what I did."

"What you did?" I turned and met her gaze through the window. "What you did or what you're going to do? Because you can choose to do the right thing *now*. You can redeem yourself on your own if you just fucking try."

She smiled. "That's more like it."

I rolled my eyes and turned away.

"I'm not saying this just to get a rise out of you, Laila. I respect you in long and vast measures," Nastya said. "But that passion. That drive in you. That fire behind your eyes, you have to let it shine, darling. Don't hold back, let it flow once in a while."

Just as I shook my head, the door flung inward. Jeremy's groggy, blood covered body stumbled into the wall and plummeted to the floor. A gasp left my lips. I rushed to the metal bars as the door slammed shut.

It clicked.

Then beeped.

"I'm okay," he slurred, pulling himself to his feet by grasping the metal bed.

My eyes filled with tears. I struggled to make words.

His bright blue eyes hid behind dark, crimson blood. He tried to wipe it away, sending an ache through both of our faces. I grimaced and fought the lump in my throat. His long black hair laid in blood coated locks along his swollen, already purple eye. Small cuts ascended over his skin as if he'd been beaten by something with sharp corners.

"Jeremy," was all that made it from my lips as I reached for him through the bars.

He forced what he could make of a smile, gripped the wall, and staggered across the room to me. His blood covered, sore fingers grasped ahold of the iron rail. I reached through and held his shoulders. "I'm okay." He lowered himself against the cement with a nod. "I'm okay."

"You're not allowed to heal him," Nastya said over the speaker. "If you do, he does to Micah what he just did to Jeremy."

"It's okay." He closed his eyes and rested his head against the cement wall. His voice was deep and raspy, as if struggling through the blood running down his throat. "I'm okay. Don't worry about me; I'm okay."

I clenched my chattering teeth together and reached for his face through the bars. "These weren't fists."

"Brass knuckles." He rolled his head into the metal rods between us. His eyes closed against my hand. *Pussy doesn't know how to actually fight.*

I tried to smile, but only tears came. "I'm so—"

"Shh." He shook his head against the cement. "Stop it. None of that."

I swallowed hard, trying to take him in while in this condition. I'd seen him high a few times. But never like this. Never so groggy that he could barely keep his head up and his words level. He never reached that point around me, not once. Although, I'd only ever seen him on pills. Heroin may come from the same plant, but it's a hell of a lot stronger. That's when I realized why he rationalized pills to be the better of the two evils.

I grazed his bloody cheek. "You're okay? You didn't... They didn't give you too much?"

"I'm high as shit." He wiped his bloody lips, battling to open his eyes. "But no. No, I'm okay. I don't really feel any of this, so I guess that's a positive to look at, right?" He rolled his head to face mine and lifted his hand to my arm. "Are you okay?"

I gave a quick nod.

He summoned a smile to his swollen lips. *I can handle this for a day if I have to, Lai. One of our backup plans is going to work.*

I hope.

I promised him, his thoughts fell to a near whisper. *It's... it's going to work.*

"Get some rest, Laila," Peterson's voice said over the speaker. "You're going to need it."

CHAPTER SEVENTY-ONE

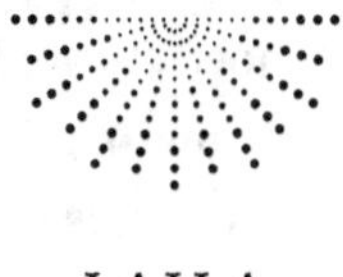

LAILA

I didn't sleep. I couldn't. Instead, I sat beside him with my hand on his chest. I counted each rise and fall. I stayed as quiet as I could to focus on that small thump-thump of his heart beneath my palm.

Finding him beneath the swelling felt nearly impossible. As the night drew on, he flinched when my hand grazed the swollen flesh. The pain gradually intensified until I pondered how he could possibly remain asleep. My entire body ached with his agony. Peterson beat the living shit out of him. But even when his swollen eyelids drifted open, a smile pulled at his lips.

"Did you sleep?" he whispered, blinking hard through the thick, crusted blood.

I forced a smile. My fingers drifted to a piece of hair plastered against his cheek. "I'll sleep when I'm dead."

"No, we'll just start this over again," he muttered with a look around. Then a smile raised up his cheeks as he touched my jaw with his thumb. "But maybe not. Maybe the cycle ends with us getting a little god damn peace."

My smile grew more genuine. I reached for his hand and touched his sore knuckles to my lips. "How do you feel?"

"I'll be alright." *You can heal me tonight.*

I smiled and gave a soft nod. *We've just got to make it that long.*

We will.

My tongue ran along my lips. I cleared my throat. "I didn't think he would look like that."

His swollen eyes turned down. "He won't for long. We'll all end up getting fat the way I know you'll feed him."

I smiled, fighting the tears that formed in my eyes.

Not yet. Peterson's words echoed through my mind.

Jeremy cupped my cheek in his hand. "None of that. That's how this ends, Laila. You'll be baking cookies while Micah and Milly play in the living room by this time next week, and I don't want to hear you say otherwise."

My thumb traced along his swollen lip. "And where will you be?"

He forced a smile. "Right beside you. Just like I am right now."

I wanted to believe that. But he looked so bad. He should have been in a hospital bed. His face was so swollen I could hardly make out his features. The whites of his eyes were red with burst blood vessels. He looked worse than anyone I'd ever seen who didn't die a few minutes later.

I pressed my chattering teeth together. He smiled back. "You're right though; he looks like me. Not me right now, but ya know. What I normally look like."

A quiet laugh left me, looking for the best in this shit situation. "We're almost there, right?"

"On the home stretch." He held his smile.

I heard a beep followed by a click. My hand instantly started to tremble. Jeremy wrapped his fingers around mine.

Peterson stepped into the room and pushed the door shut behind him.

"Get up," he said. "Both of you."

I fought the urge to swallow the lump in my throat. Jeremy kept his fingers twined between mine while he gripped the iron to pull himself to his feet. My heart hammered behind my eyes.

Peterson pulled Jeremy's blade from the back of his waist band.

He gave a nonchalant glance over Jeremy and made a gesture to the center of the iron rack where the hinges hung. "Let go of her hand and move over here."

I squeezed Jeremy's hand and shook my head. Then Peterson huffed. "Turn the monitor to face them, Nastya."

Jeremy's gaze shifted to the window to my right. A live feed appeared of Micah sitting on the floor in that shed. His little arms wrapped around his knees, only revealing his dark hair slumped above his blue scrubs. Chris was on the other side of the room with his head in his hands. Amy sat between them and smiled up at the camera with a wave of each of her fingers.

My heart raced. Jeremy squeezed my hand before letting go. My hands trembled as he sent me a gentle smile. He walked to Peterson.

Beep. Click.

I jumped.

A piece of the iron gate between us swung inward. Jeremy spun to look at the opening.

"Trade places," Peterson said.

"No," Jeremy said. "No."

Peterson sighed and turned his gaze to the camera. Amy stood from the chair in the middle of the room and gently touched Micah's shoulders. His head shook against his knees. She grasped ahold of his hair and ripped his head upward. She slammed him to the ground.

"Stop it." I shook my head, rushed to the cell door, and joined them on the other side. "Make her stop."

He gave a nod. I looked back to the camera. Amy stood and put her hands at her hips. Then Chris felt his way toward Micah's sobbing body on the floor.

Jeremy put his protective, comforting hand at my waist.

Peterson sighed again. "I'm going to have her be more brutal if you keep making this so difficult. All of this is going to be over soon; just do as I say and make this as easy as possible for all of us."

"It's okay." I looked up at him. "It's okay."

He clenched his jaw, breaths growing heavy.

"Now, Jeremy."

When he stood still, Peterson took a step forward and shoved him toward the doorway. He grasped ahold of the bar before he fell forward. He turned over his shoulder with gritted teeth and took a step inside.

The door swung shut and clicked into place. Peterson smiled at me. "It feels like centuries since I looked into those eyes of yours, doesn't it?"

I firmly planted my teeth together.

"Nastya was right." He pushed his glasses up his face. "You're awfully more quiet than I remember you."

"What do you want me to say?" I said. "Want me to beg? I've done that. Want me to yell? I've done that too. What am I supposed to say to you, Peterson?"

"You could start by calling me by my name for once." He smiled. "I prefer my first name to my last, you know."

I gritted my teeth. "Well, what would you like me to say, Robert?"

"Something." His face was screwed up in genuine confusion. "Be you. Hit me. Call me a name."

"I'm not giving you a reason to hurt my son. I'm going to do what you say until I have my baby back. I'll be the same old Laila you once knew. 'Til then, I'm going to be on my best behavior."

His head tilted, and his brow arched. "You're willing to cooperate with me this time."

"If it means my son stays alive."

"Laila," Jeremy said.

"That's where I went wrong, isn't it?" he murmured. "That day. When you woke up. After you gave birth to him. I should have put a knife to his throat then, and you would have stayed. I shouldn't have told you that he died."

A slow breath left my nostrils.

Yes. I would have. I would have done whatever he said. I wouldn't have sent word to Jeremy until I had a plan worked out that kept Micah safe.

But that was just it.

Had I been in his custody, there would've been no keeping me from

Micah. I'd have manipulated the shit out of him. I'd have been sweet as pie. I'd have let him believe he'd broken me, trained me like a rehabilitated animal. I'd have seduced him if I had to. I'd have done anything to get my baby in my arms.

And the moment I had my son, I'd have destroyed the man who stole him from me.

Peterson raised the hand with Jeremy's knife to his mouth. His thumb ran against his chin, wrinkled eyes shifting between mine. "Why did he tell me to then? It—It doesn't make sense. You... The mother in you, of course that's the route I should have taken. But then why did—No, that can't be right."

"I don't know what you're talking about, Peterson."

He glanced me over for a moment. He fell utterly silent, clearly in a deep thought. Then his lips turned up in a soft smile. A quiet laugh left him.

He looked at Jeremy over my shoulder and turned back to me. "You'll do whatever I say?"

Fuck.

My heart picked up speed in my chest.

"Then turn around." He smiled.

My teeth began to chatter before I pressed them together. My hands shook, but I clenched them to fists. My legs trembled, and I tightened the muscles within them.

I did what I had to do.

I turned around.

Jeremy looked between my eyes through the bars. His head shook, breaths short. I felt Peterson's hand pull hair behind my shoulder. I smelled his sulfury breath at my neck.

My stomach churned when I felt his hand touch my hip.

Jeremy grasped ahold of the bars in front of him. "Get off of her."

Peterson's hand at my hip drifted toward my thigh. His hand holding the knife raised to my neck. As that cold metal touched my skin, a feeling of numbness washed through me.

The sulfur-like smell of his breath and cologne. The feel of his fingertips. The cold metal against my skin. The aching pain over my whole body, but this time echoing from Jeremy's.

That feeling of powerlessness unlike any other.

Jeremy angrily shook the bars in front of him. "Get your fucking hands off of her."

Uneven breaths started bouncing from my chest.

He pushed his head into the side of my neck. I closed my eyes and looked away. "You smell better this time." His lips touched my neck. Jeremy yelled something on the other side of the room. "Cleaner. And is that perfume?"

I couldn't make words leave my lips. I was sure I knew what was about to happen, and I made the choice not to fight back to right the wrong I made three years prior. Micah was in that room because of me, but I wasn't going to let him die because of me too.

His hand at my thigh grasped ahold of the white night gown and lifted it up my body.

"I swear to god," Jeremy said. "I swear to god I'll fucking kill you."

"Will you?" Peterson asked. "This moment, I mean? Because I know that you will. But look at that poor little boy over there, Jeremy. You're going to force me to kill him?"

"It's okay," I whispered through chattering teeth.

"Baby—"

"So you won't fight me?" he whispered at my ear.

"Get the fuck off of her!" Jeremy yelled.

I tightened my jaw and opened my eyes to look at Micah crying in Chris's arms beside Amy on the cement through that little computer monitor. Tears warmed my chilled cheeks.

I shook my head.

"No," Jeremy said. "No, god damn it!"

I felt his hands throb as he hit them off of the bars.

"You know what's funny, Jeremy?" Peterson's cold hand touched my bare hip. "That day, when you had my soldier in your basement. You said I didn't break her. But would she have let me do this if I didn't?"

Suddenly his cold fingertips touched my underwear.

My stomach lurched. I swallowed vomit that rose up my esophagus. But the rest of my body went numb. Paralyzed, practically.

"She's not letting you do shit, you aren't giving her a choice."

He pushed the blade at my neck into my throat until the skin broke. I clenched my chattering teeth together. His lips lowered to my ear. "You have a choice, don't you, Laila?"

I looked at Micah on the monitor, heaving in deep, erratic breaths.

"Tell him you have a choice." His lip grazed my ear and my head pounded.

My eyes closed. *I'm sorry.*

"Lai," Jeremy barely whispered. *No. No,* I'm *sorry.*

Inside his mind, he was practically in tears.

I read once: *allow your body to do whatever it instinctively does when you're in a moment like this. Vomit, piss, shit yourself. Cry. Anything they might find repulsive.*

But I couldn't do anything. I'm not even sure I breathed.

And then, a loud sound I can't quite describe cracked through the air around us, sending a spasm through the atmosphere and the hair on my arms to its ends.

It wasn't a bang. I couldn't describe it as a roar either. But it forced a gasp from Peterson's chest.

I heard him murmur something entirely inaudible.

Peterson dropped my skirt. "Fine."

A breath of relief fell from my lips.

Then the blade at my neck slowly slid down the length of my torso.

I held my breath as the tip touched my belly button. He grasped ahold of my hair and turned my gaze to meet Jeremy's. My hand raised from my side to his, holding my husband's knife to my stomach. My trembling fingers fought to pull it back, but I could barely breathe through the anxiety.

When my shaking hand grasped ahold of his wrist, he tightened his hand in my hair. "Does this look familiar to you yet, Jeremy?"

"Put her down." He shook his head, fast breaths leaving his lips. "Please just put her down."

"Don't fuck it up this time," Peterson spat.

He grabbed ahold of my shoulder and slammed the blade into my stomach.

"No!" Jeremy yelled.

A slow, shocked breath left my lips. The real pain began as he slowly inched the knife out of my flesh.

He dropped the blade to the ground and threw me forward. I hit my face on the metal rods. Jeremy reached through. He tried to grab my shoulder, but I tumbled to the cement.

"What did you do?" Jeremy said with wide eyes, reaching for me through the bars. "What—I can't heal her. I can't—She's—She'll die."

"Figure it out," Peterson said.

Beep.

Click.

"Baby." Jeremy struggled to reach for my shoulders through the gate. "Baby, roll over. I have to put pressure on that."

"I-I..." Fast, shallow breaths left my lips. I tried to move my hands but felt entirely numb. I didn't even feel the bleeding hole that led to my intestines. I felt nothing.

Then the door between our cells swung open. Jeremy's hand left my arm. He darted through the doorway and lowered himself to the ground beside me. "Laila."

His hand twisted around my back, rolling me over to face him. His reddened, brilliant blue eyes widened with fear. He wadded up my dress and shoved it into the wound.

"Laila, talk to me. Talk to me, baby." He touched my face and looked between my eyes. "Talk to me."

CHAPTER SEVENTY-TWO

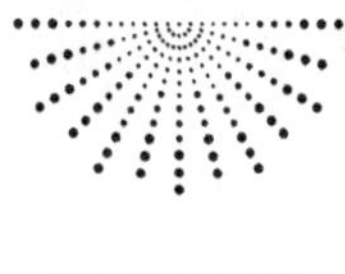

JEREMY

"Am I b-breathing?" she whispered.

I pulled her into my lap. "You're breathing." I pushed my hand into the warm, wet hole in her stomach. Her face collapsed to the palest white I ever saw. She fought a deep cough that left blood splattering from her lips to the shaking hand she lifted to her face.

"I-I-I think—I think I'm i-i-in sh—shock."

"Let's just breathe for a second." I looked down at our bloody hands against her abdomen. "Just—just take slow, deep breaths. You just have to breathe."

Her breaths grew short and close together as her hands began to violently tremble. "I'm going to die."

"No. No, you—"

"You said it," she whispered through chattering teeth. Her gaze stayed steady with the blood oozing around my hand as my stomach sunk. "I-I'm gonna die."

Shit. Why the fuck did I say that?

You just have to make it until tonight, I said into her mind. *Just a few hours.*

It's only been a few hours, Jeremy. We have at least another fourteen until night fall, and we both know I'm not going to make it that long.

"Stop it." I shook my head against hers. "Stop it. Don't say that."

She turned her gaze up to meet mine, and my heart shattered. The only way to tell where her lips ended and her skin started were the streams of bright red blood that speckled around them. All of the color in her face receded. She looked as white as paper against the dark locks around her cheeks. Purplish circles suddenly hung below her green eyes that usually glowed like light bulbs and sparkled like emeralds. But they looked dull.

Dying.

The life was slowly draining from her shaking body as she looked between my eyes.

Her bloody hand reached up to touch my face. Bright white light erupted from it before I grasped it and pulled it away.

"Very smart, Jeremy," Nastya's voice said over the speaker.

"Aren't you hurting him enough?" Laila struggled to raise her voice.

I wrapped my fingers around hers. I didn't even feel my pain anymore; all that I felt was my hammering heart.

Shit. Shit, I didn't know how to fix this. Even if I had a needle and thread, it wouldn't matter. I didn't know how to sew organs. A flesh wound, I could handle, but this cut hit intestines at the least, possibly her appendix. It was low; it could've hit her uterus too.

"Go ahead, Laila," Peterson's voice said gently. "If it'll make this easier for you."

She clenched her jaw, pulled her fingers from mine, and touched my cheek. I closed my eyes and tried to think of a plan. I tried to figure out a way to get her out of this.

But I tried teleporting, and there was a barrier around the room just as there was around Micah's shed. Laila could take it down, but it wouldn't be easy with or without a gaping hole in her stomach. She wouldn't have the time to get it down before they killed Micah. Helena was going to do the spell soon, but she already lost a lot of blood. There was no way she could make it 'til midnight our time. Six hours, tops. If we were lucky. The blood didn't seem to be pouring, more of a slow ooze. But still. Not enough time.

I pulled her hand from my face and grabbed the bottom of her dress. "I need to see where it is, okay?"

She nodded as her shaking hand wrapped around my bicep. I raised her dress and looked over the flowing wound at her stomach. It was positioned perfectly just below her belly button. He knew what he was doing; he wanted to give her time. My knife was nearly six inches long. But he couldn't have pushed in more than three. Which was good, that meant he probably didn't hit the aorta or IVC.

As a doctor, he knew just how to stab someone and make their death as slow and agonizing as possible.

But that was a good thing; it gave us time.

"I don't know if this'll work, but I have an idea," I murmured. "It's going to hurt whether it works or not."

She licked her dry lips and gave a nod.

I shifted her weight against my bicep. My legs moved so that one rested beneath her back and the other over her thighs. "I don't want you to move because I have to be really careful."

She nodded, cool sweat rushing down her cheek. "I know. You're about to electrocute me."

"I've singed you before." I pushed hair behind her ear and ran my thumb along her cheek. "We can't cauterize it with your fire because you're immune to it. But this might buy us some time."

She pressed her trembling lips together. "Move this leg so I can lie down. Then lift my knees to get blood—"

"Flow back to your head when you faint. I know, baby."

I lifted my leg to her side. She said, "I'll try and hold still."

"It's okay." I helped her lie back. Her jaw clenched together. Tears burned across her eyes. I held her chin. "We're walking out of here together, Laila. Just don't let go."

A smile tugged at her mouth. She gave a quick nod. I pulled her fingers to my lips and forced a smile. I carefully released them. I lowered myself to her thighs and put a hand on her shoulder. A slow shaking breath left her lips before I realized I was holding mine.

I exhaled slowly and turned my gaze to the hole in her stomach. My shaking hand moved above it. A small, single line of electricity danced from my palm. She gave another nod and closed her eyes.

I turned the tiny bolt of lightning to her stomach. As my hand approached her skin, I felt her body tighten. I gently slid my fingertips along her shoulder in a soothing motion. I felt the sting of electricity touch her flesh. I felt it in my own and fought with everything inside of me to keep my hand steady. Her body trembled beneath me as the smell of burning flesh touched my nostrils.

Despite the shaking, she stayed far steadier than I expected her to. Far calmer than I was.

I never hurt her, not on purpose. Not once. But watching that pain on her face and smelling the scorching skin brought tears to my eyes and a gurgle to the pit of my stomach. Hers stayed closed, but her shaking hand lifted to mine against her shoulder. She twined our fingers together as if I were the one who needed comforted. Although, I suppose that I was. She handled a crisis way better than I did, at least, that particular crisis.

I felt their gazes on me and had to fight the urge to scream profanities.

He stabbed her just to watch me suffer. To watch me scramble and search for a way to save her. To watch me fight for her life.

I should have known she was what he would use to hurt me. Nothing hurt more than fearing for her life for the millionth time, and he knew that. That's why he let her heal me. Because he saw that I could get past my own physical pain. But losing her, losing the mother of my children, that was the only thing he could do that would hurt as much as losing them.

Just before the wound cauterized shut, her trembling slowed beneath me. My heart hammered against my ribs as I climbed off of her and checked her pulse. It thudded fast but faint beneath my fingertips.

"Should stop the external bleeding," Peterson said over the speaker. "But what are you going to do about that internal bleeding?"

I clenched my jaw and carefully lifted her knees beneath my arm to get blood flow back to her brain. My fingertips grazed her paper white cheek.

"Might buy you a few more hours. But even so, we're looking at five, maybe six tops before she's gone. And there's no way that sister of yours is making it in here. Not without Laila, at least. Got to think of something more long term."

My face screwed up in confusion as I turned my gaze to his. He knew Hannah was a necromancer?

How could he know?

He raised a brow. A smirk pulled at his lips. "What? You thought I didn't know about her? I told you, Jeremy. Everyone knows you where I come from."

My breaths grew short as I turned back to Laila. I kept my fingers against her fast-racing pulse and looked back to meet his gaze. "How could you do this? You... You love her, how could you..."

"I don't enjoy this, Jeremy," he said. "I do love her. That's why I hope that you're as strong as I know you can be today."

"I'm not a healer, you know this. I can't heal her. You're a doctor. You worked on her leg; you can fix this." I licked my lips, feeling her pulse pick up a bit under my fingertips. "You said that you would never let her die—"

"I said I wouldn't kill her," he stated. "I didn't say that I wouldn't let her die."

"You just stabbed her—" I yelled.

"But if she's not here tomorrow, it'll be because you didn't save her," Peterson said.

My mouth fell open. My head shook. "You locked me in a fucking room with no medical supplies, how could this be my fault?"

He sighed, head shaking slightly. "Remember, Jeremy. I know you've had fleeting memories but this... It should have come back to you by now."

I clenched my jaw.

He knew far more than we thought he did. He'd only been telling us what was to come. But he didn't only know about our future. He also knew about our past.

Understanding how the two connected couldn't possibly process through my brain as I held my barely conscious, blood covered wife on the cool cement of that tiny cell. But soon, I'd understand exactly what he meant.

CHAPTER SEVENTY-THREE

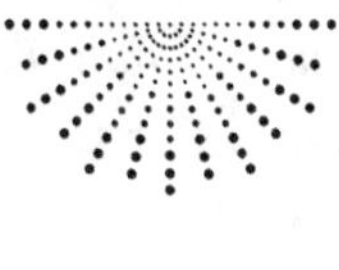

JEREMY

"Hey, beautiful." Jeremy's warm, calloused hand held my cheek. I struggled to see through my heavy eyes. He forced a pained smile to his lips.

The stabbing pain ripped up my stomach as I shifted, trying to bring myself vertical against his chest. "How long was I out?" I whispered.

"Felt like years." He carefully soothed his hand against my hair. "No more than a couple hours though."

"Maybe it worked." I fought to raise my sandpaper eyelids. "Stomach wounds usually kill pretty quick, right?"

"It worked," he said.

Neither of us believed it. It kept the blood inside. But judging by the gelatin sensation through my extremities, I was on borrowed time.

"It worked; you're going to be fine." Jeremy looked between my eyes. "You're fine."

I forced what I could of a smile and nodded.

"How do you feel?" His fingertips grazed the hair along my face, watching me the way I stared down at that single photo we had of Micah. Stricken with guilt, and fear, and love, and pain, all at once. "Do you... Does it hurt?"

"Kind of," I murmured. "Like an aching pain if I move. But mostly pretty numb."

"The bruising on your stomach isn't really bad yet. I... I asked him for a transfusion kit, but I was high a few hours ago. And you lost a good bit of blood, and that dose wasn't low, and I don't know if the two would correlate, but he made it sound like they would. And you're a lot smaller than me too, and you've never done opioids—"

"It's okay," I whispered as my fingers found his. "It's okay." *I just have to make it a few more hours. I hold Nastya back while you go into Micah's head and get a message to Chris.*

What am I supposed to tell him?

I thought for a moment. Could Chris kill Amy? She definitely had a weapon. And he was blind; I wasn't sure if he'd even learned to navigate on his own since he'd been stuck in tiny cells since his eyes were removed. I was sure he'd know those rooms like a dog knew every cranny of its cage, but getting a weapon off of anyone is a challenge. It doesn't go the way it does in the movies. It gets messy. I learned that firsthand when I saw Adam struggling to get that knife off of Adrian all those years ago and again today when I attempted to pull that knife from Peterson's hand.

Then a thought I didn't want to think traced across my mind.

Micah could kill her effortlessly.

What are you thinking?

A slow shaking breath left my lips. *At midnight, you'll be linked to Helena and Micah.*

His nostrils flared slightly. *I can't go into Micah's body to kill her, Laila.*

They're going to kill him. If we don't stop them, they're going to kill him, Jeremy. Isn't traumatized better than dead? And we have a million psychics. One of them can wipe the memory if I can't. Either way, we can make this whole ordeal feel like it never happened.

His jaw tightened. *You want me to go into our two-year-old's head and have him murder someone.*

I want him to live. I want him to get the fuck out of here. Tears brimmed my eyes as my trembling hand reached for his. *Amy dies first.*

Me or Leah will have a hold on Nastya long enough for me or you to send the message to Helena the moment that binding goes through. We tell her to send Kai and one teleporter for backup to get the shield down and grab Micah and Chris. They bring them back to the house. And you grab Peterson. He has no powers; he's no threat without Amy and Nastya. You take him back to the house and tie him up in the basement. If I'm still here, I take care of Nastya.

"Laila." He sent me a firm gaze, head shaking slightly. *You're going to be here.*

But if I'm not. If I'm not, this plan will work without me.

His jaw clenched. I felt him fight the urge to cry. His usually husky voice sounded so soft as it shook. "You're going to be fine."

Did you hear the plan, Jeremy?

He was silent for a moment. *Yeah, Lai. I got it.*

I smiled. He looked between my eyes for a moment. My gaze shifted to the window on the other side of the room where Peterson sat in an office chair watching us like animals at the zoo. He chewed the nail of his thumb, fingertips coasting along his five o'clock shadow.

"Is that what he's been doing this whole time?" I asked.

Jeremy glanced that direction before turning back to me. "Every time I looked that way. I've been trying not to. Trying really hard not to lose my temper and get our son killed."

"Looks like he's enjoying it." I tried to swallow between my dry lips and instead found myself coughing. His hand kneaded my shoulder as my stomach surged with stabbing pain. My face screwed up in a grimace.

"He's waiting for something." Jeremy glanced at him. "Look how focused he is."

I clenched my jaw and looked back at Jeremy above me. "Did you hear that sound?"

He turned to meet my gaze. "What sound?"

"When he…" I paused. "Right before he stabbed me. There was this sound. Or vibration, or something."

He pushed hair behind my ear. "All that I heard was my head pounding."

I was a little delirious, but I remembered that sound. And if I lived long enough, I was going to figure out what the hell it was. But if I didn't, I wanted to clarify one thing with Jeremy first.

I wrapped my hand around his. "I didn't... You know that I didn't want that, right?"

He frowned. "Obviously I know that, Laila." His hand at my cheek slid to my chin, raising it to meet his gaze. Those sad blue eyes looked between mine for a moment. My hand moved to his wrist. "I'm so sorry."

I forced a smile. "None of that."

Jeremy chuckled, but his eyes were so sad.

My eyes were so heavy. And my body felt like it was full of sand. His chest was so warm, so comforting. I nuzzled my head into his T-shirt. Despite the blood, he still smelled like cologne.

I loved that smell. Almost like oranges or lemons, but not quite so sweet. It mixed with musk, and maybe a touch of some type of essential oil. A drop of sage, perhaps.

It was so homey. Safe. Even in there, he could make me feel safe.

"I think I need a nap," I murmured.

"I think you need to stay awake," Jeremy said.

"Just a little one," I muttered. "Just... Just check my heart rate and if I flat line, shock me back."

"Laila." His head shook as he took my chin. "Please stay awake."

But my eyes had already closed.

CHAPTER SEVENTY-FOUR

JEREMY

They were performing the spell just after sundown in the time-zone we were in. But Peterson took my watch and phone from my pockets. Laila and I had both been unconscious for an unknown span of time from midnight on. There were no windows in the little cement room so I couldn't figure out any way to measure how long we'd been there.

But the sound of her heart thumping sounded like the tick of a clock. More like the tick of a clock on a bomb than the kind that hang on walls though.

Since that knife pierced her abdomen, I watched her slowly deteriorate. Dark purple bruises from her internal injuries gradually formed over her lower stomach that I knew I couldn't sew or singe back into place. As the thumps of her heart treaded along, the already colorless skin of her face drained. Looking down at her brought me back to the day we put my aunt in the ground.

I didn't want to go to Annie's funeral, but Adam insisted that I had to. I always hated seeing dead people and still do. The way Annie looked in that casket stayed with me forever. Brody said it looked like she was sleeping, but that's bullshit. She looked dead. A lifeless corpse. Just the shell of what the person I loved once lived inside of.

And that's how Laila looked in my arms. Dead. Lifeless. A slow emptying shell.

"It really hasn't come back to you yet?" Peterson said behind the glass.

"I've seen her die a thousand fucking times. I know this has happened before, Peterson. I've helplessly watched as she died life after life after life—"

"And you don't have to watch it happen again," he snapped. "You were never helpless. You didn't have to watch it all of those times either. Wake up, Jeremy. *Wake up.*"

"I can't just remember the other lives," I said. "There've been thousands of them. She's died *thousands* of times; I can't pinpoint the one time that you find fucking relevant."

"Am I going to have to come in there and stab her again—"

"You're not going to fucking touch her." I gritted my teeth with wide eyes. "I'm not letting her go. You'll have to pull her out of my arms, and we both know that you can't."

He grew quiet for a moment. His scheming little eyes flicked between mine. All I wanted to do was beat his fucking face off the cement and slam my knife through his chest. But I couldn't. I had to stay as calm as I could because he had my son's life in his hands. And I knew he'd take him from me too.

"That's what bothered you the most." He smiled. "Not that I stabbed her, but that I *touched* her."

My teeth ground together so tight, I thought I might break one.

He laughed. "For such a progressive, sensitive man, you sure are territorial."

"It's not about territory," I snapped. "It's about the fact that you hurt her more than anyone else ever has. And if she's going to die again, your face won't be the last one she sees."

"So that's how you feel," he murmured. "You're just going to let her die."

My jaw clenched even tighter, and my head shook.

"It's been about four and a half hours. She has another hour max until all that internal bleeding drains her," Peterson said. "Are you going to do something, Jeremy?"

"What the fuck am I supposed to do?" I yelled, turning to look at him. "If you let me out of here, I can take her to someone to be healed, but you won't let this wall come down. She could take it down if she weren't dying, but you won't let us do that either. I'm not a fucking healer; I'm a teleporter. I can't fix this. You know this, Peterson. You fucking know this. Quit pretending like I can make this better to try and make me pity myself—"

"I'm not pretending; you're just stupid," he snapped. "How can you have this magnificent bond and not see it? Are you really that dense?"

"Not see what?!" I screamed. "I see my wife dying in her worst fucking nightmare. That's what I see. Another tragic fucking ending."

"Then you don't deserve her." His nostrils flared, and his jaw tightened. He leaned toward the glass. "This is exactly why you've never deserved her. You're supposed to take care of her, and you've failed time and time again since the beginning. She saves you over and over, but you never balance the scale when it matters. You were stronger then too; you could have saved them all and you failed. That's all you ever do is fail. She finds her true self every single time, but you never do. You fail her life after fucking life, and you don't deserve her!"

"And you think that you do?!" I screamed back. "You think that you're better than me? You genuinely believe that you're a good person? You think that *this* makes you worthy of her?!"

He exhaled a slow, calming breath. His tense jaw softened. He took a step away from the window, rubbing his mouth. But his gaze stayed on mine. After a moment of silence, he said, "No. No, I don't, Jeremy. I wish that I were what she deserves, but I never will be. Truthfully, neither of us ever will be, at least not in our eyes. As I've said, I know where my fate lies. I know who I am, what I've done, and what I'm still doing. But you don't and that's what today comes down to."

"But why?" I asked. "Why are you doing this? You love her, why would you want to hurt her? Why would you kill her?"

"Do you think this is what I truly wanted?" He leaned forward and looked firmly between my eyes. "Do you believe I did these things for the sheer joy of it? Is that truly what you believe?"

"You kept the videos for a reason." I tightened my hand to a fist. "You're a sadistic pervert."

His gaze narrowed. "I shouldn't have done what I did that day. That's why I didn't do it today. That was not a part of the plan, and it shouldn't have happened."

"That doesn't change the fact that you're a sadi—"

"I didn't do this for sexual pleasure, Jeremy." His face said that offended him. "Surely, you aren't stupid enough to believe that I travelled back in time with hundreds of soldiers just to fuck your wife and jack off to people getting their backs torn apart. I did this because it had to be done, just as I've told you both a thousand times now. I did this because it's a necessary piece of history I was predetermined to be a part of just as the two of you were."

Predetermined.

Destiny.

Maybe it wasn't on our side after all.

"Who sent you to do this? Who told you that you were a part of this? You're human; you couldn't have figured this out yourself. Somebody told you that you're a part of this."

He sighed slowly once more and lowered himself back to the chair.

"Why won't you just tell me what the fuck happens?"

"Because the events have to happen as they're meant to," Peterson said. "They have to happen in the right order, in the right sequence. I have to help you remember so that you're ready for what happens next."

My mouth dropped open. "So that I'm ready to watch her die again?"

He drew out a slow breath and gave a gentle nod. "Yes. And for what comes after."

CHAPTER SEVENTY-FIVE

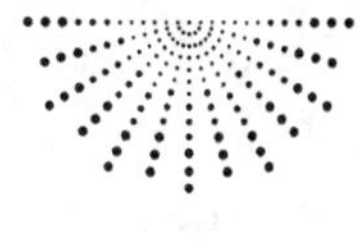

JEREMY

*D*on't listen to him, Laila's voice whispered into my mind. *I'm going to be fine, remember? I just have to hang on a few more hours.*

I pressed my trembling lips together as her eyes struggled to peel open.

Don't look at me like that either.

Like what?

Pitifully. I'm gonna be fine. But if I do go down, I did it trying to bring Micah home. And you've got a plan to do just that. So don't look at me like I'm just a victim.

I smiled and blinked at the burn in my eyes. *I would never.*

She made what she could of a smile. A slow, shaking breath left her lips. *You've got to do something for me though, okay?*

What's that?

If I don't make it out, you've got to keep being a good dad. With or without me, you've got to be a good dad to our kids.

You just said you're going to be fine.

But either way. You've got to keep being a good dad.

My tongue ran along my lips. *I'll always be there for my kids, but that's not your cue to go dying on me.*

A real smile that time. Her hand found mine. Her eyes fluttered shut, and she whispered, "I'm not going anywhere. But it hurts to talk."

Tears burned across my eyes. "That's okay."

We both knew the same thing that Peterson did. We were running out of time. If it'd only been four hours since she'd been stabbed, that meant it couldn't be more than noon or one at the latest.

She wasn't making it to midnight.

It's funny how when someone is near death or in some other crisis, we lie. We tell them they'll be fine even though we know that they won't. They know it too. She'd died at least three times in this lifetime alone. She knew this feeling. But she pretended not to.

Or maybe the slur of time that occurred left her thinking nightfall was a few minutes away. Maybe she did believe that she would survive.

I tried to believe that she'd make it, but she already looked gone. Her pulse barely tapped against my fingers. In that moment, I realized that I would lose her again. I'd watch her heart stop beating for the millionth time.

And I broke.

Tears poured down my cheeks.

I expected her to wake up as I lifted her against my chest and wrapped my arms around her shoulders. But she barely fluttered her eyelids.

Her voice tried to leave her lips but faltered through her dry mouth. *Can you sing me something?*

"I don't think the acoustics are great in here," I murmured at her ear, throat so stiff it was hard to form words.

"That's okay." She tried to make out. Her shaking, blood covered hand reached for mine and pulled it into her chest. *I just want to hear your voice.*

I tightened my hand around hers. "What do you want me to sing?"

"Anything," she murmured. "Or just talk. I just..." Her words slurred, head rolling from my chest to my shoulder.

"Wanna hear my voice," I murmured. I combed my hand along the back of her hair and took in the feel of her warm body against mine. My tongue ran along my lips. "Ask me something."

"Like what?"

"I don't know." I gave something of a laugh. I closed my watering eyes to blink the sting away. "I don't know, just ask me something. Anything."

She struggled to open her eyes. A soft smile came to her pale lips. "What... Wa-wa—" She stopped herself and pressed her trembling lips together. *What was your first impression of me?*

I laughed and ran my thumb against her abnormally cold cheek. "If I remember correctly, Adam was showing me a picture of Adrian that you were in. And I said I'd hit it."

Her smile widened.

"I asked for your number, and he told me no. He wouldn't even tell me your name." I smiled at the vague memory. "You're the reason I came to pick you guys up, you know that?"

What do you mean?

"He said that Adrian's car broke down, and I told him to have fun getting a cab. He said that his girlfriend's cute friend, the one whose number he wouldn't give me, also needed a ride home. And I said let me get some pants on."

Something that almost sounded like a laugh released from her lips. Then we both grimaced at the pain in her abdomen.

"Or did you mean when I actually met you?" I pressed my lips to her hair. She nodded slightly. "Well, I was kind of a whore back then."

"Same," she muttered.

A chuckle left my lips. I held her tighter. "I thought that you were human, and I wasn't really looking for a relationship or anything. I was clean and everything, but I didn't particularly want to fall in love. Never had a lot of luck in that department before. And I was just... I was just having fun. I was only twenty, ya know?"

She gave a soft nod against my shoulder.

"And honestly, I didn't think I'd want anything other than that from you until I pulled up to that car, and you refused to leave that damn deer." She exhaled a quiet breath that seemed as close as she could get to a laugh. "You were just so sweet. But fiery. And angry. Adam told you to get in the car, and you yelled at him to leave without you if he was in such a rush to go get his dick sucked." She squeezed my hand. Her smile stretched wider. "I think that I recognized you. The you I knew in the other lives."

I think I did too.

"Guess you can't call it love at first sight if you've seen each other a million times before, right?" I smiled and squeezed her hand.

But she didn't squeeze it back.

My heart fell.

"Laila," I said. "Laila, wake up." Her eyes struggled but shifted slightly beneath their lids. "Come on, baby. You've got to stay with me, okay? You have to hold on, and you can't let go."

She moved her head a bit. *How much longer until they cast the spell?*

I clenched my teeth together. *Not long. I—I don't think it'll be long.*

You're lying, huh?

A quiet chuckle left my lips. I ran my hand along the side of her face. *I don't know how long, baby.*

She took in a slow, shaking breath. *I think he wants you to see what I saw the other day. Me dying when we were the Elders.*

I did see that.

Yeah, but we both only saw a snippet. He wants you to see something else. Maybe after I died, maybe that's why I didn't see it. Maybe you won't remember until I die.

Stop talking like that. You don't get to give up. We had a deal. We hold on and we don't let go. We walk out of this together.

I'm not giving up. But maybe that's what he's thinking. That when I die, you'll remember. Maybe this is the end of my part of the story. Maybe you're the hero the rest of the way.

My jaw tightened. I took her chin beneath my finger. "Stop it, Laila. Stop it."

Her eyes wouldn't even open. I felt her soft, barely there pulse beneath my fingers at her neck and more tears fell down my cheeks.

Tell me you love me.

You know that I love you.

But I want to hear you say it.

"I love you." I lifted her face closer to mine. "I love you, okay? Now open your eyes. You have to hold on, Laila."

"I love you too," she barely whispered.

And then, I felt that now well-known feeling of her soul lifting from her body.

CHAPTER SEVENTY-SIX

JEREMY

My heart raced as I lowered her to the ground, placed my left hand over her right breast, and the other on the left side of her ribs. I'd defibrillated people before, and it worked. But I didn't know them, and my entire world wasn't riding on saving their lives.

The thing about a standard defibrillator is the fact that it monitors the rhythm of a heart to see if a shock will even help and how much energy to administer. And on just about anyone else, I'd know how to feel those vibrations. I'd pick up on those tiny electrical rhythms within their body. But I could barely process what I was doing. There's a reason medical personnel can't work on their loved ones because your world stops spinning and spirals at the same time when the heart of someone you love stops beating.

But I did it anyway. I sent a shock of hot energy through her body and felt her corpse jump up toward me from below.

No gasping breath left her lips. No small pump resumed in her chest. Her eyes didn't move behind their lids.

So I did it again. Only to have the same result.

Then again and again and again. I must have shocked her ten times.

But nothing.

I saw on a documentary once that people can survive hours as long as you keep their heart pumping. You keep the heart pumping, you keep blood flow to the brain, and you keep the person alive.

So that's what I did. I slid my hands from her breast and ribs to a fist at the middle of her chest and began pumping.

"If defibrillation doesn't work, CPR won't either," Peterson said. "They teach you that in standard first aid classes."

"Shut up." I listened to her voice in my head, always reminding me to pump my fists to the beat of *Staying Alive* when giving CPR before laughing at the irony.

"She's gone, Jeremy."

"Shut up!" I screamed, glancing at him. My voice startled him, and he stumbled back a bit.

"It's not going to work," he muttered.

"Then why did you do this?!" I yelled so loud that blood vessels popped in my eyes. "Why did you kill her?! Why the fuck did you do this?!"

My yells turned to sobs as I lifted her dead, lifeless corpse to my chest.

I shifted and pulled her over me. My chest was so tight, it felt like I couldn't breathe. My stomach ached. My throat felt like it was sealing shut. I held her so close, as if squeezing her tight enough would bring her back to me.

"Why would you do this," I sobbed.

"Save her," Peterson said. "For once, do it right. Fix it. Save her."

"I can't fix this! She's gone. She's—She's dead." My lip quivered as I brushed my fingertips over her cold, lifeless cheek.

As I pulled her head into my chest and closed my wet eyes, it came back.

Still, the clear, whole image of what happened that day in the Elder's Hall wouldn't come for several years. But suddenly, I found myself reliving the first time that I lost her.

I held her just as I had a moment earlier in my arms. Her head rolled into my chest, her arms swung lifeless to the floor beneath her, but I didn't feel the same agonizing heartbreak. Instead, I was livid. Not hurt but angry. Annoyed.

My arms circled her, and I murmured something in a trembling voice. I carefully lowered her to the ground. I looked over those marble floors coated in at least a quarter inch of blood. My star and smoke-like energy danced above it. My hand took hers, and I kissed those bloody knuckles. I closed my eyes and focused.

As he, or I, technically, moved into a part of my mind that I didn't realize existed, something shifted inside of me.

Suddenly, I wasn't in my body. Nor was I in his. We were both somewhere else.

Somewhere mostly dark but speckled with lights like that of the night sky. For a moment, I thought that's where we were. Space. But regardless of where we were was *what* we were.

I could see, but I had no eyes. I was moving, but I had no legs. I had no body at all; I literally became the energy that radiated from my skin.

As we spun violently through that dark space, I felt like we were searching for something, but I didn't grip what at first.

Then a voice spoke in the hall, pulling us from the dark dimension we raced through.

My head raised from Laila's body in my arms to the man in a white tunic near the door.

I'm not sure what he said, but it sent a boil to my blood. In response, I spat words from my lips like the roar of a lion.

I took in that man's overall persona, trying hard to remember it rather than focus on the words my past-self shared with him that I couldn't understand.

His skin shimmered a soft golden color like the sun or shores of a beach. Short blond hair laid just above his eyes and around his ears in small, waving curls. His brown eyes looked like a tree's bark painted with even strokes of gold.

He looked like Lucifer.

As he spoke, his hand shook like a glass of water in an earthquake. His head shook back and forth, and his brows raised over his wide, watering eyes. He felt remorse, I could see that as I looked at him looking at Laila in my arms. But it was just that, remorse. I didn't know much of what any of what I saw meant at the time, but it proved what Heylel said to be true.

He killed us.

As I brought myself to my feet, the man's eyes widened in terror.

And I slammed back to my reality.

CHAPTER SEVENTY-SEVEN

JEREMY

As my eyes flung open, as I looked down at Laila in my arms, it clicked.

I'd been through that dark space with twinkling lights more times than I could count, in the most literal definition of that phrase. I hadn't remembered it until I'd seen it, but now it was crystal clear.

The most recent time I went there, Hannah pulled me back.

Seeing it through his eyes felt like a door opening inside of my mind.

When that door opened, I jumped into it.

Suddenly, I was there. Not in a body, only that grayish black smoke speckled with blue and silver. Floating through blackness.

It was like driving down a dark highway during a blizzard, but each snowflake shined its own hue like tiny brilliants suns, some colors I didn't even know existed.

The concept on Earth proved the same there, much to my surprise. I focused hard enough, and my body practically willed itself toward her.

And I saw her. But not technically her, but who she was within the shell that held her. A glowing light brighter than any of the ones around her, gleaming an inviting golden color swirling with rays of violet and speckled with white.

I can't even describe how I actually did it because both of us were a form that I can only explain in our level of existence as gaseous. Perhaps light is a better word for it. We were light. Even that isn't an entirely accurate depiction of the matter we existed as without a body to house us.

But somehow, I grasped ahold of her.

It was as though my soul engulfed hers.

And we flung to our bodies like the kickback of a rifle.

A long, heaving gasp dropped into her lips. She began to gurgle on her blood, probably as a result of how hard I pushed into her chest when I gave her compressions.

Still, describing what I did is near impossible. But somehow, I felt some part of me holding her soul in her dying body.

Her wide green eyes met mine, blood splattering from her lips. My head shook as fast, uneven breaths heaved in and out of my chest. I had no idea what to do next or how I held onto her the way that I did in that moment. It felt like being completely frozen in time.

She grasped ahold of my hand and pushed it into her stomach.

Bright white light from her palm radiated into the back of mine. Suddenly, her hand returned to normal and mine radiated bright white light instead. My eyes shot open in shock.

That's when I understood what the purpose in that little stunt had been to Peterson. He wanted us to see what we were capable of when our souls touched. In that very moment, I grasped it.

He had two objectives that day. First, to show me that I was far more like my little sister than I realized. Second, to show us what we could do when our souls made contact.

My soul held hers into her body; that's what gave me the capability to borrow her abilities to heal the wounds that I just watched take her life.

It all happened so fast, but it felt like a lightbulb turning on after sitting in darkness for centuries.

I hated that man with every fiber of my being, after that more than ever before. But he only took her from me for a moment. I got her back.

I would *always* get her back.

CHAPTER SEVENTY-EIGHT

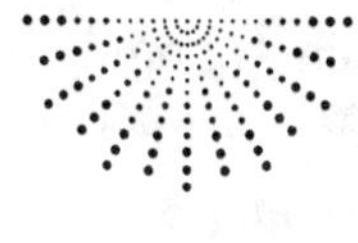

LAILA

Deep gasps collapsed into my lungs as Jeremy's glowing white hand melded the wound on my stomach back into place. For the first time since Peterson stabbed me, it really fucking hurt. But Jeremy's eyes were broader than the sky, his mouth fell wide open, and his bright white palm vibrated like a teenager's cellphone on a Friday night. I wanted to scream, but I knew that if I did, Jeremy would jump and lose his hold on whatever the fuck he somehow managed to pull off.

After a few writhing and excruciating moments, the only pain came from the light itself. When it reached that point, I grabbed ahold of his hand, flung it away, and lifted my arms around his shoulders. His palms opened against the back of my ribs, pulling me as tight to him as we could get.

"How the fuck did you do that?" I whispered with wide eyes, meeting Peterson's smiling gaze in the window.

"I have no clue," he murmured.

"Well done, Jeremy." His voice rang over the speakers as his hands drew together in a clap. "You had me worried there, but you got it. You finally got it. That ability of your baby sister's is hereditary after all."

"I pulled you back," Jeremy whispered.

"You sure did." Peterson smiled and leaned over the desk in front of him. "Then you healed her."

Jeremy looked down at his shaking, crimson covered hands. He reached out and touched my face with wide eyes. Admittedly, I didn't feel half as shocked as one might expect to feel after resurrecting from the dead. But after three times, it'd kind of lost its wow factor for me.

"I—I used your powers." He blinked hard, looking from my eyes to my hand and then my stomach. "Should I have asked first?"

My lips pulled into a smile. I leaned forward and wrapped my arms around his back. *A few more hours. Then we're getting our baby and going home.*

He laughed quietly at my ear. His hands tightened at my waist, pulling my body firmer into his.

"What a beautiful moment to witness," Peterson murmured. "I should take a picture. Might be worth a lot of money one day."

I can't wait to punch his stupid fucking face, Jeremy's voice echoed through my ears.

The rest of the hours we spent in that room felt like ecstasy compared to the ones that preceded them. Our arms stayed around each other every second from the moment that I woke up to the moment that we got out of that room. But we existed in each other's minds during that time.

We didn't speak a word to each other out loud. We didn't need to. Everything that we had to say could be said through the energy that danced between our minds.

From that moment on, I felt a connection to him that I hadn't in any of the lives I lived before, aside from the first. When he showed it to me from his perspective, I understood why. Our souls were always bound together, but they made contact that night. That taught us that when they touched, they acted as one.

It occurred to me in that moment.

The two of us together... We were invincible. One day, I'd have the ability to grant eternal life. And he was now of the few that could take it away.

Balance.

A perfect equilibrium of life and death.

CHAPTER SEVENTY-NINE

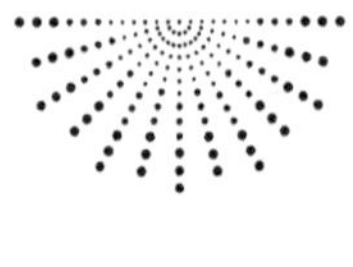

LAILA

Just after dusk, Peterson left the box attached to our room. Whether he went to piss or get ready for bed, I don't have a clue, but it timed out perfectly. Because not more than a moment after that door shut, I felt the sudden surge of energy as my mind laced between Nastya and Helena's.

The moment Helena finished that spell, I saw a gasp enter Nastya's lips.

And a smile pulled at mine.

Our gazes met through the glass window, and I saw a fear unlike any other flash through that cold gaze. They knew we wouldn't be here long, but they didn't know how we'd get out. She didn't know I'd be hopping into her head just like she'd been helping Amy and Peterson hop into Chris and whoever the hell else they wanted.

As I felt my thoughts connect to hers, I fought the urge to see what was inside. I could, but that's not why I was there. My objective was simple. Keep her from moving, taint her mind into believing I wasn't within it, and leave her thoughts in a simple state of awareness that wouldn't alert Amy of what Jeremy was about to do.

My gaze shifted between her trance like stare, and I knew it worked.

"Now," I whispered to Jeremy.

His eyes closed, focusing hard.

She stared into my eyes. Her thoughts stayed at a steady, synthetic pace as I struggled to convince her that I wasn't doing what she felt me doing. Some part of her deep down fought my hold over her mind. That fraction proved the hardest to hold down.

But we had it. We were there. Once Amy was out of the picture, I could handle the two of them. I could handle them as soon as that knife at my son's throat fell to the ground.

The longer I held onto her thoughts, the harder that small part of her that knew something felt off fought. Jeremy couldn't have been more than two minutes sending his message to Helena and speaking with Micah and Chris. But after the first minute, the weight of her fight against my mind made my hands tremble and my jaw clench as if lifting a car above my head.

Just when I felt like I was about to lose my hold, Jeremy said, "Amy's taken care of. The others are coming. Get this shield down."

CHAPTER EIGHTY

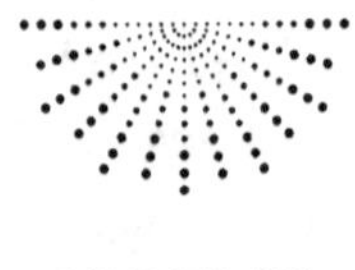

JEREMY

"Now," Laila said.

The second that wave of Micah's energy washed over me, my body was enveloped by the strength of his soul. Once that bond solidified, tapping into it felt as simple as grabbing ahold to a toy float and coasting along a whirlpool.

Suddenly, I looked out of my son's eyes at Amy in the center of the small shed. His body jerked back at my sudden presence in his mind.

It's just me, I said into his thoughts.

He took in a gasp that sent Amy's gaze our way. I felt her in his mind and knew I had to act fast. Just as she stood, I forced Micah's eyes shut and hoped like hell that Chris wasn't close behind her.

I did something that still shakes me to my core. I used my almost three-year-old son's body to murder his captor. I'd make sure he forgot it, but I saw no other option. Originally, I planned to piggyback onto Chris's thoughts from Micah's and have him do it. But the moment she stood, I had to act.

I shot some form of energy from his hands, although I'm not sure what because I kept his eyes sealed shut. She screamed. Micah tried to pull his eyes open, but I squeezed them harder together. Chris gasped on the other side of the room. I kept Micah's hands held up toward her until I'd used enough energy to take down an elephant.

What's happening? Micah's shaken voice thought.

We're coming. We're coming right now. But I need you to keep your eyes closed and hug Uncle Chris, okay? I felt his hands tremble, and I continued, *I know this is scary and you're confused, but this is going to be over soon. You're coming home.*

"Micah." Chris's hands slid along his shoulders. "Micah, what just happened?"

"He says they's coming," Micah whispered. "He says not to open my eyes."

I'll see you soon, buddy.

I hopped into Helena's mind.

Send Kai and one teleporter. Be ready to take on a couple guards. Micah and Chris are in the shed from the images we looked at yesterday. Amy's gone; Laila's got Nastya for the moment. If Kai can get that barrier down around Micah and Chris, Laila can get us out of here. I'll bring Peterson back to the house where I need Wyatt to tie him up and kill him if he tries to get away.

Jesus, that's a mouthful. But I got it, kid. Is Laila okay? I felt—

We're good, but I don't have time for chitchat.

Right. Five minutes tops.

See you soon.

My eyes opened. I looked at Laila. Blood spilled from her nose as her teeth clambered together. "Amy's taken care of. The others are coming. Get this shield down."

She released a deep breath. Nastya gasped.

"No!" I heard her exclaim through the glass before taking off out of the room. Laila stammered to her feet and walked to the wall. There, she murmured incantations at it as glowing golden light emitted from her fingertips.

Suddenly, like the vibrating glass that encased Micah's room, a thin, translucent layer around the walls vibrated. Laila's hands shook for a moment. Blood dripped from her nose to her trembling fingers.

Then the quivering of the shield around the walls began to crack, fracturing in every direction. It looked like ice on a small pond where a large rock fell to the surface. I expected it to fall on us and put my arms around Laila as a shield. But instead, each piece gradually turned to dust, sprinkling around us like snow.

I squeezed my arms around her and teleported as far as my body would allow, which took us to the next hallway.

"I'll lead the way. Get a message to Chris, tell him we're almost there."

I nodded and closed my eyes.

CHAPTER EIGHTY-ONE

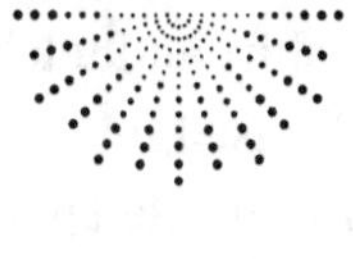

LAILA

The system of barrier spells around the warehouse seemed far less complicated than the one at the first compound had been. The aspect that made it difficult was the use of multiple forms of magic that barricaded the building. Some were Elvan, some used ancestral magic, others composed of black magic.

But the one around the shed outside was more complicated than all of them combined. I had faith in Kai's ability to take it down, but I worried about the time that he had. Nastya knew those halls, and she'd surely just alerted every guard left of our escape. They knew where we were going, and they got a head start.

In that moment, Kai and whoever came with him was our only hope. They had to get Micah out before either of them got to him.

As I swung down door after door of the complicated concrete hallways and pulled Jeremy along behind me, the only thought running through my mind was my son. I didn't note that I had yet to encounter a single person or that Jeremy could barely keep up while trying to get a message to them.

We were running out of time. They'd sacrifice him or they'd be damned. They saw it as some form of metaphoric cleansing of their souls, and they wouldn't stop until my son took his last breath.

"Somebody's trying to get in. I don't know if it's Kai or if it's them, but we have to—"

A loud, deep gurgling scream sent a swirl to the pit of my stomach.

"Get behind me," I said.

Jeremy turned his back to mine. I spun the air around us and carefully directed toward the weakest part of each wall. The door.

He grasped ahold of my shirt and nearly fell as they slammed open and clanged off the cement walls they were fastened to.

He grabbed a hold of my shirt and teleported to the end of the hall where the next barrier laid. I raised my hand to it and hurried straight through. We bolted through it and teleported up the flight of narrow steps.

As we landed at the top of the staircase, I looked up out of an open cellar door to the night sky. A thin film—similar to the Elvan border used around the shed outside and around the perimeter of our cell— separated us from the cool spring air. I raised my hands to the border and recited the spells Helena and I practiced for the past several months.

In moments, it fell to dust around us. Then Jeremy grabbed my hip, and we teleported to the grass outside. As I peered at the shed in the distance, Kai's cold, empty green eyes rolled to meet my gaze.

Brody stood beside his body with a gun aimed at a guard that held his hands above his head in front of the shed door. He said something, but Brody pulled the trigger and we appeared beside Kai. Blood puddled from a hole in his chest. Jeremy grabbed ahold of his wrist. I raised my hands to the wound as he closed his eyes and Brody shot his gun again.

A moment later, Kai took a heaving gasp of air before writhing against my hands. I climbed over his hips to pin him down. Jeremy grabbed ahold of his arms and pushed him to the ground.

"Well, look at you two go," Nastya's voice said behind me.

"He's alive; take him to Leah." Jeremy grabbed my arm and pulled me to my feet. Brody leaned down and took Kai's hand.

My jaw clenched. I looked at the three of them inside the little shack.

Micah lay in the middle, Nastya to the right, and Chris to the left. Each of them lay with their arms and legs outstretched and a blade in their right hand. Both Micah and Chris appeared to be in a peaceful sleep, but Nastya was incredibly conscious. Sitting upright, eyes against mine in the flickering yellow luminance above.

I tried to go into her mind as I raised my hands to the barrier around that shack but doing both at once was impossible. The magic of the spell that fought to maintain all of the energy within that shed made it even harder. Although weak, I had little experience with Witchcraft at all, let alone Elvan magic. If Kai were there to help, I may have had it down in time.

"Great show." Her voice echoed against the metal rafters. I raised my hands and began chanting toward the shield around the room. "But the curtain's closing now, darling."

Then, the three of them raised the blades in their hands and lifted them towards their neck. I wish that I could say that I was strong enough to keep my eyes open, but the second that blade started lowering toward my baby's throat, all that I could do was scream.

Just as my eyes sealed shut, a white light brighter than anything I'd ever seen soared from inside the shed like its own sun. Even with them closed, it still made my eyes ache.

CHAPTER EIGHTY-TWO

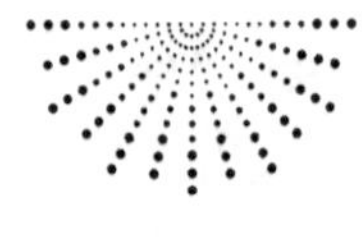

LAILA

Jeremy brushed past me and slammed his hands into the vibrating glass wall. I glanced into the shed and saw blood spraying in the air before quickly turning my gaze to the field. Deep, heaving sobs panted into my lips while he yelled and smacked his fists into the glass like forcefield.

My breaths grew close together. I braced myself against the building with one hand and pulled the other to my chest above my racing heart.

My baby was dead. He was fucking dead. All of this, and we hadn't prevented the sacrifice.

"It's down," Jeremy yelled. "It's down, heal him."

She was what held it up. Now that she was dead, it was down.

I turned and sprinted through the doorway.

I didn't take time to pay attention to the slit across my son's throat. I didn't take time to note the blood at my feet. I saw it, but we were going to fix this; I couldn't focus on it. Jeremy grabbed his hand, and I pushed my palms into his wet throat. White light shined from my skin into his as Jeremy's eyes closed.

I looked up at him. Looking at Micah hurt too much so I looked at him. I watched his careful, focused expression while he fought as hard as I did to bring our son back to his body.

Those short moments felt like years. But after a minute, Micah's brilliant blue eyes flung open.

And I realized that my hands were holding my son.

His eyes widened in fear, writhing against the pain from my hands. But Jeremy took his face in his palms. That shimmering gray light layered with blue smoke and glitter of silver and white slid from Jeremy's skin to Micah's.

His terrified expression gradually softened to a state of gentle bliss as he looked up at his dad.

"I know it hurts but it's almost over." Jeremy's hand pushed matted hair from Micah's dirty face. "It's almost over, and then we get to take you home."

A deep gasp sounded behind me.

"Go get Hannah," Celena said, passing Jeremy a crystal necklace for Chris.

Micah looked over and met my gaze as I held my skin over his throat. Tears trickled from his eyes, but his lips lifted into a smile. My eyes did the same and my lips curved up a bit. "Almost there, buddy. Almost there."

His eyes looked between mine, then between Jeremy's. He held his smile as the wound molded shut. Then Celena lowered herself to the ground beside me, and Micah looked at her with terror in his gaze. But she smiled and extended her arm out to touch his shoulder.

The moment I felt the slit beneath my hand mend shut, Jeremy teleported beside Chris on the ground to my left, leaving a cloud of gray and blue energy behind.

"Where's Peterson?" Celena said.

My palm moved from Micah's neck to his hand.

I shook my head, barely hearing a word over the sound of my heart racing in my chest.

Every single thing in that room disappeared into a grayish cloud around my son. Literally, the world looked just as it had a moment before. But from where I stood, he was the only thing visible.

Those big blue eyes filled with confusion and fear, yet awe and joy. His little panting lips that curved up in a smile as he looked between my eyes. Then the feel of his arms around my shoulders as he leaned forward and wrapped them around me.

Everything else blurred. Nothing else mattered. Nothing else even existed for that moment.

Suddenly, I didn't care about the curse. I didn't care about vengeance. I didn't even care about Chris on the floor beside him.

We made it. He lived. He died, but he lived. Just like I did, just like his dad did. We all died, but we came back. And we were finally fucking together.

A gasp dropped into Chris's lips.

"Celena," Jeremy said. "I need you over here."

She rushed to her feet and crouched over Chris gurgling blood on the ground. Micah gasped but I lifted him in the air and turned him away from Chris's seizing body. I locked my arms around his back and held him as tight as I could. My gaze shifted over Celena's hands at Chris's neck while Jeremy pushed his flailing arms to the concrete.

"I'm scawed," Micah whispered at my ear.

"It's okay. I got you, everything's okay." I brushed my hand along the back of his hair and felt my head move in a nod. "Everything's okay now, baby, we're going home."

His arms tightened around my neck and a quiet breath of relief left my lips.

Only for a moment.

Because just as Chris's gurgles turned to screams, blood began to spew from Nastya's lips. Then Amy sat forward. And then the guard laying on the ground just outside with a bullet in his head groaned.

My eyes shot open.

"Jeremy," I yelled as Amy brought herself to her knees.

Hannah and Brody appeared just outside the shed beside the moaning man struggling to his feet. Brody jerked back, pulled Hannah behind him, lifted a gun from his waistband, and fired it at the guard's head again and again. The guard jerked with each bullet but kept struggling to his knees.

Jeremy stood just as Celena pulled her hands from Chris's neck.

"What the fuck did you do?" Hannah's wide eyes shifted to the bodies rising from the ground.

"Take Micah," I blurted. Micah leaned toward Jeremy. "Everybody go. Go!"

Jeremy leaned down, placed a hand on Chris's gasping chest, and the other against Celena's wrist. I glanced at Brody who took Hannah's shoulder and disappeared. Just as Amy started toward me.

"I'm coming right back," Jeremy said.

Purple fire shot up my arms. "Land at a distance."

Then they were gone.

My gaze met Amy's. A smile pulled at her lips. "The shift has begun."

CHAPTER EIGHTY-THREE

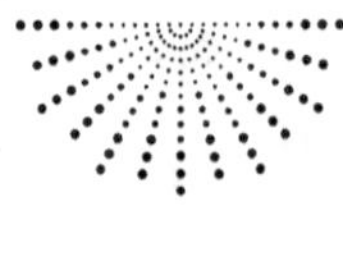

JEREMY

The four of us landed in the kitchen of the main house with a thud. Micah's arm tightened around my neck as I stumbled. Leah heaved in a deep gasp, Milly erupted in tears, and Adam laughed.

"You fucking did it, bro." Adam slammed his hands together in a clap. "Holy shit, you did it."

"Not yet." I pulled Micah from my chest and brushed hair from his face. His wide, scared blue eyes looked between mine. "Are you okay?"

He bobbed his head in a nod. "Whewe awe we?"

Chris struggled to sit up.

"You're home," Leah said with tears in her eyes. She collapsed to the ground beside our brother.

"We've got to go help Laila. Celena, you stay here with Chris and Micah," I said quickly. "Wyatt, I need you to help me track Peterson."

"No." Micah grasped my hands. "You has to stay."

"I'm coming right back." I touched his cheek. I brought a smile to my lips. "I'm going to get Mommy, and then we'll be right back."

"I don't know what the hell you did, but I have to go and help you fix it," Hannah snapped. "How many people did you bring back?"

"Bring back from what?" Wyatt asked.

Kai rubbed his chest, eyes meeting mine. "Jeremy's a necromancer."

"You stay with Uncle Chris and Aunt Leah, I'll be right back," I told Micah. Tears pearled down his little cheeks, and I smiled. "I keep my promises, right?" He gave a slow nod as Chris's hand reached up to feel around for him. Chris's hand found his shoulder while I gave another nod. "Everything's okay. You're home, buddy. You're home. You're safe. I'll be right back; I'm just going to get Mommy. Okay?"

"Be caweful."

"I got him," Chris said. "Go get your wife."

I stood and put my hand on Wyatt's shoulder. I turned to Hannah and Brody. He gave a nod. We all simultaneously appeared in the woods just outside of the open field. Bright orange and yellow fire licked the air as smoke billowed to the sky.

"Leave it to Laila to go out with a bang," Brody muttered.

"How many people did you bring back, Jeremy?" Hannah said. "Two? Three?"

I counted in my mind. Laila. Kai. Micah. Chris.

"Four," I said.

"Jesus." She walked my way and extended her palm. "Give me your hand. Now."

I joined mine with hers. "What did I do?"

"For a lack of better terminology, you left the door open." Hannah's eyes closed, and she squeezed her fingers around mine.

"Do you smell Peterson?" I asked Wyatt.

"I smell smoke," he said. "But I hear someone running."

"We got him," Brody said. "Just get Laila and get back to your kids."

"If it's him, he'll be in the basement in five minutes," Wyatt said.

"If it's not, then we kill him and bring the body back to be burned." Brody grabbed a hold of Wyatt's shoulder. "Where to?"

Wyatt gestured to his left. "Maybe six hundred yards that way."

They disappeared just as Hannah's eyes opened. "It's taken care of. But you've got a lot to learn, Jeremy. You can't bring that many people back at once, and if you really have to then you've got to make sure you do it like you're walking on glass."

I made a face. "It was your fiancé, my wife, my son, and our brother. I didn't have a choice, Hannah."

"Then do it right. They have legends about what we can do for a reason. It's dangerous. For every action, there is an equal and opposite reaction. You can't bring back every person that dies, Jeremy. You just can't."

"I just couldn't let them die, Hannah."

She looked over me with an expression of dismay, lips pursed, head shaking. All of a sudden, the roles reversed. My baby sister became my teacher. "Well, let's get Laila and figure out what we're going to do about the feds. Then we'll go over the basics of necromancy."

My tongue ran along my lips. I gave a nod.

I focused on her energy for a moment and looked out over the field. I saw her holding her hands over her naked arms, struggling to retain warmth, stepping from the smoldering shack. I took Hannah's shoulder and teleported to her.

Laila met my gaze. A slow, exerted breath left her smog covered lips. "Micah's home, right? He's okay?"

I nodded. Hannah pulled her jacket from her arms. "Wyatt and Brody are getting Peterson right now."

"You got the zombies?" Hannah asked.

Laila lifted the jacket over her bare shoulders. "Any that I saw," she said. "The four guards we got last night came out of nowhere, the two Brody and Kai got were a little slower, but I got 'em. Nastya and Amy are gone too."

"Just Peterson then," Hannah said. "Then this is over."

Laila's eyes widened, shooting up to mine. Her lips heightened in a wide grin. "They got him. They're going back to the house now."

The deepest breath of my life left my lips.

A smile came to my mouth. I reached forward and wrapped my arms around my wife. She laughed as I lifted her in the air and spun in a circle. I felt the warmth of her skin radiate into mine. Hannah chuckled behind us.

"We did it," I whispered. My lips pressed into her hair. "We finally fucking did it."

CHAPTER EIGHTY-FOUR

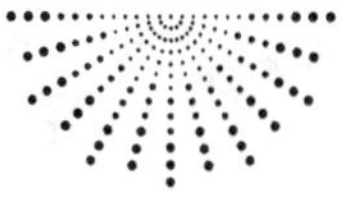

LAILA

We landed facing Chris's back and Leah's profile in the kitchen of the main house. Micah sat in Chris's lap with a hand on his uncle's cheek and a soft smile against his lips. Our brothers and sisters huddled around the three of them in awe, looking up to meet mine and Jeremy's gaze with wide, dumbfounded eyes.

My head tilted before Micah said, "Is you bettew now?"

Then Chris breathed out a soft, billowing laugh. His arms wrapped around Micah's shoulders. He pulled him tight into his body. A wide grin lifted at my son's lips.

"What just happened?" Hannah asked.

Chris turned.

And my jaw hung to the ground just as everyone else's.

A smile came to Chris's lips, extending up to his bright, shining blue eyes. "Have I ever told you how much I love this kid?"

"Did he..." Jeremy began. "Did you just..."

"Talk about healing the blind," Celena muttered.

"You grew his eyes back," I murmured to Micah.

That... that wasn't possible. The most any healer I'd ever met could do was mend a broken bone or repair a stab wound. But he... He literally gave him his sight back.

He was the most amazing thing in the entire world. Next to his sister, of course.

Micah's eyes glistened with water. His head lowered. "Am I in twouble?"

"No." I teleported across the room and collapsed to the ground with a wide smile. "No, that's amazing. You're amazing."

He smiled back, hand reaching up to touch my cheek.

Jeremy lowered himself to the ground beside us. "You're the coolest kid in the world."

Micah's smile widened, and Jeremy put his hand on his shoulder.

The door from the basement slammed shut. Brody stood on the other end. He wiped his brow. "For such a little guy, that fucker put up one hell of a fight." Then his gaze shifted to Chris, and his eyes peeled open. "You... You can see."

"I can see." Chris laughed as he looked around. "I can see."

"It's over." Leah's hands moved to her brothers' shoulder. "It's over, you're home."

He laughed, leaned forward, and put his arms around her. Adam joined in, then Hannah and Brody.

Jeremy and I wrapped our arms around Micah. Celena chuckled, situating Milly on her hip. Tink came running down the steps and licked mine and Jeremy's face before doing the same to Micah. He laughed as she lapped the blood from his neck.

He rested his head against my shoulder. I met Jeremy's gaze around Micah's messy, bloody hair and smiled. Joyous tears spilled down my cheeks. He wiped the salty water from my face with his dirty, blood and smog covered thumbs.

He smiled the largest, sweetest smile. "We broke the cycle."

We sure the hell did.

Our baby was home, and we'd never lose him again.

But breaking that cycle was the equivalent of pressing the biggest nuclear button of all time.

The story continues in *Sacred Sins*. Turn the page for a sneak peek, or click the link below to download now:
https://www.amazon.com/dp/B0956PTMBX/

Sign up for Charlie's newsletter and receive a free copy of the Eluding Destiny prequel, *Blood Bar*:
https://liquidmind.media/eluding-destiny-prequel/

If you enjoyed this story, please consider leaving a rating or review on Amazon:
https://www.amazon.com/gp/product/B095J135H4/

Join Charlie's private reader group on Facebook and discuss all things Eluding Destiny and Charlie Nottingham:
https://www.facebook.com/groups/661440911724435/

SACRED SINS CHAPTER ONE

JEREMY

My head rested against the messy, dust and blood covered hair hanging from my son's neck. All I could hear was the pounding of my heartbeat in my ears and Laila's relieved, yet tense, uneven breaths beside me. Micah stunk so bad, like a combination of urine, feces, and dirt. But Jesus Christ, he was alive, and that was all that mattered.

We did it. Three god forsaken years later, and we finally brought our son home.

"Is everyone okay?" Hannah asked from the breakfast nook.

I pulled back and looked between Laila and Micah. Stars in the royal blue sky twinkled around his head before the glass patio doors. This wasn't how I envisioned my son looking when I met him for the first time. Still dripping crimson, muddy, cheeks hollowed. But somehow, that view of him standing in front of the glass window was the most beautiful thing I'd ever seen.

I cupped his bloody cheek, and a smile came to my lips. "You're okay, right?"

He smiled and bobbed his little head in a nod.

Chris turned to me and Laila. He smiled, eyes filling with tears. "Yeah, I think everyone's okay."

Eyes. His *eyes* filled with tears.

He had eyes again.

How the fuck did he have his eyes back? How did Micah do that?

"Mommy," Micah said. His hand lifted to Laila's face. She looked at him in awe, or maybe disbelief, as salty water flowed down her cheeks. "Mommy, why awe your cwying?"

She let out a quiet laugh and wiped her cheeks. "I'm just so happy."

"Everybody's hungry, right?" Leah rubbed her watery eyes and smiled between the four of us. "We—me and Hannah, I mean. We made cookies this afternoon, and I think there's still pizza on the stove."

"What time is it?" Chris glanced around. "McDonald's isn't open, is it?"

"Yeah, you'll have to wait on that Big Mac." Laila smiled.

"Pizza 'll do then." He smiled at her. He looked at Leah. "Do you have Sprite?"

She helped him to his feet. "We have Sprite, and Jeremy brought you some clothes over before they left. We'll all get something to eat, and then you guys can all get cleaned up."

"Should we do that?" Brody asked. "The cops are going to be involved soon; we can't have him wearing Jeremy's clothes."

"We can't really show up in these either." Chris looked down at his ruined scrubs. "Where did this come from anyway?"

"You don't remember?" I asked.

He shook his head.

Well, at least that crossed one thing of the list of things we had to worry about. Chris didn't remember slitting his own throat. That meant that Micah probably didn't either.

Laila blew out a sigh. Her gaze shifted over Micah before sliding back to Chris. "We'll talk about it later."

Leah put some pizza into the microwave. Hannah tossed Laila a pair of pants. "Might want to put some clothes on, lady."

"Oh, shit." She looked down at the hoodie covering her torso, tele-ported the sweats over her legs, and started to her feet.

She lifted Micah with her, his legs tightening around her hips. He smiled at me over her shoulder. I smiled back and put my hand on his arm. He was half her size in height; they looked a little silly like that. But it was still the most perfect sight I'd ever beheld.

My wife, holding my son. It was a dream come true. Even if we were all covered in blood and smelled like shit.

"You guys can get cleaned up and take a breath of fresh air for a while," Laila said. "Everybody can get something to eat, get cleaned up, and breathe for a minute. Then we'll get some clothes from the hospital everyone was taken to after the first compound. You guys can change, and then we'll... we'll figure out a way to involve the police and get you guys back onto the radar."

I looked at Chris and back to Micah. "How did you do that, buddy?"

"My eyes?" Chris asked.

I nodded.

Micah moved his shoulders in a slow shrug. "I just did."

"He did it before." Chris cleared his throat. Leah handed him a cookie. He smiled at her before looking back to me. "We can talk about that another time, okay? Let's just... Let's just catch up."

If he'd done it before, that meant that Peterson had cut out my brother's eyes not once, but twice. He didn't have to relive that memory to me. I was dying to know how my son could've done it, but they didn't call him the savior for nothing. It must've just been one of his many, many abilities.

I summoned a smile.

Christ turned and gazed over the small crowd with a smile. "I know you guys; you haven't changed much." He looked between Leah and Adam at the other end of the granite island. He turned to Brody and Hannah. "And I think that you're my little brother and sister, but you don't look so little anymore."

Hannah grinned. "You look a lot like you did then."

"You look a lot better than you did the last time I saw you." Brody smirked.

"That was you," Chris said. "I thought so, but I wasn't sure. Puberty changed your voice a lot."

Brody was quiet for a moment. "Yeah. Yeah, that was me."

"And who are you guys again?" He turned to Celena and Kai.

"This is my little sister, Celena." Laila gestured between them at the breakfast nook to my right. Milly was in Celena's arms, wide eyes shifting between us all. "And this is my twin brother, Kai."

"You're the one who's dating Hannah, right?"

Hannah grinned, lifting her ringed finger toward him. "Engaged, actually."

"Aye." Kai stood and wrapped an arm around her waist. He kissed the top of her head, extending his hand toward Chris. "I've heard only good things."

"Yeah, likewise." Chris smiled and shook his palm.

"You remember Wyatt, right?" Hannah asked. Chris nodded, and she said, "Celena is Wyatt's par animo."

He knitted his brows, glancing at Celena. "No shit."

Huh. I thought that Laila told him that when they were in captivity together. Then again, he probably hadn't believed that the par animarum even existed then.

"Well, that's pretty crazy," he muttered. "I'm sorry, how old are you?"

"Twenty-one," Celena said.

"Where's Helena?" Laila looked around.

"She fainted when she saw Micah grow Chris's eyes back." Adam chuckled. "I took her to the couch."

I laughed. I walked toward Celena and lifted Milly from her arms. "You don't want to get cleaned up first?"

Hell no. I'd just seen four of the people I loved most in the world die and come back to life. I wanted to hold my baby girl.

I squeezed her into my chest. She tightened her legs around my ribs. Her always big green eyes were a bit wider than usual, but she gripped my shirt so tight. I walked to Laila and Micah with a smile. "You wanted to meet your little sister, right?"

A big grin pulled at his lips as he reached out to touch her hand. His dirty fingers grazed hers, and those wide eyes softened. She smiled back.

It wasn't one of those 'bring the new baby home from the hospital and introduce her to her big brother' sort of things. But in a way, it was much more beautiful. He'd been anticipating meeting her just as much as he would have if he'd have seen Laila's belly slowly grow to the size of a basketball. She didn't really understand what was happening, but it was still a wonderful moment.

"What's her name?" Chris asked.

"Milly," Laila said

"Like Mom?"

I smiled. "Like Mom."

"Your other nephew's sleeping with his mom upstairs," Adam said.

Chris's face said he wasn't sure he believed that. "You've got a kid too?"

Adam smiled. "Luka."

"Sorry. We didn't have much time to fill you in," Laila said.

Chris smiled and bit into a piece of pizza. "God, this is better than an orgasm."

I heard them all talking, but it wasn't really registering. All I was thinking of was my son. How happy I was to have him home. That sweetness in his eyes as Milly wrapped her fingers around his thumb and bashfully buried her head into my chest.

And how frail he looked.

His clavicle practically broke the skin of his neck beneath his mess of black waves. The cheeks that reminded me so much of Laila in the astral reality we'd visited him in now hollowed into his mouth. His scrubs hung loosely on his bony shoulders—just as Daniel's had all those years ago.

Why was he so thin? Why was he treated the way that he was? When we'd found the last compound, and the one before that, he had an entire nursery fit for any normal child in the world. What changed?

"Are you hungry, Micah?" I put a hand on his shoulder. "Do you want something to eat?"

He smiled and looked up from his sister. "I'm stawving."

I chuckled and ran my hand over his messy black hair. "Let's get you something to eat, okay?"

He grinned and gave a nod.

I kept Milly on my hip and started to the pizza on the counter. But Chris caught my hand and awkwardly cleared his throat. Then his voice lowered. "He... he's not going to be able to eat that."

My brows fell with confusion.

"He doesn't really know how to chew."

He'd be three in two months. And he didn't know how to chew.

Why? What the fuck had he been eating then?

"That's okay," Leah said. "That's okay, we have other stuff. There's leftover mashed potatoes in the fridge. And bananas. A banana would be okay, right?"

"A banana should work," Chris said.

"No, I got this." Adam brushed past me to the fridge. He pulled out the freezer drawer and grabbed a tub of chocolate ice cream. He turned to Laila and Micah with a grin. "Have you ever had chocolate, buddy?"

Micah shook his head from Laila's lap at the breakfast nook. I was still holding the piece of cold pizza. She and I exchanged a look of grief before she pushed a smile.

He's home. And we get to be with him for all the best firsts, she said into her mind.

She was right. At least he was home. He'd be with us for the rest of forever.

But he still should've been able to eat that damn piece of pizza.

SACRED SINS CHAPTER TWO

LAILA

"This is so good." Micah shoved his spoon into the tub of chocolate ice cream on the table before us. I forced a smile as he raised the spoon to me. "Do you want some, Mommy?"

I kissed the top of his head. The knot in my throat swelled, and I swallowed it back down. "No, that's okay. It's all yours, kiddo."

My stomach danced with butterflies over holding my son for the first time. His warmth and purity on my lap was the best feeling I ever had. But I hated that looking at him made my stomach churn with guilt. I had to clench my hands together to keep sparks from leaving my fingers when I saw his feeble hand struggle ice cream from the tub.

This whole thing was fucking bullshit. I wanted to grab one of those knives from the butcher block, run downstairs, and slit the throat of bastard responsible for it. My baby, my sweet little baby, should have never been where he was. He should have always been right here on my lap with his father beside me.

But Micah just smiled and turned back to the container.

I let that feeling wash away.

He was home. He hadn't been, but he was now.

Jeremy caressed my bicep. I turned to meet his gaze. He smiled and reached out to cup my neck in his hand. "We should go to the house and get cleaned up soon."

"After he eats." I twined my fingers through his. "Micah and Chris can go first, then you. I'm not too bad. The fire kind of charred everything."

"I'll come with." Chris glanced at Micah and gave a smile. "Might help with the adjustment a bit."

"Sure." Jeremy smiled. "Sure, thank you."

He smiled and dipped his head in a gentle nod. "Where are you guys living? Did you get a little house in town?"

Jeremy laughed.

Leah smiled. "They're living in the cabin."

"The cabin," Chris said. "Dad's little hunting cabin? The one I was conceived in?"

"What's conceive?" Micah asked.

Jeremy laughed. "Ask me that again in, like, twelve years."

Micah turned back to his ice cream.

Smiling, I raised a shoulder. "We renovated a bit."

"A bit." Kai scoffed. "All the bloody hours ye had me breaking my back. And ye say a *bit*."

I laughed and looked at Chris. "We basically built a new house around the fireplace."

"It's beautiful," Leah said.

"Ya know, we were actually talking." I looked from Jeremy to Chris. "We're all on the same property and everything. But we set up a bed in the guest room beside Micah's. If you want, maybe you could stay with us for a while. We're here a lot anyway but..." I glanced at the basement door.

He turned toward it and cleared his throat. "He's down there."

"He is," Brody said.

Chris was quiet for a moment. His fingers around the glass of Sprite trembled. I wasn't sure if in fury or fear, but he set it down and turned back to us. "Yeah. Yeah, I'll stay with you guys. It'll be nice for Micah and everything too."

"Who?" Micah looked up at me and Jeremy. "Who's down thewe?"

I cleared my throat and tried to speak, but I found myself sitting there with my mouth open.

"Don't worry about it, kiddo." Chris smiled. "Just grown-up stuff."

"Oh." Micah took another bite of ice cream. "Mommy, can I have some watew?"

"How about some juice?" Leah asked from the counter.

"What's juice?" Micah asked.

"You'll like it." Chris smiled and turned to Leah. "He'll need a bottle."

I clenched my jaw and looked down at the messy little boy in my lap. The sweet, innocent child who did no harm to anyone yet had been treated like a prisoner of war since his birth. A prisoner to his parents' war, I suppose.

He deserved so much better than he'd been given. By three years old, he should have been long off a bottle. He should have known how to chew. He was smarter than any three-year-old I ever met. But he was so far behind where he should have been in almost every other milestone.

"Maybe we should walk down to the house," Jeremy said. "It's dark, but we could all probably use some fresh air. Huh, Chris?"

He smiled wide. "I'd love a walk in the moonlight right now."

"My belly huwts a little," Micah muttered with a hand on his stomach.

"Well, that's what happens when you eat a lot of ice cream." Jeremy grinned and poked his tummy.

Micah giggled, and I blinked hard at the water forming against my irises.

Another thing I hadn't considered. Micah had never been full before he ate that half tub of ice cream. He'd never eaten a real meal. He'd only had the bare minimum to survive.

After discovering the second compound and then seeing him through our astral communication, I believed they treated Micah well. Like a child. Far from normal, but decent. Lydia wasn't malnourished when we found her. She was odd, but cared for. In that last compound, Micah had a room with painted blue walls and fluffy white clouds, framed photos of his mother, and a crib with a real mattress.

And it dawned on me.

We'd found them. We'd found their cushy, renovated torture chamber. And then they had to hide.

They moved fast and frequent because they knew we'd find them if they stayed in one place for too long. As they travelled, they threw my son and his uncle into little sheds, basements, and God only knew what else. Anything small.

Smaller confines are easier to cast complex perimeter spells around. The smaller they kept their prison, the better they could fortify it. And the harder it made it for us to break.

"I like that big white dog." Micah pointed out the patio door. Tinkerbell lay on the porch, panting as she gazed out over the blue, moon lit field. "What's hew name again?"

"Tinkerbell." Jeremy smiled. "But we call her Tink."

"Tink," Micah murmured. A smile spread across his lips, and he giggled. "She's funny."

I raised a brow. "What do you mean, kiddo?"

"She's just funny."

Chris laughed too. "Micah does this thing you guys should probably know about."

"What's that?" Jeremy asked.

"I talk to aminals," Micah said.

An odd laugh left me. "And do they talk to you?"

"Not weally."

"They communicate some way or another," Chris said. "We had this little mouse at the last place, huh, bud?"

Micah nodded and grinned up at me. "I called him Stew."

"I actually called him Stewart. Ya know, like Stewart Little." Chris smiled. "And Micah couldn't say Stewart. So. Stew."

This kid was Fae alright. And I couldn't think of a worse way to torture a person with a deep connection to animals and nature than to lock them in a place with access to neither.

Fucking Christ, why? Why do this to him? Peterson couldn't have found him a stray cat to care for? Or a hamster? He couldn't have given his supposed savior one source of happiness in there?

"Well, you'll really like playing out in the woods here then." Jeremy gave a playful grin. "We've got all kinds of little critters out there. Once we figure things out, we'll go down to the creek and catch frogs. Might even be able to find a mouse or two."

"What's a fog do again?" Micah asked.

Chris opened his mouth to answer, but I beat him to it with a croaking, "Rib-bit."

Chris sent me a sad, almost apologetic smile. Neither of us could say it. But I resented him so much at that time. I was eternally grateful and forever in his debt. Still, I found myself more jealous of him than I'd ever been of anyone in my entire life.

Obsessed with *Sacred Sins*? Click the link below to download now!
https://www.amazon.com/dp/B0956PTMBX/

ALSO BY CHARLIE NOTTINGHAM

The Eluding Destiny Series

Eluding Destiny

The Horrors That Created Us

Aftershocks

The Precipice

Land of Light

The Quiet Army

Sacred Sins

Flash Back

The Shift

Lost to Time

Gods Among Us

The Cover Up

Blank Slate

Eluding Destiny Prequels

The Last Beginning

Blood Bar

Raven's Cry Series

(MMFM Paranormal Romance)

Raven's Cry

Raven's Song

Celena's Story Duology

(Completed—paranormal romance, urban fantasy)

New Normal: Celena's Story Part 1

Reprisal: Celena's Story Part 2

Origins of the Gods

(Completed Trilogy—fantasy romance, more information on the origins of the Fae and Angels, how life began on earth, where Guardians came from, and—most importantly—a badass forbidden romance)

Origins

The Thrones of Ore and Ice

Creation

Stand Alone Novels

Curse of the Gods: The Bridge Between Origins of the Gods and the Eluding Destiny Series

Sign up for Charlie's newsletter and receive a free copy of the Eluding Destiny prequel, Blood Bar:

https://liquidmind.media/eluding-destiny-prequel/

ABOUT THE AUTHOR

Charlie is a... Okay, talking about myself in third person is weird.

Nice to meet you! My name's Charlie Nottingham, and my whole world revolves around fantasy. When I'm not writing a new book, I'm either hanging out with my dogs, talking with my fans online, or reading some amazing urban fantasy, paranormal romance, or fantasy romance series (always a series, never a stand-alone, because I hate to fall for a character and never see them again). Or re-watching some Buffy or Supernatural. (They never get old!)